In the Wilds

of

Derbyshire

by

Jann Rowland

One Good Sonnet Publishing

By Jann Rowland
Published by One Good Sonnet Publishing:

PRIDE AND PREJUDICE VARIATIONS

Acting on Faith
A Life from the Ashes (Sequel to *Acting on Faith*)
Open Your Eyes
Implacable Resentment
An Unlikely Friendship
Bound by Love
Cassandra
Obsession
Shadows Over Longbourn
The Mistress of Longbourn
My Brother's Keeper
Coincidence
The Angel of Longbourn
Chaos Comes to Kent
In the Wilds of Derbyshire

Co-Authored with Lelia Eye

WAITING FOR AN ECHO

Waiting for an Echo Volume One: Words in the Darkness
Waiting for an Echo Volume Two: Echoes at Dawn
Waiting for an Echo Two Volume Set

A Summer in Brighton
A Bevy of Suitors
Love and Laughter: A Pride and Prejudice Short Stories Anthology

THE EARTH AND SKY TRILOGY
Co-Authored with Lelia Eye

On Wings of Air
On Lonely Paths
*On Tides of Fate**

*Forthcoming

This is a work of fiction based on the works of Jane Austen. All the characters and events portrayed in this novel are products of Jane Austen's original novel or the authors' imaginations.

IN THE WILDS OF DERBYSHIRE

Copyright © 2017 Jann Rowland

Cover Design by Marina Willis

Published by One Good Sonnet Publishing

ISBN: 1987929659
ISBN-13: 978-1987929652

To my family who have, as always, shown
their unconditional love and encouragement.

CHAPTER I

*I*t has long been said that change can be a harbinger of better times to come, but Elizabeth Bennet of Longbourn in Hertfordshire could hardly believe that to be the case.

It was the spring of the year eighteen hundred and twelve, and the previous year had brought changes, such changes in such a brief period that it seemed nothing familiar had been left behind. That this upheaval had been brought about by the most wonderful events was an irony not unknown to Elizabeth, and though she felt lost in the aftermath, she could not deny that her family's situation had been improved or that certain of their members had been blessed as a result.

The previous autumn had seen the arrival of several new acquaintances, two of whom would change Elizabeth's life forever. The first was, of course, the new master of Netherfield, a Charles Bingley by name. Though Mr. Bingley was the son of a tradesman, a man who had worked all his life to allow his son to rise in society, his five-thousand-pound income guaranteed the approbation of the residents of the neighborhood, and the eyes of every young woman in the village were turned to him. His appeal was also enhanced because of his handsome countenance and amiable nature, and in the eyes of society he was in possession of every virtue.

Though every young maiden dreamed of drawing Mr. Bingley's attention to herself, it was not a surprise, to Elizabeth at least, that it was her elder sister, Jane, who immediately captured his attention, and if the other ladies were honest, they must not have been surprised either. The only one who expressed any doubt at all had been Jane herself.

"Well, Sister dearest?" Elizabeth had asked her sister one night after Mr. Bingley had given a spectacular ball in which Jane had been the exclusive focus of his attention. "When will Mr. Bingley confirm what all of us have known for some time now?"

Jane, in her usual modesty, had not understood Elizabeth's question. "Of what confirmation do you refer?"

"Why, when he confirms his love for you!" exclaimed Elizabeth as if it were the most obvious thing in the world. To her it was.

"He has said nothing of the kind, Lizzy," replied Jane, though Elizabeth thought she sensed a hint of pleasure in her sister's manner.

"He does not need to say it out loud for me to see it. It is evident in his manners, in the way he looks at you, in the way he defers to you and listens to everything you say as if they are the most important words ever spoken. I declare, Jane, that if he does not ask for your hand in marriage when he returns from his business in London, I shall think him a simpleton."

"But I have nothing to offer him."

"You, yourself, are more than enough. Anyone admitted to the pleasure of knowing you must know your worth, and I am sure Mr. Bingley knows it better than any other."

Though Jane protested Elizabeth's words, they were proven true, as Mr. Bingley had returned to the neighborhood within five days, and on the sixth, he had requested a private audience with Jane, and then her hand. Elizabeth had looked on with no small measure of smugness, not least of which because the man's sister, Miss Caroline Bingley, had looked on with barely concealed anger. Elizabeth was certain that the woman, who had followed her brother to town the day after he departed, had spent the entire time attempting to convince her brother against his inclinations.

Elizabeth kept this observation from her dearest sister, knowing that it would serve little purpose to attempt to inform Jane of Miss Bingley's true nature. Jane was an optimist through and through, and though she was more than intelligent enough to understand that not everyone meant well, she chose to attribute the best of motives to everyone she met. Mr. Bingley had shown himself to be constant and true and would no doubt prove to be an able protector. Elizabeth thought he would not tolerate any foolishness from his sister.

At the same time as Mr. Bingley was so assiduously courting Jane, another man arrived at Longbourn, though this man was as repulsive as Mr. Bingley was engaging. Mr. Collins was her father's cousin, several times removed and, perhaps more importantly, her father's heir to the estate, owing to the births of five daughters in succession, with no hint of an heir to protect his wife and children from an unfortunate entail in the event of his untimely death.

Mrs. Bennet, Elizabeth's mother, was a nervous woman, frightened by the prospect of losing her home to the unknown man. The Bennet sisters had little in the way of dowry, with nothing more than their mother's five thousand pounds for their support should their father pass early. Mrs. Bennet's brother, a Mr. Gardiner, a successful man of business, promised to provide them all with a home, should it become necessary, but fearful of losing her status, and that of her daughters, Mrs. Bennet was convinced that the only way to avoid such an ignominious fate was to see them all married as advantageously as possible.

Elizabeth, the same as all her sisters, had been brought into their local society at the tender age of fifteen and thrown into the path of any available man. Unfortunately, the strategy had proven fruitless until Mr. Bingley's arrival. With the wealthy man paying such exquisite attentions to her eldest, one might have thought Mrs. Bennet's mind would be eased, her worry for her future mitigated. Elizabeth had surely thought as much. What she had not counted on, however, was the lure of having a daughter married to Longbourn's heir, thereby enabling her to live out her life on the estate which had been her home for almost five and twenty years.

Mr. Collins had come in all his servile splendor, all eager to extend his olive branch and offer for one of his fair cousins, making sure to inform them all that it was at the express wish—command—of his patroness that the notion had come into his mind. Besides the man's incessant veneration of a woman Elizabeth thought likely was little more than a meddling virago, Elizabeth found him to be of suspect hygiene, stupid and servile, with little in the way of redeeming qualities.

Of course, it was to Elizabeth herself that Mr. Collins turned his attentions, no doubt on the recommendation of her mother. Not wishing to stir up a hornets' nest unless she was required to, Elizabeth endured the man's silliness as best she could, but in the end, had had no choice but to refuse—several times, as it turned out—Mr. Collins's proposal. A hornets' nest was a mild description of the furor which ensued, but as Mr. Bennet sided with Elizabeth as she had known he would, Mr. Collins was forced to withdraw his suit. That did not stop the injured glares he directed at Elizabeth at every opportunity, but Elizabeth chose the simple expedient of ignoring him.

Mrs. Bennet, however, still managed to obtain the desired son-in-law, as she was able to turn his attention to Mary, Elizabeth's younger sister. Mary, solemn and moralizing, was the perfect bride of a clergyman, and they were soon engaged, though Mary showed no pleasure that Elizabeth could detect. Elizabeth accepted Mary's choice with philosophy, deciding that her sister had consented to the engagement with her eyes open; if she was making a mistake, then it was hers to make. A little more reflection on the matter, and Elizabeth decided with a stifled laugh that they were even better suited than she had previously thought—they were both pompous, full of ponderous statements and little sense—and they likely deserved each other.

But Elizabeth learned that Mr. Collins also possessed a vindictive side, though at first the matter did not give her the slightest concern. It was at Mary's wedding breakfast that she made this discovery. Though Jane was acquainted with Mr. Bingley longer than Mary with Mr. Collins, the Collinses were married first, with an almost unseemly haste, which might have suggested a different and more pressing need to marry had they both not been far too priggish for any such behavior to have taken place.

Finding herself standing near to Mr. Collins by chance, Elizabeth, feeling it incumbent upon herself to say something, observed: "I offer my congratulations, Mr. Collins. I am certain Mary will make you an excellent wife."

Mr. Collins, who had hardly spoken a word to Elizabeth since his failed proposal, looked away. Then, however, a thought seemed to come to him, and he turned back to Elizabeth.

"I am certain she shall," said he, his tone haughty. "Perhaps it is fortunate it all worked out in this manner, for I do not doubt that had *other* arrangements come to fruition, I would have discovered, to my detriment and eternal dismay, that I was caught in a nightmare, from which there was no escape."

Though Elizabeth knew he meant his words as an insult, she could not have agreed more, though she would dispute *who* would be caught in the nightmare. As she had escaped his noose, it was of little matter.

"I cannot but agree. I wish you all the happiness in the world, sir."

Then Elizabeth turned to depart, having had more than enough of his brand of civility, only to be forestalled by him moving in front of her.

"Cousin, if I might impart a little advice?"

Elizabeth was certain there was nothing her cousin might say that she would wish to hear, but she gave him a curt nod and waited for him to speak.

"I would advise you," said he, his customary foolishness replaced by a gravity colored by spite, "that you look carefully for your own companion in life, little likely though you will actually find someone. Remember that I am to inherit all this estate, and after what has passed between us, I doubt we would be comfortable living in this house together."

Elizabeth took the man's meaning in every particular. She decided that there was no reason to be angry, though she was amused at a supposed man of the cloth speaking to a family member with such uncharitable words. It was more amusing to reflect on how he had surprised her—it was the second statement he had made in as many minutes which was actually sensible!

"You may be assured Mr. Collins," replied Elizabeth in a frosty tone, "that I agree with you completely. Now, if you would excuse me, I believe we would be better off if we avoided further words. I would not want an argument to mar my sister's wedding breakfast."

It was clear that the man was not of mind to remove himself from her path, so Elizabeth chose the simple expedient of stepping around him. She did not look back and did not farewell the Collinses when they departed after the conclusion of the wedding breakfast. But Elizabeth could feel the man's eyes on her form as she walked away, and it was only with a supreme force of will that she did not show him her discomfort.

Refusing Mr. Collins the way Elizabeth did was not without consequences, though it might be debatable whether these consequences were detrimental to Elizabeth's peace of mind. Quite simply, with Elizabeth's refusal to marry Mr. Collins, her mother stopped attempting to arrange a marriage for her second daughter.

"I wash my hands of you, Lizzy," she was told. "I have more important things to do with my time than to attempt to see an ungrateful daughter situated in life. You will shift for yourself."

Since Elizabeth did not appreciate her mother's propensity to put forward anyone wearing pants as an eligible husband, the matter caused her little concern. After Jane was married early in the New

Year, life at Longbourn went on much as it ever had, though now, of course, two of the family had departed for their own homes. But despite that lack, Mr. Bennet still hid in his library, Mrs. Bennet remained invariably silly, and Kitty and Lydia, Elizabeth's two youngest sisters, were still improper and loud, flirting outrageously with any man in a red coat. As a regiment of militia had taken up residence in Meryton for the winter, they had ample opportunity to embarrass their still unmarried sister.

But for Elizabeth, the loss she felt most keenly was that of her eldest sister. Jane and Elizabeth had always been the closest of siblings, the ties between them profound. When Jane married late that winter and soon after left on her wedding trip with Mr. Bingley, Elizabeth found herself without her best friend. Charlotte Lucas, who had been a close friend for years, attempted to fill the gap, but it was not the same, even though Elizabeth loved Charlotte dearly.

When Jane returned, however, Elizabeth's mood did not improve. She had hoped that when Jane made her way back to Netherfield that the sisters could once again enjoy each other's company, though they would still be separated by their different homes and Jane's new responsibilities. But the Jane who returned from her wedding trip was not same person who had left Longbourn only months before.

"There is some great alteration in your sister, Lizzy," said Charlotte Lucas one day when they had gathered at Lucas Lodge for dinner.

"Well do I know it," replied Elizabeth. "She appears to have acquired a certain air about her, one which I would never have expected Jane to possess."

"You mean she has become more like Miss Bingley."

Elizabeth scowled, and her eyes found Mr. Bingley's younger sister. The woman was even now sitting next to her sister by marriage, and every so often she would lean over to Jane and make some observation. Jane's countenance did not change—she was so inscrutable that even Elizabeth, who knew her better than any other, had difficulty interpreting Jane's thoughts. Whatever Miss Bingley was telling her sister, Elizabeth did not believe it was benign in nature.

"I do not know what to think," replied Elizabeth. "I have never known Jane to be this way. She does not display her feelings, but she seems almost . . . contemptuous of the company."

"I rather thought I detected a sadness in her eyes," replied Charlotte.

Elizabeth turned her attention to her sister's face, but she could not make out anything extraordinary. "Perhaps you are correct, though I cannot say for certain."

"Being the wife of a rich man has gone to her head," observed Charlotte.

Turning a glare on her friend, Elizabeth waited for an explanation, which Charlotte did not hesitate to give.

"She would not be the first to succumb to such thinking after having the good fortune to come into riches."

"No, but then she would not be Jane."

Charlotte obviously knew when to hold her tongue, and she did so with nary another word. Elizabeth watched her sister, and the more she did so, the more she became convinced that Jane had, indeed, acquired a hint of superiority in her manner, though Elizabeth would have thought Jane to be the last person in the world to behave in such a way.

But the evidence was right there before her eyes. Jane spoke little to anyone in her family and only slightly more to those of the neighborhood. Ladies with whom she had been friends all her life were treated to nothing more than civility, and though she was never rude with them, she also made it clear that she did not wish to continue in close association.

One day, Mrs. Bennet approached Elizabeth, clearly uncertain, her countenance troubled. "Lizzy, have you noticed anything . . . different about your sister?"

"If you mean Jane, then yes, Mama," replied Elizabeth. There was no reason to belabor the point, and Elizabeth did not wish to provoke her mother's hysterics by being anything less than honest.

"I do not understand," said Mrs. Bennet, twisting the handkerchief she held in her hands this way and that in her agitation. "She has always been such a dutiful daughter. Now, when I visit her, I encounter little more than hostility."

"It seems that our Jane has acquired a taste for higher society," said Elizabeth, giving voice to the suspicion Charlotte had planted into her mind. It somehow made it seem more real when she stated it out loud. "Perhaps the Bennets are not high or fashionable enough for her any longer."

The look of horror which fell over Mrs. Bennet might have filled Elizabeth with mirth in another situation. As it was, Elizabeth could do nothing other than sympathize with her mother.

"My Jane would never behave in such a way," said Mrs. Bennet, though her voice lacked any conviction.

"And yet, it appears she is," replied Elizabeth. "Jane has had little more to say to me since her return than she has anyone else in the family, and as you know, we always were close."

That evening at dinner, a visibly distressed Mrs. Bennet brought the matter before her husband. Mr. Bennet did not even bother to tease or vex his wife, as was his usual custom; instead, he only sighed and informed them that he had seen the same thing.

"Can we not do something, Mr. Bennet?" asked Mrs. Bennet.

"I do not know what you expect," said Mr. Bennet. "Jane is now under the protection of Mr. Bingley, and if that is how he expects his wife to behave, there is little we can do to influence her."

"But surely you do not expect Mr. Bingley, of all people, to instruct his wife to cut us," exclaimed Elizabeth.

"I would not have thought so, no. But he does not seem to have put a stop to it. I am not certain what other interpretation we can put on her behavior."

Mrs. Bennet appeared lost, but then she straightened her back and sniffed with disdain. "If that is how she wishes it to be, then I suppose we can do nothing. I will say that she is a most undutiful daughter. I can only consider it fortunate that Mr. Collins was induced to offer for Mary. At least with that, our futures are secure."

It required no greatness of mind to infer that Mrs. Bennet's final comments were an indirect barb at Elizabeth, but she paid her mother no mind. It was fortunate for Mrs. Bennet, as she would have a home, regardless of whether Jane continued in her present behavior.

As the days rolled by, however, Elizabeth's reflections on the matter informed her that her situation was, perhaps, the most precarious of them all. Elizabeth had always known that her chances of marrying were not at all good, and though she had always wished to be married, she had thought she might find other ways to find fulfilment in life if she was not so fortunate as to find a man she could love. Jane's marriage opened the possibility of her living with the Bingleys if she did not marry, a subject about which the sisters had spoken on several occasions leading up to Jane's marriage.

Now, however, that option seemed less certain, given Jane's disinclination for her company. And whereas her mother and younger sisters would have a home at Longbourn should Mr. Bennet pass away, that option was almost certainly denied Elizabeth, given Mr. Collins's final words to her.

It was the combination of the situation with Jane, which did not improve through the passage of time, and the uncertainty about her future, which provoked Elizabeth's malaise. The dream of marrying for love had never felt so unattainable as it did during those days; there was no man in Meryton who interested her, no one she thought she would be able to love one day, and no one who paid her any attention regardless.

The eldest Lucas, Samuel, who Elizabeth had known all her life, spoke with her one day on the very subject, a conversation which Elizabeth was grateful did not make its way back to her mother.

"Your sister appears to have acquired an air of haughtiness," observed he one Sunday while they were standing outside the church after services. Elizabeth was not surprised that others had begun to notice Jane's behavior—she and her new family had left almost directly after the service had ended and without saying much of substance to anyone.

"I do not doubt Miss Bingley has been tutoring her," said Elizabeth. "The woman makes it an art form."

Samuel laughed. "I dare say she does." Then he turned to look at her, speculation evident in his manner. "What shall you do now, Elizabeth? You have always been so close to Jane; I imagine you are not happy about this change in your sister."

"No, but there is little to be done about it."

"I dare say there is not." Samuel paused and Elizabeth detected a hint of his sudden embarrassment. "You wish for your own home, do you not?"

"If I could find a man I could love, I would be happy to have my own home."

"And you would make any man a wonderful wife. Perhaps there is something close to home?"

It took Elizabeth a moment to understand Samuel's meaning, and she turned her astonished gaze on him, wondering what he was about. "I hope you do not take offense, but I do not think we would suit."

A visible sense of relief came over him. "I am not offended, as I know you are not either. But I believe you know that my mother has always wished to have you as a daughter, and neither she nor Charlotte would leave me be until I promised to broach the subject with you."

Laughing in understanding, Elizabeth patted his hand, while directing a brilliant smile at him. "I can imagine. But you and I were playmates as children, and I doubt we would ever be able to change our opinions of the other. I would always remember Sammy the pirate and the floggings I gave you."

Samuel joined her in laughter. "And I would remember the Pirate

Captain Lizzy the Black, scourge of the seas."

"Perhaps if that did not lay between us, we might suit," replied Elizabeth. "But as it is, I think we had best remain friends."

"Agreed," replied Samuel. "I will inform mother and Charlotte that we have spoken and the results of our conversation."

"Perhaps then they will cease to pester you!" said Elizabeth.

"One can only hope."

The two then parted, secure in their mutual admiration for the other, and the knowledge that it did not extend past friendship. But the conversation did not lighten Elizabeth's sense of melancholy, nor did it give her any peace of mind. She was content to keep Samuel as a friend and nothing more, but it underscored how there truly were no prospects for her to consider in a serious light. Kitty and Lydia might be content to waste their hours chasing after officers, flirting, and all other forms of nonsense, but Elizabeth had no interest in officers, other than as young men with whom to hold a pleasant conversation on occasion. None of them held the key to her happiness, she was certain, and so she did not pay them much attention.

By the time the weather started to improve and the trees to begin sprouting their spring greenery, Elizabeth felt lost in a sea of indifference and regret, and even the warmer temperatures could not improve her mood. She found herself wandering the paths of her youth with more and more frequency, but all she saw had no interest for her. Even the summit of Oakham Mount, her favorite place in all the world, could bring her no pleasure or relief. At times, she wondered what her purpose could possibly be, or if it was her fate to live and die this way, unmoved by life, drifting along as a twig in a river, not caring where she went, at the mercy of the flowing water.

In late March of that year, a letter arrived for her father from his brother-in-law, who lived in the north with his family. Mr. Drummond had married Mr. Bennet's younger sister, but as their situation was relatively modest, there was little in the way of communication between the families other than the occasional letter. Elizabeth had met them only once or twice in her life.

Had this been a typical letter, Elizabeth might have remained ignorant of its arrival, for her father was not in the habit of sharing his correspondence with his family. But that day, Elizabeth was summoned into her father's study, and when she entered, he bade her sit, and then regarded her for several long moments. Elizabeth bore it with patience, knowing that her father had noted her poor spirits, and assuming he had called her into his study to discuss them. It was, therefore, a surprise when he spoke on the subject of his letter.

"A letter from Uncle Drummond?" asked Elizabeth. "What does he have to say?"

In all truth, Elizabeth had no interest in the subject, and she thought her father was aware of that fact. He watched her for several more moments before he spoke again.

"As you know, the Drummonds have a daughter about Kitty's age. My brother writes me to ask if one of my daughters would like to go to the north and stay with them to be a mentor to her."

Elizabeth nodded, understanding the reason for his summons. "You could hardly ask Kitty or Lydia to mentor her, not when their own behavior is so lacking."

"That is true," replied Mr. Bennet. "But that is not the whole of it. I have noticed your lack of spirits, Lizzy, and I can guess the reason for them. I can write my brother and inform him that none of you are available if you prefer, but I thought a change of scenery might be to your benefit."

"It might," agreed Elizabeth, though she was not at all certain anything could pierce this shroud of melancholy which had fallen over her.

"Before we speak any further, I should warn you that your uncle's house is not the same as Longbourn." Mr. Bennet paused and grimaced, though Elizabeth was not certain why. "Mr. Drummond's estate is small, and though he does have a tenant or two to farm parts of his land, most of his land is taken up by the home farm, to which he tends himself. Their children, while technically considered the progeny of a gentleman, help on the farm and in the house, as the Drummonds cannot afford to employ many servants."

Nodding slowly, Elizabeth said: "I would be expected to assist where asked."

Mr. Bennet returned her gesture with a tight nod of his own. "My sister would no doubt insist on it. Drummond tells me that his primary motivation is to ensure his daughter is given the best possible opportunity to make a good marriage, and for that she will at least require the proper manners. I do not suppose she will have a large dowry, so she will only have herself on which to rely."

"I do not have a large dowry myself, Papa," said Elizabeth, smiling to inform him she was not attempting to be critical of his management. "I imagine I am as well qualified as any to assist her."

"That you are, Lizzy," replied Mr. Bennet. "I will not insist on your going, but I believe you may wish to consider it. I have visited

Drummond on occasion, and I am familiar with the neighborhood. There are several large estates in the area, and many potentially eligible gentlemen live nearby. You might be able to find a husband there, where there is little chance of it here."

Elizabeth smiled. "But my disadvantages will still exist in the north, Papa. I have no objection to going, but I will not entertain such thoughts at present. I will, instead, resolve to enjoy some months with my relations, with no expectation of anything more."

"Good girl," said Mr. Bennet. He appeared as if he wished to say something further, but in the end, he only smiled and said: "I will inform your uncle that you will stay with him for a time."

Nodding, Elizabeth stood and made her way to her room, after thanking her father. Perhaps a change in society would be beneficial for her after all, and as she did not know this branch of the family well, she was interested in meeting them.

CHAPTER II

The letter was dispatched and a reply came soon after, and it was decided that Elizabeth would attend her relations before the middle of April. With this in mind, Elizabeth began to prepare her possessions for the journey to the north.

Though Elizabeth was not certain what her future held, by her father's testimony she knew that there would be much society in the north, and as her avowed purpose of staying in her uncle's house was to mentor his daughter, she was certain she would be much involved. As such, she packed a selection of day and evening dresses, as well as some frocks which she had owned for some time and thought would be suitable for whatever chores her aunt saw fit to assign to her. Those items of a sentimental nature she also stowed in her cases, though she did not take everything by any means.

All might have gone well had she not been subjected to a continuous stream of commentary from Kitty and Lydia—though mostly from the younger girl—when their attention was not on the officers. Much of their conversation touched on such subjects as her reasons for going, why she would find journeying to the north interesting when there was a regiment in Meryton, and other assorted inanities. These were, of course, accompanied by continual requests for Elizabeth's possessions, which no amount of refusal induced Lydia to abandon.

"If you do not mean to take that bonnet, you should give it to me," said Lydia one spring morning. "It will look so much better on me anyway."

"No, Lydia," replied Elizabeth, for what seemed like the hundredth time. "Just because I will not take it with me does not mean I do not wish to keep it. I will be returning to Longbourn, you know."

Lydia only sniffed. "I do not know why you would. There are rumors that the regiment is for Brighton this summer, so there shall be nothing left to return to."

"As you know, I care not for the regiment," replied Elizabeth, as she folded and laid another dress in her trunk. "The officers leaving the neighborhood is of no interest to me."

"I am not sure why you have suddenly become so serious, Lizzy," said Kitty. "You liked the society of the officers well enough when they arrived."

"And I still do like them. But I can be happy without them too."

"Then you should give me that bonnet," said Lydia, "if you are set on becoming an old maid."

"That is enough Lydia," said Elizabeth with a glare. "I tire of your constant demands for my personal effects. I will be returning and will require my possessions. You may not have anything."

Lydia sucked in a breath to retort, but at that moment, Mrs. Bennet stepped into the room.

"Leave your sister alone, Lydia," said she, surprising all three sisters. Mrs. Bennet rarely reprimanded Lydia, her favorite daughter, and would almost always take her part against any of her sisters in any dispute. "I wish to speak with Lizzy. You and your sister may go and find something to occupy your time."

Though Lydia appeared ready to argue the point, she saw something in her mother's countenance which persuaded her to hold her tongue. Whatever the reason, Elizabeth was happy to be rid of her when she flounced off the bed and stalked from the room, Kitty following close behind.

When they had departed, Mrs. Bennet closed the door and stepped close to Elizabeth, looking at her efforts to make ready for her departure. It appeared like she was satisfied, for she soon turned her attention on Elizabeth.

"I see you have made progress."

"I have, Mama. Everything will be ready when Papa and I depart in two days."

Mrs. Bennet directed a long look at Elizabeth before sighing and sitting on the edge of the bed. "I still do not know why you wish to go."

This had been a common conversation in the past days since Elizabeth had declared her intention to accept her uncle's invitation. "Because there is nothing for me here, Mama. With Jane's betrayal, I find myself blowing in the wind with little to anchor me."

Mouth tightening at the mention of her eldest, Mrs. Bennet said: "I understand Jane's behavior has hurt you. But surely we are not so much changed here at Longbourn."

"Perhaps that is part of the problem." Mrs. Bennet looked at Elizabeth with curiosity, prompting Elizabeth to sigh and sit down next to her. "There simply does not seem to be anything here for me, Mama. The society has become so familiar as to be irksome, I am confronted with Jane's indifference whenever we are in company, and there is a dearth of gentlemen in Meryton, which will make it difficult to ever marry."

The last point Elizabeth made quite deliberately, as she knew her mother would understand that, if nothing else. It was not a surprise when Mrs. Bennet seized on that point.

"You wish to find a husband in the north?"

"I cannot say that, Mama," replied Elizabeth. "Papa seems to think it is a possibility, but at present I have no knowledge of society there. Should the opportunity arise, I will not allow it to pass by."

Doubtful, Mrs. Bennet said: "Like you did not with Mr. Collins?"

"I apologize for upsetting you, Mama," replied Elizabeth, calmly, but giving no ground, "but I require something more in a marriage than Mr. Collins was offering."

A shaken head was Mrs. Bennet's response. "I have always tried to do my best by you girls, Lizzy. But I have found you to be particularly incomprehensible. I do not understand what you wish to find in marriage, and I do not know why Hertfordshire is suddenly not enough for you."

"I just feel like there should be something more in my life than I have found here," replied Elizabeth.

"Do you think you will find it in the north?"

"I cannot say. At the very least, a change in scene and society will not be unwelcome."

"You may find yourself regretting such sentiments," muttered Mrs. Bennet. When Elizabeth shot her a questioning look, Mrs. Bennet sighed. "Your aunt has always seemed like a hard woman to me, and she was particularly ungracious after I married your father. I wonder if your time with her will be pleasant."

"At the very least, Uncle appears to be a good man, according to Papa."

"Perhaps," replied her mother, though it was clear she was doubtful.

"Well, it is decided regardless," said Elizabeth. "Perhaps I shall have very great luck and meet a man I can tolerate. Once Papa passes on, there will be nothing for me here, so I had best try to find a home of my own."

"You speak of Mr. Collins's words to you at the wedding breakfast?"

Shocked, Elizabeth gaped at her mother. Mrs. Bennet only shook her head. "I overheard what that wretched man said to you, Lizzy, but you need not fear *him*."

"He was very clear, Mama."

"Perhaps he was," said Mrs. Bennet, the disdain she felt for the man evident in her tone. "But I dare say that between Mary and myself, we will ensure you will always have a home at Longbourn if you choose." When Elizabeth looked doubtful, Mrs. Bennet grasped her hand and squeezed it. "Can you imagine Mary standing by and allowing one of her sisters to be homeless when she had the power to prevent it?"

A giggle escaped Elizabeth's lips, and she shook her head. No, Mary, pious as she was, would never allow such a thing, and now that Elizabeth thought of it, Mr. Collins was a weak-willed man and would no doubt defer to his wife, little though he might like it.

"To tell the truth," said Mrs. Bennet with a laugh of her own, "I did not care for Mr. Collins either. There is something . . . most disconcerting about him. But he is the heir, and he is easily led, which will work to our advantage."

Mother and daughter shared a laugh, and Elizabeth reflected that she had never felt so close to her mother before.

"I would not wish to discourage you from finding a husband, Lizzy," said Mrs. Bennet, "but you should always remember that you will have a home at Longbourn, despite whatever foolish notions William Collins gets into his head. You should think on it no more."

"Thank you, Mama," said Elizabeth quietly. "I do not know if a husband awaits me in the north, but I shall do my best to find him if he exists."

"Then that is all I ask."

Then in a business-like manner, Mrs. Bennet arose and looked about the room. "It seems you have everything in hand, Lizzy. Please do not worry about your possessions, for I will see to it that Lydia does not take anything."

And with that, Mrs. Bennet let herself out of the room, leaving a bemused Elizabeth behind, watching as she departed. Elizabeth had no memory of ever having such an exchange with her mother, and she was gratified that at the very least, they would part on amicable terms. They were very different people and there would undoubtedly still be times when they would vex each other, but she hoped that this was the start of a new relationship between them.

Elizabeth's leave-taking with Jane was everything she had grown to expect, though only a few months before she would never have been able to fathom such coldness from her sister. She had been reluctant to meet with Jane at all, as she had no desire to be once again beset by the loss of the sister who had become a stranger to her.

"You were always the closest of sisters," said Mrs. Bennet. "Though Jane has changed since her marriage, I believe you should not cease your attempts to bridge the distance. Besides, if you went away without any word to Jane, it would spawn gossip in the neighborhood."

The schism between Jane and her family was, by now, quite well known in Meryton, so Elizabeth did not consider that to be a valid argument. But her mother was right—regardless of how Jane might choose to conduct herself, Elizabeth would not allow her own behavior to be dictated to her. However, the sight of her sister's indifference might affect her, Elizabeth would not descend to Jane's level.

Netherfield was much the same as Elizabeth had remembered it. In one of the last happy memories Elizabeth had of her sister only days before her wedding, she had declared her intention to avoid redecorating Netherfield. At the time, she was uncertain of her future husband's intentions regarding the estate and did not wish to commit any money to such an endeavor until such time as their plans were set. As the rooms were all quite handsome, Elizabeth thought it a prudent decision, and, indeed, it seemed like Jane had kept to her resolution.

The Hursts were not present, having returned to Mr. Hurst's family estate after the wedding. Elizabeth had heard talk of a long-awaited heir, which meant that they had not seen Mr. Bingley's elder sister and her husband since that time. As Elizabeth found the woman nearly as intolerable as her sister and the husband naught but a drunkard, she did not repine the loss of their society. Thus, it was only Mr. and Mrs. Bingley and Miss Bingley who were there to receive them.

"Elizabeth!" exclaimed Charles when Elizabeth was shown into the room. After their marriage, he had insisted that she address him informally. "How do you do? I have heard from your father that you are bound for Derbyshire to visit with some relations."

"I am, indeed, Charles," said Elizabeth. Though her sister had changed into an almost unrecognizable person, at least Charles was still engaging and pleasant. "My Aunt and Uncle Drummond have invited me to visit, and I am happy to accept."

"Your sister informed us that your uncle lives near the town of Lambton, Eliza," said Caroline, interrupting her brother when he appeared like he was about to speak again. Elizabeth had never cared enough to ask her to stop using that moniker, little though she appreciated it. "We are quite familiar with the area. Many well-situated families live there, but I must own that I do not recall meeting anyone by the name 'Drummond.' What is the name of your uncle's estate?"

"Indeed, we are a little familiar with the neighborhood," said Charles. He glared at his sister, warning her to be quiet, but Caroline simply continued to regard Elizabeth, insolence in her air. "Of course, we do not know everyone."

"But you are known to some?" asked Elizabeth, interested in spite of herself.

"My friend owns an estate situated not five miles from Lambton," replied Charles. "We have been great friends since university, and a better man you cannot find."

"Ah," replied Elizabeth. "I remember you speaking of this Mr. Darcy on occasion."

"I am sure you have." Charles grinned. "I have often relied on Darcy for advice, as he is both intelligent and experienced in matters in which I am not. He would have joined us at Netherfield last fall had other matters requiring his attention not arisen."

"Then I shall be happy to make his acquaintance. If *you* recommend him as a man worth knowing, then I am certain I cannot find him anything other than amiable."

Charles beamed, but Caroline only snorted. "Perhaps you shall not make plans so quickly, Eliza. Mr. Darcy is very discriminating about those with whom he will associate. I doubt he moves in the same circles as your uncle."

"Given the Drummonds' proximity to Lambton, I have no doubt

that Darcy is known to them," said Charles. He directed another quelling glance at his sister. For her part, Caroline scowled, but she subsided.

"There is a possibility we might visit Pemberley this summer," said Charles, turning back to Elizabeth.

"Then perhaps I shall see you there." She turned to Jane who had been sitting and watching them all without saying a word. "I shall carry your greetings to Uncle and Aunt Drummond for you, Jane."

"Of course," replied Jane. She opened her mouth to say something further, but after a moment's hesitation, she subsided, leaving whatever she had been about to say unsaid.

"Will you not anticipate a visit to Derbyshire?" said Elizabeth, trying to induce her sister to say something more. "Neither of us has gone since we were little girls."

"I suppose Edward must be nearly grown now," said Jane, with a diffidence Elizabeth was not certain was entirely due to her sister's usual manner.

"I believe he is a year younger than I," said Elizabeth.

Jane smiled, but it was one devoid of any warmth. Elizabeth wanted to shake her sister, to discover what had become of the woman she loved more than any other. By her side, Caroline regarded her with a hint of a satisfied smirk she reserved solely for Elizabeth. Elizabeth wanted nothing more than to slap the haughty woman.

She made polite conversation with the Bingleys until the time came for her to depart, though to own the truth, her conversation was mostly with Charles. Jane and Caroline rarely had anything to say, and when they did, Jane was distant and Caroline was snide. Elizabeth bore their incivility with grace, never giving any indication that their manners hurt her. In Caroline's case, they did not—she had learned to expect nothing more from the woman.

When at last fifteen minutes had passed, Elizabeth rose to depart.

"We wish you a safe journey and a pleasant stay with your uncle and aunt," said Charles, as he rose with her. "If our footsteps should happen to take us to Derbyshire, we will be happy to see you there."

"Thank you, Charles," said Elizabeth. "I hope to see you there too."

Then Elizabeth turned to Jane and wished her well, before turning to depart without waiting for Jane's response. It was becoming too painful for Elizabeth to face her indifferent sister. She wished for nothing more than to be out of her company.

But she chanced one last look back at Jane before she quit the room. She was standing, watching Elizabeth as she left, but though Elizabeth thought she saw a glimmer of some remorse in Jane's eyes, she did not speak a word. Then Caroline said something to her in a soft tone, and the two women turned and sat back down on the sofa.

With quick steps, Elizabeth moved through Netherfield, intent upon departing from the house as soon as could be arranged. The Bennet carriage was waiting for her in front of the entrance, and seeing her arrival, the footman opened the door for her to enter. She was just about to do so when she was halted by the sound of someone calling her name.

"Wait, please, Elizabeth!"

Though every instinct screamed for her to enter and depart without a second glance, Elizabeth turned and noted Charles's quick approach. She stopped and waited for him, equal parts thankful and devastated that it was not Jane who had chased after her. The look of compassion he bestowed on her almost caused her to become undone.

"I wanted to again wish you a safe journey," said he, as he stopped in front of her.

"Thank you, Charles," said Elizabeth, not certain why he had thought it necessary. "As you know, my father is to journey with me. I am certain I shall be quite safe under his protection."

"I am certain you will," replied Charles. He hesitated for a moment, then in a manner typical to his behavior, said with an impulsive sort of eagerness. "Do not worry, Elizabeth. Jane will eventually return to what she was."

Though surprised, Elizabeth directed a pleading look at her brother-in-law. "Do you know why she is acting this way?"

"I do not."

Disappointment flooded through Elizabeth. She almost wished he had not said anything, for she had allowed her hopes to rise at his words.

"It is most unlike her," said Charles, his brow furrowed in confusion. "I had thought she was eager to return to see you all, but then when we returned, everything seemed to change. I have asked her what is the matter, but she has only said she requires time to adjust."

"Time to change into a proud woman who wants nothing to do with us," said Elizabeth bitterly.

Charles shook his head. "As I said, I do not understand it, nor can I refute your words. But she loves you, Elizabeth. I am certain that much has not changed. Perhaps when you return you may speak with her and understand what has distressed her."

"Or perhaps when you come to Derbyshire."

"Yes, that is exactly it!" He paused and, grasping Elizabeth's hand, he bowed over it. "Please enjoy yourself in the north, Elizabeth. And if you do happen to meet Darcy, please give him my best regards. I am certain everything will work out."

Though Elizabeth was not nearly so confident as Charles was himself, she felt a little lighter in spirit. One could hardly remain cast down when faced with Charles's eternal optimism and cheer.

Elizabeth stepped into the carriage with Charles's help, and she began her journey back to Longbourn. Tomorrow she would leave the neighborhood, and who knew when she would return? But she was determined to do as he suggested. The sense of malaise she had been struggling under had not left her, but perhaps, with her new brother's assistance, it had just grown a little lighter.

Pemberley was a grand old house, with centuries of history embedded in its very stones. A large, stately house built of the grey stone which was so plentiful in the vicinity, Pemberley had stood for centuries, a visible, imposing reminder of the stability of the Darcy heritage which had presided over the land for longer than the house had been in existence. It was often said that Pemberley compared favorably with many of the great houses in England, and this was a source of pride for the generations of its owners.

The current master of the estate was a young man, not yet eight and twenty, who had inherited far earlier than he would have expected due to his father's early death. With both of his parents already passed on to their eternal reward, he was left as the guardian of his much younger sister, though he was grateful that his father had possessed the foresight to appoint his cousin Anthony Fitzwilliam to share in Georgiana's care. There were times when Darcy did not know what he would have done without his cousin's support.

It was Georgiana who was on Darcy's mind at present. Like Darcy himself, Georgiana was much more comfortable at Pemberley than anywhere else in the world. But though she gave every indication of contentment, Darcy was not certain he could trust what his eyes were telling him.

It was Wickham's fault. The very thought of the man was enough to fill Darcy with rage. He almost wished that he had allowed Fitzwilliam to follow through with his threat to call Wickham out and solve the problem once and for all.

"Why do you scowl so, William?"

The sound of his sister's sweet voice pulled Darcy from his ruminations, and he realized he had allowed his dark thoughts to show on his face. A glance at Fitzwilliam told Darcy that his cousin knew exactly of what he had been thinking—Fitzwilliam was watching him, his own manner a little grim.

"There is no reason for you to concern yourself for me any longer," said Georgiana when he did not immediately reply. "I am quite recovered."

"I would hope so, dearest," replied Fitzwilliam. "It *has* been eight months."

"Believe me," said she, so quietly that Darcy had difficulty hearing her, "I have more than learned my lesson."

"I should hope so," said Darcy. "We have discussed what you did wrong at length, so I see no need to belabor the issue. I just wish for you to return to what you were before."

"I will. It will simply take time." Then Georgiana smiled at him, a mischievous sort of expression he had not seen in far too long. "Truly, you might have accompanied Mr. Bingley to Hertfordshire. But I suppose any excuse to avoid Miss Bingley must be grasped with both hands."

Fitzwilliam let loose a hearty guffaw, and Georgiana let out a little giggle at her own quip. Darcy supposed that he should take her to task for saying such a thing, though it was far truer than he would wish to reflect. In the end, however, he did not have the heart to censure her.

"I was happy to spend the autumn and winter with you, Georgiana," said Darcy at length. "My feelings for Miss Bingley have nothing to do with the matter."

"Neither do hers," interjected Fitzwilliam, "though I caution you to ensure Miss Bingley does not hear you speak of *any* feelings for her."

Fitzwilliam laughed again at the face Darcy made, but in the end, he decided that it would be best to simply ignore his cousin. Furthermore, it was nothing less than the truth, for Miss Bingley would take any perceived compliment he gave her and turn it into a reason to purchase her trousseau.

"I think . . ." Georgiana fell silent, and she appeared to be struggling with some great weight. In the end she sighed, then looked up at Darcy from behind long lashes. "I simply wish I had a friend."

"And this you do not find in your brother or me?" asked Fitzwilliam. "Or my sisters, for that matter?"

Georgiana colored, but she did not back down. "You are all wonderful, of course. But it is not the same. I had difficulty making friends at school, and there are not a lot of young ladies my age in this district."

"That is true," said Darcy. Georgiana suffered from the same affliction as Darcy did himself, though in his case it was simple reticence and a desire to avoid being the focus of attention, rather than Georgiana's sometimes crippling shyness.

"A friend with whom to share confidences would be lovely. But I know no one so well as to allow for such intimacy.

"Do not lose hope, Poppet," said Fitzwilliam. "You are growing into a young lady, and confidence will come with experience. I have no doubt you will make more friends than you can count."

"Thank you, Anthony," replied Georgiana with a slight smile. "Now, if you gentlemen will excuse me, I believe I shall retire."

Later, Darcy and his cousin retired to his study, and it was while they were lingering over glasses of port that a subject came up which had been on Darcy's mind for some time.

"You know, Darcy, if you were to take a wife, Georgiana would have at least one friend."

"*If* I chose the right woman. I sincerely wish it were that easy."

"Come now, Darcy," said Fitzwilliam with that insouciant grin which told Darcy he was about to make sport with him, "your marrying is the easiest thing in the world. All you need to do is stop running and allow Miss Bingley to catch you."

"As I said, *if* I choose correctly." There was no point trying to admonish Fitzwilliam or respond in a like fashion, as it would only spur him on. "As you know, Georgiana dislikes Miss Bingley almost as much as I do."

"Clever girl," murmured Fitzwilliam while taking a sip of this drink.

Darcy flashed his cousin a quick grin and turned his attention back to his own drink. "But you are right in essentials. This marriage business is the easiest thing in the world. Choose a woman of good dowry and impeccable connections and marry her."

"And then spend the rest of your life miserable," snorted Fitzwilliam.

"That does seem to be the problem."

Darcy was silent for several moments, thinking about the situation. It was not as if he had never had any interest in a woman. Unfortunately, his interest usually did not survive a little time in the woman's company, and the revelation that she was dull and unintelligent, interested in nothing more than fashion gazettes and the latest additions to her wardrobe or was an unrelenting shrew, clever and hard—or as Fitzwilliam had declared, the kind of woman who would make the rest of his life miserable. There simply did not seem to be much in between the two extremes.

"What of you?" asked Darcy, turning his attention back to his cousin. "You are two years older than I, and yet you remain unmarried yourself. Now that you are naught but 'Mr. Fitzwilliam,' should you not be looking for a wife yourself?"

Fitzwilliam sighed and set his glass down, rested his chin on his hand and stared into the fire. "I am in the same position as you, though there are some differences, as you know. I am both higher in society, being the son of an earl, and less in consequence, not being the heir. Father is interested in alliances and would marry me off to an earl's daughter without a second thought. But most earl's daughters have no desire to live on a small estate in the hinterlands of the kingdom."

"Thorndell is a good estate, Fitzwilliam. There is nothing wrong with it."

"No, there is not," replied his cousin. "I dare say I shall be quite comfortable there, though my income will not be a vast sum. But it is not Chatsworth either, and most young ladies of a certain level of society have been reared to expect Chatsworth rather than Thorndell."

It was nothing more than the truth, and Darcy conceded the point with a nod.

"Besides," said Fitzwilliam, his eyes staring into the fire such that he appeared mesmerized with the snap and hiss of the logs and the merrily dancing flames, "I wish for something more from marriage. It is more important to me to have a wife who is compatible with me than to have great riches."

"And what of love?"

Fitzwilliam turned a wry smile on Darcy. "Love is, indeed, a valuable commodity. However, I believe I will settle for compatibility if necessary. Love would be akin to the cream on top of the strawberries."

"True," replied Darcy. "And very well spoken. You know I wish you the best of luck."

"And I, you." Fitzwilliam turned back to Darcy and grinned, the serious moment seemingly forgotten. "Perhaps we shall have the very great fortune to find two sisters who will suit us. We have always called each other cousin, but perhaps a change to 'brother' would be welcome."

"You know I would never disagree with that," replied Darcy.

They stayed in the study speaking for some time before they sought their beds. Though the subject was not broached between them again, Darcy thought of the matter on several occasions. And he knew that Fitzwilliam thought about it as well, for there was some truth to the maxim of a man in possession of an estate being in want of a wife. Darcy certainly was himself. He simply had no idea where he should look for one.

CHAPTER III

$\mathcal{T}$he journey to Derbyshire was accomplished over the space of more than two days. Elizabeth had never journeyed north of Longbourn or further than Stevenage, so she spent much of her time looking out through the window at the passing scenery, noting the rolling hills, fields, and forests of central England with interest. At the beginning of her travels, she did not note much difference between what she was seeing and the beloved scenes of her home.

As they continued toward the north, however, she began to notice gradual changes in the land. It was, for the most part, tamed, as much of England was. The fields showed recent signs of planting, and those which were left to such crops as clover were showing the brilliant green she so loved. But though the changes were subtle, she noticed the rolling hills gradually grew more rugged and the land, less tame, and the appearance of rocky outcroppings and wilder forests grew more common.

"It almost seems like a different country," murmured Elizabeth late on the second day. They had passed through two counties already and were on their way through a third before they would finally reach Derbyshire on the morrow.

Her father, who had been engrossed in his book, looked up and said: "You were not unaware of the changes in the terrain. I have found you poring over my atlases many times."

"I did know it, Papa. But knowing and seeing are quite different, you must acknowledge. I have not been north of Hertfordshire before."

"That is true."

Elizabeth was grateful for her father's presence. Mr. Bennet's aversion to travel was something of a legend in the family, and Elizabeth had thought he might be content to send her in the Bennet carriage with a maid for company. Instead, he had declared his intention to see her to his sister's house himself.

"The land gradually continues to become more rugged the further north we go. Your Uncle Drummond, for example, lives not far from the Peak District, and you will be able to see some of the peaks in the distance from his house on a clear day. But for the truly rough country, you would have to travel to Scotland, land of the mountains, valleys, and lochs."

"Have you ever been there?" asked Elizabeth, curious about his response. Her parents did not often speak of their personal history, likely, Elizabeth thought, because their marriage was not the happiest.

"I have," replied Mr. Bennet. "In fact, your mother and I spent our wedding trip in the north." He paused and seemed to further consider the matter before he changed the subject. "But Derbyshire is a lovely county."

"Or so Aunt Gardiner always waxes eloquent."

Father and daughter laughed together. "Yes, Mrs. Gardiner's affinity for Lambton is well known. You will be staying not far from that town, so you will be able to judge for yourself."

Nodding, Elizabeth turned her attention back to the window. She wondered at the reason for her father's reticence on the subject. She was certain he had been about to say more before he decided differently, but what it was, she could not guess.

"Lizzy," said Mr. Bennet, "I wish for you to enjoy yourself in Derbyshire."

"I believe I shall, Papa. I imagine there will be society aplenty, given Mr. Drummond's reason for inviting me."

Mr. Bennet nodded, but his countenance remained stern. "You were quite young the last time we met the Drummonds so you will likely not remember much. Your uncle is an amiable man, and I believe you will like him a great deal. But my sister . . . Let us just say that Claire's life has not turned out the way she might have expected, and she has become quite bitter as a result."

Frowning, Elizabeth looked at her father askance. "Do you refer to some specific event?"

"I believe it is best not to be explicit," said Mr. Bennet after a pause. "If my . . . if my sister decides to tell you, then that is her prerogative, but I believe I shall be silent on the matter. What I wished to say is that you should not allow her to disparage you or make condescending remarks about you."

"She would do that?" asked Elizabeth with wide eyes.

Mr. Bennet shook his head. "Not so openly, I should think. Her opinions—brought about by her disappointments in life—are not precisely hidden. Though I have not seen her in many years, when last I was in her company, she was openly critical of gentle-born ladies in general, especially those who are not aware of their privilege."

"But that is nonsensical, Papa! She is gently-born herself."

"I am aware of that." Mr. Bennet paused for a moment, seeming to consider his words. "Bitterness can do that to a person. Sometimes the change in fortunes can cause a person to become unreasonable, where their opinions take such a radical shift as to be ridiculous. Your aunt has had a harder life than she would have expected as the daughter of a gentleman, as the size of her husband's estate has meant that she is quite low in society. I know that you are well able to fend for yourself, and Drummond has pledged to protect you. It is for his daughter's benefit that you go, after all. But you may expect cutting comments at the very least from your aunt."

"I receive those at home," replied Elizabeth. "I doubt a little vitriol will cause me to dissolve into tears."

"No, but then again, your aunt possesses more intelligence than your mother, which may make her more difficult to endure. You will be required to help with their chores, I would imagine, though Drummond will likely wish you to be primarily concerned with his daughter's education."

"Then I shall do what is necessary to promote harmony with her." Elizabeth paused and directed a serious look at her father. "I shall be well, Papa. There is no need to worry."

"Excellent! Now, I will also leave a certain stipend with your uncle, in case there is anything you should require, as well as an amount of money which will assist them in feeding another mouth. It is possible Drummond may attempt to refuse it, but I shall leave it with him all the same. That money will be available to you too."

"I brought everything I require, Papa."

The fondness in Mr. Bennet's gaze made Elizabeth feel warm all over. "I know you have. But there may be some occasion for you to purchase finer clothes than you now possess, as there are several wealthy families in the neighborhood. The money will also allow Olivia to make some purchases, if required."

Knowing her father would not give way, and understanding that he was likely right, Elizabeth thanked him and returned her attention to the passing scenery. They stopped soon after and took their rooms at the inn her father had chosen before starting once again early the following morning.

It was early afternoon on the third day when her uncle's house came into view. They had passed beyond a small strand of trees swaying gently in the breeze when they came over a low hill to see the manor house standing not far distant before them. It was, to Elizabeth's surprise, quite large—larger than her father's house, though smaller than Netherfield. It was built of stone and featured a large portico which sheltered the front door from the elements, with ivy running up the side of one wall. The driveway through which they drove was packed gravel and appeared well maintained, and the park in which the house was built was neat and clean. Had Elizabeth not had her father's words on the matter, she would have thought the estate was large and prosperous.

When the carriage rolled to a stop in front of the portico, Elizabeth saw the family emerge from the door. The carriage door was opened, Mr. Bennet stepped out and helped Elizabeth down, and then they turned and greeted the family.

"Bennet," said a tall man, stepping forward to grasp her father's hand. He was strong and lean, possessing a full head of dark, wavy hair greying a little at the temples. "Welcome to Kingsdown."

As her father greeted his brother-in-law, Elizabeth happened to be looking at her aunt, and the woman's look at her husband was no less than a sneer, though Elizabeth could not quite determine what prompted it. Startled at such an indecorous display, Elizabeth stared at her for a moment, until her aunt realized it and returned it. A look passed between them, and Elizabeth felt a hint of challenge from the other woman. There would undoubtedly be arguments between them in the future.

"This is Elizabeth," said Mr. Bennet, drawing Elizabeth's attention back to the two men, who had completed their greetings and were now proceeding to the introductions.

Mr. Drummond stepped forward and grasped Elizabeth's

shoulders, regarding her with a wide grin. "Little Lizzy. When I last saw you, you were a little sprite, in braids and a little green dress. I see you have grown into a beautiful young woman."

"Thank you, Uncle," said Elizabeth. "I am very happy to see you."

Turning, Mr. Drummond motioned to his family. "You may not remember her, but you have met your aunt, Claire. You also met Edward, my eldest son. The rest of Edward's siblings are Olivia, Thomas, David, and Leah."

Elizabeth curtseyed and greeted her cousins. Olivia was a girl of about Kitty's age, tall and pretty with long dark hair. Her younger brothers appeared to be between ten and thirteen years old, and appeared as most young boys were—mischievous and active. The younger girl was a little darling, her cherub face peaking up at Elizabeth from behind her elder sister's skirts.

"Well now, we should enter the house," said Mrs. Drummond, her words short and her manner abrupt. "There is little sense in standing out of doors."

So saying, the woman turned and began to make her way into the house. Out of the corner of her eye, Elizabeth witnessed her father and uncle sharing a shaken head, and she wondered about it. What would Mrs. Drummond say if she knew that Elizabeth's favorite pastime was walking country paths, drinking in the scents and sounds of the serenity of nature? At that moment, Elizabeth's two young cousins approached her, and she turned her attention away from her aunt.

"Elizabeth," said Olivia, as she curtseyed shyly. "Leah and I are happy to make your acquaintance." Leah, still clutching her sister's skirts, stared at Elizabeth, and she was not certain the girl was at all happy to see her.

Smiling, hoping to put her cousins at ease, Elizabeth replied: "And I am happy to make yours. You have a lovely home. I cannot wait to begin to explore the paths I am certain you have in abundance."

"Mama does not approve of our walking," blurted Leah. Then she blushed and hid behind her sister.

Elizabeth smiled and crouched down, catching Leah's eye when she dared to once again look at Elizabeth. "Perhaps I may show you the joys of nature, then. I am quite familiar with the paths around my father's estate, and the prospect of new places to explore has me quite breathless with anticipation."

The girl attempted a half smile, but soon her eyes darted up to her sister. Olivia, for her part, appeared bemused by the exchange. She reached down and took her sister into her arms, lifting her up and settling the girl on her hip. Leah, still shy, attempted to bury her head in her sister's shoulder, but Olivia coaxed her from hiding her face, instead encouraging her to face Elizabeth, though she appeared ready to hide again at any moment.

"She is right, though," said Olivia. "There is much to do on the farm, and if we spend all our time walking, I am certain Mama will be upset with us."

"Of course, I would never suggest that we neglect the tasks which must be completed," replied Elizabeth with a sage nod. "But surely there must be some time for leisure. As I understand, I am here to assist you as you begin to move in society, for you are almost of age to come out. Your father must have other activities in mind than simply working on the farm."

For a moment, Elizabeth thought Olivia might say something in response, but she decided not to. Instead, she turned and led Elizabeth into the house where her pelisse was divested and hung neatly in a closet, and the two girls showed her to her room. It was similar to her room in Longbourn, with a bed along the far wall, a small vanity on the other side, and a corner closet for her clothes.

"There is wash water in the basin," said Olivia, pointing to a large bowl on a small table sat beside the bed.

"Thank you," said Elizabeth. "I will refresh myself and be down directly."

With a nod, the other girl left, taking her sister. Elizabeth sighed and began to divest her clothes for something fresh. Inside, she was already wondering if it had been a good decision to come here.

When Elizabeth made her way down to the sitting-room before dinner, it was there that she noticed for the first time that the estate was not so prosperous as the outside might suggest. The sitting-room was large—larger than her mother's room at Longbourn. But it was also not in the latest fashion, the furniture showing signs of wear, and the wallpaper peeling in places, though she could see evidence of repairs having been completed at times in the past.

Elizabeth took a seat close to where Olivia sat with Leah by her side, and she turned, noting that her aunt was scrutinizing her. Mrs. Drummond appeared to possess more than a hint of sardonic amusement, and though Elizabeth wondered what the woman was about, she only nodded and attended her father's conversation with her uncle.

"Do you plan to stay with us long?" her uncle was asking her father.

"Perhaps a week," replied Mr. Bennet. "I will need to stay long enough to rest the horses, but I cannot be away for long. My youngest are likely to cause untold havoc if I did."

"Papa!" admonished Elizabeth. But her father just grinned.

"Are *all* your daughters that . . . high-spirited, Henry?" drawled Aunt Claire.

"Only my youngest," replied Mr. Bennet, unaffected by his sister's ironic tone. "My Lizzy is a lady through and through, though I will own that she tends toward playful manners."

"Excellent!" said Mr. Drummond, shooting a quelling glance at his wife. "I am certain the girls will get on famously."

"What can you tell me of society in this area, Uncle?" asked Elizabeth.

A shrug was Mr. Drummond's response. "I am certain it is much like that to which you are accustomed in Meryton. There are young girls and young men aplenty, vying for one another's attention, dancing the complex courtship rituals, not to mention men with their interest in estate matters, shooting, fishing and matrons with nothing in their heads but gossip."

"But my father said there are some large estates in the vicinity."

"That is true." Mr. Drummond paused and seemed to consider the matter for a few moments. "Though not all of them attend events at Lambton, there are a number of affluent families in the district. The closest to us are our neighbors to the north, the Darcys. At present, the family consists of naught but the master and his much younger sister."

"They are far too proud to associate with the likes of us," said Mrs. Drummond with a derisive sniff.

"I have always found Darcy perfectly unassuming," contradicted Mr. Drummond. Elizabeth did not miss his wife's annoyed glare, but if her uncle did, he ignored it. "His father before him was an excellent man, and Lady Anne Darcy was everything genteel and polite.

"He does, however, possess connections to the nobility, as his mother was the daughter of the old Earl of Matlock. The Fitzwilliams live further to the south, and I have always found them to be excellent people too."

"It seems we have a little knowledge of your neighbors, Drummond," said Mr. Bennet. "As you know, our Jane married a Mr. Bingley in January, and Mr. Bingley claims this Mr. Darcy as one of his closest friends. It seems Mr. Darcy was to come to Hertfordshire to assist his friend before a sudden change in plans kept him in Derbyshire."

"Then Jane has made a fortunate alliance," replied Mr. Drummond. "Darcy does not bestow his friendship lightly, but when he does, it is immovable. He is highly regarded in London society, from what I understand, and his influence is extensive."

Elizabeth shared a glance with her father, and she was certain they both knew what the other was thinking. It may have been a fortunate alliance, but with Jane's unforeseen behavior since her marriage, it was uncertain just how fortunate it was to the rest of the family.

"As your father no doubt informed you," continued Mr. Drummond, looking at Elizabeth, "I hope you will take Olivia under your wing and assist her transition into society." Mr. Drummond paused, and she witnessed the first hint of self-consciousness in his manner. "Kingsdown is a small estate, and we must fend for ourselves to a large extent. Thus, Olivia has not had the opportunity to attend school, though we have educated her to the best of our abilities. If what my brother Bennet says is true, he considers you the most intelligent of his daughters, the most widely read, and the most educated."

Elizabeth looked down, feeling a little self-consciousness herself. "I do like to read, Uncle, though I cannot speak to my own education. Do you have a pianoforte?"

"We do," replied her uncle, "though it is an older instrument. Olivia plays a little, but she has not had masters, nor the opportunity for much practice."

"I would not consider myself a proficient," said Elizabeth, "but I do like to play. Perhaps we may play together. I would be happy to help wherever required."

"Before you begin to plan to waste your time while you are here," interjected Mrs. Drummond in a severe tone, "you should remember that this is a farm, and we all do our part. If you mean to while away your hours here on nothing more than the pianoforte and other such frivolous pursuits, then you may as well return to your idyllic existence with your father."

"Claire," said Mr. Bennet, his eyes narrowed, "my Lizzy has never shirked her share of responsibility, but I did not bring her here to be your scullery maid."

"Of course, you did not," added Mr. Drummond. His glare at his wife was even more pointed than his previous looks were, but she returned it with a mutinous glint.

"I apologize, Bennet," said Mr. Drummond, turning to Elizabeth's father. "I did not bring you here under false pretenses. My primary motivation is to provide a good example for Olivia, as I have stated.

There may be some occasion for Elizabeth to assist in the running of the farm, but I have no desire to fill her day with chores."

"I am capable of assisting, Uncle," said Elizabeth, speaking hurriedly to relieve the tension. "I have assisted in the stillroom at Longbourn, and I visit the tenants regularly."

"There are only two tenants at Kingsdown, child," sniffed Mrs. Drummond with disdain. "And they are well able to fend for themselves. We do the work of the farm here, and I have no doubt that your pretty little hands have never seen the kind of work we do. If you do not mean to help in the real work, then you should return to your home."

"That is enough, Mrs. Drummond," growled Mr. Drummond. "We have already discussed this, and I will not have you plaguing our niece with this nonsense."

Though the tension in the room was thick, Elizabeth noted the lack of any reaction from the children. Edward, the eldest, watched behind a passive façade, while Olivia seemed almost annoyed. The younger boys were engaged in a game of their own and were not paying any attention, while Leah continued to cling to her sister's side, watching all through wide eyes. Clearly, the Drummonds' marriage was not any happier than Elizabeth's own parents' marriage was. But while Mr. and Mrs. Bennet tended to hide their lack of felicity behind her nerves and his sardonic amusement, it appeared the Drummonds often descended into open conflict.

"I am certain it will all work out," said Elizabeth. "As I said, I have no objection to assisting. If Olivia means to become comfortable in society, then we must have a certain amount of time to attend to those things she must learn."

Elizabeth turned to her aunt. "You might consider them frivolous, Aunt, but there are certain skills which are expected of a young gentlewoman, and Olivia must at least possess a passing familiarity with them."

"Olivia is not a gentlewoman," snapped Mrs. Drummond.

"I own an estate, do I not?" replied Mr. Drummond. Though he was a genial man, Elizabeth could see that his patience was almost exhausted. "I have tenants. Though I farm part of the land myself, that does not make me any less of a gentleman."

"You are as much a gentleman as any," said Bennet. His own gaze at his sister warning her to cease her comments.

It seemed like Mrs. Drummond realized that her husband and her brother were not to be pushed any further, for she looked away and did not speak again.

"Then it is settled," said Elizabeth, eager to leave the argument in the past. "I am very much looking forward to our time together." Elizabeth looked at her young cousin warmly, gratified when Olivia returned her smile with a timid one of her own.

"Excellent!" said Mr. Drummond. "Then perhaps we should all go in to dinner. There will be time for more conversation later."

They did as he suggested, and for a time, there was peace and harmony. Mrs. Drummond, however, was watchful, and Elizabeth thought that she herself was the primary target. There was, however, a liberal sprinkling of reproachful, even approaching disdainful, glances at her brother during the course of the meal. There was something strange happening, but Elizabeth, not knowing the whole of the history, could not understand it. Mrs. Drummond seemed to hold some sort of a grudge against her brother. Elizabeth hoped her time here would not be too uncomfortable, for if Mrs. Drummond continued in such a manner, it might very well be.

Chapter IV

*M*r. Bennet did, indeed, stay in Derbyshire for a week complete. It was during this time that Elizabeth came to understand more of the family's routine and was able to gain a certain insight into their characters, though much remained hidden.

As it turned out, Elizabeth's duties with respect to the house and its operation were less onerous than she thought Mrs. Drummond would have wished. Though she assisted in the gardens with the weeding and digging, most of her responsibilities revolved around the children, primarily the youngest girl. With the gardens, Elizabeth assisted without a hint of regret, for though they were vegetable in nature, rather than the flowers she and Jane had cared for at Longbourn, it was familiar work, and something she enjoyed. The seeds had only recently been planted, so there was little to do besides a little weeding, as most of the plants were in the early stages of growth.

Similarly, Elizabeth's care of the younger children was not at all arduous, and she found that they were dear children. The boys were, confirming Elizabeth's first impression, rambunctious and active, and part of her duties were to assist them in their studies, drilling them in math and reading their books with them. Mr. Drummond, she soon discovered, insisted that his children receive as much learning as he could provide, and when he discovered that Elizabeth was conversant with those subjects he had been teaching them himself, he was happy to cede their instruction to her.

As for Leah, Elizabeth soon discovered that the girl was shy, but intelligent, sweet, yet with a mischievous streak of her own. She also seemed to view her mother with some hesitation, which was far from a normal healthy relationship between parent and child. Elizabeth could not quite understand a parent behaving in such a way as to make a child wary, but she soon came to understand that it was her aunt's usual behavior.

Elizabeth also soon learned that what her aunt had said when Elizabeth had first arrived was nothing more than the truth—everyone on the estate assisted with the work which needed to be done, even down to little Leah. The boys all assisted their father in the fields—Edward shouldering much of the work as the eldest—while Olivia and Leah helped in the house, whether it was cleaning, in the kitchens, or whatever else needed to be done.

There actually were servants in the employ of the Drummonds, though not as many as Longbourn boasted, and they all performed several tasks. The maid, for example, also served as the housekeeper, in that she answered the door and planned much of the menus for their meals in addition to her duties cleaning and assisting the ladies when they dressed. They had a cook, but the girl who handled the cooking also helped in other aspects of the running of the house. There were also two farmhands who helped her uncle in the fields, the stables, and the other work such men often did, but one of them also acted as her uncle's coachman, and the other did much of the carpentry and other assorted work which was done on the estate. And contrary to her aunt's assertions, Olivia and Elizabeth visited the two tenants within a few days of her arrival, finding them to be pleasant people who seemed to be content with their lives.

"You are different from what I expected," said Olivia.

After their visit to the two tenants, the two girls were walking back toward the manor house. Elizabeth had been thinking of the mystery of her uncle's family when her cousin spoke and interrupted her thoughts.

"Oh?" asked Elizabeth. "What did you expect?"

The girl seemed a little embarrassed, but she lifted her chin and met Elizabeth's eye. "My mother said that young gentlewomen are insufferably proud, and consider themselves to be quite above those beneath them."

"You are not beneath me, Olivia," said Elizabeth. "Your father is a gentleman, though his estate is small. You must remember that my father is not a wealthy man either. By the strict interpretation, you and I are both the daughters of gentlemen, which makes us equal."

"I can see that now," said Olivia. "I sometimes think . . ."

"Yes?" asked Elizabeth when her cousin trailed off.

Olivia ducked her head. "It is just that Mama is so very angry. She has been as long as I can remember. But are we not more fortunate than the tenants we just visited?"

Elizabeth sighed. She did not wish to speak ill of her aunt to her aunt's daughter, but she did not wish to speak falsehood to Olivia either.

"I do not know what has happened in her life to make her so, Olivia," said Elizabeth. "I do not understand it. If it is a matter of her station in life, I cannot see that it is very much lower than it was when she was living at Longbourn with my grandfather."

"I shall no longer listen to her about you, Elizabeth," said Olivia, with all the confidence a young girl of seventeen can muster. "I would like to be your friend, as well as your cousin, if you will allow it."

"I would like that too," said Elizabeth. "But my friends call me 'Lizzy.' If you are to be my friend, I should like you to do the same."

A shyness settled over her young cousin, but she nodded. "I shall, Lizzy."

"But what shall I call you?" mused Elizabeth, a hint of teasing in her voice. "Livy, perhaps?"

"Oh, Lizzy!" giggled Olivia. "If you do that, then we shall simply confuse each other, as they sound so very much alike."

"Then I suppose you shall be bereft of your own nickname. Olivia it shall be."

The two girls returned to the house in high spirits, and though Elizabeth recognized the pinched look of displeasure from her aunt, she decided it was best to ignore the woman's ill humors. She could hardly be here for months without befriending her cousin. Was that not why she had come in the first place?

By contrast, her uncle was delighted. "I see you girls have become good friends."

"Yes, Papa," said Olivia. "Elizabeth is so very interesting. I am glad she has come."

"So am I, my dear."

Mr. Bennet spent most of his time with Mr. Drummond during his stay in Derbyshire. The two men it seemed were completely at ease in each other's company, and that led to a camaraderie that Elizabeth did not think she had ever seen between her father and any other man, except, perhaps, for Mr. Gardiner and maybe even Sir William. They spent time together in the fields, and Elizabeth even saw her father assisting with the work.

Though he was not in company with his sister much, other than at mealtimes, Elizabeth saw him speaking to her at times and in places where she suspected he thought it unlikely they would be overheard. He did not share the contents of those conversations with her, but she was certain he was warning her about her behavior toward Elizabeth herself. He might not have bothered—Elizabeth thought she was well able to care for her own concerns—but she was still grateful that he thought enough of her happiness to take a hand in it where his sister was concerned.

Elizabeth had little direct interaction with her aunt. Mrs. Drummond often directed her when she thought that something needed to be done, but she did not speak with her in any other fashion. Given Elizabeth's impression of Mrs. Drummond's character, she was quite happy with this state of affairs.

While Elizabeth had her chores and her cousin had hers, Mr. Drummond insisted that Elizabeth take some time to begin educating her cousin in some of the skills he knew she would need to move in society with a degree of credit. Although Elizabeth could not call herself an expert in all these subjects, she endeavored to instruct Olivia as best she could and soon discovered that her cousin was an intelligent girl and a quick study.

Though Elizabeth had a good knowledge of French and Italian, Olivia had not much talent for languages. Consequently, they did not spend much time in those studies. But her playing, though unrefined, as could be expected since she had had little instruction, was good for someone who had learned through her own study. She had a good notion of fingering and could pick out a tune by sound alone. Elizabeth thought she would be more proficient than Elizabeth was herself, if she practiced and received some instruction.

They also practiced dancing, and Elizabeth found that her cousin anticipated the upcoming amusements with an excitement which reminded Elizabeth of her younger sisters. The girls spent several pleasant hours going through the steps, laughing and giggling among themselves. They also had, for company, Leah, who was determined to learn to dance herself.

"What are assemblies like, Lizzy?" asked Olivia one day during one of their sessions. Since there was no one to play the pianoforte while they were dancing, they practiced by means of Elizabeth keeping a beat which she encouraged Olivia to follow.

"I believe you might end up disappointed," said Elizabeth, flashing her cousin a mischievous smile. "Assemblies can be dull affairs, especially when the number of young ladies exceeds that of young men, as is typical in Meryton."

"But surely they are not all like that," protested Olivia.

"Of course not," replied Elizabeth with good humor. "I quite enjoy dancing as a rule. There is something freeing in moving about a floor with nothing in mind but the next steps, and it can be agreeable, indeed, with a partner who is kind and amiable."

"I can hardly wait." The girl was staring off into the distance, seemingly alight with dreams of a handsome prince come to take her hand for a set.

"It is great fun. But do not forget your position in society and your status as a young gentlewoman. There is a certain level of behavior expected, and though we dance to have enjoyment, among other things, we must always remember to uphold that expectation." Elizabeth grimaced. "My youngest sisters, who are entirely too exuberant for their own good, often forget to behave with decorum."

"I will not forget, Lizzy," said Olivia. "I wish to make both you and my father proud of me."

Elizabeth put an arm around her cousin's shoulder. "I know you do. And I have no doubt you will be successful. If there is one thing I can impress upon you is that you must always be aware of your behavior and that of those around you. We, neither of us, possess a large dowry to induce young men to propose to us. That can be a blessing, as it will deter those who marry with only fortune in mind, but it can also be a curse, as many perfectly acceptable young men will not even look in your direction."

"What do you see it as?" asked Olivia, her curiosity evident.

"A bit of both," said Elizabeth. "I have always wished to marry for the deepest of love, and the lack of a dowry keeps fortune hunters at bay. I have striven to remember that I have only my charms to recommend me, and I hope there is a man in the world who can see that I am worth all the wealth in the world. But in our society so much is made of fortune that I fear it may be difficult to find that one man."

"Then your sister Jane has been fortunate."

A pang of regret pierced Elizabeth's heart at the thought of Jane. She had attempted to avoid thoughts of her sister in the days since she had come to Kingsdown, but the thought of her was still enough to fill Elizabeth with sorrow at the distance which had sprung up between them.

But this was not something she would share with her young cousin. It was far too private for that.

"She has, indeed," replied Elizabeth. "She is doubly fortunate because Mr. Bingley is such a good man, and he positively dotes on her. I very much wish for the same myself."

"Then I shall hope for the same," declared Olivia. "My brother will say I am foolish to harbor such wishes, but I do not care."

"If it if foolish to have dreams, then I prefer to be a fool," said Elizabeth. "It is our dreams which allow us to have hope in the future. Life is very dull without them."

Olivia agreed, and they turned their attention back to their practice. Their developing closeness was a source of pleasure for Elizabeth. In some small way, Elizabeth thought her closeness with Olivia was filling the hole left in her heart by Jane's defection.

The time soon came for Mr. Bennet to return to Longbourn, for, as he put it himself: "I do not know what Kitty and Lydia have got up to in my absence, and I cannot count on your mother to limit their behavior to any great extent."

Elizabeth shook her head. "I would prefer you take them in hand yourself, Papa. They will ruin us all if they are not checked."

"Perhaps you are correct, Lizzy. But can you imagine the commotion which would ensue if we were to restrict Lydia's fun?"

"It would undoubtedly be unpleasant," said Elizabeth, not giving an inch. "But if they ruin us all, then none of us will ever make a good marriage."

"But would it not be amusing to see Miss Bingley's reaction to it?" chortled Mr. Bennet. "I imagined Miss High-and-Mighty would be taken down a notch or two if our family was embroiled in scandal."

All Elizabeth could do was shake her head. She knew that Mr. Bennet had no more desire for scandal than Elizabeth did herself, but he loathed noise in his house, and the quickest way to disturb whatever peace he possessed would be to restrict Lydia. He would hear it not only from his two youngest daughters, but also, undoubtedly, from his wife. Given Elizabeth's conversation with her mother before her departure, she wondered if her mother might not be brought to see reason. Either way, there was nothing she could do about it at present.

"Regardless, I did not wish to speak of Lydia," said her father. "I wished to discover how you have found your stay in this house, Lizzy."

"It is different from Longbourn, to be sure," said Elizabeth. "But I like Olivia very much, indeed, and Leah is a dear, sweet girl. The younger boys are prone to mischief, the same as all such boys, but they are good lads, I dare say. My uncle is all that is kind and attentive, and I could not be happier with him."

"You do not mention your aunt and her eldest son," observed Mr. Bennet.

Elizabeth sighed. "My aunt is difficult, as I am sure you know."

"I do."

"It seems to be best to simply avoid her," said Elizabeth. "As for Edward, I hardly know what to make of him, as he rarely ventures an opinion of his own. Underneath his reticence, however, I sense a hint of the same discontent which rules his mother's life."

With a nod, Mr. Bennet said: "I knew you would notice it. Edward has said little to me either, but I have also seen his discontent."

It did not signify, so Elizabeth only shrugged. "The rest of the family is delightful, so I confine my attentions to those who wish to be pleased. It is clear that my aunt and eldest cousin do not wish it, so while I will return civility for civility, I believe I will be content with Olivia and those who do wish it."

Mr. Bennet watched her for several moments, apparently considering something, before he spoke again. "Lizzy, I do not wish you to be in circumstances you find uncomfortable. If you would prefer not to stay, we will make our excuses and return to Hertfordshire."

"I believe I have already committed to staying, Papa," said Elizabeth quietly.

"That commitment may be broken," was her father's short reply. He sighed and was silent for a moment before he spoke. "There are many things about your aunt that you do not understand, Lizzy, and I have been loath to inform you of them, as I wished you to form your own opinion of her without my interference."

"Then you know why she is so bitter?"

A grimace was preceded by Mr. Bennet's softly spoken: "I know of the genesis of it, yes. As you are aware, I have not met with my sister in many years, though I do correspond with your uncle. I had not realized that she had become so . . . openly dissatisfied. The last time I was in her company, I knew she was discontented, but she was accustomed to hiding it behind a façade. Much has changed since then."

"She seems to have some specific grudge."

"Toward me," said her father with a nod. "She was happy and bright as a child. I would never have thought she would end this way, no more than I would have thought she would transfer her animosity to one of my children."

"I will be well, Papa," said Elizabeth. This talk of her aunt had caused her to hesitate, but it somehow felt right that she would stay here for a time. Perhaps in helping Olivia, Elizabeth could somehow help her aunt to become more contented in her life. Elizabeth almost laughed at the absurdity of such an arrogant thought, but there it was. Either way, she would not be chased away by a bitter woman.

"Are you certain?"

Elizabeth turned a fond smile on her father. He could be considered lackadaisical and indifferent at times, and he had a disturbing tendency to laugh at the actions of his daughters and wife, but he was always quick to defend them at any sign of trouble, especially Elizabeth, who was his favorite. She had always tried, with a healthy measure of philosophy, to appreciate his good qualities.

"I am," replied Elizabeth, with growing conviction. "I am certain that I will have my uncle to turn to, should my aunt become difficult, and I am very fond of Olivia and Leah already. I am content with my decision to stay here, Papa."

Mr. Bennet looked on her fondly. "You are determined, Lizzy. It has always been my opinion that is one of your best qualities. I will inform your uncle. I am certain he will be happy with your decision."

The next day, Mr. Bennet boarded his carriage and began the long journey back to Longbourn. She had not told him, but part of her decision to stay in Derbyshire was due to the desire to avoid Jane's continued distance—she already felt happier here in her uncle's house, felt like she had some purpose other than the trivial, dreary concerns she had felt eating away at her patience when she was in her home. Elizabeth still looked on the prospect of finding a husband in Derbyshire with more than a little skepticism, but she decided she would not make herself unhappy about it either.

Though Elizabeth might have thought that her father's departure would have released all her aunt's unpleasantness with cutting words and little insults, in fact the opposite was true. Her brother's departure seemed to settle Mrs. Drummond, and though she was no more amiable or kind to Elizabeth—or even to her own family—Elizabeth witnessed less of the overt hostility which had been such a large part of her interactions before.

It happened not a day after her father's departure that Elizabeth was given the first glimpse of the society of Derbyshire. There were no events for them to attend yet, but on a day when the sun was shining, Mr. Drummond had a visitor come to the house, and Elizabeth saw the man of whom she had heard so much, though they did not exchange words.

Having stepped outside to enjoy a short constitutional around the grounds, Elizabeth and Olivia had completed a circuit of the back lawn and come around the house to see a young man dismounting from a large grey stallion.

"Darcy!" they heard Mr. Drummond's voice as he exited the house. "How are you today, young man?"

"Very well, thank you," said Mr. Darcy in response. He stepped toward Mr. Drummond and the two men shook hands. "I have come to discuss the fence at our border."

"Of course. If you will wait for a moment, I will have my horse brought around and we can go there directly."

With a bow, Mr. Drummond moved toward the stables to the side of his house to retrieve his horse and Mr. Darcy stood there for a moment waiting for him. As he had not noticed Elizabeth and Olivia, Elizabeth was able to take her first impression of him, and she was not at all disappointed. He was tall and lean, with wavy dark hair which settled over his forehead and tickled the collar of his jacket. His clothes seemed to be of fine quality, though they were not ostentatious, consisting of pants, shirt, waistcoat, and jacket, clearly made for riding. He also wore a leather overcoat, unfastened in the front, which undulated around his legs in the breeze. His boots were black and shiny, and Elizabeth though the man's valet must have polished them until they gleamed.

In all, Elizabeth thought he was the most perfect specimen of masculinity that she had ever seen. Even Mr. Bingley, who Elizabeth had acknowledged to Jane several times was well-favored, was nothing to Mr. Darcy.

"Is he not frightfully handsome, Lizzy?" asked Olivia by her side.

"I dare say he is," replied Elizabeth. "This is not the first time you have seen him?"

Olivia shook her head. "He comes to speak with my father on occasion, and I have seen him in Lambton. I care not what Mama says, but Mr. Darcy has never displayed a proud or haughty manner to me or my father."

Elizabeth was forced to agree with her cousin. Mr. Darcy, though he stood with seeming unconcern, did not give a hint of distaste in his surroundings; in fact, as he glanced about, it seemed to be with interest, rather than pride or disapproval. By contrast, on the occasions when Mr. Bingley had forced his sister to come to Longbourn, the woman's thinly concealed contempt had been plain for all to see, and she had much less reason to be proud than Mr. Darcy, Elizabeth was certain.

He seemed to become aware of them, and he smiled and tipped his hat, and Elizabeth and Olivia responded by curtseying in his direction. But Mr. Drummond led his horse out at that moment and the two men rode away.

"I think a woman would give much to be the subject of Mr. Darcy's attentions," said Olivia.

"Do not allow such nonsensical thoughts into your head, girl!"

The sound of the loud voice close behind them startled both girls, and they jumped in unison. Behind them stood Mrs. Drummond, arms akimbo, glaring at them.

"The likes of Mr. Darcy do not pay attention to the likes of you, Olivia." Then Mrs. Drummond turned to Elizabeth. "My husband has decreed that you are here to teach my daughter to be a lady." Mrs. Drummond's scoffing tone instantly put Elizabeth's back up. "But I will thank you not to fill her head with such nonsense."

"Elizabeth said no such thing, Mama," cried Olivia, her manner screaming her defiance. "I only said that Mr. Darcy was handsome and that it would be pleasant to receive his attentions."

While Elizabeth would have thought Olivia's rebellious words would earn her mother's ire, Mrs. Drummond only shot them a sneer and turned away. A moment later, she was gone, leaving Elizabeth and Olivia to themselves yet again.

"I hate her!" cried Olivia, and though her voice was quiet, there was no lack of fervency in it.

"Olivia!" admonished Elizabeth. "You should not say such things about your mother."

"But I do," averred Olivia. "She is malicious, she treats my father with contemptuous ridicule, and she is so mean-spirited that Leah is afraid of her."

"But she is your mother, and you must respect her as such," said Elizabeth. "Come, let us go into the house. I believe a little time in more sedentary pursuits would do us both a world of good."

Though Olivia still glared with mutinous disgust after her mother, she allowed Elizabeth to persuade her into the house. Elizabeth was glad that her cousin had already started to defer to her; she would clearly have some work to do to keep the peace between mother and daughter.

CHAPTER V

$\mathcal{E}$ lizabeth Bennet considered herself something of an expert on the subject of difficult relationships with a mother. As far back as Elizabeth could remember, Mrs. Bennet's attention had been fixed on Jane and, later, Lydia. Jane was the eldest, the most beautiful, the sweetest, and Lydia was the liveliest, the most liked in company. Mrs. Bennet had lived with the entail for so long that she had hung her hopes on Jane, the most beautiful daughter, and loved Lydia because she was so like her in essentials.

As the second daughter, Elizabeth had never quite measured up to Jane in Mrs. Bennet's opinion. She was not as beautiful, she insisted upon unfashionable activities such as walking and reading, and she was far too intelligent and outspoken—the latter being the greater sin—for any man to look upon her with any serious consideration.

Though she had never resented Jane for being the focus of Mrs. Bennet's hopes, Elizabeth had not missed the times her mother disparaged her or voiced her despair that Elizabeth would ever find a husband. At times, her mother's words had hurt. At times, she had wondered how she could ever measure up to her elder sister. At times, she had wondered what she had done to earn her mother's scorn.

It was a matter of supreme irony that Mary, a child even more ignored by her mother than Elizabeth, should have been the one to save the family from the entail. And with Jane's defection, it appeared like Mrs. Bennet would be forced to rely on Mary's generosity and sense of duty to keep her housed and clothed should her husband pass away first. Elizabeth's improved relationship with her mother in the days before she left was welcome, but she did not forget what it was like when Mrs. Bennet's approbation was withheld.

In the days after her father left, Elizabeth observed the Drummond family, and to a large degree, she realized that Olivia had been correct when she had made her comments concerning her mother. Elizabeth had never met such a bitter and sometimes mean-spirited woman as Mrs. Drummond. She largely ignored all the children, and when she did speak to them, it was to snap at them for some perceived wrong or to berate them for only she knew what.

What was more heartbreaking was the fact that Mr. Drummond was not insensible to his wife's behavior, but he presented the image of a man who had long despaired of changing it to any degree. When she spoke to his children in that sharp voice of hers, he would make a comment to her, inducing her to silence—and not a little sullenness— and she would be silent for a time, only for the scene to play out again at a later time.

The children had varied methods of dealing with Mrs. Drummond's ill humors. The eldest, Edward, strangely escaped being a target of her vitriol. They were not precisely close that Elizabeth could see, but when she spoke with him it was with a softer tone, while he replied with respect, but with evident distance. Olivia glowered at her mother when she spoke—and when she was not looking—but she seemed to ignore everything the woman said. The two younger boys simply shrugged her off and looked to their father.

But in Leah, Elizabeth saw the truth of what Olivia had told her— the youngest child was afraid of her mother. Her propensity for clinging to Olivia's legs was born of her fear of Mrs. Drummond, not shyness, and Elizabeth began to see that Mrs. Drummond resented the child, though she could not understand why that should be. There was very little interaction between them, other than a curt word from the matron on occasion, and Leah normally stuck close to her father and her eldest sister. That seemed to suit Mrs. Drummond quite well, as she rarely went out of her way to do anything other than sneer at her youngest.

The situation in the house was trying on them all, and they all had various ways of relieving that tension. Mr. Drummond and his sons spent time out of doors, working in the fields or stables. Mr. Drummond would often ride the grounds with his sons, so they were able to escape for much of the day. Olivia and Leah, however, were often bound to the house where there was no escape. Thus, Elizabeth began to devise some means by which they could be away, at least for a little while.

"I believe that we should go on a picnic today," said Elizabeth, one morning a few days after her father had departed. Mr. Drummond was present, and by now Elizabeth had learned that she should make such suggestions in his presence, as Mrs. Drummond would invariably object. "Do you know of any good locations we could use?"

Olivia shot her mother a hesitant look, but Mr. Drummond immediately spoke his approval for the scheme. "And excellent idea. Perhaps the hill on the norther border would be a good location?"

"Oh, yes, that would be lovely," replied Olivia. "It has a good view out on Mr. Darcy's lands."

While Olivia was speaking, Elizabeth noted her uncle watching his wife, as if daring her to protest. Mrs. Drummond grimaced at the mention of the Darcys, but she did not protest, contenting herself with a grunted: "As long as your responsibilities are completed in advance."

"Of course, Aunt," said Elizabeth.

When everything had been prepared, the three girls, with a basket in hand, filled with simple fare obtained from the cook, set out toward the hill. Elizabeth had not yet walked out in this direction from the farm, and she was anticipating the new sights which awaited her. The ground to the north was rockier, with strands of alder and beech, intermixed with gorse and other low standing bushes. To the west of them some little distance, a creek bubbled and gurgled on its way to its meeting with a larger waterway, which Olivia informed her lay some distance away near the house at Pemberley.

Soon they were climbing the small hill, and when they crested it, the valley spread out in front of them, moving down through the ever-present trees to the cultivated farmland below. At the top of the hill there were a few tall trees which provided a little shade from the sun, and it was next to these trees that they lay down their blanket, removed their bonnets, and began to eat their meal.

"The land to the north all belongs to Pemberley?" asked Elizabeth as she took a bite of her cool cucumber sandwich.

"It does," said Olivia. Between the two young women, Leah sat with her own sandwich. The girl was quiet and focused on her meal, but though she did not speak much, Elizabeth was of the impression that very little escaped her notice.

"How far distant is the house?"

"I have never been there myself," confessed Olivia. "But Papa says that it is some five or six miles from our house to Pemberley manor. I understand that it is down in the valley," Olivia waved her hand toward the gently sloping land, "but it is off to the left, behind some of those trees, and therefore not visible from here."

The girls were silent for some moments, concentrating on their meal, when Olivia once again spoke, saying: "Papa says that our land used to extend down into the valley."

"Truly?" asked Elizabeth.

Olivia nodded. "I do not know the whole of the story, but Kingsdown was once a larger and more prosperous estate. Hard times came upon my ancestors, and slowly the estate was reduced to what it is now. That land to the north was sold to Pemberley to help keep the estate solvent, and other tracts in other locations were sold as well."

"That would explain why the house is much larger than an estate of this size would usually support."

"It does," agreed Olivia. "You have not been to the servants' quarters. Much of it is unused, with only the two maids and the two hands to live in it. And many of the rooms in the main part of the house, especially above stairs, are closed." Olivia paused and then directed an apologetic look at Elizabeth. "Before your coming, your room and your father's rooms needed to be cleaned, as they had not been used in many years. We keep the dust from building up and the maids will go in and beat the mattresses to keep them from rotting. Mama was not pleased the work had to be done. I think she prefers to forget about all the extra rooms we do not use."

With the greatest of care, mindful of not hurting her cousin's relationship with her mother any further, Elizabeth said: "Olivia, do you know where your mother's bitterness originates?"

A shadow settled over Olivia. "She has always been like that." Olivia's tone was dead and allowed for no dispute. "Ever since I can remember she has been angry. I try to stay away from her as much as I can."

"Mama is always angry," added Leah, pressing herself into Olivia's side. "She does not like us."

Elizabeth's heart melted at the girl's solemn surety of her mother's indifference. "I have not known her for long, but she may surprise you someday. I am certain she loves you, as any mother would love their child."

The open skepticism of the younger girl broke Elizabeth's heart, but though Olivia scowled, she seemed to understand that it was best to stay silent and say nothing. It seemed like the subject of their mother was best left alone, so Elizabeth began speaking of her own family, relating some anecdotes of her own childhood in Hertfordshire.

'You climbed a tree?" asked Olivia with shock when Elizabeth mentioned one of the more infamous stories from her childhood.

"When I was younger, I often could be found in the branches of a tree." Elizabeth paused and laughed. "Or rather, I took great care not to be found, for my mother would surely be overcome with paroxysms, should she find me in so unladylike a position."

"But this time you were not careful?"

"The kitten was stuck in the tree," said Elizabeth with a shrug. "I could hardly allow it to languish there and perhaps injure itself attempting to climb down."

"Could your father not have ascended with a ladder to rescue it?"

"That is what Papa said. But at the time—and you must remember I was naught but seven years of age—I thought I was the creature's last hope, so I climbed up to retrieve it."

"Can I assume your mother found you?"

With a rueful nod of her head, Elizabeth said: "You must understand that my mother has little love for nature. I was far enough away from the house that I was certain I was safe from her prying eyes. Unfortunately, she chose the moment when I was reaching out for the kitten to scream at me."

Olivia winced, no doubt thinking of the times her own mother had raised her voice. "Did you fall?"

"No, but it was a near thing. When I had balanced myself, I glared down at my mother, displaying my most imperious expression and said: 'Do not disturb me, Mama. The fate of the kitten is at stake.'"

By now both of her cousins were laughing at her description, Olivia in genuine amusement, while Leah looked on with no little awe.

"Once I retrieved my precious package and descended, I was hurried back to the house for a bath and a dressing down. My dress was in a passable state to me, though my mother did not see it the same way—she examined it and exclaimed over every blemish. I was sent to bed without dinner, and told my mother would disown me if I should ever dare to climb a tree again."

"At least your final adventure into the branches of a tree was memorable," said Olivia, still laughing.

"Who said it was my last adventure?" asked Elizabeth with exaggerated nonchalance. "I merely confined my exploits to trees situated further from the house."

The girls descended into hilarity again, and it was several moments before they recovered enough to speak.

"Can you teach me to climb trees?" asked a wide-eyed Leah.

"I am sorry, my dear," said Elizabeth with an affectionate smile, "but my tree climbing days are many years in the past. Besides, I do not believe your parents would be pleased with me if I taught you such skills."

Olivia grimaced. "I believe you are correct." She turned to Leah and said: "You should keep the stories Lizzy tells us to yourself, Leah. Mama would not like hearing them."

The solemn manner in which Leah agreed to keep Elizabeth's secrets again prompted Elizabeth's regret. She could not understand how they endured the situation.

"It appears as if you girls are enjoying yourselves."

As one, the three girls looked up to see Edward watching them, the hint of a smirk displaying his amusement containing a bit of a sarcastic edge. By her side, Elizabeth could feel Olivia stiffening, and she noted that Leah also regarded her eldest sibling warily.

"I suppose we have," said Elizabeth, deciding to bear the burden of the response. "I enjoy your sisters' company very much, Cousin."

Edward regarded them for several moments, before he motioned them to rise. "It is time to return to the house. In the future, I would appreciate it if you would limit these outings. I have tasks to complete, and I must put them off to fetch you."

"You need not bother," said Elizabeth, glaring at him and daring him to disagree. "We are not so far from the house that we cannot make our way back without your assistance."

Though Edward pursed his lips, he did not respond. Knowing there was nothing to be done, Elizabeth assisted Olivia in packing the remains of the lunch back into the basket. It did not escape Elizabeth's notice that Leah held her sister's hand tightly and stayed close to her as they walked. Edward, it appeared, did not notice her behavior. In fact, he seemed to have something to say to Elizabeth herself, as he deliberately slowed his steps and allowed his sisters to continue ahead.

Her conjecture was proven correct when he turned to her after some minutes and said: "You should not fill my sisters' heads with dreams and fanciful notions."

"Oh?" asked Elizabeth. "I was under the impression that was why your father asked me to come to Derbyshire. It seems to me that preparing for her coming out would fit *your* idea of a 'fanciful notion.'"

Rather than becoming annoyed as Elizabeth might have thought, Edward only shook his head. "Why raise their hopes, only for them to be dashed?"

"Are you so certain they are destined to be dashed?"

"You are familiar with the world in which we live, Cousin," said he, throwing her an exasperated glance. "There are no men who will consider my sisters as partners in marriage when they come with no dowry and connections to naught but a man of business, a country squire, and a farmer who gives himself airs of being a gentleman."

"You are harsh on your father, are you not?"

Edward grimaced. "I simply understand the reality of the situation. The best my sisters can ever hope for is a country parson, perhaps. I would not be surprised if either of them make no more favorable match than a tenant."

"I am sorry, Cousin, but I do not subscribe to your pessimism." Edward's eyes darted to Elizabeth, and she showed him that she was not impressed by his manners or his attitude. "Perhaps you have chosen to believe this, but I choose to believe that there are men in the world who are not ruled by greed and shallow desires."

"I suppose you believe that some wealthy man will offer for you, elevate you to the status of a duchess." The sarcasm in her cousin's voice was unmistakable, and his gaze raked over her with evident disdain for her naïveté. "Or perhaps great wealth alone is enough. Shall you throw yourself at Darcy? He has remained inscrutable to all—perhaps he is waiting for just such a fortune-hunter as you."

"If you mean to provoke me to anger, Cousin," replied Elizabeth, "I shall not oblige you. I have no such thoughts in mind. All I ask from a husband is love and respect, and I am determined that I shall not enter into marriage if I cannot have them."

"Then you shall die an old maid."

"That is possible." Elizabeth shrugged. "If that is to be my fate, then I accept it willingly. But I shall not compromise my principles in favor of a comfortable situation, and I will not teach your sisters to have no hope."

The look Edward directed at her sent shivers down her spine. His behavior was not objectionable—not like his mother, for certain—but she did not quite know what to make of him.

"When I heard you were coming," said he after a moment's silence, "I had thought to explore whether we were compatible as marriage partners."

"You may dismiss such a notion completely," said Elizabeth. "I do not think we would suit."

"In this, I can agree with you. I believe I will require a practical wife. Practicality is something you do not seem to possess."

"I do when the situation is right." Elizabeth turned to her cousin and stopped walking, forcing him to stop if he wished to continue to speak with her. "I have no desire to argue with you, Edward. I can see there are differences in our opinions, and I would not bring more discord into your father's home.

"I will promise that I will not teach your sisters to hope without reason, nor will I instruct them to reach further above them than is wise. But I will also not teach them to be completely without hope. Can you accept that?"

Edward eyed her for a moment before he looked away. "I wish, Elizabeth, that I could give my sisters everything their hearts desire— my brothers too, for that matter. But I cannot. My father is not a wealthy man, and neither will I be wealthy when I inherit. I do not wish to see them disappointed by life."

"Disappointment is part of life, Edward," said Elizabeth. "No one, not the wealthiest man in the world, has everything he wishes. But to me, the worst fate is to live, having no faith, no expectation of joy. One can strive for a better life, for better circumstances, or even just for one to love, as I do. Disappointment will inevitably strike us during our lives. It is how we deal with our disappointments that define us, that define our happiness."

"Very well, then," said Edward. "A truce it is." He attempted a smile. "Olivia and Leah have been happier since you have come, and I do appreciate that. I will support you however I can."

"Thank you," said Elizabeth, appreciating her success in coming to a détente with her cousin.

They walked back to the house in silence, eventually overtaking Olivia and Leah, who had stopped, wondering what had become of them. Elizabeth saw the girls looking at her with curiosity and gave a minute shake of her head. There was no need for her to concern herself, it seemed. Perhaps Edward would be an ally after all.

"You did not tell me that such beauty could be found in the wilds of Derbyshire, Darcy."

Darcy looked away from the retreating forms of the two ladies, the young girl, and his neighbor's eldest son, to see Fitzwilliam grinning at him.

"Can I assume you are acquainted with these people?"

With a shrug, Darcy said: "The young man is my neighbor's son, Mr. Edward Drummond, while the younger girls are his daughters, Miss Olivia Drummond and Miss Leah. The other I do not know."

"And she the jewel of the group, I dare say," replied Fitzwilliam. "The distance makes it difficult, but she was slender, and her hair appeared to be a lovely shade, and I would not be surprised if she was pretty, indeed. Perhaps you should ask for an introduction."

Darcy scowled at his cousin. "I know nothing of her."

"What better way to learn than to be introduced?"

A grunt escaped Darcy's lips, and he turned away from his cousin, heeling his horse to return to Pemberley, sensing Fitzwilliam following him. It had been the merest chance that had led him to this far flung part of the estate, and he had not expected to see the ladies there, nor the young man who had, it seemed, come to collect them. From his experience, the Drummond children were immersed in assisting their parents care for the estate, which had dwindled to little more than a farm. Drummond was a good man, though, and Darcy esteemed him for that fact alone.

"I have seen her once before," said Darcy, giving voice to his thoughts. "She was at Kingsdown two days ago when I visited."

"And?" prompted his cousin.

Darcy only shrugged. "I know nothing of her. Drummond and I needed to speak of the fence between our properties. The young miss never came up in our conversation."

"Do you think she is some relation?"

"I do not know. I have never heard of any relations of the Drummonds, but then again, they have not spoken much of themselves the times I have been in their company. Furthermore . . ."

"Yes?" asked Fitzwilliam when Darcy remained in his thoughts for several moments.

"Perhaps I should not speak so," said Darcy, "but Mrs. Drummond has always given the impression of a woman who is not content with her lot."

A frown was Fitzwilliam's response. "There may be many reasons, if she is discontented."

"That is true. I do not mean to cast aspersions on her character, and she has never been anything other than proper in my presence, and I have never had to concern myself with the prospect of her pushing her daughter on me."

Fitzwilliam laughed and shook his head. "It always comes to that, does it not?"

"I would be very happy if it did not, but society mothers are relentless."

Though he continued to shake his head, Fitzwilliam said nothing further on the subject.

"I shall depart on the morrow for Thorndell."

Darcy nodded. "You will return, though?"

"Of course," said Fitzwilliam with an expansive grin. "The society you keep here is more interesting than any I have experienced at Thorndell. I have a few details to see to—when they are complete, I will return directly. I should be gone no more than two or three days."

"Then God speed, Cousin. Georgiana and I will anticipate your return."

CHAPTER VI

*T*wo days after their picnic, Mr. Drummond asked Elizabeth and Olivia if they would like to accompany him to Lambton.

"I have some business in town, and I believe there are some items for you young ladies to purchase."

They were sitting at breakfast, and Elizabeth had been contemplating what she planned to do that day. The invitation to go to Lambton had taken her by surprise.

"I would like to go, Papa," said Olivia. "But to what items do you refer?"

"A visit to the dressmaker would be in order, for one," replied her father. "As you know, there is an assembly next week, and as it is only an informal gathering at Lambton's assembly hall, I believe it would be a good opportunity for you to have your first taste of society."

A movement out of the corner of her eye caught Elizabeth's attention, and she caught a glimpse of her aunt's grimace. The woman did not say anything, leading Elizabeth to believe that the subject had already been canvassed between them, and her aunt had already been informed of Mr. Drummond's plans for this outing. She did not seem to be pleased, but she did not protest.

"And, there are other activities in which to indulge in Lambton."

Mr. Drummond smiled at Elizabeth. "My brother Bennet led me to believe that his second daughter is a great reader, indeed, and yet she has not yet entered a bookstore since her arrival in Derbyshire."

The quiet scoffing of the Drummond matron was universally ignored. Instead, she fixed a stern look on her uncle.

"I am not a great reader. You should not pay any attention to my father, as he has a propensity to tease."

"Perhaps that is true, Lizzy," replied Mr. Drummond, not at all put off. "But I believe today is an excellent opportunity to go to Lambton and enjoy yourselves." Elizabeth had the impression he was avoiding a glance at his wife when he added: "Of course, there are tasks which must be completed before we depart."

"Of course," replied Elizabeth smoothly.

"Papa," asked Leah with a fearful look at her mother. "May I go too?"

"You may," replied Mr. Drummond. "Attend to your lessons with Elizabeth this morning, and there may be a treat for you when we are there."

The vigorous nod from the girl prompted a laugh from Mr. Drummond, and he held his youngest child to his side. Elizabeth was struck by the contrast between them. Her uncle obviously loved his children and wanted the best for them. Elizabeth could not quite determine what her aunt wanted for her children, but she seemed to have little affinity for them. Not for the first time, Elizabeth wondered at her behavior, wondered what could have happened to have turned her into the woman she was.

But there was no understanding to be had, so Elizabeth put it from her mind. She spent some time in the garden that morning, and then attended to the younger children's lessons, while Olivia assisted the maid, and then late that morning, the Drummond's old carriage was brought from the stables, and they set out on the short journey.

Lambton was a small town in the manner of Meryton, existing for the purpose of the movement of goods and supplying the nearby estates with that of which they stood in need. But physically, Lambton was quite different from the town near Elizabeth's home. It was built on the side of a hill, for one thing, and though it had a wide main thoroughfare where the bulk of the town's traffic was concentrated, it also boasted winding side streets, paved with grey cobblestones. It seemed to Elizabeth that this particular stone was abundant in Derbyshire, as the house at Kingsdown was built with the same material. The town itself was quaint and possessed a friendly atmosphere, and Elizabeth soon realized why Mrs. Gardiner found it to be so charming.

"It is quite different from Meryton," said Elizabeth, as they disembarked from the carriage near the edge of town.

"Yes, I dare say it is," replied her uncle. "Meryton is built entirely on a flat plain, whereas there is very little area of flat terrain in Derbyshire."

Elizabeth looked at her uncle with interest. "You have been to Hertfordshire?"

"I have," said her uncle, though it came with a tightening around the corners of his mouth. "Your aunt and I traveled there once not long after we were married, and I had occasion to visit before."

It was nothing more than a suspicion, but given her uncle's reaction, Elizabeth thought that he did not wish to discuss the matter further. Mindful of his privacy, Elizabeth allowed the subject to drop.

Mr. Drummond's business consisted of some purchases from the general store in Lambton, which he arranged to be delivered. Once they were finished there, they left, walking down the street for a short distance before he led them down a narrow side street to a door with a painted sign of a woman in an evening gown on it. Olivia suddenly brightened in excitement.

"Yes, my dear," said he with an affectionate squeeze of her shoulder. "It is time we ensure you are properly outfitted for your entrance into our society."

He led them into the shop where they were greeted by a plumb matron with a kindly face and dark hair, greying at the temples. "Good morning, Mr. Drummond," said she. "I see you have brought your daughter as promised. And who is this young lady?"

"I have, Mrs. Richards. This is my eldest daughter, Olivia, my youngest, Leah, and this is my niece, Miss Elizabeth Bennet. She is staying with us for a time."

The ladies curtseyed to one another—Miss Leah Drummond giving a credible attempt at a proper curtsey—before her uncle turned his attention to the matter at hand.

"As I explained before, Olivia will be coming out into local society and will require an assortment of dresses for day and evening wear. Also, I would like to commission an evening dress for my niece."

Elizabeth had not expected such generosity from her uncle, and she was quick to protest. "I have several evening gowns with me, Uncle. There is no need for you to purchase dresses for me."

But Mr. Drummond was not to be deterred. "Please allow me to do this for you, Lizzy. You have been so good as to travel all this distance to be of use to Olivia, and I would like to show our thanks in whatever manner possible. I will pay for this dress, and we will hold the funds your father left in reserve for the future." Mr. Drummond grinned. "I have no doubt that you will require more as the young men begin to flock around you."

Though Elizabeth was of mind to protest further, she knew her uncle would insist, so she agreed. Furthermore, she felt the heat of a blush creeping up her cheeks at his reference to the admiration of young men, the redness staining Olivia's cheeks the match for her own.

"Papa!" exclaimed Leah at that moment, tugging on her father's coat. "Shall I have new dresses too?"

Mr. Drummond smiled down at his youngest and crouched down until he was eye level with her. "Perhaps just this once, Poppet. These dresses are for your sister to make a good impression upon the young men of the area when she begins to attend the events of society."

"It is not fair," said Leah with an adorable pout. "I want to come out too."

A laugh escaped Mr. Drummond's lips, and Elizabeth and Olivia shared a private smile. Olivia bent down to catch her sister's eye, and she said: "You are not ready for such things, Leah. But if you mind Lizzy and Papa, you will be ready when you reach my age."

"But that is so very long from now!"

"It will be here before you know it," said Mr. Drummond. He caught his daughter up into his arms and held her as he turned to the seamstress, who was looking on with amusement. "Perhaps a light summer dress for my daughter?"

"Of course, Mr. Drummond." She turned her attention to the young girl, who still wore the trace of a pout. "I dare say you will be the most beautiful young lady to come out in many years. But you have much growing to do before you are ready. For now, let us make a special dress, just for you."

With a shy smile, the girl assented.

"Now, if you will all come back, I need to take your measurements."

Thus began their time at the dressmaker's, a time enjoyed by them all, Elizabeth thought, though Mr. Drummond was not so interested in the process as the young ladies. Mrs. Richards and her assistant soon had them measured, and they were poring over style magazines, looking for the perfect gowns. Elizabeth settled on a gown of light rose, with little lace, as was her preference, and a wrap of a slightly darker shade. For Olivia, there were a variety of light summer day dresses and several evening gowns in a similar style to Elizabeth's. For Leah, a bright summer dress in a soft floral print—the girl squealed at the sight of the fabric, and Elizabeth thought her disappointment at what she perceived as her sister leaving her behind was more than made up for with that pretty little dress.

There seemed to have been some further prior communication between Mr. Drummond and Mrs. Richards, for the lady was careful to steer them toward certain fabrics which, though Elizabeth thought to be good quality, were not the most expensive the shop boasted. Most Olivia's dresses would be created from a selection of soft muslins, though one or two of her evening gowns were designed with other fabrics in mind. She was also careful to lead Olivia toward certain modest styles which were appropriate for a young girl her age just coming out into society.

As the time wore on, Elizabeth discovered a curious thing about herself. She had never liked to shop—her aversion to the activity was infamous among her friends and family. And perhaps most of all, she had never liked being fitted for new gowns, along with the accompanying fabric and style selection.

But she found herself enjoying the time in that shop, and as her cousin was looking over the various styles, she realized that she had more positive feelings toward this outing because she was not constantly forced to contend with her mother over her choice of fashions. Mrs. Bennet had definite opinions about what would assist her daughters in catching husbands, and those opinions differed greatly from Elizabeth's. But in this instance, she had the opportunity to make her own choices, and furthermore, she found herself engaged in assisting her cousin to determine her own preferences. Not even on the occasions she had gone to a dressmaker with her Aunt Gardiner had Elizabeth enjoyed herself so much. She attributed that to the presence of her cousin, who was so near her in age.

In all, they spent some two hours in Mrs. Richards's shop, and by the time they were prepared to depart, Elizabeth was certain that the day's entertainment had lightened her uncle's pocketbook considerably. But he only beamed at his daughters—it was clear that the sight of their happiness was much more important than the money he spent making them happy.

"If you will bring the ladies back on Friday," said the matron when they were prepared to leave, "we can have the final fitting for Miss

Bennet, and two day dresses and an evening dress for Miss Drummond."

"What of my dress?" demanded Leah.

Mrs. Richards laughed and said: "Yours too, Miss Leah." Then she turned back to Mr. Drummond. "The rest of Miss Drummond's dresses will be ready within two weeks."

"Excellent!" He turned a sly grin on his eldest daughter. "Your evening gown will be ready just in time for the upcoming assembly."

Though she blushed, it was clear that Olivia was pleased. Elizabeth found herself interested in Derbyshire society and anticipating the upcoming assembly. Hopefully, she and Olivia would be able to make the acquaintance of other young ladies their age.

The Drummond party said their farewells to the matron, and soon they had departed from the shop, through the maze of streets, and back to Lambton's main street. From there, Mr. Drummond took the three girls to a nearby inn, where they ate a pleasant lunch in one of the inn's back rooms.

"Now," said Mr. Drummond as they finished their meal, "I have some business at several establishments which I know you young ladies will not find at all interesting. Perhaps you will wish to look in some of the shops while I am about my business?"

"Does Lambton have a bookshop, Uncle?" asked Elizabeth.

Mr. Drummond chuckled. "It does, and if what I suspect of you is correct, I can just complete my other business while you three browse for books."

He led them out of the inn and down the street a short distance to a small, nondescript building, with a large sign proclaiming its purpose to all who passed by. There, Mr. Drummond stopped and smiled at them.

"I will return here in half an hour. If you wish to go somewhere else, please return at that time."

The girls assured him that they would, and he stepped away, walking down the street, a cheerful spring in his step.

"Will you help me choose something, Lizzy?" asked Olivia.

"Of course," replied Elizabeth, and they entered the building.

The shop was small, with bookshelves taking up every available space along the walls and several situated in the middle of the room, leaving narrow aisles in between for customers to navigate the proprietor's selection of works. The man at the counter — a cheerful, thin man of perhaps thirty years — greeted them and invited them to peruse his shop, then proceeded to return to some ledgers in which he was making careful notations. For the next several moments, Elizabeth amused herself and her cousins, showing Olivia some of her favorite books, and looking through beautifully illustrated children's books with Leah.

When they had made their selections, Elizabeth guided the two girls to the counter, insisting that she would purchase their books for them. Leah clutched an illustrated selection of fairytales to her breast, enchanted with the colorful pages and depictions of some of Elizabeth's old favorites. Olivia, however, looked at her book—a copy of *Gulliver's Travels*—with some trepidation.

"Are you certain, Lizzy?" asked the girl. "Papa will return and purchase these books for us."

"I am quite happy to do it, Olivia," said Elizabeth. "Please accept it in thanks for your family's warm welcome."

She allowed for no further argument and stepped toward the counter, holding in her hand a copy of Blake's *Songs of Innocence*. There, standing at the counter, was a young lady, perhaps a year younger than Olivia, but tall and flaxen-haired, with a handsome countenance. The proprietor and the girl both looked up as they approached, though the girl immediately looked down in seeming embarrassment. On the counter in front of her, Elizabeth could see some sheet music.

"I will be with you momentarily," said the man.

"Of course, sir," said Elizabeth. Then she smiled at the young girl, who was looking at them out of the corner of her eye, and said: "Herr Mozart's Sonata in C Major. An excellent choice."

Though she seemed startled that Elizabeth had spoken to her, the girl shot her a bashful smile. "I love to play. My brother has recently purchased a new pianoforte, and I cannot allow it to go to waste by not playing it regularly."

Elizabeth laughed. "That would be a shame, indeed."

They waited while the girl paid for her purchase, and Elizabeth noted her cousins looking at the girl with some awe. Indeed, her dress was obviously made of costly material, and she carried herself with the grace of a truly well-bred woman. And though she was still young, she was handsome, and her form was developed and womanly.

Before long, the girl stepped back and Elizabeth approached the counter to pay for their books. "Perhaps we should consider purchasing some music ourselves," said she to Olivia. "Though perhaps not the sonata." Elizabeth smiled at the girl, pleased when she returned the gesture. "I believe it might be a little beyond my poor capabilities."

"Oh, no, Lizzy," said Olivia. "Perhaps next time."

"Very well. I shall ask my sisters to send me some of the music we have at Longbourn, so that we may practice."

"You play as well, miss?" asked the young girl, a timidity in her voice Elizabeth might not have expected from what she thought was such a wealthy young girl.

"Aye, but very ill, indeed," replied Elizabeth. She leaned close, as if to impart a secret, and said: "I have far too many other interests to spend much time practicing. It is a failing, perhaps, but I own to it without disguise."

The girl giggled. "My aunt informs me at every opportunity that I should practice diligently. If not for the obvious wisdom in the advice, I might be inclined to ignore her, for she has never learned, though, as she also informs us all, she would have been a true proficient if she ever had."

The image of such a pompous old woman struck Elizabeth as rather droll, and she laughed along with the girl. Olivia laughed as well, though her mirth seemed to have a hesitant quality inherent in it.

When the purchases had been completed, Elizabeth led the sisters out onto the street, accompanied by the girl to whom she had spoken in the shop. It seemed like the girl, once they were outside, realized that she had been speaking to someone with whom she was not at all acquainted, as her timidity returned in full force. To put her at ease, Elizabeth smiled and introduced herself, saying:

"It seems we have made one another's acquaintance, and yet there is no one to properly introduce us, so I fear we shall have to introduce one another. I am Elizabeth Bennet, from Longbourn estate in Hertfordshire. These are my cousins, Miss Olivia Drummond and Miss Leah Drummond, from Kingsdown estate, not far from here."

Though the girl appeared a little shocked, she soon recovered and curtseyed. "Miss Bennet, Miss Drummond, Miss Leah, I am Georgiana Darcy from Pemberley, also quite close by."

Olivia gasped, but Elizabeth looked on the other girl with interest. She had not thought to come across Miss Darcy, of whom she had heard so much, in a bookshop in Lambton.

"We are happy to make your acquaintance, Miss Darcy," said Elizabeth. "But I, at least, have the advantage of you, for I have heard much of you."

Startled, the girl looked at Elizabeth, her eyes suddenly shuttered and wary. "Oh?" asked she.

"Yes," said Elizabeth, hastening to put Miss Darcy's mind at ease.

"For you see, I have some neighbors in Hertfordshire who claim an acquaintance with you. A Mr. Bingley, along with his two sisters, took up residence at an estate close by my father's last October. Earlier this year, Mr. Bingley married my eldest sister, Jane."

"Oh!" repeated the girl, eyes widened. "But Mr. Bingley is my brother's closest friend!"

"So I have understood," agreed Elizabeth. "In fact, Mr. Bingley had much to say of you. Given how enthusiastic he was concerning your brother's merits, I almost wondered if such a perfect man could possibly exist."

The girl giggled in response to Elizabeth's sally. "I have no doubt of it. Mr. Bingley looks up to him, for William is experienced in society and in the running of his estate."

"I dare say that is correct."

"But why would Mr. Bingley speak of me?"

Elizabeth smiled and winked. "It was not Mr. Bingley who spoke of you, but rather his younger sister." A roll of Elizabeth's eyes told the girl exactly what she thought of Miss Bingley, and as she expected, Miss Darcy commiserated with a similar response. "According to Miss Bingley, you are the closest of friends, and she has never met anyone so accomplished, so talented, and at such a young age! She could not speak enough of you or of her connection to your family."

The girl shook her head with rueful exasperation. "Miss Bingley's imagination concerning our relationship in no way matches the reality. I have met her only a handful of times, and I found her . . ." Miss Darcy's cheeks suddenly flooded red, and she ducked her head, only daring a bashful look at Elizabeth from behind long lashes. "She is quite determined, you see, to become *my* sister."

"Believe me, Miss Darcy," said Elizabeth with a laugh, "I understood that within a few minutes of hearing her speak of you."

They shared a laugh, and then Miss Darcy, seeming to regain her confidence, turned to Olivia, who had been watching them with a faint sense of astonishment.

"You are Mr. Drummond's eldest daughter?" When Olivia replied in the affirmative, Miss Darcy said: "I have seen your father, though I have never made his acquaintance. William, I believe, has a high opinion of him."

"Thank you," replied Olivia. "I believe Papa returns the sentiment."

"Do you often come to Lambton, Miss Darcy?" asked Elizabeth.

"Yes. It is the closest town to my home, and there are shops here which are quite charming, indeed." Miss Darcy paused. "There is another town on the other side of Pemberley called Kympton, but it is a smaller town, with not so much of interest."

Unaccountably, Elizabeth experienced the vague notion that she had heard of Kympton in the past, but she could not remember exactly where. It was of little matter, so she shook it off, focusing her attention back on her new acquaintance. They stood in the street speaking for some moments, and Elizabeth's initial impression of the girl as one possessing little experience with others not of her family circle and an excess of shyness was confirmed. Still, the longer they spoke and the more they shared of themselves, the more at ease she became, until she was speaking with calmness and composure, though perhaps not with the same animation Elizabeth, or even her cousin, possessed.

When they had been speaking for some five or ten minutes, Elizabeth noted the approach of a gentleman, and she looked up, seeing Mr. Darcy striding toward them. And it was at that moment that she was forced to concede that he looked even better than he had only a few days before.

"Brother!" called Georgiana as soon as she caught sight of Darcy approaching.

"Georgiana," replied Darcy, favoring her with affection. "Miss Drummond," added he, bowing a little to the girl's curtsey. "And, Miss Leah, of course."

The youngest Drummond giggled and imitated her sister's curtsey, though with little of the grace her elder sister had displayed. Then Darcy turned to the other young lady of the group, noting that she had been watching his interactions with her relations, not to mention her look of amusement, which displayed not a hint of embarrassment.

"Perhaps one of you ladies will do me the honor of introducing your companion?"

"Of course," said Miss Drummond. "This is my cousin, Miss Elizabeth Bennet, who is visiting us from Hertfordshire."

Interested by the information, Darcy turned to Miss Bennet. "I apologize, Miss Bennet, but I was not aware of any relations of the Drummonds."

"My father is Mrs. Drummond's brother, Mr. Darcy."

"And your father also is a gentleman?"

"Yes. My father's estate is called Longbourn. It is not that far distant from Stevenage."

"Stevenage?" repeated Darcy. "Are you, by any chance, familiar with Netherfield? I understood it was quite near Stevenage. My friend is leasing it, at present."

"I should hope I am," said Miss Bennet, flashing him a mischievous smile. "My sister is now the mistress of the estate."

"Bennet!" exclaimed Darcy, before he realized that the young miss must think him quite daft for suddenly blurting out her surname in such a fashion.

"I apologize, Miss Bennet. You must understand that though my friend informed me of his engagement and marriage, his penmanship is atrocious. Through the blots, I was unable to determine if his new wife's maiden name was Barnet, Bonnet, or *Bon Nuit*. I can see now that I was mistaken on all three counts."

To Darcy's gratification, Miss Bennet laughed at his sally. "So I have come to understand, Mr. Darcy. In fact, one night while I was in company with them, Miss Bingley lamented on her brother's carelessness in writing." She shot him an arch look. "I distinctly remember *your* name being referenced as a standard to which he should aspire."

Darcy shook his head while his sister giggled in response. "I can well imagine it, Miss Bennet. I hope Mrs. Bingley is adjusting to her life as a married woman with ease?"

A shadow seemed to pass over Miss Bennet's face, but she quickly recovered. "With a husband as amiable as Mr. Bingley, I do not doubt that her adjustment period has been easy."

"Will you be in Derbyshire for long?"

"Lizzy has come to help me become accustomed to society," said Miss Drummond. She then ducked her head as if embarrassed. "My Papa intends for me to attend some society events in the area in the near future."

"And shall you attend the upcoming assembly?" asked Darcy, attempting to put the girl at ease.

"I shall. Lizzy and I were being measured for some dresses today. I am very much anticipating it."

Darcy was certain the girl was, but her lack of coquettishness was refreshing, as it was in her elder cousin. This was clearly a lady of some substance, one he would not be averse to knowing better.

They spoke on the street for some more moments before Drummond came to collect them. But Darcy was surprised by his sister, for she spoke to them before they could depart.

"I would like to continue our friendship. Might I invite you to come to Pemberley and visit me in the next several days?"

Though it was clear that Miss Bennet was delighted with the offer, she hesitated a little, shooting a glance at her uncle for his concurrence. Immediately understanding the gesture, Darcy felt obliged to speak up.

"We would be happy to send a carriage."

"Thank you, Darcy," said Drummond. "If the situation demands it, I would be happy to accept your generous offer."

Saying that, the Drummond party departed.

"What pleasant people," said Georgiana, as she watched them board their carriage. "Miss Bennet, in particular, is quite delightful. I believe I would like to have them as friends."

"And so you shall, Georgiana," said Darcy.

He steered his sister away toward their own carriage, and he reflected on the introductions which had just taken place. When Darcy had heard of his friend's marriage, he had wondered if Bingley had finally been captured by one of his many angels. But if Mrs. Bingley was anything like her sister, Darcy thought it likely that Bingley had made a good match, though he did not know anything about her fortune or other connections. In the end, it was none of Darcy's concern, so he decided to think instead upon how lovely Miss Bennet had appeared and how fine her manners. Perhaps he would do more than avoid dancing at the upcoming assembly.

CHAPTER VII

"Miss Elizabeth Bennet, you say," said Fitzwilliam. "And her sister is now married to Bingley?"

"It appears to be so," replied Darcy. He raised his drink to his mouth.

"Is she as promising up close as she was from a distance?"

"More so," replied Darcy, thinking on his impressions of her. "You know that much of society will not consider any woman beautiful unless she is tall and blonde. Miss Bennet has neither of those traits, yet she is as fine a woman as I have ever beheld. She is petite, but her figure is womanly and attractive, her complexion fair, and her eyes are possibly the most glorious that I have ever beheld."

"Shall I receive an invitation to the wedding?"

Darcy rolled his eyes, turning his attention away from his contemplation of the girl whose acquaintance he had made that day. "Not if you persist in making such comments."

"Oh ho!" cried the Colonel. "You did not deny an interest in her."

"Neither did I confirm one. I merely turned your impertinent remark away with a jest of my own."

Fitzwilliam shook his head. "I know you better than you think, Cousin. You never speak of a woman—other than to express your exasperation concerning that Bingley woman. I must, therefore, assume she has caught your interest."

"I do not deny that, though I will assert that I have met her but once."

"So you have."

"Tell me of Thorndell," said Darcy, changing the subject. "Might I assume everything is well at your estate?"

They continued to speak for some time about the colonel's short journey, and Darcy was pleased at having been able to deflect his cousin. The teasing would undoubtedly resume at some later time, but for now, Darcy was content. The woman had impressed him, he was forced to confess, but he preferred there to be a reason for Fitzwilliam's teasing, rather than his typical insouciance.

The night of their return from Lambton, Elizabeth found herself unable to sleep, which was an unusual situation—Elizabeth rarely found herself suffering from insomnia. She was not certain she could pinpoint the reason herself—it seemed a combination of restlessness, thoughts about the acquaintances she had made that day, and the particularly handsome visage of Mr. Darcy. She did not know, but her thoughts swirled inside her mind, and no matter what she did, she could not induce them to settle.

After lying in bed for some time, she decided that it was useless to fight it. She reached to her side table for the book she had purchased that day, intending to allow Blake to sooth her mind and prepare it for the blissful release of sleep. Unfortunately, it was not there, and a moment's thought on the matter confirmed to Elizabeth that she had left it behind, likely in the sitting-room.

Rising from her bed, Elizabeth slipped on her robe, and crossed her room to the door, opening it slowly to prevent any squeaking from the hinges, and slipped out through the narrow opening. The darkness of the night and the moonlight shining in through the window at the end of the hall gave it a ghostly sort of luminescence. Elizabeth hurried along toward the stairs, intent upon retrieving her book and returning to her room as soon as may be. She was arrested by the sound of voices.

"Elizabeth is nothing but trouble." The voice belonged to her aunt. "You should never have invited her to come here. We should send her back to Hertfordshire as soon as may be."

"In what way has she been trouble?" asked the mild voice of her uncle.

"She is filling our daughters' heads with dreams and frivolities.

They need to remember the reality of their situation and not be distracted."

"We have discussed this before, Claire." The warning note in her uncle's voice was easy to discern.

"Perhaps we have," responded she. "But I no more agree with you now than I did then."

"I noted your objections then and I do so now. But they have no effect on me. I cannot see how Leah and especially Olivia do anything other than benefit from Elizabeth's presence. She is easy in company, intelligent, and she is kind and friendly to them. Elizabeth is a true lady, by any measure, and I would ask you to remember that."

"You should not have taken them to Lambton. And you should not have spent so much of our money on clothes which will make no difference in the end."

"Again, your objections are noted, Wife. Is there anything else?"

Elizabeth heard footsteps, and for a moment she thought to flee, when she realized that her aunt had started stalking the floor. Her tone was ever more exasperated, and Elizabeth was certain that she flailed her hands about in the air, attempting to make her points.

"You are being foolish! Our girls have nothing with which to recommend themselves, and your idea of bringing my *brother's* offspring here to teach them manners is laughable, considering the woman he married. All you have done is to burden us with another mouth to feed, one who does nothing to improve our situation. What must I do to make you understand this?"

"You cannot," was Mr. Drummond's short reply. "For you are wrong. Burden us? Elizabeth has willingly taken on duties in our household, leaving us both free to attend to other tasks. And has she complained about doing so?"

"She does not do enough," muttered Mrs. Drummond, her voice just audible to Elizabeth.

"I did not bring her here to be your maid. And you heard your brother—he would not have allowed her visit if you meant for her to spend her days in the scullery."

"She should do more."

"She does everything we ask with little complaint. How many other ladies of her station do you think would do as much as she does without protest?"

They were silent for a moment, and Elizabeth began to wonder if she should not depart. She was not accustomed to listening at doors and knew it to be the height of bad manners, but in this instance, she felt herself a little justified, given the faults her aunt was laying at her door.

"She is a gentlewoman, Claire," said her uncle at length. "I will see her treated like a gentlewoman. Do not allow your own disappointment in life to provoke you to mistreat our niece. I will not have it."

At that moment Elizabeth decided that it would be best to retreat. Now knowing that a book would not hold her attention, she decided it was best for her to return to her room before her aunt caught her in the hallway. She certainly did not need the woman to think more poorly of her than she already did.

The next day, Elizabeth made certain to go about her daily tasks in a quick and efficient fashion, though she noted, with no little cynicism, that she had never done anything else, regardless of what her aunt thought of her. It helped that Elizabeth enjoyed the work she was doing; she found it no hardship at all to serve as teacher for the younger children, and nothing about her other tasks was onerous.

Mrs. Drummond watched her, much as she watched any other day since Elizabeth had arrived, but Elizabeth did not notice any difference between that day and any other, so she ignored the woman as much as possible.

Though only three days north of Hertfordshire, Derbyshire's climate was different from that to which Elizabeth was accustomed. For one thing, though it had already been warm, with life sprouting all around in Hertfordshire before Elizabeth had left, in Derbyshire the nights were still chilly, and the buds had only begun to sprout after Elizabeth's arrival. It had been pleasant, but it was on that day that Elizabeth began to truly see the much sought-after signs of spring.

Olivia seemed to be in fine spirits that morning, and Elizabeth found herself caught up in her cousin's enthusiasm, even if the worry about her aunt was still present. And that night the conversation turned to the subject for which Olivia, at the very least, had been waiting.

"The assembly is to be held on Tuesday week. I suppose you exist in a state of keen anticipation."

Olivia, to whom her father's words had been directed, returned his smile, though she attempted a demure calmness. "Indeed, I am, Papa. It will be my first assembly, after all."

"Indeed, it will. It will be your first taste of local society."

"Shall you be the belle of the ball?" asked Edward, his tone teasing.

"Shall you dance all night until dawn? Or perhaps you will instead leave at midnight with the prince chasing after you."

"Edward," said Olivia in a warning tone, but Edward only grinned at her, completely unrepentant.

"I shall merely emulate Lizzy," replied she with airy unconcern. "Then I shall be certain to make a good impression on our neighbors."

The soft snort which proceeded forth from the lips of Aunt Claire did not escape anyone's attention, but Elizabeth ignored the woman. Her uncle shot her a glance and said:

"Excellent idea, my dear. I am certain your cousin will not lead you astray."

"Perhaps I shall stay at home with the younger children," said Aunt Claire.

"They will be very well with Marie and Betty," said Mr. Drummond of their two maids. "This is Olivia's first assembly. It would not do for you to be absent."

The admonishment was spoken in such a way as to refuse any possibility of disagreement, and her aunt subsided, though with evident ill grace. Elizabeth considered her aunt. It was clear she was not happy in her life, and she made no attempt to assume even the veneer of complacency. Her aunt's discussion with her uncle gave some tantalizing hints of the woman's character and the reasons for her disillusionment, but the truth of the matter was still out of reach.

It was the day after their discussion regarding the upcoming assembly that the promised note arrived from Georgiana, inviting Elizabeth and Olivia to Pemberley for the afternoon. Given Mrs. Drummond's seeming intent to deny her daughter and niece any ability for activities which might have brought them pleasure, Elizabeth would have thought the woman would protest their going, but instead she only shook her head and allowed her husband to approve of the outing without comment.

At the appointed time, a carriage pulled in front of Kingsdown, and a liveried footman descended to open the door for them. Olivia gazed at the carriage with awe, and Elizabeth was forced to concede how impressed she was by its elegance. Even Mr. Bingley, whose fortune was greater than her father's, had not possessed a conveyance to match what she saw before her.

"Enjoy yourselves, girls," said Mr. Drummond.

"Thank you, Papa," said Olivia, throwing her arms impulsively around her father's neck. "Miss Darcy is so kind. I am sure we shall become great friends."

"I know you will." Then he helped them both in the carriage and took up his youngest daughter in his arms, comforting her and drying her tears with loving care. Leah had protested her own desire to accompany them, but Mr. Drummond had promised her part of his time that afternoon to make up for her inability to go.

Then the carriage lurched into motion and the estate faded away behind them. The outward beauty of the vehicle was further supported by the comfort of the seats and the smoothness of the ride. It was the most relaxing experience Elizabeth had ever had in a coach.

"Now, I seem to remember your informing me that you have never visited Pemberley?" said Elizabeth, turning to her cousin.

"I have not. Papa has told me that it is a beautiful place, but I have never been there myself."

"Then I am happy that we are to see it today." Elizabeth smiled. "I do not know if you are aware of it, by my aunt, Mrs. Gardiner, who is my uncle's wife, is from Lambton, and she has seen the estate herself many times. She declares it the finest she has ever seen."

"I have heard my father speak of your aunt. But I was very small when she left Lambton for London, and I do not know her."

"I hope you will have occasion to meet her someday," said Elizabeth. "Aunt Gardiner is a wonderful woman, and I am excessively fond of her."

The girls passed the carriage ride in this attitude, alternating playful conversation with watching the scenery as it rolled by. The road to Pemberley was well-maintained, and had obviously been travelled extensively. The woods to either side often crowded in about the road, making it seem like they were winding through a narrow maze, rather than a country road.

When they had climbed a hill of some natural prominence, the woods to the left side of the road fell away, opening out into a little valley. There, in the center, like a large jewel set into a pendant, stood a large, handsome building, overlooking a lake and a winding stream gleaming in the distance. Elizabeth gasped; this was a house beside which Netherfield, the largest estate near Meryton, paled by comparison. No wonder Miss Bingley desired to be mistress of this place above all other things.

"*That* is Pemberley?" asked her cousin, her voice strangled with disbelief.

"I believe it must be," said Elizabeth. "Unless the coachman does not know the road to return to his master's estate."

A giggle escaped Olivia's lips, though she attempted a severe look to cover her mirth. Elizabeth's comment served its purpose, however, as she noticed that Olivia was relaxed rather than disbelieving about the fineness of the house.

"Do not say such things, Lizzy," whispered Olivia. "I am certain I shall burst out laughing and make a fool of myself!"

"Do not worry, dearest," replied Elizabeth. "I am certain you will do very well. Miss Darcy does not strike me as the kind of girl to judge."

The carriage, by now, was proceeding down the long drive which led to the entrance of the house, and the closer they came, the grander it appeared. It was a three-story building, situated on a little rise near the lake, which would protect it should the spring rains be heavy enough to overflow the banks. It was built of stone and boasted two long wings to either side of the main entrance, with large, spacious windows. Just to the rear of the house, she could see the beginnings of a formal garden and, perhaps, a hedge maze, which promised to be delightful. Here and there, leading off into the trees, Elizabeth could see the beginnings of several paths, leading Elizabeth to believe that the walks were extensive. How much she would like to walk those paths, to become as familiar with them as those who lived in this magnificent place!

Elizabeth reined in her emotions, cautioning herself against excited displays, and avoiding the appearance of covetousness. This house, no matter how large and imposing, was nothing more than a home to their hostess, and Elizabeth well knew how tasteless a person could appear if they displayed an unseemly level of enthusiasm when touring another's home. Mr. Collins's performance when he had come to Longbourn was certainly not an example she wished to imitate!

At length, the coach stopped in front of those imposing double doors, and there on the steps waiting for them was Georgiana Darcy. The girl was dressed in an elegant but simple gown of yellow, showing yet again that even having been raised amid great wealth, she was naught but a young girl, and one who was shy at that. The step was lowered for them, and Elizabeth and Olivia were helped from the carriage by the footman, and they approached their hostess.

"Miss Darcy," said Elizabeth with a smile and a curtsey. "How do you do?"

"Miss Bennet, Miss Drummond," said Miss Darcy, returning her gesture. "I am very happy to see you. Welcome to Pemberley."

"We are happy to be here," said Olivia. "Thank you for inviting us."

A grin settled over Miss Darcy's face, though she ducked her head in apparent embarrassment. "Come, let us go inside. I have been anticipating your visit since word arrived yesterday that you had accepted. I am so excited!"

They were led into an entry hall, large and imposing like everything else about this place. A massive stairway led up to the upper apartments, wide and spacious, and there were passages leading away from the room in every direction. Elizabeth thought that she could become quite lost in this place very quickly if she had no guide!

Miss Darcy led them away to the left, where they passed a short distance down a hall which stretched off some ways, until she opened a door to a room set against the front of the house. Inside was a lovely arrangement of furniture, tastefully elegant and well-constructed, and on the far wall stood a fine pianoforte. The sunlight shone into the room from the large bank of windows, making it light and pleasing, a truly lovely room. There they were introduced to a handsome older woman by the name of Mrs. Annesley, Miss Darcy's companion.

"So this is the infamous pianoforte of which you have told us," said Elizabeth, after the pleasantries with Mrs. Annesley had been exchanged. "It does appear to be a superior instrument, but I believe I would like to judge based on hearing you play."

"Perhaps you would like a turn on it yourself," said Miss Darcy.

Elizabeth laughed. "But Miss Bingley has informed us of just how accomplished you are. I doubt my poor attempts could possibly measure up to your talents."

"You are familiar with Miss Bingley?" asked Mrs. Annesley in a way which led Elizabeth to believe that the woman suspected her of being of similar ilk. She had obviously had enough contact with the woman to be disapproving of her, though her manner could not be said to be disrespectful.

"I am, indeed," said Elizabeth. "Miss Bingley, you see, came to the neighborhood in which I was raised last autumn, when her brother leased an estate adjacent to my father's. Earlier this year, my elder sister, Jane, was married to Mr. Bingley." Elizabeth turned to Georgiana with chagrin, saying: "I know I mentioned this before, Miss Darcy, but I now have a permanent connection with Miss Bingley. If you do not wish to associate with me any longer, I understand."

Olivia gasped, but Miss Darcy burst out laughing at Elizabeth's jest, and even Mrs. Annesley, who appeared to be somewhat less amused than her charge, still nodded at Elizabeth.

"You are very droll, Miss Bennet," said Miss Darcy. "But though a connection with Miss Bingley is, indeed, a serious drawback, I believe

I will maintain your acquaintance."

"Miss Darcy," said Mrs. Annesley in a warning tone.

"I apologize for making such a jest, Mrs. Annesley," interjected Elizabeth. "I understand and applaud your desire to teach your charge proper manners. But since you are obviously aware of the . . . want of subtlety in Miss Bingley's behavior, I wished to assure you that I do not behave in a similar way. I will not praise Mr. Darcy to the skies, nor will I ingratiate myself with his sister to promote myself to him."

"Very well, Miss Bennet," said Mrs. Annesley. "Let us leave the subject, then."

"I have heard from my brother," said Georgiana, eagerly grasping at Mrs. Annesley's suggestion, "that it is possible that Mr. Bingley and his new wife will visit Pemberley this summer. Perhaps your visit will coincide with your sister's."

"Mr. Bingley mentioned the possibility to me as well," said Elizabeth, avoiding the thought of her sister. "I hope they do come, for I will be happy to see them.

"Now, since we are in the music room, what say you of music? Do you have a favorite composer?"

It turned out that Elizabeth's choice of subject was an inspired one, for Miss Georgiana Darcy was a music enthusiast and was more than happy to speak of her great love for it, forgetting all about the thorny subject of Elizabeth's elder sister. And it was clear that the girl was knowledgeable too, and her opinions were near enough to Elizabeth's that there was something of which to discuss.

"Bach, without a doubt," said Miss Darcy. "His harmonies are sublime, and his music is a joy to play. I have been practicing his Toccata and Fugue in D Minor recently, though I will own that I still require practice."

"I am not much familiar with Bach," said Elizabeth, "though I have heard the Toccata and Fugue. You have just revealed the disparity in our levels of ability. I would hesitate to even attempt the Fugue. The Prelude in C Major is much more gratifying, for I can actually play it!"

"Lizzy has been teaching me to play," said Olivia in a quiet voice. "I still have much to learn, but I find that I am enjoying it very much."

"Then your talents must not be nearly as modest as you would have us believe," said Miss Darcy to Elizabeth. "To take on a student is no small matter."

Elizabeth laughed. "I do not think I would refer to it in such a grandiose manner as having taken on a student. But I do have some small ability, and I am happy to share it."

"And who is your favorite composer, Miss Bennet, Miss Drummond?" asked Miss Darcy.

"I am partial to Mozart and Beethoven," said Elizabeth.

"I very much like what I have heard of Herr Mozart," said Olivia. Elizabeth smiled at her cousin; there had not been much use or time for music in the Drummond residence, and as such, Olivia had relatively little experience.

"That is an odd duo, is it not, Miss Bennet?" asked Miss Darcy. "Mozart's style is light and airy, and some might even suggest unserious. No one could ever consider Beethoven unserious."

"On the surface, yes," said Elizabeth with good humor. "But underneath Mozart's soaring, airy melodies, I fancy I can hear his love of music, though his style is for the most part light. But when Mozart's style gets a little too much, it is lovely to turn to Beethoven and enjoy his grander and more serious style."

"Well said, Miss Bennet," murmured Mrs. Annesley. Elizabeth exchanged a look with the other woman, and had the sense that she had stated the companion's opinion on the matter with succinctness.

The conversation wound on from there, touching on different aspects of music and performance, and she was happy to listen to Miss Darcy—though she did so with an air of self-consciousness. In fact, Miss Darcy was quite talented, in Elizabeth's opinion—much more than she was herself. If the girl made any mistakes in her playing, Elizabeth was not able to hear them. Furthermore, she played with feeling and verve, displaying a love for the music which could not be feigned.

By contrast, when Elizabeth played, she felt even more awkward, knowing that her own performance could not measure up to the younger girl's. And yet, Miss Darcy complimented her so sincerely, assuring her that her playing brought much pleasure.

When Elizabeth stepped away from the pianoforte, she realized that another had entered the room and was watching them as they interacted around the pianoforte. He was tall and broad-shouldered, a truly large and imposing man, though his countenance shone with good humor. He greeted them all pleasantly and requested an introduction. When Georgiana did the honors, he was revealed to be a cousin, Colonel Anthony Fitzwilliam.

"In truth, my cousin is no longer a member of the army, for he retired several months ago," said Miss Darcy with more than a measure of pride. She turned to him and said: "It is well that the custom is to continue to refer to you by your former title, Cousin, for I am so accustomed to thinking of you as a colonel."

"I am accustomed to thinking of *myself* as a colonel," replied Colonel Fitzwilliam with evident good humor.

"Oh, it is unfortunate you are not in the army any longer," said Elizabeth, directing a mischievous grin at him. "My younger sisters admire a man in the scarlet uniform. They would have been pleased to make your acquaintance."

"But now," said Colonel Fitzwilliam, "given I am naught but *Mr. Fitzwilliam*, I assume I would not be worth their time?"

Elizabeth laughed. "I see you have seen their like before, sir."

"Indeed, I have," replied he. "Far more often than I would like to confess. My experience tells me there is naught of harm in such girls, but the squeals of delight often grate on the nerves."

The tea service Miss Darcy had ordered moments before arrived then, and Colonel Fitzwilliam sat down to tea with them, entertaining them with stories of his time in the regulars. Elizabeth listened with interest and laughed at his words, but she was certain that many of his stories were, at the very least, embellished upon, though she would not accuse him of making them up out of whole cloth.

Elizabeth did, however, watch Olivia, who appeared to be entranced by Colonel Fitzwilliam's genial manners and interesting discourse. Olivia seemed to have taken an instant fancy to the man, and though Elizabeth was not affected herself, she could understand why her young and inexperienced cousin would feel so intrigued. She thought of speaking to Olivia on their way home, but she soon decided there was no reason to do so. Girlish infatuation was an affliction often experienced by young girls, and it would almost certainly fade away with time.

For her part, Miss Darcy laughed at her cousin's tales as much as Elizabeth or Olivia did, though she had obviously heard some of them before. Underneath it, Elizabeth thought she sensed a hint of exasperation for him. The girl, though she had been brought up by doting guardians intent upon seeing to her every need, was more than a little lonely, Elizabeth realized. She likely had interacted with few girls her own age and had formed few friendships as a result. Elizabeth had no frame of reference, not having a brother, but though her sisters exasperated her at times, it would be much more difficult to try to share confidences with a much older brother.

At length, the time for their return arrived, and Elizabeth and Olivia rose to take their leave.

"Thank you for inviting us, Miss Darcy," said Elizabeth. "I believe

I may speak for us both when I say that we have been happy to make your acquaintance."

"I certainly am," added Olivia. "We live so close together that it is strange we have never met."

"I must apologize for my brother," said Miss Darcy. "He had intended to be here to greet you, but an unexpected situation arose among the tenants to which he was obliged to attend."

"We understand. Needs of the estate must take precedence."

"And my cousin is nothing if not dutiful," added Colonel Fitzwilliam.

"You will see him at the assembly anyway, as he and my cousin will attend."

"You will not be attending yourself?" asked Olivia.

"I am still not out, Miss Drummond. My brother has told me that I might begin to attend some small events next year, but for the present, I do not."

"This assembly is to be Olivia's first," said Elizabeth.

"Oh!" said Miss Darcy, clapping her hands. "Then you must tell me of your experience!"

"I would be happy to," replied Olivia.

They made ready to depart and their hostess, in the company of her cousin, escorted them to the entrance where they took their leave. It was with an almost diffidence that Miss Darcy addressed them as they strode down the stairs to the waiting carriage.

"I look forward to continuing our acquaintance in the future," said Miss Darcy. The girl hesitated and ducked her head. "In fact, since we are now friends, shall we not dispense with the formalities? I would like very much if you would call me 'Georgiana,' if you will afford me the same privilege."

"An excellent idea," said Elizabeth. "My sisters and friends often call me 'Lizzy,' but I will answer to 'Eliza' as well, if that is what you prefer. My cousin, however, objects to 'Livy,' as it sounds too much like my preferred moniker."

"Oh, Lizzy!" exclaimed Olivia while Georgiana giggled.

"Livy and Lizzy, eh?" asked Colonel Fitzwilliam, his eyes gleaming with mirth. "Perhaps you should run away and become actresses. I do not doubt you would be a sensation."

"I believe, sir, that I am quite happy where I am," replied Elizabeth.

"That is truly the trick, is it not, Miss Bennet?"

It was, Elizabeth thought, thinking of her aunt and her obvious dissatisfaction with her life and situation. But not wishing to cast a pall on their leave-taking, she pushed such thoughts to the corner of her mind. Before long, she was ensconced with her cousin in the coach headed back toward Kingsdown.

CHAPTER VIII

The next few days passed in much the same manner as many of the previous ones, with the exception that for the first time since Elizabeth had come to Derbyshire, they were subjected to several days of almost constant rain. As a young lady who loved to be out of doors, Elizabeth found the weather trying—it confined her to the house, except for a short constitutional in the immediate vicinity on the rare occasions when it relented for a time. Soon the ground became a sodden mess, and even that was denied her.

They did not see Miss Darcy again, but that did not mean that Olivia and Elizabeth did not have much to occupy their time. There were the ever-present tasks which needed to be completed, Olivia's continuing instruction in both the pianoforte and the dance steps, and the final fittings for their gowns which were to be ready for the assembly.

Elizabeth was confident that her cousin would acquit herself well on the dance floor, as well as in conversation with the other young ladies who would be attending. It would be some time before she was ready to perform in front of anyone, but she did seem to possess a certain aptitude for the pianoforte, which would blossom if it was nurtured correctly.

The promise of an assembly was certain to make young maidens, alight with the excitement and expectation of a new experience, eager for the activity to commence. As such, the days leading up to the activity were filled with Olivia's speculations and anticipation, which, while charming, at times reminded Elizabeth of her younger sisters' less than proper behavior. She had no fear that Olivia would behave in a like matter, but her constant chatter on the subject wore at Elizabeth's nerves at times.

At length, however, the appointed night arrived, and with it, a cessation of the rain. There were still intermittent showers, but the sun had begun to peer through the low cover of clouds, though her uncle opined that it would likely be at least a day or two before the sun began to shine in earnest. That evening, the four eldest Drummonds, with Elizabeth in tow, made their way to the carriage for the short journey to Lambton's assembly hall. Her cousin, Edward, Elizabeth was forced to concede, looked quite well in his suit which, while it was not the highest of quality, was still well-made and becoming. Her aunt and uncle had dressed up in their own finery, such as Elizabeth had never seen them wear.

"We shall arrive in less than a half hour," said Mr. Drummond as the carriage set off. "If you can maintain your composure that long, you shall have the promised amusement."

Olivia blushed, but she looked at her father with affection and gratitude. Mr. Drummond had seen his eldest daughter's behavior these last days and had obviously recognized it as well as Elizabeth had.

"And let me take this opportunity, my dear," continued Mr. Drummond, "to solicit your hand for the first dance of the evening."

"Of course, Papa," replied Olivia, with a hint of a giggle.

"After, I shall take you to my friends and introduce you," said Edward. "You will also make the acquaintance of their sisters, which should be of as much interest for you as dancing."

"Thank you, Edward. Will you do the same for Elizabeth?"

"Of course."

The relationship seemed to have become a little closer since the conversation Elizabeth had with Edward on the day of the picnic. She could not claim to be the instigator of such better relations, but Elizabeth wondered if Edward had begun to see his sister as the woman she was becoming. Either way, she could not help but rejoice—would that Elizabeth had an elder brother and protector!

"Elizabeth, will you dance the first with me?"

With a smile at her cousin, Elizabeth indicated that she was happy to do so. Indeed, knowing no other man who would be in attendance—other than Mr. Darcy and Colonel Fitzwilliam—Elizabeth thought dance partners might be a little scarcer than she usually expected.

The carriage moved along rather slowly, as the horses strained to pull it over the soaked road, which, though Elizabeth had thought was well-maintained, appeared to allow the carriage passage only with the greatest reluctance. There were ruts which jostled the occupants about, and more than once Elizabeth thought she heard a sucking sound, as the wheels were pulled free from the mud which held it in its grip.

The first sign of trouble was when the carriage lurched violently to one side, throwing Elizabeth and Olivia against her brother. It seemed to rock in place for a moment, and then came to a sudden stop, though by this time it had been going so slowly that the girls did not fall to the floor. Outside, Elizabeth could hear the driver urging the horses forward, but though the horses whinnied and strained, the carriage shuddered and did not move.

"Wait here," instructed Mr. Drummond, before he opened the door and pushed his upper body out, and for a moment, Elizabeth could hear a murmur of conversation with the driver.

"The carriage has become stuck in the mud," said Mr. Drummond when he re-entered.

"Can the horses not pull us out?" asked his wife.

"The carriage is too heavy. We will have to step out to lighten the load."

Though Elizabeth could easily see that her aunt was not impressed with her husband's words, she seemed to sense that there was little reason to argue. Elizabeth's uncle stepped down from the conveyance, and after him Edward alighted, and they turned to help the ladies. After Mrs. Drummond was helped to the ground, Elizabeth stepped down herself, noting that it was fortunate that the carriage had become stuck on one side of the road, as there was a grassy section not far away. Her uncle held her up in his arms and deposited her in the relatively cleanliness of the grass and smiled at her.

"If you ladies will wait here a moment, we shall see if the horses can pull the carriage from the mud. As an intrepid young lady, I am certain you will not be put out by a little wet grass."

"No, indeed, Uncle," replied Elizabeth.

Elizabeth stood with her cousin and watched as the driver urged the horses on with cracks of his whip. The two animals strained against the cross piece to which they were attached, but though the vehicle shuddered and their muscles strained under their sleek coats, the coach did not budge.

"I suppose there is no help for it," said Mr. Drummond with regret. "Edward and I will need to push to try to dislodge it."

"You will become muddy yourselves," said his wife.

"I know, but there is nothing else to be done. The horses by themselves are not enough to free the carriage. Edward and I can return to Kingsdown and join you after we change."

Though it appeared like Mrs. Drummond wished to say something further, she held her peace. For Elizabeth, she realized that the time consumed in such an endeavor would mean they would arrive very late, but there seemed to be little that could be done, as her uncle had indicated.

"At least it is not raining at present," said Olivia in a quiet voice to Elizabeth. Though Elizabeth agreed with her, she was not confident it would not begin yet again.

The sound of another carriage approaching caught the company's attention, and they looked as one as a large coach and four appeared out of the gloom. Though the light was poor and the approaching carriage was mired in the darkness, Elizabeth could see the faint gleam of enameled lacquer, the intricate filigree which adorned the doors and her attention was caught when one of the horses stamped and snorted. It rolled to a stop behind the Drummond carriage, and the side door opened, allowing two men to step down. They approached the waiting party, and a moment later, their identities were revealed as Mr. Darcy and Colonel Fitzwilliam.

"Drummond!" exclaimed the former. "It seems as if you are having a spot of trouble."

"More than a spot, sir," was Mr. Drummond's reply.

"This section of road has been a problem for some time," said Mr. Darcy. He sounded exasperated. "I may have to do something about it myself."

"I apologize for delaying you and your cousin with our difficulties."

Mr. Darcy only waved him off. "There is nothing you could have done about it, sir. Let us push your vehicle out so we can get you on your way to the assembly."

"I would not wish for your clothing to be soiled dealing with our problem, sir," said Mr. Drummond.

"If someone is to become soiled, it makes greater sense for it to be me. Pemberley is much closer, and my conveyance, pulled by four horses, is better equipped to go through this area than yours. Come, sir, I insist."

There was little Mr. Drummond could do but thank Mr. Darcy for his civility. The two men took their positions behind the carriage, and with the assistance of the two footmen from Pemberley, they began straining against the rear of the old equipage. The horses squealed and the men shouted as they heaved against the heavy bulk, and for a time it stubbornly refused to move. But then with a great sucking sound, the carriage broke free of the mud and lumbered on for a few feet until it reached a section of the road which appeared to be a little firmer. It was a miracle that none of the men had fallen when it had suddenly moved.

"I believe a change of pants is necessary, at the very least," said Colonel Fitzwilliam, as he looked down ruefully at his trousers. Indeed, though the man's jacket seemed to have escaped unscathed, he was speckled with mud below his waist. Mr. Darcy was in the same condition.

"Not until we are certain the Drummonds will have no further trouble," replied Mr. Darcy.

"Thank you, good sirs," said Mr. Drummond. "We would have been in a fix, had you passed this way before us."

"It was our pleasure, sir," replied Colonel Fitzwilliam.

"Now, let us get you underway," added Mr. Darcy.

The gentlemen escorted them to the side of the equipage where they saw them seated in the coach. Mr. Darcy extended his hand and assisted first Olivia and then Elizabeth up, and then bowed and stepped away. "I hope you will arrive with no further mishap. I know how ladies love to dance—you might still even arrive in time for the first."

"Thank you, sir," said Elizabeth. "Are you, perhaps, as eager as your friend Mr. Bingley?"

Mr. Darcy laughed, a rich deep sound. "I cannot claim any such eagerness, Miss Bennet. I believe there are few who can. But I will attempt to do my duty when we arrive."

"I shall hold you to it, sir."

Mr. Darcy bowed and stepped away, allowing the rest of the Drummond party to enter the carriage, and with a spoken word from the driver and a shake of the reins, the horses once again began to pull them toward their destination.

"Now, Mrs. Drummond," said Mr. Drummond, "does Darcy still seem like an insufferably proud and disagreeable man? How many of his station would insist upon pushing us from the mire himself?"

Mrs. Drummond did not respond, and well she did not, as there was nothing for her to say. For her part, Elizabeth found herself warmly disposed toward Mr. Darcy, and not only for coming to their rescue that evening. In fact, she had found him to be gentlemanly and warm, and she hoped to learn something more of him during her stay.

When the carriage came to a stop in front of the assembly hall, the gentlemen disembarked, turned to assist the ladies, and they all entered. The hall was larger than Meryton's and, as a consequence, could accommodate more dancers, and since the hall was already filling up, Elizabeth thought that was likely for the best. They stood as a party for several moments, speaking softly amongst themselves, and watching others enter.

It was interesting for Elizabeth to witness those arrivals. There was a much greater variety in the situations of those in attendance, she thought, than existed in Meryton. In the neighborhood with which she was familiar, most of the landowners presided over small estates, her father and his two thousand five hundred being the largest of those permanent residents of the area. The one larger estate, Netherfield Park, had not been occupied since Elizabeth was a girl, and the man who finally leased it was certainly wealthy, but descended from a stock of tradesman, though that fact did not make him any less worthy in Elizabeth's eyes.

This neighborhood, however, seemed to have a much wider variety of residents. There were other gentlemen of Mr. Drummond's general consequence, or so they appeared by their clothing and demeanors, while there were others of gradually greater exalted stations, all the way to whose deportment and dress practically oozed wealth, and whose manners spoke to pride aplenty.

Her uncle obviously had many acquaintances, for he spoke with several other gentlemen, and it did not seem to matter if they were higher in consequence than he was himself—he seemed to be respected, regardless. Likewise, Elizabeth saw that Edward had many acquaintances of his own, and he seemed to be equally accepted among them.

By contrast, however, Elizabeth witnessed more than one look of complete disdain directed toward her aunt—those who deigned to notice her at all—though the woman affected no notice of them. There were some few other women with whom her aunt stood and spoke, but unless Elizabeth was mistaken, it seemed like they were mostly of her own general consequence. It seemed rather incongruous that her uncle and cousin should be accepted by all, while her aunt was held in thinly concealed disdain by those higher than she. Elizabeth suspected it was the woman's own doing.

As promised, Edward introduced Elizabeth and Olivia to his acquaintances, and through him, they gained some introductions to their sisters, who took their standard up from there. Soon Elizabeth had been welcomed to the district many times over, and Olivia had been welcomed to society.

It was due to a chance remark on Elizabeth's part that the adventure of the evening became known to the locals.

"Mr. Darcy and his cousin assisted you?" asked one young lady with wide eyes.

"He is frightfully handsome," opined another.

"That does not make him amiable," added a third.

"Perhaps not, but he has never been anything other than a gentleman," said a fourth.

Elizabeth, trying to follow this conversation as she was, hastened to assure her new acquaintances of how she had always found Mr. Darcy to be perfectly amiable.

"He rarely dances," said the first young lady with an annoyed sniff.

"He usually dances with only those with whom he is particularly acquainted," corrected another. "When he does dance, he is attentive and civil."

"I suspect he does not wish to raise expectations," said a new voice. "Most young ladies of any station would immediately raise their expectations from a dance to matrimony, if he were to be any more than civil."

The newcomer was tall and handsome, perhaps a year or two older than Elizabeth, with her exquisite blonde hair tied into an elegant knot at the back of her head. Her dress was made of costly material and of a fashionable design, and her ears and neck glittered with jewelry which appeared to rival to Mr. Bennet's annual income. Elizabeth did not miss how the other young ladies, even those who gave themselves airs, deferred to her.

"Why should he need to avoid raising expectations?" asked a persistent young lady, a Miss Burbage, by name. "I have heard that his aunt claims him for her daughter, and that there is an engagement in place."

"All the more reason for him to avoid being entrapped by one of you," replied the regal lady. "But I have it on good authority that this engagement of which you speak is nothing more than the wish of his aunt. Furthermore, this cousin of his is a woman who is already five and twenty. Do you not think they would already be married had he intended to offer for her?"

The looks of hope that appeared on several faces almost caused Elizabeth to laugh, and she was certain the newcomer had not missed them either. But she ignored them, instead fixing her attention on Elizabeth.

"Will you ladies do me the honor of introducing your new companion to my acquaintance?"

The introductions were readily taken up by Miss Burbage, and the woman was introduced as Lady Emily Teasdale, the daughter of the Earl of Chesterfield. Elizabeth curtseyed to the lady, and received a smile in return.

"Welcome to our society, Miss Bennet, Miss Drummond. I hope your presence will enliven the society we keep.

"As for the rest of you, though I doubt Mr. Darcy will marry his cousin, you would do well to remember that though he is a gentleman, he also possesses connections to the peerage, and his lineage is ancient and respected. He can expect nothing less than a wife of society, one with a splendid fortune and lineage herself. The daughter of a duke is not beyond his reach."

And with that, Lady Emily directed a pleasant nod to Elizabeth, and she turned away, leaving the ladies chastened behind her.

"Who does she think she is to speak for Mr. Darcy in such a way?" demanded Miss Burbage, though Elizabeth noted the woman had kept her voice quiet.

"She is the daughter of an earl," said another woman, a Miss MacDonald. "I dare say she may speak however she wishes."

"Perhaps she is. But I do not care for her. Too high and mighty by far."

As the young ladies stood and spoke amongst themselves, Elizabeth watched as Lady Emily walked to some other ladies of her acquaintance and began speaking to them. Whatever her new acquaintances said, Elizabeth did not find the lady's manner to be overly proud or disagreeable. Indeed, she had less overt conceit than Miss Bingley and Mrs. Hurst, with much more reason.

The result of Elizabeth's comment about Mr. Darcy was that before long the news flew through the halls on the wings of gossip. It seemed like it was not long before the story was on everyone's lips, with such a speed as to lead Elizabeth to believe that her uncle and cousin must also have shared the story. It seemed like many waited for the arrival of Mr. Darcy with bated breath, though she was certain that it would be some time yet before he would arrive.

At length, the musicians began playing the overture for the first dance, and Elizabeth took her place with her cousin. But when Elizabeth made her observation to Edward, he disavowed any culpability in the matter.

"Mr. Darcy is well known as a man who demands his privacy, and he does not appreciate those who intrude upon it. I do not know the man well enough to speak of the matter, knowing that word of it will make its way back to him. And I am certain my father would not have spoken of it either."

"Perhaps I should have held my tongue," said Elizabeth. "I had no intent to gossip."

Her cousin only shrugged. "I have not much experience with Mr. Darcy, so I cannot tell you how he will react. But I would not expect him to think ill of you for nothing more than a casual comment."

Elizabeth hoped that to be the case. For the present, however, she put the matter from her mind and concentrated on the dance and the rest of the company. Other than the words exchanged at the outset of the dance, Edward did not seem eager to speak, and so Elizabeth's attention was free to wander about the room. Nearby, Olivia danced with her father, and if her laughter was any indication, it seemed the girl was enjoying her first taste of society.

Elsewhere it appeared like those in attendance were eager to take to the dance floor. The attendance was much greater than what Elizabeth would have seen in Meryton, with couples spread across the length of a floor which was at least a third longer than the assembly hall near her home. Furthermore, there was no Kitty or Lydia to run amok, drawing attention to themselves and embarrassing Elizabeth.

Once the first dance was complete, Elizabeth lined up for the second with her uncle, while Olivia lined up with her brother. Thus began a whirlwind night for Elizabeth. Contrary to what she might have believed, she had no shortage of dance partners that evening, and she rarely had to sit out a dance. There was something intangible about the evening, something she could not quite put her finger on. The gentlemen were interesting and the ladies, though it was true that some were gossipy and even silly, were amiable and welcoming. It was possible that the simple fact of associating with people with whom she had not previously been acquainted was the reason. But Elizabeth found herself enjoying herself more than she had at an assembly for many months.

The evening was perhaps half gone when Elizabeth was approached from an entirely unexpected quarter and solicited for a dance. When she thought on the matter, she could not even remember noticing when the gentleman arrived. But the seriousness with which he approached her when she did notice him was unmistakable.

"Miss Bennet," said he as he bowed to her. "Might I solicit your hand for the next dance, if you are not already engaged?"

Something in Elizabeth trembled at this man's earnest entreaty for her hand.

"I am engaged for the next, sir," said Elizabeth, wishing with sudden irrationality that the young man who had requested it had found someone else instead. "But my next dance after that is still free."

"Then I shall await it with much anticipation."

Then, bowing, Mr. Darcy stepped away from her to allow her next partner to approach. It was fortunate Elizabeth was so familiar with the steps of the dance, for she had not a hint of attention to spare to her feet. Her partner fared little better, as though he appeared to be an amiable man and he spoke to her with congenial interest, Elizabeth could not keep her focus on him. She must have responded in an appropriate manner to his words, for he seemed content, at the very least, with their interactions.

Soon the set was complete, and Mr. Darcy approached to claim Elizabeth's hand. She bestowed it willingly, attempting not to give in to the embarrassment which spread over her, its source nothing that Elizabeth could define. The man himself was graceful on the dance floor, moving through the forms with precision and flair. Elizabeth had never danced with such a fine dancer as Mr. Darcy.

In the first few moments, nothing was said between them. Elizabeth was feeling unaccountably bashful in his company, not a comfortable feeling for a normally self-assured woman. For Mr. Darcy's part, he was either cognizant of Elizabeth's feelings and determined to allow her the opportunity to collect herself or taking the opportunity to inspect her. The very thought that the man was scrutinizing her with such intensity ultimately caused Elizabeth to break the silence between them.

"I can see that Miss Bingley was, indeed, correct about you, Mr. Darcy."

It seemed like Mr. Darcy caught Elizabeth's playful tone, for he raised an eyebrow and said: "That is interesting, Miss Bennet, for to be honest, I am not at all well acquainted with the lady."

Elizabeth feigned astonishment. "Truly? She spoke of you and your sister as if you were the most intimate of acquaintances."

"I am quite close with her brother," replied Mr. Darcy. "But though I have often met with his sisters, I would not say that I know them well. That might have been different had I been at liberty to travel to his estate last autumn. I am curious as to what knowledge of me my friend's sister possesses."

"Only that you dance exquisitely, sir," replied Elizabeth.

"Dancing is a subject of which many young ladies love to wax poetic," observed Mr. Darcy.

"Many ladies do, indeed. But in this instance she was entirely correct. But I must own that your friend gave you a more flaming character."

"Oh?"

Elizabeth could not determine if Mr. Darcy was amused or offended at this observation, but her impression of him as a reserved, yet amiable man, gave her the courage to continue speaking.

"He claimed that you almost never dance, sir. And yet your civility in requesting my hand suggests that Mr. Bingley exaggerated."

A fleeting smile passed over Mr. Darcy's countenance. "How well Bingley knows me."

"So you own to it?" asked Elizabeth.

"I do, but not to the extent that Bingley insinuated. I will confess that I rarely dance twice with a young lady at one event, and I often prefer to converse with friends, rather than attending young ladies on the dance floor."

"That *is* shocking, sir!" exclaimed Elizabeth. "Should I feel offended for the sake of young ladies everywhere?"

"I think not. In fact, it is simply because I do not feel comfortable in company I do not know and wish to refrain from raising the hopes of young ladies. I am much more at ease when I am particularly acquainted with my partner."

"Ah, then I suppose you are not at ease with me! We are not well acquainted."

"No, we are not. But I find that I am quite comfortable, Miss Bennet."

"Is that so?"

"Yes. Perhaps it is because you have spoken of my friend with such familiarity."

"Perhaps that is it," replied Elizabeth.

Their conversation, carried on in fits and starts due to the demands of the dance, was interrupted by a long interlude in which the steps took them away from each other. Mr. Darcy was nothing like Elizabeth would have expected, and given Miss Bingley's description of him, Elizabeth might have been prepared to dislike him.

But Elizabeth had long known that Miss Bingley was not to be trusted, and her professions of intimacy with the Darcys had been disproven with her meeting with Georgiana. Furthermore, Elizabeth had long known of Miss Bingley's pretensions and ambitions toward high society, and the woman's words had rung with the faint tones of desperation. Either way, Elizabeth would not judge the man by the brush strokes Miss Bingley had used to paint his likeness.

As they came together again, Elizabeth chanced to notice a cluster of young ladies, and she was startled to see the eyes of Lady Emily watching them as they danced. It was difficult to discern what the woman was thinking, but Elizabeth wondered at her scrutiny, as for several moments it never wavered, even when the woman saw Elizabeth watching her. Perhaps she was thinking that Elizabeth was reaching above herself, given her newness to the neighborhood and relative position in life.

But then Mr. Darcy was once again before Elizabeth, and she decided she must make a disclosure before the man discovered the matter for himself.

"I must inform you, Mr. Darcy," said she, feeling her former nervousness return, "that the incident from earlier this evening was made known to those in attendance due to a careless remark I made myself."

The man's eyes bored into her, and Elizabeth began to feel even more uncomfortable. "You are referring to the fact that the Drummond carriage became mired in the mud?"

"Yes, sir," replied Elizabeth. "I had no intention to speak of it, but when I made an oblique reference, several of our new acquaintances would not rest until they knew the whole of the matter. I apologize, sir, for I understand your wish to maintain your privacy."

"My privacy is, indeed, something I treasure." Mr. Darcy's expression softened. "But it does not follow that I blame you for it. The matter is, after all, something which occurred in your presence, and I doubt you possessed any ulterior motives in making it known. It likely would become known anyway, as I plan to speak with several others about that stretch of road, for it has become something of a hazard to those of us who use it frequently."

Relief settled over Elizabeth and she inclined her head. "Thank you,

Mr. Darcy, for granting me clemency. I assure you that I am not one who is prone to gossip."

"Miss Bennet, I hardly think clemency is mine to grant. Come, shall we speak of other things?"

"Certainly, sir. But do not be surprised if I tease you on the subject of your gallantry in the future. It is not a matter nearly so inconsequential as you would have me believe, and I am afraid I will be required to remind you of it in the future."

Mr. Darcy laughed at Elizabeth's sally, and shook his head. "I believe being teased by you, Miss Bennet, would be an exhilarating experience. I look forward to it."

Thus, was Elizabeth's opinion of the man reinforced, and when they separated after the dance was finished, she found her head to be full of him. It was, perhaps, not the most sensible thing to espouse such feelings for a man of Mr. Darcy's stature, but she could not help it. And she felt certain that the future would prove him to be even more amiable than he had hitherto shown himself to be.

CHAPTER IX

Anthony Fitzwilliam sat at the table of the breakfast parlor at Pemberley vastly amused. Though his cousin had often given him reason to be amused—mostly it was because of his reticence and ability to offend without trying—Fitzwilliam thought he had never enjoyed himself quite so much as he was now. For though Darcy was often focused to a fault and had often been referred to as a force of nature when pursuing some objective, he ate his breakfast that morning with a distracted air, often pausing between bites or staring at something only he could see.

"The assembly last night was a success, was it not?"

It seemed like his cousin had forgotten that he was even there, for he started a little. "It went well enough, though we were not there for the first half of the evening."

"I think that suited you very well, indeed, Cousin."

Rather than give Fitzwilliam any further reason to make sport with him, Darcy only grunted and returned to his sausage.

"You must have felt the loss of half the evening keenly," said Fitzwilliam, still attempting to provoke his cousin to respond. "I dare say that you have never danced so much as you did last night."

But Darcy only shrugged. "I behaved much as I ever would."

"I disagree, Darcy. There was Miss Pearce and Miss Dawson and Lady Emily. And of course, Miss Drummond and Miss Bennet. How can you account for such liveliness?"

"You forget their situations, Cousin. Miss Pearce is betrothed and Miss Dawson is all but engaged. As for Lady Emily, she is her father's only child, and her sons are set to inherit the earldom. She has no need of my money and no interest in me at all."

Though Fitzwilliam privately thought Darcy was mistaken about the earl's daughter, he ignored her for the moment. "And Miss Drummond and Miss Bennet?"

"Miss Drummond is only just out in society and not looking for a wealthy husband. Miss Bennet is quite engaging and does not give the impression of being a fortune hunter."

"I will certainly not disagree with you on that front, though I will say that many ladies are able to hide their designs behind fluttering eyelashes, or even wit, if it comes to that. But I will do you the favor of agreeing with you—I also found Miss Bennet to be quite delightful, so I will not say anything against her."

That prompted a response, as Fitzwilliam had known it would. Darcy turned a level gaze on him, his eyes questioning, quite obviously trying to ferret out Fitzwilliam's own level of interest in Miss Bennet, interest that Fitzwilliam was convinced that his cousin possessed in large measure. Fitzwilliam decided to twist the knife just a little.

"In fact, I am quite certain that she would make an excellent wife, and as you know, I am quite independent."

"You have only met the woman twice, Fitzwilliam."

There was the infamous Darcy displeasure. Fitzwilliam was delighted.

"Twice is more than enough. Do not mistake me, Cousin—I know she would make a good wife; I do not know if she would make a good wife for me."

"Then you mean to court her?"

"That is premature." Fitzwilliam paused, looking at his cousin. "With this inquisition, I might have thought you have some interest in the lady yourself."

Darcy scowled and turned his menacing glare on Fitzwilliam. Had he not already had many years to become used to his cousin's humors, Fitzwilliam thought that he might be intimidated.

"You do not need to say anything, Darcy, for your response betrays you. I have no particular interest in Miss Bennet, other than as a pleasant young lady with whom it is a pleasure to converse."

"Then why do you speak in such a manner?"

"To see if I can provoke a response, old man. And you have not disappointed."

"Perhaps you should keep your clever remarks to yourself."

"Perhaps I should. If you do decide to pursue the lovely Miss Bennet, you will have no competition from me. But what of Lady Emily?"

Nonplussed, Darcy stared back at Fitzwilliam. "What of her?"

"She would be an excellent match, the kind of match not even Aunt Catherine could speak against. She has beauty, accomplishments, dowry, and your firstborn would be an earl. Have you considered her?"

Darcy shrugged. "I have not. She is an intelligent woman, but she does not have that spark which intrigues me. Furthermore, I do not think she considers me in such a light."

He turned back to his breakfast, indicating the conversation was over, and Fitzwilliam regarded him for several moments. Perhaps Darcy did not think Lady Emily considered him in such a fashion, but Fitzwilliam was certain his cousin was wrong.

The trouble with Darcy, mused he, was that he was adept at spotting a fortune hunter, but when it came to a predatory woman who was *not* motivated by social advancement or fortune, it seemed he was blind. From what Fitzwilliam had seen the previous evening, he was certain that Lady Emily had been anything but indifferent to Darcy as a potential mate, and given the way her gaze had stayed on Miss Bennet, he did not think the lady was inclined to be defeated by a young woman of little standing.

Thus, it was up to Fitzwilliam to see to his cousin's interest. Contrary to others in his family—and Aunt Catherine in particular— the only hope he had with respect to Darcy's future was to see his cousin happy. Happiness had often been in short supply in Fitzwilliam Darcy's life. But the right companion would change that, and if Miss Bennet held the key to Darcy's happiness, Fitzwilliam would do everything in his power to see that his suit was successful.

The morning after the assembly was an opportunity for young ladies to discuss the night before, speak of the gowns of the ladies attending, the handsome countenances of the gentlemen, the dances and the conversations, and to relive once again the magic to which they had been introduced. Elizabeth had often engaged in such conversations with her sisters, but primarily with Jane and Charlotte, her two closest friends. Had Olivia not been full of vigor, eager to speak of what she had seen and done, Elizabeth might have found herself quite lonely for Meryton.

As it had been her first time in society, Olivia more than made up for the lack of Elizabeth's dearest friends, for from the time they arose and began their daily tasks until that evening, her mind was full of nothing but the assembly, a never-ending stream of words falling from her mouth. Elizabeth thought that she might have been rather fatigued by it all, were she not so amused.

"It seemed to me that you were the author of many conquests, Lizzy," said Olivia after they had sat for some time at the pianoforte. Ostensibly they had been practicing, but in reality, there had been little practice as Olivia's tongue had not stilled for two minutes together.

"I know nothing about conquests, Olivia," said Elizabeth. "I welcomed the amusement, especially since it is quite different from the assemblies in Meryton."

Olivia was taken aback by the statement. "Surely it resembles them. They cannot be much different."

"Of course," replied Elizabeth. "But there are differences. For one, there were many more people in attendance than one would see in Meryton. Also, Meryton does not have a vast array of situations as I saw last night."

"Situations?" asked Olivia, cocking her head to the side.

"A disparity of wealth," said Elizabeth. "Near Meryton, the only large estate does not begin to compare with Pemberley, and almost all the rest are smaller than Longbourn, my father's estate."

"Oh. So there are no earl's daughters or ladies of Miss Darcy's station?"

"No. The Bennets are one of the foremost families in the district, though we are naught but minor gentry. In this neighborhood, there are several families of like circumstances, but there are also many of much more wealth."

"Foremost families!"

The words, spoken with such force and contempt as to leave those hearing them with no doubt as to their meaning, startled both girls, and they turned as one to see Mrs. Drummond standing in the doorway, arms akimbo, glaring at them.

"Though your father might wallow in his fantasy world, content to imagine that he has upheld the honor and credit of the family, I know the truth. The Bennets have fallen far. You would do well to remember that."

"Considering how you have not visited Longbourn in my memory, I cannot imagine to what you refer," said Elizabeth, her offense overriding her desire to refrain from being at odds with her aunt. "I hardly believe you are in any position to judge the state of my family's respectability."

"You may believe that, if you wish," was Mrs. Drummond's frosty reply. "But however you wish to think of your family, it is not that which has prompted me to speak to you today. It is your own conduct—behavior which provides proof of my assertions—of which I wish to speak today."

"My conduct? I cannot imagine of what you speak."

"I am certain you do," said Mrs. Drummond. "To whit, your shameless manners, the way you flirted with every man in attendance, the way you threw yourself at Mr. Darcy and Colonel Fitzwilliam. I will not have this shameless behavior in my home."

"Mama!" cried Olivia.

"Aunt Claire," said Elizabeth at the same time, stiff with affront, "my behavior in no way resembles the charges you have laid at my door. I have done nothing improper."

"Of course, you would feel that way," said her aunt, her tone a sneer. "Given the example you have been given, it is not to be wondered at."

"My father does not take issue with my behavior, and neither does *your* husband. I have no idea what *you* consider to be good behavior, but whatever it is, I cannot think there are many who agree with you."

"With this impertinence, I am not surprised you see nothing wrong with the way you act. It was a mistake to bring you here. I knew it from the start."

"If you think it was so," said Elizabeth, clenching her fists to keep her temper, "then I will return to my home at any time convenient. It is clear that at least *one member* of this family does not wish for me to be here, and I will not stay where I am the subject of baseless attacks."

The gasp from Olivia almost broke Elizabeth's heart. She knew her departure would be hard on her young cousin, and Elizabeth herself felt little desire to be separated from the girl she was coming to esteem highly. But her character would not be maligned in such a way without response. Luckily, the conversation was interrupted before anything else could be said which could not be taken back.

"That is enough, Mrs. Drummond." Mr. Drummond stepped into the room and glared at his wife, and though she gave every indication of defiance, Elizabeth could see it was more bravado than anything. "In fact, *I* invited Elizabeth here, and *I* will decide how long she is welcome to stay. Furthermore, as far as I am concerned, there is nothing wrong with her behavior."

"You did not see her flirting with every man present last night?"

"I hardly think that her playful manner constituted flirting, Mrs. Drummond." Mr. Drummond's voice cracked like a whip. "In fact, I believe that Olivia cannot but benefit by having such a vivacious example as Elizabeth to guide her in our society. The fact that Elizabeth was so widely accepted last night by so many is a testament to her ability to put others at ease and recommend herself to new acquaintances."

Mrs. Drummond smirked at Elizabeth. "Or perhaps it is a way of letting all the young men know that she is—"

"Enough, Madam!" roared Mr. Drummond. "You claim to be genteel yourself and you insinuate such vile innuendo? If your brother knew you were speaking of his daughter in such a manner, he would slap your mouth, and I would not prevent him!"

The couple glared at each other, but Mrs. Drummond was the first to look away.

"Elizabeth," said her uncle, turning kindly eyes to her, "I cannot begin to express my mortification at the attacks to which you have been subjected in my own home. I can only apologize sincerely and beseech you to remain with us. Though there are *some* who have apparently allowed longstanding grudges to affect their judgment, I assure you that everyone else in this family values you as one of our own. I beg for your forgiveness."

Though Elizabeth eyed her aunt with some distaste, she directed conciliatory words back at her uncle. "Uncle, I have been happy to be here. You have all been welcoming, and I have come to think of you as my family in reality rather than simply in name. Olivia has become as dear to me as my own sisters.

"But I cannot—I will not—be the subject of such attacks. Should she speak in such a way to me again, I will write to my father, begging to be allowed to come home."

Mr. Drummond replied with a curt nod, though his eyes never left his wife. "It will not happen again. You have my word.

"Now, Wife—I would speak with you in our chambers. Come with me now."

The look Mrs. Drummond directed at Elizabeth was pure poison, but she did not gainsay her husband. When they had gone, the silence in the room was almost deafening.

"I hate her!" exclaimed Olivia, and she collapsed onto a nearby sofa and burst into tears. "She cares nothing of any of us. All she wishes is to make all our lives miserable!"

Though Elizabeth had no cordial feelings toward her aunt at that moment, she sat beside her cousin and drew her into an embrace. "Though I will own to having no knowledge of what motivates your mother, I cannot think her completely without feeling. Her disappointments in life have made her bitter, it seems."

"She should be happy with what she has. She makes my father miserable, and I cannot bear to see it."

There was nothing Elizabeth could say to Olivia's words, as she knew it was nothing more than the truth. As Elizabeth thought back on the confrontation, she realized that Mrs. Drummond had almost certainly attempted to offend Elizabeth enough to make her wish to return to her home. The reason for such an attack eluded Elizabeth at that moment, but she was almost certain that she was correct.

Further consideration told Elizabeth that she herself was almost incidental to the woman's enmity. She did not dislike Elizabeth particularly; rather, her antagonism was directed more at Elizabeth's father than Elizabeth herself. She was incidental—nothing more than the target of Mrs. Drummond's ire because of the simple fact of her presence.

But she would not allow Mrs. Drummond to hurl such vile insults as the one she had been about to say when her husband had stopped her. If she was forced to return home, perhaps Olivia could go with her to visit Longbourn. Even with the situation with Jane, her mother's nerves and Kitty and Lydia's silliness, it would almost certainly be more comfortable for them both than to be constantly on their guards against a bitter woman.

Later the day of the unpleasantness with Mrs. Drummond, Elizabeth had taken some time to herself to reflect on all that had happened since her arrival in Derbyshire. By now, Elizabeth adored Olivia and Leah, she respected and esteemed her uncle. She was coming to appreciate Edward as well and had nothing but fondness for his younger brothers. The countryside was beautiful, and though she could not walk as much as she would have in Hertfordshire, still she appreciated what she could see.

As for Mrs. Drummond herself, whatever threats her husband had used to force her good behavior seemed to be efficacious—at least at present. Elizabeth could not state with any degree of certainty that the woman's good behavior would last, but other than a few dark looks in her direction, Mrs. Drummond appeared intent upon ignoring her. Elizabeth found that she could bear the woman's indifference quite cheerfully.

"I understand you and my mother had a disagreement today," Edward had said the previous evening. Aunt Claire had not descended the stairs for dinner, allowing for a peaceful meal and a momentary cessation of her attacks.

"We did," replied Elizabeth, though she truly did not wish to speak of the matter.

Edward sighed and shook his head. "If it is any consolation, I do not believe her ire is directed at you in particular."

"I believe I have already apprehended that fact."

"And you did not take offense?"

"On the contrary, I took great offense. Your mother was about to accuse me of vile actions before your father put a stop to it. But as the matter has already been dealt with, I do not consider it useful to dwell on it."

"That is wise," was Edward's quiet reply.

When Elizabeth returned to the house after her constitutional, she found that Olivia and Leah were together reading, and as she did not wish to disturb them—and more importantly, wished to continue her privacy for a time—Elizabeth climbed the stairs to go to her room. But before she could enter, she was stopped in the hall by her uncle, who beckoned her into a nearby sitting-room, one which was all but unused.

"Elizabeth," said he, as he turned to face her, "I wish to take this opportunity to again apologize to you for your aunt's conduct. I have known since the time of our marriage that she was not happy and did not consider me enough of a gentleman for her tastes. But she has never mortified me to the extent that she did yesterday."

"As I said before, Uncle, I do not hold you to blame for her words. You have been nothing but welcoming since I came to Derbyshire."

"It is a credit to you, Elizabeth."

Mr. Drummond sighed and sat down on a nearby chair, motioning for Elizabeth to do the same. The thought was incongruous at the moment, but Elizabeth noted that the furniture in the room was old, though it did not show overt signs of the wear she would have anticipated in pieces which were greatly aged. It seemed clear that the family had simply ceased using this room at some point in the past, either when the furniture had fallen out of fashion and could not be replaced, or because of diminishing circumstances.

"I know your aunt offended you grievously," said Mr. Drummond after brooding about it for a moment. "But you should not take her words to heart. It seems like there is little which does not offend her these days, but I do not think her words constituted a disapproval of your manners. Her target was, in fact, something quite different."

"That was quite evident, Uncle." Elizabeth paused, wondering how she could raise the matter without prying or insulting, when she decided that it was best to simply ask her question. "Why has she become like this?"

"She has been disappointed in life. I do not wish to unearth old grievances, Lizzy, so I prefer not to speak of it."

"If you will forgive me, Uncle, Aunt Claire is more than willing to not only unearth those grievances, but also to wave them about like a flag."

"That is true. But let us not descend to her level. My primary motive is to protect my children from her vitriol, and, indeed, to protect you as well. Though my wife rarely listens to me, I can still command her, and in this instance, I have done so. She will not attack you again with such spurious charges, or she will reap the consequences."

"Thank you, Uncle Drummond," said Elizabeth, putting her hand on his arm. "I appreciate your support."

"And I appreciate yours. Your presence has been wonderful for my daughters. I would not wish for you to be made uncomfortable or made to flee by the accusations of a bitter woman."

After exchanging a few more words, Elizabeth parted from her uncle and retired to her room for some rest. She was still annoyed that he would not explain the reason for his wife's objectionable behavior, but she understood why he did not wish to speak of it. Perhaps she should write to her father, demanding that he explain what had happened to his sister. She would have, if she thought he would respond.

CHAPTER X

*I*t was with great relief that Elizabeth left the tense circumstances at Kingsdown, including the brooding person of her aunt, behind to attend Georgiana at Pemberley. The girl, who had not been able to attend the assembly, sent them a note, and in reading between the lines, Elizabeth was able to determine that she was all afire with curiosity for an account of the evening. Thus, the day after Elizabeth's confrontation with Mrs. Drummond, she embarked in the Darcy carriage, sent for their use, for the short journey to visit their friend.

"It is unfortunate that Georgiana cannot participate in society yet," said Olivia once they had set out.

"She is still only sixteen, Olivia," reminded Elizabeth. "I have experience with coming out too early. It is better that she wait for another year and gain more maturity."

Olivia cocked her head to the side. "You have told me about your coming out, but you did not say much of your impressions."

Elizabeth sighed. She had not spoken of her family much, not wishing to give her cousin a poor impression of their behavior. Perhaps now was the time to do so.

"Every one of my sisters came out at the age of fifteen," said

Elizabeth. "I dare say Jane handled it with her usual calmness, while I managed by laughing away my insecurities. But Mary was lost, and Kitty and Lydia much too immature for it. Trust me—it is better that you waited until seventeen, for you are much better able to understand how you should behave."

"You have spoken of your sisters before," observed Olivia.

With a sigh, Elizabeth shot her cousin a smile and said: "Kitty and Lydia were both much too young. Add to that an indulgent mother who does not completely understand how a gentlewoman should behave herself, and you have a pair of girls who are completely wild.

"And though I have not been part of that world myself, I am certain that young women do not come out in London until they are at least eighteen. Anything younger would be unseemly. Thus Georgiana might begin to partake in some country society next year, but in London she will need to wait another year."

"I suppose I will not have to concern myself with such things." Olivia shot Elizabeth a smile. "Papa is not wealthy enough to give me a London season."

"From what I have heard, my dear Olivia, I do not think that is much of a loss. Be content with what you have and those you will meet here. Regardless of what your mother says, I think there is a good chance you will find someone to love and to live in a state of bliss for the rest of your life."

The girls laughed together, and Olivia grasped Elizabeth's hand with fervent affection. "I am so glad you have come, Lizzy. I have never had so much confidence as I have now. I do not know what I shall do when you leave."

"Then I shall simply have to stay," replied Elizabeth. "I believe I would be happy to live the rest of my life in Derbyshire."

The carriage soon stopped in front of their destination, and Olivia and Elizabeth were treated to the sight of shy, reticent Miss Georgiana Darcy hopping from foot to foot in her excitement. They laughed as they stepped from the conveyance, greeting her exuberance with fortitude and not a little amusement. Only the presence of Mrs. Annesley by her side kept Miss Darcy from demanding an immediate account of their experiences, Elizabeth thought, though it did not take long after they were seated before they were inundated with questions.

"Were you not informed of the events of the evening by your brother?" asked Elizabeth.

Georgiana only rolled her eyes. "My brother does not enjoy society and cannot be bothered to pay attention to anything that is of any interest to me. He would not even tell me with whom he danced!"

"He danced with Lizzy," said Olivia, turning a sly eye on Elizabeth. "I have it on good authority that he enjoyed it very much, indeed."

A joyful clap of her hands accompanied Georgiana's exclaimed: "Oh, I knew he admired you! Now I shall have a sister!"

Elizabeth felt her jaw drop at such a pronouncement, and by her side Olivia was in much the same straits. She was about to reprimand her friend when she saw a mischievous gleam in Georgiana's eyes and the twitching of her lips. And then her friend could not hold it in any longer, and she laughed out loud, drawing Olivia and Elizabeth — though much more restrained — into her mirth.

"You should have seen your countenance, Elizabeth," said Georgiana between gasps of laughter. "I thought you were about to expire from mortification."

"I will own to being surprised," said Elizabeth.

Georgiana eyed her sternly, though underneath Elizabeth could see the same playfulness. "Should I be offended for my brother that you do not see him in such a way?"

"Oh, Georgiana," said Elizabeth, shaking her head. In truth, Elizabeth was not enjoying her new friend's mirth — Mr. Darcy *was* an amiable man, and Elizabeth thought she could esteem him quite easily. But she would not allow herself to be lost in dreams of a future with this man when, in truth, he was far above her, both in consequence and birth.

"Miss Darcy," interjected Mrs. Annesley; her frown of disapproval spoke volumes as to what she felt about her charge's jest. "I believe you owe Miss Bennet an apology."

"I am not offended, Mrs. Annesley," said Elizabeth quickly. "I understand that Georgiana was teasing."

"I know, Miss Bennet," said Mrs. Annesley with a nod at Elizabeth. "But it is still not something of which she should jest. If someone were to overhear, it might cause rumors to be started which could damage both yourself and Mr. Darcy."

Elizabeth nodded, knowing that Mrs. Annesley was, in part, attempting to teach her young charge, and in part protecting her employer. The woman was loyal, which spoke well to her character.

"I do apologize, Lizzy," said Georgiana, in a tone which almost managed to convey contriteness. "I know you have just met William. It is just . . ." The girl paused and ducked her head, suddenly shy. "I have longed for a friend, and now that I have you — and Olivia too — I am loath to lose you. You must understand that I will use every stratagem I can devise to keep you in Derbyshire."

This time they all laughed together. "I am quite happy to be your friend," replied Elizabeth. "I shall be here for some months yet, and even when I do return to my home, I will continue to be your friend. And Olivia will remain when I am forced to return to my home."

"I will," said Olivia, though in a quiet and shy tone.

"Then I shall be content with that," said Georgiana.

They continued to speak for some time, Elizabeth and Olivia sharing with Georgiana some of the impressions they had of the assembly. The girl listened to them with rapt attention, and it was clear that she wished she could have been there herself. It was hard, Elizabeth knew, for younger girls to hear of such things and not partake in them themselves, but Elizabeth knew Georgiana's patience would be rewarded in the end.

When they had been speaking for some time, Mr. Darcy and Colonel Fitzwilliam came in to greet them, and they sat down to visit. When they had been engaged for some minutes Elizabeth could not help but tease her host.

"So, have you gentlemen assisted any other travelers in distress? I would not be surprised if it has become a habit."

"No, Miss Bennet, it is not a habit. In fact, I believe the episode the other night was the first time I have ever found myself in such a situation."

"What is this?" demanded Georgiana. "You did not speak a word of it, Brother."

"That is because there was not much to tell."

"On the contrary, sir," said Elizabeth, shooting him a reproachful frown, "I have rarely seen such an act of bravery, such sheer compassion for the welfare of others. I dare say the bards would make an epic of it, if only it were known!"

"Then you must share it with me, Lizzy!" exclaimed Georgiana.

"And share it I shall," replied Elizabeth, arching an eyebrow at Mr. Darcy, daring him to object.

Mr. Darcy only waved her on. "I am certain only you can do the story justice, Miss Bennet."

"Then you had best prepare for something shocking, Georgiana, for your brother and cousin displayed a heroism far from the common sort. For you see, on the way to the assembly, a group of common people, numbering among their number two damsels, who were most assuredly in distress, encountered more than a hint of trouble. While they journeyed, they were betrayed by treacherous rain-soaked roads, which rose to prevent their ever arriving at their destination.

"The horses screamed and strove against the sucking muck, which clutched at the wheels and held them, like some demon, jaws gaping with dripping fangs to pull them down to the depths of hell. In a panic, those in the stricken carriage alighted, hoping to escape the awful damnation which awaited them, leaving the horses to strive against the weight of their doom. But it was all for naught, for though the horses strained against the grasping fingers of the mud, it held fast, preventing their escape.

"At last, when all hope seemed exhausted, another carriage happened upon them, and when it had rolled to a stop, two young men, alight with the fire of courage and determination stepped down, insisting upon offering their assistance. With the help of their trusty men at arms, these mighty men strove with the very lieutenants of hell and prevailed, with naught but a few specks of mud on their trousers to mark their struggle. And so all were saved — the damsels to the assembly, where they danced the night away, while the two young men returned to their estate and from thence to the assembly hall, to pay homage to the young maidens with all the humility of truly heroic young men." By the time Elizabeth finished her tale, the entire company was laughing at her story, even Mr. Darcy, who had struck her as more stoic than mirthful. Colonel Fitzwilliam slapped his knee and Olivia and Georgiana leaned against each other, giggling, each supporting the other in her arms.

"Did it truly happen that way, Brother?" gasped Georgiana.

"More or less," said Mr. Darcy. "Miss Bennet *might* have embellished the tale slightly."

"Aye," chortled Colonel Fitzwilliam. "She has the soul of a storyteller, I dare say."

"My cousins have always enjoyed my stories," replied Elizabeth modestly. "A story devoid of embellishments is akin to a bowl of strawberries without cream. Yes, you can eat and enjoy it, but it is so much more interesting when combined with something sweet."

"And make it better you did, Miss Bennet," said Mr. Darcy. "Even Fitzwilliam, who I am absolutely certain has not done half of the things of which he boasts, cannot spin a yarn so well as you."

"Darcy!" exclaimed Colonel Fitzwilliam. "Do not say such things! I will have you know that everything I have told you is nothing but an exact account of my experiences!"

"I think my cousin has become addled by the rigors of command," said Georgiana *sotto voce*. "No one could ever believe all the outlandish blandishments which come out of his mouth."

Elizabeth covered her giggle with a hand, noting the severe look Colonel Fitzwilliam was directing at his cousin. She only looked calmly at him, though her amusement danced in her eyes.

"I believe it might be prudent for you to take care as to whom you allow to influence your sister, Darcy," said he. "She seems to have acquired a hint of teasing in her manner which is quite unseemly."

"I actually rather enjoy it, Fitzwilliam," said Mr. Darcy, leaning back into the cushions of the sofa. "It is amusing to watch you receive a taste of your own medicine from time to time."

"Cut to the quick!" exclaimed Colonel Fitzwilliam, raising a dramatic hand to his chest. "And to think that it is my own cousin who has wounded me so."

"I agree with William," said Georgiana. "You *do* deserve to be teased in return."

They all laughed and then moved on to other topics. Elizabeth participated, but underneath she was considering all that had happened. She had enjoyed relating the story of Mr. Darcy's heroics and was certain it would become a favorite story with which to tease him in the future, but she was still not certain what to think of Georgiana's comments. It seemed clear that the girl thought much of her, for which Elizabeth was grateful, for she was quite fond of Georgiana too. But Mr. Darcy had shown no noticeable interest in Elizabeth, and she did not mean to make herself unhappy over him.

Of the utmost importance, however, was Elizabeth's wish that Mr. Darcy never learn of the jest his sister had made. Elizabeth could not imagine the mortification she would feel should he become aware of it, and she would not wish him to be put into a position where he felt he had no choice but to marry her. As an amiable man, Elizabeth had no doubt he would make the best of it in an admirable fashion, but the thought of taking another's choice away was more than she could bear. She determined to have a word with Georgiana before they parted to make certain she understood this.

After some time had passed, the girls agreed amongst themselves that they would go together to Lambton to peruse some of the shops. It was so similar to a common occurrence between herself and her younger sisters at Meryton that Elizabeth could not quite stifle a grin. The gentlemen insisted upon accompanying them, and soon they all set off in the Darcy carriage for the small market town, the rumbling of the wheels accompanying their continued lively banter.

In town, they separated for a time, the gentlemen indicating that they had some business to conduct while the ladies visited some shops that interested them. There was nothing in particular that any of them wished to purchase—instead they browsed and talked and laughed amongst themselves, enjoying their time together as ladies friendly with one another often do.

It was while they were engaged in this attitude that they came across an acquaintance, though Elizabeth could not determine if the woman was happy to see them. The three girls curtseyed to Lady Emily, which she returned with a nod and a smile.

"I had not thought to meet you here today. It seems to me that you three have been together much of late."

"Miss Bennet and Miss Drummond have become very dear friends," said Georgiana. "I am very happy to have them call on me, for they have told me of the assembly. My brother does not care for such things, so their intelligence was welcome, indeed."

Lady Emily smiled, an indulgent sort of gesture. "I dare say gentlemen will not pay any attention to the kind of details that would interest a lady."

"That is exactly it," agreed Georgiana.

Lady Emily turned to Elizabeth. "Have you become accustomed to Derbyshire yet, Miss Bennet?"

"It is different from my home," replied Elizabeth, "but I find myself quite content here. There is nothing wanting in the locale, to be sure."

"I have passed through Hertfordshire. I am certain it contains many beauties of its own."

"It does, and I am quite fond of it. I believe we all possess an affinity for our own homes, but there are many beauties in the world, and I am happy to see whatever I can of it."

"I agree." Lady Emily paused and after a moment she again spoke to Elizabeth. "I would be happy, Miss Bennet, if you would visit me when the opportunity presents itself. I would like to know you better.

"Of course, I am happy to welcome you all," continued she, addressing Georgiana and Olivia. "I mean no disrespect for your excellent companions, but as we are closer in age, I believe we have much in common."

The girls were quick to indicate that they were not offended, to which the lady smiled. For Elizabeth's part, she was flattered by this unlooked-for bit of civility, and she agreed that she would, to which Lady Emily smiled and thanked her. "If your means of coming to my house is a problem, please let me know and I will send a carriage."

"Thank you, Lady Emily," said Elizabeth. "I will speak with my uncle."

"There you are," a voice said, hailing them, and the gentlemen joined them, bowing to the newcomer. "Lady Emily," said Mr. Darcy. "How good it is to see you."

"Mr. Darcy," replied Lady Emily. "I was not aware that you and Colonel Fitzwilliam were also in attendance."

"Miss Bennet and Miss Drummond were visiting Georgiana at Pemberley before we came to Lambton," said Colonel Fitzwilliam by way of explanation. "We, in turn, had not expected to see you."

There was something of challenge in Colonel Fitzwilliam's tone, but though Elizabeth did not understand it, it was equally clear that Lady Emily either did not notice it or she simply ignored it. She turned her eyes back on Mr. Darcy and her gaze almost seemed to be possessive, though that was not quite the correct word either. There did seem to be admiration inherent in it, though Elizabeth was forced to own that she did not know Lady Emily well enough to be certain of anything she was seeing.

"Did you find anything of interest, Miss Bennet?" asked Mr. Darcy, drawing Elizabeth's attention back to him.

"Several things of interest, sir?" said Elizabeth. "But I have made no purchases."

Mr. Darcy shook his head. "You share the same affliction as Georgiana. I cannot count the number of times I have conveyed her to Lambton—at her insistence, I might add—only to have her purchase nothing."

"Then you should be thankful, Mr. Darcy," replied Elizabeth. "Instead of merely browsing the shops, she might be more predisposed to purchase everything she can lay her hands on."

Seeming amused, Mr. Darcy said: "You believe her predilection to be a virtue then?"

"I do not believe it can be anything else. Georgiana has become a dear friend. I must defend her against all naysayers."

Colonel Fitzwilliam laughed. "Those you will not find here, Miss Bennet. I dare say that I have never seen two siblings as devoted to each other as Darcy and Georgiana."

"Of course, they are," said Lady Emily. "And it is to their credit." Lady Emily turned to Elizabeth. "I look forward to your visit, Miss Bennet. For now, I bid you all good day."

After the lady departed, the company soon broke up themselves, the residents of Pemberley to return thither, while Elizabeth and Olivia were conveyed in a carriage graciously provided by the Darcys to

Kingsdown.

"I am quite glad you have come, Lizzy," said Olivia when they were seated in the carriage on their way back to the Drummond home. "I love my sister, but it is wonderful to have a companion my own age with whom to converse."

"The benefits of having a sister close in age are, indeed, many," replied Elizabeth. "There are vexations, of course, but I believe the benefits outweigh whatever drawbacks there are."

"I have not had any yet," averred Olivia. "I am perfectly content with your presence."

Laughing, Elizabeth embraced the younger girl about her shoulders. "Perhaps you have not experienced any of them, but I assure you there will be vexations. It may be best to have our first argument as soon as may be arranged, so we can make up and be friends again."

"Oh, Lizzy! It is exactly that playful conversation to which I referred. It is delightfully droll to have another young lady, for it can sometimes be dull without. I hope you never return to Hertfordshire!"

"We shall have to see," said Elizabeth.

Though unbidden, the picture of Mr. Darcy, his handsome countenance in the light of the sun, his hair tousled by the gentle breaths of wind, entered Elizabeth's mind, and no matter how much she tried to tell herself that he could never possess any interest in her, the image would not leave. So she allowed her imagination full rein. Being the object of such a man's affections would be something marvelous — of this she was absolutely certain.

As the coach drove down the road, Darcy watched it go, his mind with one of the young ladies contained therein. Miss Drummond was an admirable sort of girl, and he had a high opinion of her, but Miss Bennet was a breath of fresh air, a veritable diamond in a sea of opals, a woman so unlike any other that Darcy had never seen her like. It was beyond comprehension that he might ever have managed to resist her siren call, for thoughts of her filled his mind and fired his imagination.

As he stepped into his carriage with his sister and cousin, he was content to allow Georgiana and Fitzwilliam to carry the conversation between them, inserting a word or two here or there where he thought it least likely that he would be required to speak more. His mind was full of *her* and he would not have it any other way. The attraction he had felt for her was stronger, more powerful than anything he had ever felt, and he found himself wondering what it would be like if he was never required to watch her return to her home at night—if her home was *his* home.

It was fortunate for Darcy that he escaped his relations' teasing, for if they recognized his distraction, he had no doubt they would make sport with him with merciless abandon. Through dinner and their time in the sitting-room after, his thoughts remained half on Miss Bennet, even as he played cards with his sister and cousin and listened to Georgiana play the pianoforte. But though he thought much on her, the weight of duty stayed on his shoulders, and he was nowhere equal to the task of determining if his duty to his family or legacy would be broken by expressing a firmer interest in Miss Bennet.

"It appears to me that your thoughts have stayed with the lovely Miss Bennet since our parting," observed Fitzwilliam as soon as they were ensconced in his study upon Georgiana's retiring that evening.

Darcy directed a piercing glance at his cousin. It appeared his attempts to hide his distraction had not been nearly as efficacious as he had thought. Furthermore, the fact that Fitzwilliam had not seen fit to tease him about it—and the fact he was not teasing now—suggested some measure of seriousness in his cousin's manner. Darcy was wary, wondering if his cousin was merely saving his wit for some moment in which he could embarrass Darcy and derive the most amusement from it.

"Perhaps my mind has been on other matters," said Darcy.

Fitzwilliam snorted and looked skyward. "I am afraid I understand you far too well to believe your obfuscation, Darcy. There are many little clues which betray you—if you took the time to think on them yourself, I am certain you would recognize them too. What I would like to know is what you think of her."

"She is an amiable, intelligent woman," replied Darcy, his shrug indicating a lack of concern for this subject. It was also completely false.

"That she is. But I am more interested in whether you intend to act on your attraction and pursue her."

"How do you know I am attracted to her?"

"Please, Darcy," growled Fitzwilliam, "do not insult my intelligence. I knew almost as soon as I saw you together that you found her irresistible."

Darcy did not even attempt to deny it, knowing its futility. "Attraction for the girl is one thing. We often feel attraction we do not act upon."

"Forgive me for saying as much, but you are more of a simpleton than I would have ever thought if you allow this woman to slip away."

"Peace, Fitzwilliam," growled Darcy. "I have owned my attraction to her. But there are more facets to marriage than a simple attraction, and I have not known her long, after all."

"Yes, it is prudent to come to know her better. Just make certain you do not allow *other* matters to interfere with your choice."

"As I said, there are many facets. I will consider them all ere I make a choice."

Fitzwilliam drained his glass, and he stood, his gaze falling heavily upon Darcy. "You are careful, Cousin, as always, and it does you credit. But I will remind you of one matter before I leave you for the night: remember that there are many of our sphere—including my brother—who have married with nothing in mind but wealth and status. If you recall, James is miserable, and though I cannot speak for each of my acquaintances in turn, my general perception is that most are not happy with their arranged wives, and several keep mistresses, or engage in even greater debauchery to fill the void."

"And you think I would behave as such?" asked Darcy, feeling affronted at what his cousin was suggesting.

"I *know* you would not, which would make it much more difficult for you to bear. I only counsel you to marry the girl if you possess any affection for her, and live happily with her. Why does it matter if she does not possess connections or fortune? The last I heard, you were flush with both of these things. A wife with a compatible temperament, a passionate nature, intelligence and wit—she must be prized above the value of rubies. Make your choice based on these things, not that which society deems most important."

"It is yet early for such talk. I must know her better."

"Then make certain you move quickly. Such a woman as Miss Bennet cannot remain in obscurity for long. She will attract suitors to her like flies to honey. Do not wait so long that you lose her to someone else."

Fitzwilliam turned and strode from the room, whistling a jaunty tune as he went, leaving Darcy to his brooding thoughts.

CHAPTER XI

❧⟨♥⟩❧

For the next several days, Darcy thought about his cousin's words, and his thoughts were colored by his own impressions of Miss Bennet.

Fitzwilliam had always been more impulsive than Darcy. He had always charged headlong into everything, be it pranks, racing on his horses, or often fisticuffs with the steward's son, not that Wickham had not deserved the thrashings he had received.

Darcy, by contrast, had always been of a more sober, thoughtful nature, always thinking carefully about any decision before committing himself, always weighing every angle in search of the best understanding of the problem. Fitzwilliam had, at times, decried him as over-cautious when a problem presented itself, and Darcy had, more than once, acceded to the justice of his opinion. But he could be no other way, as such caution had been ingrained in him by his father as a child.

It was nothing more than expected that Fitzwilliam should urge Darcy to proceed with all haste when the subject was matrimony. But should he not take care when considering a matter as important as the identity of his future wife? It was perhaps the single most significant choice he would make in his entire life. Such consequence necessitated a careful examination of the woman, his own desires, and whether they were in any way compatible. Surely Miss Bennet, if she was at all attracted to him, was considering the same factors as he was himself.

"You said *what* to Miss Bennet?" asked Darcy, startled to hear such things from his self-effacing sister. It was the morning after Miss Bennet and Miss Drummond had visited, and they were sitting down to breakfast, and Darcy was not certain he had heard his sister correctly.

"I teased her about being my future sister," said Georgiana with blithe unconcern.

"Why would you do such a thing?" demanded Darcy. On the other side of the table, Fitzwilliam was chortling at the scene, and though Darcy glared at him, it had little effect. "That is not proper, Georgiana."

"As I told her at the time," said Mrs. Annesley, her countenance set with displeasure.

"I do not think you need to concern yourself with propriety, Mrs. Annesley," said Fitzwilliam. "Miss Bennet strikes me as the kind of woman who would be diverted by such silliness."

"Perhaps she would. But there are many reasons why such statements should not be made."

"I agree," said Darcy, feeling more than a little cross with his sister.

Georgiana, however, only rolled her eyes. "I know Lizzy well enough to know that she was not offended. She *was* surprised, but she recovered quickly."

"Still, that is not the kind of statement you should make."

"I will guard my tongue, Brother. You may be assured of it."

Her manner was anything but contrite, but Darcy decided against reprimanding her any further. It truly had been a minor misstep, after all, one between young ladies who were, by all accounts, becoming fast friends. Georgiana's behavior had never been a problem before, so there was little reason to make an issue of it now.

"But now that you mention it," said Georgiana, a mischievous glint in her eye, "I believe I would like to have Lizzy as a sister very well, indeed. When were you planning on paying court to her?"

By this time Fitzwilliam was almost falling off his seat, he was laughing so hard. Mrs. Annesley still watched her charge with disapproval, though Darcy could easily sense a hint of amusement in her manner as well. For his part, Darcy was wondering what had happened to his sister.

"Are you truly Georgiana?" asked he, though not without a teasing hint in his tone. "My shy little sister, who would barely speak to me only a few months ago?"

Georgiana shrugged. "I have fallen in with young ladies who are much more confident. I would think you would be happy that they have imparted to me a little of their assurance."

"The confidence I can accept. It is the impertinence that has me struggling."

"I believe Miss Bennet is to blame for that," interjected Fitzwilliam. "Miss Drummond can hardly be called impertinent."

"Neither is Lizzy," said Georgiana, frowning at them both. "She is merely lively, and I will not have you censuring her."

"We do not," Darcy was quick to say. "I have nothing but praise for the way she comports herself. But you must own that you have made a startling change. You must allow your cousin and me a little time to accustom ourselves to it."

"You have not answered my question, Brother."

"No, I have not," replied Darcy. This time his pointed look caused her to subside, though not with much grace. She was chastened, but Darcy could easily tell that she was not about to allow him to remain silent.

"I *do* find that Miss Bennet interests me, Georgiana," said Darcy at length, surrendering as much as he was willing. "But I have not decided what to do about it yet. She is everything that is good and amiable, but I do not know if we would suit or if she is equipped to be the mistress of Pemberley."

Georgiana looked skyward. "Of course, she is capable, Brother. She is intelligent. She is capable of anything she chooses to do, I am absolutely certain."

"Mrs. Reynolds will help her," said Fitzwilliam. "In your excellent housekeeper, you have the perfect situation for a young woman who has been raised in a smaller household. I am certain she will have no difficulty in training Miss Bennet."

"I believe that is quite enough, from both of you," said Darcy, bestowing his disapproval on each of them in turn. "I think very highly of Miss Bennet, but I have not known her long enough to come to any conclusions. I will not have either of you embarrass her with such talk."

"I believe we are well able to hold our tongues when in company," said Fitzwilliam, though his amusement never lessened.

"Be that as it may, I do not wish to hear of it again. Whatever happens between Miss Bennet and myself will happen at a pace comfortable to us both. There is nothing more you need to know."

Having said as much, Darcy turned back to his breakfast, intent upon ignoring his overbearing relations. He did not miss the glance of amusement which passed between them, but since no more was said, he decided to be content with that."

At Kingsdown, Elizabeth was experiencing the same frustration as Mr. Darcy, but in her case it was at the instigation of her cousin. With four sisters, it could hardly be assumed that she had no experience with the teasing of others. As none of her sisters was nearby to provide the service, it appeared Olivia took it upon herself to do it in their stead.

"You seem to be a little distracted today, Lizzy," said she the next day while they were working in the gardens. "I have not known you to be this quiet since you arrived in Derbyshire."

Elizabeth grasped at a small weed and pulled it free, tossing it to the side where the weeds they had pulled were accumulating. "This work tends to allow for introspection. Jane and I would often work in the gardens of Longbourn for some time without exchanging any words at all."

A giggle was Olivia's response. "I might almost believe you, had you not been quiet since our return from Pemberley yesterday. It is not surprising since a handsome gentleman may take many a maiden's breath away."

"Colonel Fitzwilliam and Mr. Darcy *are* handsome, indeed," said Elizabeth, hoping that her cheeks were not coloring. "But it does not necessarily follow that my thoughts were focused on them."

"If they are not, I must think you a simpleton."

"To what do these comments tend?" asked Elizabeth, beginning to feel a little cross.

"Only that you seem to like Mr. Darcy very well, indeed," replied Olivia. Her casual response and hidden grin suggested that she had not heard the warning note in Elizabeth's tone. "And why should you not? He is eligible, handsome, tall, and ever so attentive."

"And he is of a level of society much higher than the one I can boast," said Elizabeth.

Olivia finally seemed to sense that Elizabeth was a little annoyed at the teasing, for she looked at Elizabeth, a question written upon her brow. Elizabeth felt her irritation drain away; even she and Jane had sometimes exchanged such teases. There was no reason to now feel defensive because Olivia had taken up Jane's standard.

"I do like Mr. Darcy," said Elizabeth with a sigh. "But I am also realistic. Men of his level of society and wealth do not focus their attentions on penniless country misses."

"I am certain Mr. Darcy thinks of more than just those things." Olivia's tone was reproving.

"Perhaps he does," replied Elizabeth. "But it would not do to hope for such attentions, knowing that the likelihood of them ever being offered is so low. I do not wish to make myself unhappy."

These words seemed to sober Olivia. "I understand." The girl sighed. "But would it not be wonderful if he did offer them?"

"I believe it would, as long as the man is not odious or of suspect hygiene." Elizabeth giggled. "I have been wooed by such a gentleman, and it is in no way agreeable, I assure you."

"You have been courted?" asked Olivia, wide-eyed.

"If you can call it that," replied Elizabeth, shaking her head at the memory. "I believe I mentioned that my father's cousin visited Longbourn last autumn?" At Olivia's nodded head, Elizabeth continued: "He came with the intention of extending my family an 'olive branch' to heal the breach between our respective families. My father and his, you see, had argued many years ago and become estranged because of it."

"He was not agreeable?"

Elizabeth shook her head, laughing. "He is tall, but portly, his shoulders hunched due to an overly submissive nature, his hair is lanky and thinning at the top of his head, and he is perhaps the most obsequious man I have ever met. Furthermore, I believe he subscribes to a faction of the church which believes bathing to be immoral, for I could not walk downwind from him without gagging."

By the time she finished her description, Olivia was laughing with abandon. "Did you not say that your younger sister married this man?"

"Aye, she did. Mr. Collins was devastated by my refusal and waited all of a day to offer his hand to Mary, and her acceptance was given with equal swiftness. I dare say they are well suited for each other. Mr. Collins's peculiar mixture of sycophancy and arrogance are easily a match for my sister's moralistic tendencies and haughty disapproval of anything that brings one joy in life. I have no doubt that they read Fordyce's sermons together every night before they retire, and they spend several hours each day convincing themselves that the attention of a notorious busybody, whose feet my cousin kisses at every opportunity, is a blessing, rather than a curse."

"No, Lizzy!" exclaimed Olivia, gasping with laughter. "Surely you are exaggerating."

"Perhaps," replied Elizabeth, with only a hint of a smile. "But it is not far from the truth. They may be rather well suited, but for my part, I would prefer to be courted by a man who has spent more than a single day admiring me, and whose devotion is more than the work of a moment."

Olivia shook her head, her manner once again serious. "Then I hope you find it. Mr. Darcy is not the kind of man to bestow his attentions on a lady frivolously, I dare say."

"No, but thus far no such attentions have been offered, Olivia."

A snort nearby startled the girls, and they looked up to see Mrs. Drummond looking down on them, contempt in her air. She said nothing beyond that look and turned away, but Elizabeth could not help but be mortified that she had overheard them speaking.

"Do not listen to my mother," said Olivia, as she watched her mother's retreat. "I have teased you this morning, but I truly believe I have seen some measure of admiration in Mr. Darcy's manner toward you. I know not if he will act upon it, but I do not think he is indifferent."

"I am also not indifferent to him," replied Elizabeth, speaking more to herself than her cousin. "But as I have stated, I have no desire to make myself unhappy over him. If he does pay his compliments to me, I shall receive them in the spirit in which they are intended. I have nothing else to say and no expectations beyond friendship."

"I understand, Lizzy. But as you have told me, anything is possible. I will pray for this for you, for I believe he is the kind of man who can make you happy."

"And I shall pray for it for you, dearest," replied Elizabeth. "I would see you as happy."

They returned to their tasks in silence, and Elizabeth's mind was a riot of conflicting emotions. She had spoken the truth—she was not indifferent to Mr. Darcy. At times, he gave the impression of being far too sober and severe, but Elizabeth understood he was a very good man and master, a man who would answer all her desires of intelligence, companionship, and love, should he only love her in return. But something Olivia had said also rang true: she was certain that Mr. Darcy *was* the kind of man who could make her happy. One did not meet such men every day.

Later that same week brought another sojourn to Lambton. The bulk of the dresses they had ordered for Olivia were due to be completed, and she was to return for a final fitting. At the same time, they had decided to accept Lady Emily's invitation to call on her. Thus, after a conversation with Mr. Drummond, wherein they confirmed the availability of the carriage and the driver, they set out.

The business at the dressmaker was completed quickly. As Elizabeth had noted previously, Mrs. Richards was competent at her craft, and there was relatively little to be done to the dresses she had completed. Elizabeth wondered what Miss Bingley would say if she saw them purchasing dresses from a dressmaker in a country town. No doubt she would sneer and exclaim as to their country manners, insinuate that such dresses were more than good enough for those of such a low status. But then what a shock she would receive to learn that Georgiana Darcy was also a patron of Mrs. Richards's! Elizabeth almost hoped to be able to see her face should such intelligence be revealed. Surely the woman would expire from horror!

When they had completed their tasks at the dressmaker, they stepped out into the streets of Lambton once again, intending to be on their way to visit Lady Emily. It was a glorious spring day, the sun shining brightly, lending its warmth to the land below. The streets of Lambton were alive with activity, townsfolk hurrying this way and that, some going about their daily tasks, while others appeared to be engaged in nothing more urgent than a leisurely stroll. Interspersed with the townsfolk a few top hats and bonnets of gentlemen and their ladies could be seen. A tall man detached himself from the press and approached them, doffing his hat and bowing to them. It was Mr. Darcy.

"Good morning Miss Bennet, Miss Drummond," said he. "I see you are once again taking advantage of the amenities this fair town offers."

Olivia stifled a giggle and shot Elizabeth a meaningful look, but Elizabeth ignored her, concentrating on this man before them. "We were actually at the dressmaker's for Olivia's final fitting for her new gowns. A lady must have new clothes if she is to join society."

"And often when she is *not* joining society," replied Mr. Darcy, "as my sister often informs me. But Mrs. Richards seems to be more than competent at her work. I hope you enjoy your new finery, Miss Drummond."

Elizabeth could not help but smile at Mr. Darcy's endorsement, especially in light of her speculations concerning one Caroline Bingley. If the Bingleys were to come to Derbyshire, she would have to find some way to make Georgiana's patronage known to the insufferable woman.

"Thank you, sir," replied Olivia. "Elizabeth also purchased a new dress, you know. Perhaps she will wear it to the next assembly."

It was clear that Mr. Darcy did not quite know how to take Olivia's statement. A feeling of mortification stole over Elizabeth at such brazen coquetry, and she hurried to say:

"How is your sister this morning?"

"Georgiana is well," replied Mr. Darcy, seeming grateful for the change of subject. "When I left Pemberley this morning, she was engaged at the pianoforte with Mrs. Annesley."

"It seems to me your sister is almost always to be found at the pianoforte," said Elizabeth. "Have you had much luck in guiding her to other studies, or does she defy you at every turn?"

Mr. Darcy laughed. "Indeed, at times it is difficult. Georgiana loves her music and takes every opportunity to indulge in it. Fortunately, Mrs. Annesley, though not a strict taskmistress, will not allow Georgiana to spend *all* her time in such pursuits and insists on other studies as well."

"Well, it is to her credit that she is so diligent. Would that I could be half so industrious. There are far too many activities I enjoy to spend as much time practicing as I obviously should."

They spent some few moments talking on the street before Mr. Darcy excused himself, citing the business for which he had come to Lambton. Elizabeth and Olivia curtseyed and said their farewells, after which they returned to the Drummond carriage for the short drive to Lady Emily's estate.

"Surely you did not miss the way Mr. Darcy was paying attention to you," said Olivia when they had set out. "I might as well have been invisible, for all the attention he paid me."

"Perhaps he might have paid more attention to you if not for your comment," said Elizabeth, turning a pointed look at her cousin.

Olivia had the grace to appear ashamed. "I should not have said that, should I?"

"No, you should not." Elizabeth sighed and turned a wan smile on her cousin. "Olivia, you must understand that there is a time for teasing and a time to be silent. With such comments, Mr. Darcy might think that I am trying to throw myself at him."

"Surely not!"

"I do not believe he did," soothed Elizabeth, "but fortune hunters are rife in our society, and I am certain Mr. Darcy has had to endure them as long as he has been master of his estate. I would not wish him to think that of me."

"I am sorry, Elizabeth," said a truly contrite Olivia. "I had not thought of it in such a way."

"I know you did not," replied Elizabeth, grasping her cousin's hand and squeezing it, showing her forgiveness. "I know you esteem me highly and believe that Mr. Darcy would benefit from having me as a wife, and I thank you for your regard. But you must understand the way society works. I am naught but a country gentleman's daughter, and I have very little in the way of dowry. I *am* hopeful that I will find a man who will look past such disadvantages and offer for me, but I must also be wary of setting my sights too high. Mr. Darcy possesses high connections and a handsome estate—he can aspire to much more than I can offer in a wife."

"If *you* will have difficulty marrying, then what hope do *I* have?" asked Olivia, a hint of petulance in her voice.

"You always have hope, my dear cousin. There are many good men in the world. I am trying to teach you how to behave in society and to value yourself appropriately. Your chances of marrying well are as good as mine, I dare say, but I cannot promise you the hand of a duke. Instead, I would have you search for a good man, one who complements you, who will love you for who you are, rather than what you can bring to him. It matters not whether he is a parson or a gentleman. All that matters is that you are happy.

"And let me reiterate now that should Mr. Darcy turn his attentions to me, I will accept them with pleasure and gratitude, but I will not marry him unless I am convinced I am in love with him and he with me. I would rather remain unmarried than bind myself to a man with whom I will be miserable. And I most assuredly will not give him the impression that I am attempting to provoke his interest through underhanded means."

Olivia colored at the pointed comment Elizabeth made. "No more comments such as the one I made this morning, then."

"I would appreciate it." Elizabeth smiled. "Let us see what happens, Olivia. If Mr. Darcy *does* admire me, let us allow him to show it in his own way, for he has the power of first choice in courtship. If he does not choose to pursue me, then it is better that way, for I would not wish to force his hand and end with a husband who cannot respect me."

"Of course, Lizzy. I will temper my comments."

Elizabeth smiled and looked out the window. There was no harm in her cousin, but she was still young and inexperienced and prone to saying what was on her mind without considering it first. Elizabeth had not been forced to be severe with her, and yet she had learned a valuable lesson. Clearly Olivia was easier to teach than Lydia, who could never be bothered to listen to anything her elder sisters said.

For some time, the carriage drove along a country road, a pretty sight with vibrant woods closing in on either side, and a hint of the peaks in the distance through intermittent breaks in the forest. The countryside was quiet, with calls of birds competing with the noise of the wheels of the carriage in which they rode. It was a tranquil scene, beauty and serenity abounding, as Elizabeth had come to expect from the county she had come to visit. Elizabeth could not be any more content.

The thought provoked a hint of contemplation in Elizabeth's mind, and she wondered at the changes Derbyshire had wrought upon her. When she had left Hertfordshire, she had been depressed and almost fearful for the course her life would take. Derbyshire had proven to be the balm her troubled soul had needed, though that was as likely as much because of the new surroundings, distance from the familiar scenes of her youth, and lack of any possible improvement, not to mention, from the indifference of her sister. There had been trials here, and she knew there would be trials in the future, but Elizabeth felt more able to bear them, more disposed to her usual happy disposition, rather than the sullen creature she had turned into those last months in her father's home.

So intent was Elizabeth on her own musings that her cousin had to pull her from them as they approached the earl's residence.

"There it is," said Olivia. "It is not quite so . . . impressive as I might have thought."

Elizabeth looked out the window to see the house in the distance. Teasdale Manor, the unimaginatively named estate which comprised the primary residence of the Earl of Chesterfield, was an old building, its weathered stones standing defiantly against the weight of years which seemed to settle over it like a blanket. It was in some ways more of a castle than a manor house, as two towers rose at each of the front corners, looming over the rest of the house, making it seem insignificant by comparison. But a closer look at the building revealed the towers to be no more than affectations, as there were no battlements, and wide windows broke the façade at all locations, destroying any defensive value the wall might have provided in more dangerous times.

"It is certainly an interesting sort of house," replied Elizabeth. "Were you referring to something specific?"

"It is not as fine as Pemberley; do you not think?"

Elizabeth could do naught but agree—Pemberley was larger and more imposing, not to mention grander than Teasdale Manor, and more like a manor Elizabeth might expect from a great estate.

"It certainly appears to have some quirks," replied Elizabeth. "But I do not doubt it is spacious and fine on the inside."

"Should an earl's house not be finer?" asked Olivia. "I would have thought we would see a house much larger and grander than Pemberley."

"The possession of a title does not necessarily make a man wealthy, Olivia. I understand that the Darcys are an old family, and given what I have seen of Pemberley, they are quite wealthy. I know nothing of Lady Emily's family, but this house does not necessarily mean they are lacking in wealth."

Olivia did not say anything, but the way she watched the approaching house suggested she was thoughtful. The carriage soon drew to a stop in front of the house, and when they had alighted, a man of middle years approached and requested their names.

"Miss Elizabeth Bennet and Miss Olivia Drummond, to call on Lady Emily."

"Ah, yes," said the man, gesturing toward the open door with a bow. "The mistress informed me you would be calling on her. If you would step into the house?"

The inside of Teasdale Manor was, as Elizabeth had suspected, elegant and pleasing. The wide entry hall into which they were led boasted a large staircase which led to the second floor, and was sheathed in expensive tile that fairly gleamed with the polishing it received. But it was also a little quirky, as the outside of the house suggested, as though there were several exits to various parts of the house. She also noticed a door which seemed to go nowhere and a small cubbyhole behind the stairway that appeared dark and dim, not a common sight in a large house.

The butler—for that was who Elizabeth assumed had greeted them—turned them over to a matronly housekeeper, who conveyed them through the house to the sitting-room. Seeing them, Lady Emily rose and extended her greetings.

"Welcome to Teasdale Manor, Miss Bennet, Miss Drummond. I am glad you accepted my invitation to call."

She invited them to sit and called for some refreshments. Within moments the three ladies were chatting with the aid of tea and cakes to loosen their tongues. Most of the conversation was carried by

Elizabeth and Lady Emily, with Olivia adding a few comments from time to time. For the most part, she seemed to be awed at being in the house of a peer, and it induced her to more stillness than was her wont. Elizabeth, noticing this, ensured she carried the burden of the visitors' conversation, knowing that Olivia would eventually become more accustomed to her surroundings.

"I remember you telling me that you are from Hertfordshire, Miss Bennet," said Lady Emily after they had spoken for some moments.

"Yes," replied Elizabeth. "My father owns an estate not far from London."

"Hertfordshire is a handsome county," said Lady Emily. "I have a close friend who lives in the county, though toward the northern border with Cambridgeshire."

"My family's estate is not far from the village of Luton," said Elizabeth.

"Ah, I am familiar with Luton, having passed through many times. I believe you mentioned that you have siblings?"

"Yes, four sisters. My elder sister has recently married Mr. Darcy's close friend, Mr. Bingley."

"Mr. Bingley? I do not believe I have heard that name in society."

"His family is not at all prominent," replied Elizabeth, not really wishing to discuss the man's connections. "My understanding is that he and Mr. Darcy have been friends since their days in university."

"Ah, a longstanding friendship, then," said Lady Emily. She then changed the subject. "Does your father not lament the lack of a son? Is your elder sister his heir?"

"Actually, my father's heir is a distant cousin," said Elizabeth, the direction the conversation was taking becoming less comfortable the more they spoke. "His cousin has since married my younger sister, Mary, some weeks before my elder sister was wed."

The look Lady Emily turned on Elizabeth was unreadable. "That is odd, is it not? That your younger sister should be married before you and your elder sister?"

"Perhaps, when you say it in such a manner," conceded Elizabeth.

"Did your cousin not direct his attentions to you or your sister first?"

"My eldest sister was already being courted by Mr. Bingley," said Elizabeth.

She paused for a moment, wishing to speak carefully without revealing embarrassing family secrets. At least Olivia was silent by her side, seeming to understand that Elizabeth would not welcome her assistance.

"In fact," continued Elizabeth, "my cousin was inclined to direct his attentions to me initially. But I believe we both recognized that we were not well suited, and as he was suited to my younger sister, his attentions were thus redirected."

The look Lady Emily bestowed on Elizabeth was unreadable, and Elizabeth was not certain if the lady was at all taken in by her obfuscation. When she spoke, her words were no more illuminating.

"It is fortunate, indeed, that you possessed the insight to understand this, though some would suggest you are foolish for refusing what I assume would be an eligible match."

Having no notion of whether Lady Emily agreed with her stated opinion, Elizabeth nodded. "If the only goal in mind is to be married without regard for how it might be accomplished or whom one married, then I dare say you are correct—some might consider me foolish. But I wish for something more in marriage. A marriage to my father's cousin would have provided future security, but none of the companionship or even affection that I crave. To accept would have been a punishment."

Lady Emily regarded her for several moments, digesting what Elizabeth said. "Then you are to be commended. I think there are many in society whose opinions are quite the opposite of yours."

Elizabeth inclined her head and the subject was dropped. In all, it was an agreeable visit, and Elizabeth was satisfied with it. Lady Emily was, at the very least, pleasant and amiable, and though Elizabeth could not quite make her out at times, she thought there was little true harm in her.

CHAPTER XII

When Darcy found himself once more mounted on his favorite steed and on his way to Kingsdown, he found his thoughts to be quite different from the last time he had visited. Mr. Drummond was a good man, and Darcy quite esteemed him—it did not matter to Darcy that the man was naught but a farmer, for all he claimed the title of a gentleman. But the last time he had come this way, his thoughts had been colored by a hint of impatience. The fence between their two properties was an important matter to consider, but their border was not extensive and it had been little more than an annoyance.

This time, however, Darcy's thoughts dwelt on the young woman who had come to stay to Kingsdown whom Darcy had seen for the first time on that previous visit. Miss Elizabeth Bennet was unlike any other woman he had ever known, and as he was often the target of fortune hunters high and low, she was like a hint of a breeze to a miner trapped beneath the earth. His cousin and sister's words had not informed Darcy of anything he had not already known; the woman would make a good mistress—that much was not in question. The question was how they would suit. He did not know at that moment, but he was coming to the conclusion that he wished to find out.

The neat driveway before the house at Kingsdown was as well-maintained as ever, a flat loop of gravel, regularly smoothed with nary a rock out of place. The front of the house was festooned with ivy growing here and there, clean and properly washed, and if Darcy did not know that the estate was small, he might have thought Drummond had an annual income of four or five thousand. He was a good man, one who did not attempt to use the accident of being Darcy's nearest neighbor to his advantage, and one who, by all accounts, dealt fairly with all and was industrious in the care of his lands.

One of the young maids who served as the housekeeper came out to greet Darcy, informing him that the master would join him in a moment. As such, Darcy remained mounted, looking out over the estate with interest and a bit of hope. But it was to be dashed — of Miss Bennet there was no sign.

"Darcy!" Drummond rode out from the stables at the side of the house on a dappled grey horse, his smile infectious and welcoming. "Welcome, young man."

"Mr. Drummond," replied Darcy, extending his hand.

Their hands met and they shook from horseback. Soon Drummond was leading him away toward his northern boundary and the fence which waited them. Hopefully they would come to an agreement that day and allow the matter to be put to rest.

The two horses thundered across the lands of Kingsdown, like a pair of centaurs of antiquity, Darcy's stallion a little larger than Drummond's gelding, the sounds of the hooves hitting the turf echoing back to them from the trees and rocks strewn along the way. As always, when Darcy visited Drummond's lands, he was impressed by the care which the man obviously took to ensure his enterprise was well-maintained and used appropriately. The fence in question abutted a plot one of Mr. Drummond's tenants farmed for him, and they waved to the man when they passed, as the tenant was inspecting one of his fields, which had started to sprout.

As Darcy had hoped, the discussion around the fence was completed swiftly, and the costs, split up fairly. Soon they were at leisure to return to the estate. But where the journey to the fence had been direct, with no hesitation, they were easier about their return, walking rather than cantering, and it was then that the conversation turned more interesting. It was fortunate that Drummond brought up the subject of which Darcy was most interested, as he could not conceive of a way of bringing it up without causing himself untold embarrassment.

"I wish to thank you for your kindness to my daughter and my niece," said the man. "I know they have both been happy to gain the friendship of your sister."

"The pleasure is all ours," replied Darcy with all honesty. "Miss Drummond and Miss Bennet have been beneficial for my sister, as she has managed to shed some of her shyness in their company."

Mr. Drummond chuckled. "That does sound like Lizzy. My own daughter was in a similar state until Lizzy came to stay with us. She appears to possess the ability to instill timid women with courage."

"I cannot disagree," said Darcy, thinking about the recent changes in Georgiana. "Your relations are from Hertfordshire, I understand?"

"They are actually my wife's family," replied Drummond. "Claire's brother is Elizabeth's father. His estate is not far from London, and though it is nothing to Pemberley, it is one of the largest in the neighborhood."

"And has he any other family?"

"A cousin, from what I understand, who will inherit the property through the means of an entail."

Drummond went on to explain the situation of the family, including Miss Bennet's elder sister's marriage—of which Darcy was already aware—the younger sister's marriage to the heir of the estate, and the existence of two more younger sisters. He also said something of Mrs. Bennet's relations, the solicitor in the same neighborhood and the uncle in trade in town. Darcy felt the weight of the man's scrutiny as he spoke of the tradesman, but as one of Darcy's closest friends was himself only a generation removed from trade, the idea was not at all distasteful.

"Mrs. Bennet can be a little . . . silly at times," confessed Drummond. "And her sister is not much better, for all that I have seen them but rarely."

"Many society wives are," replied Darcy. "Vapidity and meanness of understanding are not singular traits."

"I would agree," replied Drummond. "But Mr. Gardiner is nothing like his sisters. A man of greater understanding of business would be difficult to find. He has built his business up from a small inheritance left to him by his father and has grown it into a profitable venture, indeed. My brother Bennet and I myself also have some little money invested with him. I have given him the authority to keep reinvesting it in my stead. I am hopeful that I will be able to provide some means to my younger children by way of his investments."

Darcy paused for a moment to digest that. Drummond was a man of prudence, but Darcy had not thought that he had any funds other than that which was required for the operation of his estate. It spoke well to the man, though Darcy did not think it likely that the money would ever amount to much.

"How long is Miss Bennet to stay with you?" asked Darcy at length.

"We have not determined an exact time for her return to Hertfordshire," replied Drummond. "I hope to have her here for some months. I requested her presence, hoping she would be able to provide some guidance for my Olivia. Thus far my expectations have been more than met. The difficulty is that she is her father's favorite, and he will likely wish for her return long before I am ready to surrender her company."

"I can see that," replied Darcy quietly. "I am not sure if Miss Bennet has mentioned it, but my friend Bingley, who is married to her sister, will likely be visiting Pemberley this summer." At Drummond's nod, Darcy continued: "Is the elder sister as lively as Miss Bennet?"

"Though I have not met her since she was a child, I remember that their characters are quite different. Jane is serene, calm, quite beautiful, and she has always tried to see the best in others. She has none of Lizzy's fire or vivacity."

Drummond paused for a moment, and then he spoke, albeit slowly. "Perhaps I am speaking out of turn, for I have no true knowledge of the situation, but you should likely know if you are to host Mrs. Bingley. I have heard something of trouble between the sisters, though they were the closest of friends before Jane's marriage."

"Trouble?" asked Darcy.

"Again, I do not know the particulars, but it seems Jane has altered since her marriage. By all accounts, she no longer sees Lizzy as her closest friend. Perhaps it is more correct to say that she no longer wishes for the closeness which existed between them before."

"It would not be the first time marriage has changed a woman, particularly when she married so advantageously."

"You would be correct. But Jane was always of the sweetest disposition. I am not aware of any specific occasions of tension between them, but I am almost positive that part of the impetus for Lizzy's acceptance of my invitation was due to problems between the sisters. It may be nothing, but if she is to be close by, you should be aware of it."

"Thank you, Drummond."

Nothing further was said, and Darcy was lost in his thoughts as they rode back toward the house. Though he was aware it was irrational, he found that he almost disapproved of Mrs. Bingley for nothing more than Drummond's brief speculations. As he had noted, a woman becoming unreasonably haughty after her marriage was not unusual, though Drummond's characterization of the woman made Darcy think it unlikely that a woman of her character would submit to such feelings. And for a moment, he was angry at her for causing her sister such pain—how a beloved sister could treat a woman of Miss Bennet's caliber so was beyond his understanding.

But to dislike a woman for nothing more than hearsay and rumor was not logical either, and Darcy firmly decided to defer making an opinion on her until he was introduced to her. It may be that it was nothing more than a misunderstanding. Surely Bingley would not marry a mean-spirited and proud woman—though his friend had often fallen in love in the past, Darcy was certain he possessed more discernment than that.

While he was immersed in these thoughts, the house came into view and soon they had reached it. There was no one in evidence in the immediate vicinity, and though Darcy strained to catch a glimpse of Miss Bennet, she did not appear. He hid his disappointment and turned to his companion to wish him a good day.

"Thank you for dealing fairly with me, Darcy," said Mr. Drummond, extending his hand. "I am glad we were able to work the matter out to our mutual benefit."

"Of course, Drummond. I appreciate your own actions in the matter."

"Shall you not stay for dinner tonight? We would be pleased to have you."

Though Darcy was tempted, he did not wish to impose on such short notice. Of more importance, he did not wish to appear eager to once again be in Miss Bennet's company.

"I am expected back at Pemberley tonight, so I shall have to decline. But I thank you for the offer."

"Very well. Perhaps some other night? We would be happy if your cousin and sister could also attend."

"Thank you, Mr. Drummond. We shall be pleased to accept."

They spoke a few more moments, confirming the date and then Darcy departed. Though he had not met Miss Bennet that day, he was pleased with the outcome. He would see her at dinner, and it was likely they would cross paths during the coming week.

Though Darcy thought the ladies were not present, he was, in fact, incorrect, as the ladies — or lady — in question were watching him and Mr. Drummond from the window of the lady's bedroom. And though he could not know the content of their conversation, he would have been highly gratified to know that the she in question was no more unaffected by him as he was by her.

"Mr. Darcy *is* very handsome," said Olivia with a sigh as she watched as he spoke with her father for a few moments. "I can see why you like him so."

"I cannot think *any* young woman would not be affected by such an eligible man," replied Elizabeth.

The two girls watched as the two men shook hands and Mr. Darcy turned his horse and began to ride away. His bearing was erect, and his hands on the reins, casual, as if he was well accustomed to his current position atop the great beast. He truly was a fine figure of a man.

"Be serious, Lizzy," said Olivia as she turned away from the window. "I am not attempting to tease you, and I would not wish you to own to anything you do not feel. But I have watched you together with Mr. Darcy, and I am certain you like him very well, indeed. Can you claim otherwise?"

Sighing, Elizabeth turned away from the window, where Mr. Darcy was naught but a speck in the distance. "I do not deny it, Olivia. As I said, I cannot imagine there is any young lady who cannot admire him. But that does not mean that I will do something so gauche as to throw myself at him or attempt to capture him. No matter how much I esteem a man, I will not remove his freedom of choice. I am not Miss Bingley."

"Miss Bingley?" asked Olivia, confused. "Your new brother's sister?"

Elizabeth could not stifle her giggle. She had not intended to make the comment, but as it had slipped out, she supposed there was no harm in telling Olivia about her new sister-in-law.

"Indeed," said Elizabeth. "She is one of the most disagreeable young ladies I have ever had the misfortune to meet. She is haughty and proud; she disdained Hertfordshire society and was particularly opposed to my sister's marriage to her brother."

"How do you know this?"

"Come now, Olivia," said Elizabeth, rolling her eyes. "I am perfectly capable of observing a person's reactions, and Miss Bingley is far easier to understand than most."

"But her background," sputtered Olivia. "Her father's fortune was made in trade, was it not?"

"It was," said Elizabeth, "not that I hold *that* against her—my mother's brother is a tradesman, as I am certain you know. She *is* an oddity. In company, she behaves as if she is Queen Charlotte herself. Though she was initially looked on with awe when she and her brother came to the neighborhood, most soon learned to recognize her disgust, and she quickly gained the reputation of being disagreeable, not that she would care."

"Your poor sister," said Olivia with feeling. "I should not like to be burdened with so disagreeable a sister."

"I cannot but agree," replied Elizabeth.

Olivia turned a severe frown on Elizabeth. "You changed the subject, Lizzy."

"I believe it was *you* who changed the subject, Olivia," replied Elizabeth. "You asked me about Miss Bingley."

"But you commented on her, expecting that I would ask."

"Perhaps I did."

"So, what *do* you think of Mr. Darcy?"

Sighing, Elizabeth shook her head at her cousin's single-mindedness. "I esteem him very much. He is a good man and quite handsome. If he should deign to pay his addresses to me, I would be happy to accept them, hoping to understand him better and determine if my feelings could be engaged. But at present, that is *all* I think of Mr. Darcy. Will that do?"

The hint of warning in Elizabeth's tone suggested that Olivia had best drop the subject, and to the girl's credit, she did so, after a fashion.

"I will not push you, Lizzy. I understand your reprimand. But I *will* say that I think his interest in you is greater than you believe at present."

"It may be. Only time will tell."

"Dinner at Kingsdown?"

The snicker which accompanied Fitzwilliam's words was roundly ignored by Darcy. His sister's response took his attention in any case.

"That is good news, indeed, Brother! I am so happy you accepted, for I am eager to see my friends again!"

"By my count you have seen them frequently already," replied Darcy.

"Yes, I have!" exclaimed Georgiana. "But I cannot have enough of their society! Olivia is so quiet and thoughtful, like me in character.

And Elizabeth is funny and happy. I cannot but think that I would learn much by watching her."

"I believe you are correct, Georgiana," interjected Fitzwilliam. "Miss Bennet is as confident a young lady as I have ever seen. She would be an uncommonly good mentor for you."

Georgiana beamed at Fitzwilliam happily, but Darcy noted the sly look Fitzwilliam directed at him, and it was all he could do to refrain from rolling his eyes. Fortunately for Darcy's peace of mind, Fitzwilliam did not seem inclined to continue in that line of conversation, though as he listened to Georgiana's continuing commentary on the virtues of her new friends, his smiles suggested continued amusement.

When Georgiana finally exhausted her store of words, she excused herself for the evening, leaving Darcy in the company of his cousin. Then, of course, Fitzwilliam's wit would not be restrained.

"So, dinner at the Drummond's with the exquisite Miss Bennet in attendance. I suppose that makes up for the fact that you did not catch a glimpse of her today when you attended Mr. Drummond."

"How do you know I did not meet her?" asked Darcy with a frown. He did not think he had mentioned it.

"For the simple reason that you did not speak of her," replied Fitzwilliam, taking a sip from the glass he held in his hand. "You usually have some comment or other to make when you have spoken to her. I have found some of her observations to be rather droll."

Darcy decided any response would open himself up to further teasing, so he remained silent.

"Have you decided on a course of action?" asked Fitzwilliam, all traces of teasing absent from his voice.

"I have not," replied Darcy. "As you have so eloquently pointed out more than once, I find her intriguing and wish to know more of her. I assume our interactions in the coming days and weeks will tell me what I wish to know."

"And Lady Emily?"

Darcy was confused. "What of her?"

"She is eligible, single, beautiful, possesses a fine dowry, and should you marry her, your eldest son would be a future earl."

"I have never paid a hint of attention to her. Why would you think that I have an interest in her, especially considering the teasing you have subjected me to regarding Miss Bennet?"

"No reason. In fact, you have only confirmed my suspicions. Most men would jump at the chance to engage such a woman, especially when she makes her interest so well known."

"You have me completely perplexed, Fitzwilliam. I know not of any interest Lady Emily has expressed in me."

"It is of no matter, Darcy. Miss Elizabeth is a fine choice. I wish you well in your endeavor to catch her eye."

Once again Darcy thought that Fitzwilliam was overstating the matter, but he decided against making any further comment. His cousin was in an odd mood tonight, and Darcy was not certain he would receive a straight answer should he inquire. They spent some little more time in each other's company until Darcy announced his intention to retire. Fitzwilliam bid him good night, but Darcy sensed that he was still distracted. Shaking his head, he left the room to seek his bed.

Fitzwilliam watched his cousin and shook his head as Darcy retreated. Darcy was a good and intelligent man, and Fitzwilliam thought more highly of him than he did of any other man of his acquaintance.

But for all Darcy's erudition, his ability to spot a fortune hunter and turn their efforts aside, Darcy had not a hint of sense when it came to a woman who was *not* a fortune hunter, but every bit as predatory as any mercenary. Lady Emily was determined to have Darcy— Fitzwilliam was absolutely certain of the fact. But she presented an opponent with the likes of whom Darcy had never crossed swords. She was rich and titled and she meant to have him for a husband, whereas most of those Darcy had fended off in the past had been more concerned about his ability to keep them in comfort.

Ah, the work of a cousin is never done, thought Fitzwilliam, indulging in an amused chuckle at Darcy's expense.

In fact, Fitzwilliam was certain Miss Bennet would be perfect for Darcy, and though Lady Emily would also make him an excellent wife, his continuing professed admiration for Miss Bennet took Lady Emily out of the picture. Fitzwilliam's esteem of his cousin would not allow him to sit idly by while Darcy ignored the viper coiled nearby, prepared to strike.

The thought caused a frown to crease Fitzwilliam's brow. It was a disservice to the lady, he thought—she might wish for Darcy to court her, but Fitzwilliam did not think she would stoop to anything underhanded to achieve her aims. Darcy's courtship would be much smoother should Lady Emily's machinations be blunted. And Fitzwilliam was just as determined that she would not interfere.

Satisfied with what he had decided, Fitzwilliam tossed the rest of his drink back and set the glass down on the table. He was certain he would need his wits about him to ensure Lady Emily was well and truly diverted from Darcy and Miss Bennet.

CHAPTER XIII

$\mathcal{I}$t was clear that Mrs. Drummond was far from pleased with her husband's invitation to the Darcy party, but just as evident that she was reluctant to protest openly. The communication was made that evening at dinner, and though her mouth was set in a firm line, her brow furrowed, Mrs. Drummond did not make any comment. Mr. Drummond, who had been watching his wife closely, nodded once in approval and turned back to the conversation.

"They are amiable people," said Olivia, sensing the discord between her parents. She must have seen it so many times — much like Elizabeth had with *her* parents — that it was easily recognizable.

"The closer connection can only do us good," added Edward. He looked down the table at his mother, his gaze almost commiserating. Mrs. Drummond nodded slowly and acceptance seemed to fall over her.

"Will our simple fare suffice for Mr. Darcy and his party?" asked Mrs. Drummond.

"You ascribe far too much pride to the gentleman," said Mr. Drummond. "Darcy *is* a very wealthy man, and he can afford the best money can buy. But I do not believe his tastes are overly extravagant. I am certain they will be quite happy with what we can produce, and

Marie is quite skilled in the kitchen."

Mrs. Drummond nodded slowly. "Then I will plan a menu with Marie's help. We will ensure there is nothing of our hospitality to criticize."

"I am certain all will be well. You will see."

The subject was dropped, and the conversation turned to other matters.

In the intervening days, however, there was not a dearth of society. Elizabeth and Olivia visited Georgiana, and Elizabeth often had the opportunity meet with other friends that she had met in the area. Furthermore, the day after the invitation to the Darcys had been offered and accepted, Elizabeth and Olivia received an invitation of their own.

"Lady Emily is inviting us to her home," said Elizabeth after she had read the note. "It seems she has invited many in the area, and it is to be a large party on the grounds of Teasdale Manor. There is to be a picnic lunch with games, and other amusements."

"When?" asked Olivia. She seemed a little too fretful for such an outing.

"The day after tomorrow," replied Elizabeth. "Do not worry, dear. I am certain it will be a diverting outing."

Permission to attend was sought and given, but an alteration was soon made to their plans. Olivia, Elizabeth discovered, was unaccountably a little intimidated by the thought of so many people in such an informal setting. A quick flurry of letters between Kingsdown and Pemberley soon revealed that Georgiana would not be attending, though both her brother and cousin had accepted the invitation. When it became clear that Olivia was not eager to attend, Georgiana invited her to Pemberley for the time the others would be at Teasdale Manor, and it was quickly—and with some relief—accepted. The Darcys offered to convey Elizabeth and Olivia to Pemberley and from thence it was determined that Elizabeth would continue to the picnic in the company of Mr. Darcy and Colonel Fitzwilliam, with a maid in attendance for propriety's sake.

On the appointed day, Elizabeth found herself in the carriage on the way to Teasdale Manor with the two gentlemen. Olivia had been delivered to Pemberley to both her and Georgiana's excitement, her position in the carriage taken by Mr. Darcy and Colonel Fitzwilliam, as well as the promised maid. The young maid was introduced to Elizabeth, and after they exchanged a few words, the carriage departed and they settled in for the journey. They were a lively party, and their wit and conversation flowed freely.

"You must ready yourself for a treat, Miss Bennet," said Colonel Fitzwilliam. "I doubt you have seen any house the likes of Teasdale Manor."

"It is quite unique, indeed," said Mr. Darcy.

"Unusual architecture can be quite diverting," replied Elizabeth. "But in this case, you shall be disappointed, for I have already visited Teasdale Manor."

"You have?" asked Colonel Fitzwilliam. When Elizabeth confirmed her experience with the place, he stayed silent, apparently contemplating something known only to him. Elizabeth was not certain why a visit to someone in the area would be a subject of such interest, but she put it from her mind in favor of Mr. Darcy's next words.

"I am not certain of the origin of the towers at the front of the house," said he, "as the earl would not be explicit. It is apparently some family secret which they will not share. I *do* have it on good authority that they are locked tight and no one is allowed into them."

"That is strange," replied Elizabeth. "One would think that they would provide a location for storage, if nothing else."

"I made that same observation to his lordship," said Mr. Darcy. "But he refused to be explicit."

"Is this one of the great mysteries of the neighborhood, Mr. Darcy?" asked Elizabeth, archly raising an eyebrow.

"I hardly think most of us are engaged in investigating the mystery, Miss Bennet. But on occasion, it has been a matter of some curiosity."

"I would not mention it, though," replied Colonel Fitzwilliam. "The family does not even like to acknowledge it, let alone answer any questions."

"Then I will keep my curiosity in check."

The carriage rolled along the same avenue that Elizabeth remembered from her previous visit, though today was not the perfect day that one had been. The air held a hint of coolness she had found to be common to the area at this time of year, and though the sun shone, isolated islands of puffy white clouds flew west in the breeze, making the chill feel even more pronounced when they passed overhead and blotted out the sun. Elizabeth observed that the day was, perhaps, a little cool for an outdoor entertainment such as a picnic, to which Mr. Darcy nodded.

"It *is*, but we Derbyshire folk have long learned to be hardy. You have been fortunate this year, Miss Bennet, as we have not had the sudden rainstorms and even late snow which are common."

"In Hertfordshire, we never see snow this late in the season," said Elizabeth, sparing a wistful thought for her home. "The paths near my home are almost certainly clear of any impediments, allowing for the enjoyment of walking, as long as there is no rain."

"You enjoy walking, do you?"

Elizabeth nodded. "It is one of my favorite pastimes. I enjoy the beauty of nature, and one can best see it where there is little sign of man's encroachment to spoil it."

"You should definitely not be introduced to our Aunt Catherine," replied Colonel Fitzwilliam. "She has never met a wilderness she did not wish to tame with a perfectly trimmed lawn or a few gaudy topiaries."

"Fitzwilliam," chastised Mr. Darcy. "Lady Catherine lives in Kent, which is a much more civilized land."

"But you cannot think that she would not remake Pemberley in the image of Rosings, should she ever succeed in hogtying Anne to you."

"That, I cannot deny." He turned back to Elizabeth. "Have you had the opportunity to walk Pemberley's grounds?"

"Not yet, Mr. Darcy," said Elizabeth. The mention of Rosings and Lady Catherine had caused her to start, though she did not think either of her companions had noticed. "I have come to visit Georgiana, and I would not be a poor guest by insisting on walking the grounds during my visit."

"I believe she would be very happy to oblige you," said Mr. Darcy, "though I sense that you would likely walk farther than she would consider comfortable. And she spends so much time at the pianoforte, that I cannot think that the exercise shall be anything other than beneficial."

"Then I shall attempt to entice her out into the gardens. I will own, however, that I would likely prefer to walk further. I am sure there are many paths to choose from."

"There are. The park is ten miles around, so I am certain you would not exhaust new sights quickly."

The mention of the size of his estate impressed Elizabeth. It was obvious that it was a great estate, but to have such a large park was almost unfathomable to a young woman who had been raised on one much smaller.

"I am curious, Miss Bennet," said Mr. Darcy. His manner seemed a little hesitant, almost bashful, which Elizabeth had never seen. "Do you ride at all?"

"I can ride a little," replied Elizabeth. "I am not by any means accomplished, but as long as the horse is gentle, I am able to keep my seat."

"Perhaps you would consent to a little instruction when you come to Pemberley? As I said, the park is large, and there are some delightful scenes at distances which are not conducive to walking. Given your love of nature, Georgiana and I would be pleased to take you to them."

Elizabeth was flattered that he should offer such a boon to her. "If it would not be too much trouble, I would be happy to accept your instruction."

"It is no trouble at all," replied Mr. Darcy quietly.

"Perhaps your cousin could be persuaded too?" asked Colonel Fitzwilliam.

"It is possible. I am not certain if she has any experience, but if she has, I know it is not much."

"Then we shall attend to it when the opportunity presents itself," said Mr. Darcy. "It should not be long before you are competent enough, as long as we are there to escort you."

"And Darcy will not miss an opportunity to display his beautiful estate," inserted Colonel Fitzwilliam.

"It is my family's pride and joy," replied Mr. Darcy, stating a fact rather than boasting. "As a lover of nature yourself, Miss Bennet, I am convinced there are few who would appreciate it as much as you."

Blushing in response to his praise, which Elizabeth sensed was anything but gratuitous, she nodded, indicating her pleasure with such a scheme. There truly was so much of Derbyshire that she had never seen that she could not but be excited at the prospect of seeing more of Mr. Darcy's estate.

Soon, the towers of Teasdale Manor rose into view, and they stopped in front of the house and were welcomed by Lady Emily. The front lawn had been decorated with streamers and ribbons, several large canvas shelters had been erected, and lawn chairs had been brought out to provide a place to rest for those who did not wish to sit on the ground. Inside those tents there were several tables groaning under the weight of a great variety of foods, the variety enough to satisfy any taste. All at once Elizabeth realized that she was positively famished, having eaten only a roll that morning.

"Welcome to Teasdale Manor," said Lady Emily when they had alighted from the carriage.

The gentlemen bowed over the lady's hand while Elizabeth curtseyed and greeted her with pleasure. "Thank you for the invitation, Lady Emily," said Elizabeth. "Everything appears to be remarkably fine."

"Thank you, Miss Bennet," said the lady, though her demeanor betrayed no hint of any emotion. "We usually do this every spring, and I must confess that it is the event I anticipate more than any other."

She turned to the gentlemen. "As you can see, most of the guests have already arrived, and many are already partaking of the food. Please do not stand on ceremony—there will be games and other entertainment after luncheon."

"Thank you, Lady Emily," said Mr. Darcy. Then he turned to Elizabeth and offered his arm. "Shall we?"

Acceding with a shy nod, Elizabeth put her hand in his arm and they proceeded to the nearest table. Elizabeth heard a snort from behind them, but when she glanced back to Colonel Fitzwilliam, he only smiled at her and rolled his eyes. Elizabeth did not quite understand what he found so amusing, but she soon put it out of her mind when they passed some of the ladies she had met during her stay, whom she greeted with her usual friendliness and exchanged some pleasantries. Soon, however, Mr. Darcy drew her away to the tables.

"Shall I fix you a plate, Miss Bennet?"

She seemed pleased by his solicitation, smiling and nodding, and she directed him to some of her favorites, surprising him by choosing some of the plainer fare—a few sandwiches, some fresh fruit, and only one small tart to go with them. When Darcy made this observation to her, Miss Bennet laughed.

"Shall you also be disgusted with the simplicity of my tastes, Mr. Darcy?" At his questioning glance, she continued: "During a dinner at Netherfield, Mr. Hurst found he had nothing to say to me when he discovered that I prefer a plain dish to a ragout. The man's contempt was quite apparent."

Darcy laughed and shook his head. "I can well imagine it. Hurst is . . . well, he is a simple sort himself. He loves to hunt, loves breeding his dogs, and can be happy at any event, as long as he has copious amounts of wine or brandy and a plate of sweetmeats all to himself."

"When I stayed at Netherfield, he was almost always sprawled across one of the couches in the evenings. That is, when he could not convince anyone to play cards with him."

Having filled her plate and his, Darcy led her to a pair of chairs nearby, ensuring she was seated comfortably before he seated himself.

Across the way, he noted Fitzwilliam seating himself close to Lady Emily, who had apparently followed them from where she had first greeted them, and he received a wink and an expressive glance at Lady Emily from his cousin. Darcy frowned—he could not imagine what that was all about. More of Fitzwilliam's typical insouciance, no doubt.

"I am sure, Miss Bennet," said Darcy, turning back to her and shunting thoughts of his cousin to the side, "that your picture of Hurst is quite accurate. Though he is not a bad sort, I find him to be more than a little bit of a bore."

"I never would have guessed, Mr. Darcy," replied Miss Bennet, her eyes sparkling with suppressed mirth.

"It is unfortunate," said Darcy. "I *had* planned to join Bingley at Netherfield myself last autumn. If I had, we would have been acquainted all this time."

She did not seem to know what to make of his statement, and Darcy himself was not certain what had made him say such a thing. She paused a moment, and then redirected the conversation.

"That is unfortunate, sir. Do you think you would have brought your sister with you?"

"Ah, pierced through the heart!" Darcy put a dramatic hand over his breast. "The possibility of making your acquaintance last year rendered palatable only because I might have introduced Georgiana to you at the same time!"

Miss Bennet giggled at his melodramatic statement, and he winked at her. "It is unlikely she would have come to Hertfordshire. At the time, she was recovering from a disappointment which she has only recently overcome. That is the reason why I decided not to go myself."

"Oh, I hope she is quite well now," said Miss Bennet, concern etched on her face. "She does not seem to be suffering."

"I think it is in a large part because of your friendship and that of Miss Drummond."

When Miss Bennet appeared taken aback, Darcy continued: "She has not had much opportunity to make many friends, owing to a shy demeanor and a dearth of young ladies her age in the area."

Miss Bennet frowned. "There seem to be many such young ladies."

"Yes, but she is exactly at the age where there are many who are her elder by two or three years, and several younger. The elder she has not the confidence to approach, while she has little interest in the concerns of the younger. Miss Drummond is the closest in age, being less than a year older."

Darcy sighed and looked away. "I should have encouraged a

friendship between them earlier, but I did not wish to push her into situations she might have found uncomfortable."

"She will never become comfortable in society unless she puts herself forward."

"You are correct, of course."

Contrary to Miss Bennet's words, there was no censure in her gaze. She watched him, her expressions showing nothing but concern and compassion. A powerful feeling welled up within him. He was unused to ladies of Miss Bennet's station looking on him with anything other than avarice and calculation. He suspected, given Drummond's intelligence, that she had little in the way of those benefits which would attract most men, but her lack of artifice and her joyful character made those concerns meaningless.

"Georgiana is the youngest of my extended family. We have some second cousins on the Darcy side, with whom we are not at all close, while only a few on the Fitzwilliam side. Fitzwilliam is one of my two elder cousins, and he has two younger sisters who are both older than Georgiana. My aunt in Kent also has a daughter, but she is closer in age to me than to my sister. So, you see, it has left my sister without a natural companion within the family. Fitzwilliam and I are jointly responsible for her care, and we have done our best. But what do a pair of young bachelors know about raising a young girl?"

"I would say you have done a marvelous job of it," replied Miss Bennet. "She is intelligent, respectful, elegant, and so very talented. Both Olivia and I are particularly fond of her.

"But your mention of your aunt does bring to mind a rather curious connection, sir." Darcy was gratified by her assessment of Georgiana but intrigued by her subsequent words. "You have mentioned your aunt, Lady Catherine—might I inquire if she is Lady Catherine de Bourgh of Rosings Park in Kent?"

Surprised, Darcy nodded. "Yes, she is. How do you know her?"

"I have never met the lady. I believe I have spoken of a cousin who is to inherit my father's estate?"

"I believe you said he married one of your sisters."

"Yes, that is correct. In fact, Mr. Collins is the rector of Hunsford, which I believe is the parish connected to your aunt's estate."

"That is a curious connection, indeed," replied Darcy. Then a thought occurred to him, and he turned a curious eye on the woman at his side. "Pardon me, Miss Bennet, but . . . I am simply wondering about your cousin. You see, I have been to Rosings many times, often in the spring—though we chose not to attend my aunt this year—and

I am quite familiar with Hunsford, and even more familiar with the kind of men my aunt prefers to install there."

A laugh bubbled up from Miss Bennet's breast, and her eyes shone with mirth. "I believe I know what you are asking, Mr. Darcy. I have never met any of your aunt's previous parsons, but I can imagine what kind of men they were. Mr. Collins is quite the most obsequious, ridiculous man I have ever met. He could not be content unless he venerated and lauded his patroness from morning until night."

Darcy joined her, indulging in a quiet chuckle. "I can well imagine it. Her previous parson, Mr. Peters, was afraid to say anything which might remotely be construed as in opposition to Lady Catherine's many opinions."

"Then I rather think she has outdone herself this time, Mr. Darcy. Mr. Collins is not afraid of opposing Lady Catherine—rather, he is eager to agree with everything she says. I dare say that he would be happy to declare the sun green, should she only decree it to be so."

They continued to laugh together, but in the midst of her laughter, Darcy thought he saw a shadow cross Miss Bennet's face. As a woman who laughed at life, enjoying it to its fullest, he would not have expected such a reaction during a mirth-filled conversation.

"Is there something the matter, Miss Bennet?"

A rueful glance was her initial response, and for a moment he thought she might refuse to answer his question. In the end, however, she sighed and looked at him, her smile more a grimace.

"The reminder of a different side of Mr. Collins crossed my mind at an inopportune time."

"Oh?" asked Darcy. He thought to be a little concerned, as he knew she was not easily intimidated, more likely to laugh if anything.

Miss Bennet tried to demure, but she seemed to sense that he was only concerned, not intrusive. She straightened her shoulders, and then she looked at him, her countenance seeming to dare him to ridicule.

"In fact, *I* was the first recipient of Mr. Collins's attentions. I could not, in good conscience, marry a man as ridiculous as he, a man I could not respect, let alone love, so I refused him, after which he turned to my sister. At their wedding breakfast, he informed me in no uncertain terms that I had best find a husband, for I would not be allowed to live at his estate in the event of my father's untimely death."

Several contrary emotions ran the gamut through Darcy's mind at her revelation: anger at the man's presumption and unchristian mean-spiritedness; offense for her sake; pride in her convictions; and a sense of undefinable sadness that he might have lost her before ever meeting her.

"You may despise me at your leisure," said Miss Bennet brightly, though he thought he caught a hint of nervousness under her nonchalance. "I have refused a highly eligible match, and must now end an old maid. But you must not fear for me, Mr. Darcy—my mother overheard Mr. Collins's words, and she was quick to assure me that she and my sister, who would undoubtedly consider it a duty, would never allow me to be put out from my home. And since Mr. Collins is probably the weakest willed man I have ever met, I do not doubt she spoke the truth."

"I hardly think it possible to despise you, Miss Bennet." Of course not. Any thought that he might still have espoused of her being a fortune hunter was now dispelled. "I cannot imagine that such a thing will ever come to pass, for I cannot imagine you remaining unmarried for so long."

"Thank you for your kind words, sir."

"It is not a kindness. It is a conviction." She lowered her gaze to the ground in embarrassment, but the pink stains on her cheeks showed that she was not displeased. "As for Mr. Collins, I can hardly fathom a man of the cloth saying such things to one who is, after all, a relation. Though my aunt is many things, I cannot imagine that she would approve of such behavior."

Seeming embarrassed by the conversation, Miss Bennet changed the subject. "You have mentioned your invitation to the Bingleys to Pemberley. Will the Hursts be included?"

"My understanding is that they are in Norfolk at Hurst's family estate. As such, I believe I will take the opportunity to avoid Hurst's company by only inviting your sister and her husband. That also means that the invitation must include Miss Bingley, as she is not welcome in Norfolk, due to a number of highly pyroclastic confrontations with Hurst's mother."

Miss Bennet laughed. "I can well believe it."

At that moment, their conversation was interrupted by the approach of the earl. Darcy rose to his feet and bowed, shaking the other man's proffered hand. "Your lordship. I had not thought you would attend your daughter's picnic."

"And you would be correct," replied the earl. "I am to go into Derby today, for I have some business there. But I noticed a young lady to whom I have not been introduced and thought to procure an introduction."

"Of course." Darcy turned to Miss Bennet, who had risen by his side. "My lord, this is Miss Elizabeth Bennet of Hertfordshire. Lately she has been visiting her uncle, Mr. Drummond, and is to stay with us through the course of the summer. Miss Bennet, may I introduce his lordship, Arthur Teasdale, Earl of Chesterfield and Lady Emily's father."

"I am charmed to meet you, Miss Bennet," said the earl. "Your uncle is a good man and a valued member of the community."

"Thank you, my lord," replied Miss Bennet.

The earl turned back to Darcy. "I did not miss the mode of your introduction, sir. I dare say you have the right of it: being Emily's father *is* as important a title as the rest of it."

Darcy laughed. "I am certain it is, my lord. She is a fine woman."

"Something of a handful since her mother's death, but I must agree with you.

"Ah, it looks as if the sports are about to begin," said the earl, gesturing at the lawn where those in attendance were gathering. "I shall leave you to it. Only remember that it is customary for a man to carry a lady's favor onto the field of battle."

With a sly wink at Miss Bennet, the earl farewelled them and departed.

Darcy turned to his companion, noting that her embarrassment had made a return. "What say you, Miss Bennet?"

"Of what, sir?" replied she, though Darcy was convinced she knew exactly to what he referred.

"Shall I carry your favor into battle today?"

Miss Bennet laughed. "I do not know if it is correct to call it battle, sir. I have naught but this handkerchief to give you, if you wish."

The piece of cloth that she produced was a lacy, frilly sort of thing, with her initials embroidered in one corner in a complex script. With a bow over her hand, Darcy accepted it and placed it carefully in the front pocket of his jacket.

"I will endeavor to win the day for your ladyship. I hope I will receive the boon of your support."

"Of course, my handsome knight. You have already come to my rescue once—I doubt there is a man in the whole of the world who could represent me as well as you."

Satisfaction swelled in Darcy's breast. He reached for her hand and bent over it, but on this instance, instead of contenting himself with a bow, he pressed his lips to her dainty fingers, lingering for a moment. Then he straightened and released her hand, and turned away to her shy nod.

"You have put on quite a show this morning, Darcy," said Fitzwilliam as he approached. "I dare say there is not a person present who did not just witness your display."

For once, Darcy decided that he did not care for the scrutiny of others. "Let them talk. It is nothing to me."

Fitzwilliam chuckled and shook his head, following Darcy to where the other men were gathering.

There were many activities for them that day. Elizabeth indulged in a game of croquet with the other ladies, pairing at one point with Mr. Darcy in a game where they alternated shots. There were other games, interspersed with walks in the park, sometimes in the company of friends, and once in Mr. Darcy's company.

Through it all, Elizabeth could not help but wonder if she was caught up in a dream. New friends, a new situation, Mr. Darcy's attentions, an event as fine and diverting as any she had ever attended — these had all changed her outlook on life as completely as if she had become another person. Though she had come to Derbyshire in a poor frame of mind, worried for the future, depressed at the rejection of her elder sister, now she could not be happier. She did not know what the future held for her, but she knew that it had been a good decision to come to Derbyshire, and she thanked her father and her uncle for their encouragement.

Later in the afternoon, the gentlemen turned their attention to an impromptu game of cricket, and they all doffed their coats in favor of the greater freedom of movement granted by their shirts and waistcoats. Mr. Darcy, Elizabeth noticed, transferred her handkerchief from his jacket pocket to his waistcoat. He looked up at her when he did so, smiling at her and nodding while patting the pocket in which the handkerchief lay. Elizabeth waved, feeling more than a little self-conscious at his obvious regard.

"It seems to me that our Elizabeth has made a rather prestigious conquest."

Feeling the heat on her cheeks, Elizabeth turned to Miss Clara Burbage, who had made the comment, noting her sly glances with Miss Fiona MacDonald, who sat nearby.

"I do not know of what you speak," said Elizabeth. She turned back and watched as the gentlemen began to play, noting the competitive fire which fueled their efforts.

"There is no need to be coy," replied Clara. "We have all seen the attentions Mr. Darcy is paying to you, not to mention the fact that he carries your favor."

"The earl suggested it," said Elizabeth. "Once he did, Mr. Darcy had little choice."

"He did not look reluctant to me," said Fiona.

"It is said that fortune favors the bold," added Clara, "and I cannot but help but think that luck has been very much on your side of late. Mr. Darcy is handsome and gentlemanly and every woman in the neighborhood between the ages of sixteen and six-and-fifty has been pining for his attentions since he inherited Pemberley."

"And Pemberley itself does no harm to the man's appeal," said Fiona. She sighed. "If only he would pay such exquisite attentions to *me*. I should be very happy, indeed."

"I rather think that possibility has been extinguished by our excellent Miss Bennet," said Clara. "I doubt the man will ever look at another woman again."

Like clucking chickens, the two ladies continued to tease, but though she made a response a time or two, Elizabeth did not hear more than one word in three. Elizabeth's mind was much more agreeably engaged — Mr. Darcy was playing cricket with the rest of the men, and she could not but notice how athletic and tall he was, how when he struck the ball it sailed over the heads of the other players, and how his countenance shone with enjoyment and vitality. Indeed, she was as agreeably engaged as she had ever been. Though Elizabeth would not think of it for several days, she never did retrieve her handkerchief.

When the day's entertainments had run their course and the parties prepared to leave, Fitzwilliam took it upon himself to stay close to Lady Emily, wary of the woman. She had not missed the display Darcy and Miss Bennet had put on before the neighborhood — no one could be less aware of it, Fitzwilliam thought. And though her countenance remained congenial and she interacted with her guests with her mask of good humor firmly in place, Fitzwilliam had not missed the gradual tightening of her lips. She had said little to Darcy or to Miss Bennet, choosing instead to immerse herself in her duties as hostess. But when they were together, her eyes followed the couple wherever they went, and Miss Bennet, whenever they were apart, considering, calculating, scheming.

"Is that truly your cousin, Fitzwilliam?" asked Mr. Dunstan, a man from a nearby estate. "I hardly recognize him. He has never so much as batted an eyelash at a woman before, and now, here he is, making love to her before the entire party."

Fitzwilliam eyed Dunstan with more than a little distaste. He was not a bad man, but both Darcy and Fitzwilliam had little to do with him, as his behavior resembled that of George Wickham far too closely.

"I hardly think he is being so open," replied Fitzwilliam.

"For a man as closed as Darcy, he is being positively demonstrative. Do not attempt to tell me you do not see it."

Dunstan turned his attention toward Miss Bennet, his gaze considering. "She is pretty, and I am sure that dress hides many delights, but I cannot see what he sees in her. She has very little, from what I understand, and as such, I doubt her connections are anything to boast of either. Or perhaps he means to make her his mistress."

"Do attempt to be more circumspect, Dunstan," said Fitzwilliam. "You are at the residence of an earl, and I doubt he would appreciate one of his daughter's guests being spoken of in such a manner."

"The earl is away from the estate."

"No, but his daughter is here, and she would not appreciate it either."

Dunstan shrugged. "It matters not. Whatever charms Miss Bennet may have are lost on me. I much prefer Lady Emily. Let Darcy have his country miss; it is obvious that Lady Emily favors him as well, but if he chooses to eschew the riches of the Teasdales and fathering the future earl, why it clears the field for me."

With a tip of his hat, Dunstan stepped away toward his own carriage. Fitzwilliam snorted to himself—he doubted very much that Lady Emily would give the time of day to a foppish rake such as Dunstan. Of greater concern was what to do about Lady Emily. She had not done anything that day, preferring to observe and scheme, but Fitzwilliam did not think that would last for long. Sooner or later she would begin her campaign to garner Darcy's attention, and though there was little chance Darcy would respond, still it would interrupt his courting with Miss Bennet. Knowing his cousin was in a fair way in love with the woman, Fitzwilliam was determined to intercede.

CHAPTER XIV

As the days passed, the date of the dinner at Kingsdown approached, and the Darcy family prepared to join their friends for dinner. Darcy was the only one of the three who had ever been there—Georgiana typically received her friends at Pemberley, though she had made mention of visiting Kingsdown, a significant step for her, in Darcy's opinion. Thus, it fell to him to make some explanation of the Drummonds' situation.

"The Drummonds are not wealthy," explained he. "At one time, the estate brought in a respectable amount, but it has dwindled to almost nothing due to mismanagement and the dissolute habits of more than one of Mr. Drummond's ancestors. Our south fields, in fact, used to be part of Kingsdown."

"Truly?" asked Fitzwilliam, interested in the tale.

"Yes, my father purchased them from Drummond's father not long after he became master of Pemberley. It is a pleasant house, but as it was built for a larger estate, you will find that it is more spacious than an estate the size of Kingsdown can normally support."

"But we shall not see much of the house," replied Georgiana, apparently a little nervous at the thought of visiting people she did not already know.

"That is true. They are good people, even though they are not truly of our circle. Drummond is friendly and obliging, his eldest son, whom I do not know well, is quiet, but seems intelligent, and Mrs. Drummond, though she often gives the appearance of coldness, is polite."

"I do not care about their status," declared Georgiana. "I am quite happy to have made their acquaintance anyway."

"I did not think you would have concerned yourself with such matters," replied Darcy. "Your friendship with Miss Drummond grows ever closer, unless I am very much mistaken."

"I *do* like her very well, Brother. She is close to my age and shares many like interests. If it meets your approval, I would like to invite her to attend the next time my music master comes. I believe she would play wonderfully, if she was only given a little instruction."

"Of course, you may," replied Darcy.

The carriage in which they sat wended its way toward the Drummond estate, and Darcy owned to himself that he was impatient to arrive. The carriage wheels rumbled along the road, the sound echoing off the surrounding hills, their pace seeming the same as it ever was, but it seemed as if they were crawling, and the anticipation of being in *her* company again was nigh unbearable. Darcy heard a snort from his cousin, most likely because he had recognized Darcy's impatience, but for once Fitzwilliam did not speak.

When at length the carriage finally entered the drive at Kingsdown, Darcy suppressed a sigh of relief. The family was gathered on the front stoop to greet them, and Georgiana exclaimed delight, charmed at the children's manners as they stood gravely, waiting for the arrival of their guests. The carriage pulled to a stop, and Darcy and Fitzwilliam alighted, Darcy turning to assist his sister, before they approached the waiting family.

"Darcy," said Drummond, extending his hand, which Darcy took with pleasure. "Thank you for joining us tonight."

"The pleasure is all ours, Drummond."

The Darcys were introduced to the Drummond children, and Fitzwilliam and Georgiana to Mrs. Drummond and the eldest son, Edward, who was yet unknown to them. Then their hosts led them into the house, and the younger children were sent off to the nursery for their own dinners. The youngest girl, Leah, left only with great reluctance, Darcy noticed, though she was eventually coaxed from the room.

After the children's departure, the company settled into

conversation, and though Darcy might have wished it were otherwise, the lines were drawn at the sexes, for Georgiana sat with Miss Bennet and Miss Drummond, Mrs. Drummond sitting nearby and listening, if not speaking much. Darcy found himself in company with Drummond, his son, and Fitzwilliam.

In truth, Darcy was hardly able to remember what was said the first moments of the conversation, for his attention was caught by Miss Bennet. She sat with the other ladies, speaking in an animated voice, and every now and then she would gesture to make some point or another. The other ladies, including his dear sister, contributed to the conversation admirably, but in that moment Darcy could not see anything other than Miss Bennet in her blue floral print muslin dress. He did not think he had ever seen such a lovely sight as she presented that evening.

"You are fond of fishing, Mr. Drummond?" asked Fitzwilliam, catching Darcy's attention.

It was soon clear that Fitzwilliam's question was directed at the younger Mr. Drummond, for it was he who responded. "I do, though I do not often have the opportunity. There is always so much to be done."

"A man of Darcy's own heart," said Fitzwilliam with a laugh. "He spends a large amount of time managing Pemberley."

"Some of us actually care for our estates, Fitzwilliam. Perhaps you should follow our example and devote some time to Thorndell."

Instead of being offended, Fitzwilliam only laughed, as Darcy knew he would. "Thorndell is quite well, indeed, as I have already told you. The society in your neighborhood is much more interesting than that in mine."

"Where is your estate, Colonel Fitzwilliam?" asked the elder Drummond.

"Southwest of here," replied Fitzwilliam. "I can comfortably travel there in half a day, though my horse might not appreciate such a pace."

"You are fortunate, then. There are many younger sons who do not inherit anything, even when their fathers are earls."

"Well do I know it," replied Fitzwilliam. "Thorndell is an inheritance through my mother's family and is not part of my father's earldom."

"My younger sons will almost certainly be relegated to the army or the clergy," replied Drummond. "I am hoping they both choose the safer option of the clergy. They will both have the power of some choice, as I have invested some money on their behalf with my brother

Gardiner."

"That is good forethought," replied Fitzwilliam. "My mother wished for me to go into the clergy, but it is far too sedate a lifestyle for me. I own that I was more interested in excitement and adventure as a young man."

"And now you have entered a sedate lifestyle akin to the one you eschewed before," inserted Darcy. "Being a gentleman is not exactly adventurous."

"I dare say it is not," agreed Fitzwilliam, amused. "But the exhilaration of being shot at quickly fades to ennui, often in direct proportion to the enemy's improving aim."

They all laughed at Fitzwilliam's jest. "You must have some interesting stories to tell," observed the younger Mr. Drummond.

"I can tell a yarn as well as the next man. But most of my experiences in the army are not grand or adventurous. Quite the opposite, in fact."

Fitzwilliam fell silent, and Darcy could see the introspection of remembrance fall over him as it had many times in the past. Fitzwilliam often told humorous stories, and embellishment was in his blood, but he could rarely be induced to speak of his more serious experiences. Darcy could not understand what he had endured, never having lived through it himself, but he could empathize with the desire to leave painful experiences in the past.

"I would not wish for my brothers to experience such horrors," said Edward Drummond.

"That is why I hope they make different choices," replied his father, "though I understand why you made yours."

"It is not all gloom and desperation," said Fitzwilliam. "I have made many excellent friends, with whom I shall ever be close, and at times the antics of the higher ranks can be positively amusing."

With that Fitzwilliam began to regale then with some of his more amusing tales, and soon they were all laughing at the silliness of the last general under whom he had served. Darcy, who had heard many of these tales before, only shook his head, wondering how much of what he said was grounded in fact.

"A certain measure of eccentricity is a hallmark of a brilliant mind," said Fitzwilliam when Edward had expressed disbelief. Then he laughed. "Of course, I do not know that I would call General Romsley a brilliant man—eccentric, yes. There are so many men who come from highborn backgrounds and purchase their way into an elevated rank."

Edward appeared confused. "You are the son of an earl, are you not?"

"Aye, I am," replied Fitzwilliam with a grin. "But I worked my way up to colonel from lieutenant. My father taught both my brother and me that though we were sons of an earl, very little in life could be handed to us without our having to work to gain it. My brother has been involved in the management of the earldom's estates for many years, and I purchased a lieutenancy instead of entering the army at a higher level, like I see so many others doing."

"That is to your credit, Colonel Fitzwilliam," said Drummond.

Fitzwilliam only waved him off. "I believe a man has no business leading men into battle unless he has some experience in their shoes. I believe the purchase of high commissions should be abolished in favor of a system based solely on merit. Sadly, I do not believe anything will change any time soon."

"I do not doubt you are correct," said Darcy.

The gentlemen spoke together for some time, and though his cousin directed expressive looks at him from time to time, Darcy thought he acquitted himself quite well. Miss Bennet did not distract him *too* much, though her infectious laughter, the sound of her voice raised in her usual wit, and the sheer *force* of her presence did capture his attention quite often. Darcy also came to know young Edward Drummond better, and the young man was as he suspected — reticent, like Darcy himself, but intelligent. He sensed that Mr. Drummond wished Edward to become better acquainted with both Fitzwilliam and himself, perhaps to become something of a mentor to him. Darcy was happy to oblige.

They went in to dinner soon after, and Darcy was impressed with the fare they were able to provide. He did not think the Drummonds possessed the resources to employ many servants, but clearly whoever had done the cooking was not unfamiliar with the kitchen. The roast pheasants Drummond had likely shot, himself, were cooked to a turn, and the assorted dishes which accompanied it would not have been out of place on Pemberley's own table.

There was one incident during dinner which surprised Darcy. As it happened, Darcy had managed to escort Miss Bennet into dinner and had thus been able to take his seat beside her. As Fitzwilliam had escorted Mrs. Drummond and was sitting to her right, Darcy was seated to her left with Miss Bennet beside him, and though he had done his best not to ignore Mrs. Drummond, he did not think the woman missed the fact that his attention was on Miss Bennet much more than anyone else in the room.

Their subjects were wide ranging and always interesting, and as usual, when in her presence, Darcy was astounded by Miss Bennet's intelligence, and her grasp of any subject, which was often more profound than that of many men with whom Darcy was acquainted. All this Mrs. Drummond observed with little visible emotion—she ate her dinner, rarely partaking in the conversation, watching them all like a governess over her charges. When she did finally speak, it was with some asperity and in a tone which was faintly censuring, though after Darcy could not quite remember exactly what Miss Bennet had said to provoke it.

"You seem to have an opinion about many things, Elizabeth. I wonder where you might have cultivated such things, for it is not usual for women to speak of the troubles on the continent."

Only those who were near enough actually heard the comment—Fitzwilliam turned and looked at the woman, and Darcy and Miss Bennet were both surprised at it, but Mr. Drummond, his son and daughter, and Georgiana continued to speak as if they were not aware of it.

"I find it rather refreshing," said Darcy before Miss Bennet could speak up. "So many young ladies these days have little knowledge of the world in which they live, and they can speak of naught more substantial than the weather. Miss Bennet is obviously well-read, and she shows an understanding which is quite uncommon."

Mrs. Drummond returned his placid gaze with one of her own, and Darcy was unable to determine what she was thinking. At length, however, she contented herself with an abruptly spoken "Quite" before she turned back to her meal. Not wishing to allow the woman's nebulous attack to dampen the atmosphere, Darcy spoke quickly to Miss Bennet, and soon they were speaking with as much animation as they had before.

The problem of Mrs. Drummond was one Darcy could not quite unravel. He had little interaction with the woman, and was not well acquainted with her as a result. Mr. Drummond was all that was congenial, but the same traits did not seem to exist in the wife. Why she had chosen to make such an oblique attack on her niece, to suggest she was a bluestocking, was beyond Darcy's comprehension. One thing was clear: she did not approve of Miss Bennet.

The meal continued with no further issue, and at length, when it was consumed, Darcy was surprised when Mrs. Drummond rose to lead the ladies from the room, leaving the gentlemen behind. Darcy had not thought that Drummond would wish to separate, given the smallness of the party and the number of younger ladies in attendance.

The four men sat about the table with some of Mr. Drummond's port—not the finest vintage, but still quite good—and spoke for some time. Though Darcy was, in all honesty, eager to return to the sitting-room to once again be in company with Miss Bennet, he held himself in check, not wishing to insult his host. Fortunately, it was not long before the reason for Drummond's actions made themselves known.

Fitzwilliam and Edward had entered into a conversation of horses, and Edward was paying rapt attention to Fitzwilliam's comments concerning some of the chargers he had ridden into battle, when Drummond turned his attention to Darcy.

"Thank you for coming tonight, Darcy. I know that we are not able to offer the same style of fare to which you are accustomed, but I hope everything was agreeable."

"Completely so, sir," replied Darcy. "The meal was exquisite, and your family everything obliging. We were happy to come and hope to be able to return the favor soon."

"And we will be happy to accept." The man paused for a moment, seeming to search for something to say, when he turned his attention back on Darcy. "I apologize in advance if I am offending you with my query, sir, but I feel that I must have this conversation. May I ask what your intentions are with respect to my niece?"

For the briefest of moments, Darcy was offended. Who was this man to question his character so?

Then sanity set in and Darcy was thankful he had not voiced his reaction born of conceit. Mr. Drummond had the care of another man's daughter, whose safety and protection was his responsibility until she was returned to her father's home. He could see Darcy's attentions, as could any intelligent man. Of course, he would wish to know how Darcy meant to proceed.

Darcy let out a heavy breath and smiled at his host. "In all honesty, Mr. Drummond, I do not know what my intentions are at present."

It seemed the man had been holding his own breath, for he exhaled and shot Darcy an apologetic look. "I do not mean to question your honor, sir."

"I understand. She is under your care, and you take that responsibility seriously."

Mr. Drummond nodded, to which Darcy replied: "As you should. I believe you already know that I think highly of Miss Bennet, and I am pleased that she has such a conscientious protector.

"The fact of the matter, however, is that I do not know my own mind at this time. I enjoy her company and I appreciate her vivacity and the way she and your daughter have befriended my sister. I *do* have some inclinations in her direction, but at this point I do not know if I will pursue them."

"It is hard, I know," replied Drummond. "We have spoken of Elizabeth's situation, and you know that she is not gifted with great wealth and she is not connected to the highest of society."

"I understand. But of her person, there is little of which to find fault. I have rarely met someone like her. I have a low opinion of much of high society, and even lower of misses who are bred for nothing more than to capture a wealthy husband."

"Then Elizabeth must be a little confusing. She is unpretentious and is more concerned with the contents of others' characters."

"I am not certain I would use the word confused," replied Darcy. "Enchanted would be closer to the mark."

Drummond laughed. "She does have a way about her, does she not? She was bright and precocious as a child, and showed great promise. I had not seen her in many years before she came to stay with us, but the potential she displayed has been exceeded in every particular."

"I do not doubt it," said Darcy softly.

For a few moments Drummond allowed him to think before he spoke up again. "I will not press you for a decision, nor will I attempt to influence you in any way. I, of course, see my niece as good enough for any man, but I will own to a little bias in the matter."

A slow smile spread over Darcy's face in response to the other man's words.

"I understand some of the pressures you face," continued Drummond. "I trust Elizabeth not to raise her hopes without foundation, and moreover, I trust that you will not trifle with her affections. The only thing I ask for is circumspection when you meet with her. Hopes can be raised unintentionally, after all, and I would not have her hurt."

"That is the last thing I wish to do," said Darcy.

"I know it is. But I would not wish to return her to the state she was when she arrived, intentionally or no."

"The state she was in before?" echoed Darcy. He was confused — Miss Bennet had never seemed anything other than happy and contented.

"This situation with her sister is part of it," replied Drummond. "She has always presented the appearance of cheer, but my brother

Bennet tells me that her spirits were quite low before she came to us. I do not know all the reasons, but I do know she has been happier the longer she has been with us."

"I promise I will take care," said Darcy.

He did not speak for a moment, thinking of his options. The fact was that though he was impressed with Miss Bennet and understood her siren call could prove to be irresistible, he was in no way ready to make any kind of commitment. But Mr. Drummond deserved to have some understanding of his intentions beyond his simple statement that he did not know yet. There was a way for him to learn his own feelings and provide the other man with that security.

"With your permission, sir, I would like to call on Miss Bennet," said Darcy, feeling immediately like he had made the correct choice. "I am not ready for anything more than that at present and I do not think that she is either. But I am aware that the more I know of her, the more I esteem her. Through calling on her with your permission, I will begin to know more of my own mind."

"Excellent, sir!" said Drummond, lifting his glass in agreement. "You have my hearty approval and consent, though I am certain you are aware that for anything further you will be required to apply to her father."

"Should it come to that, I will be happy to do so."

Darcy tapped his glass to Drummond's in a silent toast to Miss Bennet, and they both drained them.

"Now," said Drummond, rising to his feet, "I believe it might be time to rejoin the ladies. I am certain there is one with whom you would rather converse."

Nodding, Darcy followed his host from the dining room with the other gentlemen in tow. The first sight Darcy had of Miss Bennet when they entered the room was of her laughing, her mirth streaming from her gaily, showing for all to see the delight she took in life. And it was at that moment that Darcy knew that he could love her, that he could make her an offer and bring her back to Pemberley as its mistress.

They entered the room, and Darcy sought a seat by the temptress's side. As soon as he did, he leaned over and softly spoke to her: "Might I ask what prompted your mirth, Miss Bennet?"

"You may ask, but I might choose not to answer," was her arch reply.

"Ah, I believe I might understand. You have confidences concerning the gentlemen that you wish to keep."

Miss Bennet only laughed again. "So typical of your sex, sir. You imagine that the ladies speak of nothing else."

Darcy feigned surprise. "You do not?"

"We do speak of you at times," replied she, vastly amused at the conversation. "But not always. You may put your sense of superiority away, sir, for we ladies are not as affected by you as you would like to think."

"I beg to differ, Miss Bennet. I think you are every bit as affected as we might think."

"And you are not affected by us?"

"No, I believe we are equally moved by you."

"There," cried Miss Bennet. "I have induced you to own it."

"It was not difficult," replied Darcy with a shrug. "I was not the one who denied it."

"Touché, Mr. Darcy. I believe you have carried your point in this instance."

"I hope you will allow me to call on you, Miss Bennet," said Darcy, leaning toward her and speaking in a low voice. "I have a great desire to know more of you."

Suddenly shy, Miss Bennet nevertheless responded with the self-possession that Darcy had come to expect from her. "Of course, sir. I believe you are welcome to come at any time convenient."

Darcy smiled and thanked her, but he resisted correcting her implication that his intentions were anything other than directed at her. Much as he respected and esteemed the Drummonds, it was Miss Bennet whom he truly wished to see.

For the rest of his time at Kingsdown, Darcy stayed close to Miss Bennet and engaged her in conversation. Fitzwilliam's amused grin, Mrs. Drummond's stony countenance, the joviality of others—none of these could distract him from the focus of his attention.

Later, when it was time for the Darcy party to depart, they did so with fond gratitude for the pleasant evening in good company, and left promising that it would be repeated very soon. Fitzwilliam's commentary on the journey back to Pemberley was ignored, though in truth he did not say much. What stuck in Darcy's mind was the thought that Miss Bennet had been as reluctant to see him depart as Darcy had been to leave. It was with great hope for the future that Darcy retired that evening.

CHAPTER XV

Even if Mr. Darcy had not requested permission to call, Elizabeth would have known that he was developing an interest in her. His demeanor when he came, the way he fixed his attention upon her, often to the exclusion of anything else, the soft smile he often displayed for her—all these things showed a deepening regard, the likes of which Elizabeth had often despaired of ever prompting in a man.

"You seem to be a man of your word, sir," said Elizabeth on his second visit, a few days after the dinner.

"I am," replied Mr. Darcy, "though I am not certain to what you refer."

"Your request to call on me, though I do wonder if you should not raise the subject with my uncle. He *is* responsible for me while I am here."

"Indeed, he is." The smile Mr. Darcy directed at her was faintly roguish. "The fallacy in your thinking lies in your assumption that I have not spoken with Mr. Drummond."

"You have?" asked Elizabeth, raising an eyebrow at him.

"Yes," replied Mr. Darcy. "The night we came to dinner, he confronted me about my intentions, and I responded by asking if I could call on you."

"Oh," said Elizabeth, not quite knowing what to make of that intelligence.

"I would inform you, Miss Bennet, that I do not take such things lightly. I am very serious about my future and the future of my family, and I do not ask to call on just any woman of my acquaintance."

"I am certain I would not think it of you," replied Elizabeth gravely. "I feel I must ask, sir: how many other women have you called on, considering you are so fastidious about these matters?"

Mr. Darcy grinned. "I am so demanding that this is the first time I have ever asked to call on a woman."

"Then I suppose I must feel flattered."

"Flattery is not my intention, though you may feel it if you choose. Rather, I am wondering if we might find a meeting of the minds. I am hoping we do."

"Then I must wish you luck, sir. For it is what I wish as well."

Elizabeth held Mr. Darcy's eyes for several moments and they the both burst into laughter. "We seem to have descended into a little silliness this morning, Mr. Darcy."

"Only a little," replied he. "In truth, I was dead serious."

"My mother would no doubt scold me for my impertinence, urging me to show you every deference, should she witness this scene. She has often despaired of my manners."

"I do not wish for deference," replied he. "I receive enough deference from the Miss Bingleys of the world. From you, I would wish nothing but for you to be yourself."

A shyness descended over her. "Then I will endeavor to meet your approval."

"You already have."

Their conversations were not all playful bantering, though Elizabeth discovered that Mr. Darcy possessed a talent at such speech far beyond what she might have expected at her first meeting. He was obviously a man who was much more loquacious the more he came to know someone, and his comfort with Elizabeth soon increased to the point where they conversed with ease. But such playful repartee was only a part of their conversations; in fact, they spoke of many things—literature, music, common interests such as the theater—though Mr. Darcy proved to possess more of a predilection for the opera, while Elizabeth enjoyed only certain works—art, and even a sprinkling of politics. Interspersed with this, they spoke of the world and some of Mr. Darcy's travels, including his abbreviated grand tour on the continent, and Elizabeth revealed a desire to someday see some of those locations of which he spoke so eloquently.

All this the Drummonds watched with varying degrees of interest—Olivia with amusement, Mr. Drummond with satisfaction, Edward with surprise, and Mrs. Drummond with annoyance, unless Elizabeth missed her guess. But she was content to ignore the woman, and Mrs. Drummond did not display her feelings openly.

The largest surprised came from a shockingly perceptive Leah. Elizabeth had quickly joined Olivia in the girl's esteem and trust, and one morning after Mr. Darcy departed, the girl approached her shyly and sat on Elizabeth's lap.

"Lizzy, will you marry Mr. Darcy?" asked she as seriously as a child of five could manage.

Astonished, Elizabeth could not speak for a moment. "Why do you say that?" she finally managed.

"Because he loves you," replied Leah.

At her side, Olivia giggled into her hand, but Elizabeth, far from feeling amused, was only confused. "I do not think Mr. Darcy loves me, Leah."

"Of course, he does. He visits and speaks to you, kisses your hand, and listens to you carefully. Is that not what a young man does with a woman he loves?"

"I believe a young man also does those things with a woman he considers a friend."

"Friends do not look on you the way Mr. Darcy does," insisted Leah.

Though she was shocked by this entire conversation—and more than a little cross with Olivia's inability to hold in her peals of laughter—Elizabeth attempted to explain the situation to the young girl.

"Mr. Darcy is only calling on me as a friend, Leah. He is an amiable man, and that is what amiable men do."

"Mama says he is proud."

"That is only because your mama does not know him well. He has no improper pride."

"He is ever so tall and handsome."

Elizabeth smiled at the girl. "Yes, he is, Leah. But I do not think he is in love with me."

"But maybe he will be one day?"

"Perhaps," said Elizabeth, unwilling to make any further comment.

"Then when you marry him, I hope you invite me to Pem . . .

Pember . . ."

"Pemberley?" supplied Olivia helpfully.

"Yes, that is it!" cried Leah. "I have heard that it is quite wonderful, and I should like to see it."

Elizabeth decided that it was time to bring the conversation to a close. She had noticed — where she did not think the sisters had — that Mrs. Drummond had looked into the room to see what had prompted Olivia's mirth. Elizabeth did not think the woman had heard what her youngest had said, and Elizabeth was eager that she did not learn of it.

Not long after Mr. Darcy started calling on her, Kingsdown had an unexpected visitor whose appearance shocked them all. Having completed their tasks for that day, Elizabeth and Olivia had sat down in the music room, Elizabeth showing Olivia whatever her meager skills on the pianoforte would permit. The younger children were in their lessons, their mother attending them that day, while Mr. Drummond was out on the estate, seeing to some matter or another.

When the door opened and the maid who acted as the housekeeper stepped in, leading Lady Emily into the room, Elizabeth and Olivia both rose. Elizabeth attempted to rein in her astonishment and greeted the lady with perfect civility, though Olivia was not so successful. As such, Elizabeth attempted to attend to the niceties, requesting that the maid provide some tea and rolls she prepared in the morning in case they should have any visitors.

"Miss Bennet, Miss Drummond," said Lady Emily, accepting their welcome with generous civility. "Might I inquire after your families?"

"All well," replied Elizabeth, inviting their guest to be seated. "Mrs. Drummond is with the children at present, and my last letter from my mother reported nothing extraordinary. And you?"

"I am tolerable, indeed," replied the lady.

Pleasantries were exchanged for several moments, until the tea tray arrived, and Elizabeth nudged Olivia, reminding her that it was her duty to serve. The girl colored a little at having to be reminded, but she readily attended to it. Then they all sat back with their cups and the conversation began in earnest. Though Lady Emily was as amiable as ever, there seemed to be a distinct probing quality in her comments that day, making Elizabeth feel uncomfortable.

"Have you learned yet whether your sister is to come to Derbyshire, Miss Bennet?"

"I have not heard anything yet," said Elizabeth. "By all accounts, Mr. Darcy and Mr. Bingley are great friends, so I would expect that they will come at some time or another."

"You will be happy to see her."

"Of course," replied Elizabeth. "She and I have been the closest of sisters all our lives. Our separation these past months, though I have been happy at Kingsdown, have been painful. I shall be happy to have her with me again."

"You make me quite envious, Miss Bennet. I have no other siblings. My mother died giving birth to a younger brother, who also perished, and my father could not bear to marry again."

"I am sorry to hear that," murmured Elizabeth.

"I would have liked to have known my mother, but I can hardly miss what I have never known." Lady Emily paused for a moment. "I have also had cousins and aunts to fill the void, so while I feel for my father's sorrow, on the whole I have been content."

There was nothing to be said to such a statement, so Elizabeth did not reply. Lady Emily did not seem to miss Elizabeth's lack of response, for she forwarded the conversation immediately.

"I have been attempting to remember everything I can of Luton, but I cannot picture your estate. Can you describe it to me?"

"It is actually south and east of Luton, my lady," replied Elizabeth. "It is closer to a small town called Meryton, though Longbourn does have a tiny village attached to it."

"And that would mean your father possesses a living in his gift?"

"Yes," replied Elizabeth. "He has not ever exercised this ability, for our rector—Mr. Standish—has been parson there since long before I was born. But as he is quite elderly now, I suspect my father will need to appoint someone else before too many more years have passed."

That seemed to impress Lady Emily. "Perhaps you could describe some of the sights of the area? I am interested in other places, and you speak so eloquently that I suspect I will be able to imagine it from nothing more than your description."

Something about the question seemed off to Elizabeth, but she readily complied. She spoke of her father's house and the park in which it sat, described the area, including the paths she had often walked, spoke of her favorite view atop Oakham Mount, and a little of Netherfield, her sister's new home. Lady Emily listened attentively, giving the proper responses in the proper places, but Elizabeth could not help but feel that she expected to hear something particular, though what it was, Elizabeth could not quite determine.

"This Oakham Mount, you say, is on your father's estate?" asked she after Elizabeth had described the view from the summit.

"I do not believe that Oakham Mount is actually part of any of the estates," said Elizabeth after a moment's thought. "My father has always said it is of little value, unless one means to build a fort to survey and protect one's lands. The northern slope might be of some use, as it is heavily forested, but that would more properly belong to the estate to the north, which is, I believe, somewhat larger than father's. But the estates to the south, Netherfield and Longbourn, have never paid the hill much attention."

"And it is two miles to the north, you say?"

"That is approximately correct," replied Elizabeth.

"And do you journey there on horseback?"

"No, I walk."

Lady Emily's eyes widened in surprise. "You walk, do you? You must be a prodigious walker, to be able to attempt such a journey."

"I have been walking as long as I have been old enough to find my way, Lady Emily. I do not walk to Oakham Mount often, as four miles is longer than I will normally venture, but I do not think it to be more than I am capable."

"That much is evident," said Lady Emily. "And your sister's estate? Is the house quite distant from your father's house?"

"It is a little less than three miles on a direct path," replied Elizabeth. "The easiest way to go by carriage, however, is through Meryton. It is about one mile to Meryton from Longbourn, and then a further two miles to Netherfield."

"Thank you for describing it so succinctly," replied Lady Emily. "I do, indeed, have a clear picture of your home through your efforts. I hope to be able to visit you there someday."

"You would be welcome, indeed," replied Elizabeth. She could not think of anything else to say; she did not think that Lady Emily's wish—if indeed it was in earnest—was likely to be gratified.

The visit continued for some little time after, and though the conversation did not strike Elizabeth as odd as it had before, there was still something unusual about Lady Emily's behavior. She watched and listened and spoke and tried to show that she was much as she ever was, but Elizabeth could not quite determine what had prompted this oddness. Then when Lady Emily arose to depart, she did so with every indication of continued civility and friendship. It was soon clear that Olivia had seen nothing of the lady's strange behavior.

"It was very civil of Lady Emily to visit us here," said she, her voice brimming with admiration. "I would never have expected her to return our call."

"No, neither would I," replied Elizabeth, distracted by her thoughts.

"It is hardly the behavior one would expect of the nobility," pressed Olivia. "I do not know what to make of it."

"Nor do I," replied Elizabeth, pushing her concerns to the side to focus on her cousin. "I will own, though, that I have not known many of equal station to Lady Emily, so I cannot expect to predict how they will conduct themselves. I cannot think she meant anything but friendship."

"I am certain she did not," replied Olivia, though Elizabeth was struck by the falsehood in her own words. In fact, she was certain that friendship had not been the only purpose of Lady Emily's visit.

The door to the sitting-room opened, and Edward stepped in. "Was that truly the daughter of an earl at Kingsdown?" asked he in evident surprise.

"It was," said Olivia, her enthusiasm fairly gushing from her voice. "It was very civil of her to have attended us."

"She is a handsome woman, indeed," replied Edward. "Perhaps I shall stand up with her at the next ball."

Olivia giggled and put her hand over her mouth. "It seems that my brother is infatuated with Lady Emily. What do you think, Elizabeth? Does he have a chance to woo the lady, or is he destined to disappointment?"

Elizabeth could not hold the laugh which escaped from her own mouth. Edward only shot his sister a withering glare and departed from the room, with Olivia chasing close behind, calling after him in a teasing voice. Elizabeth decided not to join her — the siblings would no doubt end in an argument if Olivia persisted, and she had no desire to be drawn into it.

Besides, Elizabeth still had not determined what Lady Emily's ulterior motive for calling on them had been. It was something she thought she should likely understand, but she could not fathom it. It was some time before Elizabeth left the room, and had anyone looked in to see her sitting there, they would have seen her deep in thought.

Though Elizabeth and Olivia were more often to be found in Georgiana Darcy's company than any other ladies' of the district, it did not follow that they neglected their other acquaintances. Elizabeth especially grew close with several them — they were mostly older than Olivia, and though she was friendly with them, she did not exactly consider them to be "friends." Thus, they often visited those other estates and ladies, though not so often as they might have liked, for the hand who usually drove the carriage was much engaged in the care of the farm.

The ladies with whom Elizabeth was closest were the two she had spoken with the most at Lady Emily's picnic — Miss Clara Burbage and Miss Fiona MacDonald. There were several others in the area who became known to her, some closer than others. Unfortunately, one could not possibly hope to please everyone with whom they were introduced, and Elizabeth found that maxim to be as true in Derbyshire as it was anywhere else.

It was beyond hope, Elizabeth supposed, that Mr. Darcy's continued attentions to her might go unnoticed. The man's actions were ever more ardent, and while he was still guarded when in any gathering, his preference for her company was certain to be observed. Though most of Elizabeth's acquaintances saw this and either teased her or envied her in silence, there were a few who could not hold their tongues. Comments, mean-spirited or cutting, were to be expected. It was one of the less admirable facets of human behavior to covet the good fortune of another.

Elizabeth found that the longer she remained in Derbyshire society, the more she was the recipient of such comments, though she could not state that she was made uncomfortable on many occasions. The worst incident took place not long after Mr. Darcy started calling on her openly.

It was during a morning visit to the estate owned by her friend Clara Burbage's father. The Burbage estate, Heath Hill, was situated on the far side of Lambton from Kingsdown, which meant that Elizabeth could not visit the young lady she had rapidly come to consider a friend as often as she liked. That morning, Clara had invited several ladies for tea, and they were received with affability and good humor by her mother, a matronly and plump woman of approximately Mrs. Bennet's age; Clara's younger sister, Eleanor; and her brother, Harold, who was younger than Elizabeth, though only by a few months. After the social niceties had been observed, Clara's family went away and left her to her friends and her tea.

The guests, who consisted of Fiona MacDonald and four other ladies of the area, sat down to their conversations, and Elizabeth, in Olivia's company, was drawn to her two closest friends. The conversation was lively and interesting, and Elizabeth was enjoying herself when the incident occurred.

"You seem to have made yourself many friends since coming to the area, Miss Bennet."

Elizabeth turned to regard the young woman who had addressed her. She did not know Miss Hillary Russell well at all, nor did she know the two ladies who sat on either side of her—their names were Miss Mary Campbell and Miss Erica Allen. They had always struck her as a little incautious in their remarks, and at times, they could be deemed unpleasant. In between the two groups, the final member of their party, Miss Deborah Grant sat, looking between the two of them as if she expected some unpleasantness.

"I appreciate the welcome I have received," replied Elizabeth, not knowing the woman's intentions, but thinking that a banal response might prevent further comment. "Derbyshire has proven to be beyond my expectations."

"Yes, it is a wonderful county," replied Miss Russell. "Is your home as beautiful as that you find in Derbyshire?" She paused, as if attempting to remember something, and continued: "I am sorry, Miss Bennet, where did you say your home is?"

"Hertfordshire. My family estate is fewer than twenty miles from the outskirts of London."

"That must be convenient for the season. I assume your family has a presence in London?"

"Yours does not," replied Clara. She seemed to sense that Miss Russell was intent on some mischief, for her gaze was more than a little pointed.

"I have attended the season," replied Miss Russell, her eyes flashing with displeasure.

"When staying with Mary's family," said Fiona.

"We were happy to have her with us," said Miss Campbell. In consequence, Miss Campbell was higher than Miss Russell, whose family estate was no larger than Longbourn. Miss Allen was higher than them both, but as the girl was naturally of a more reticent disposition, she often deferred to her more vocal pair of friends.

"Well, Miss Bennet?" pressed Miss Russell. "I have not seen you in London, but I assume you have been there."

"Many times," replied Elizabeth. "My uncle owns a house in London. My father but rarely goes, as he finds London society is not to his taste."

"Then your family does not possess a house in town?"

"No, Miss Russell, we do not." A hint of impishness came over Elizabeth, and she added: "It seems we are not so different, Miss Russell, though town is more accessible to me, given my proximity."

"My family at times spends the entirety of the season in town, though this year we have not gone due to my mother's health," ventured Miss Allen. "My mother and father are both very fond of society."

"I believe we have all attended events there," said Clara. "My favorite is the theater, though I do enjoy balls and parties too."

For a time, Clara's attempt to change the subject was successful, for the ladies' conversation concerned what they had done in London, what events, what activities were favorites. But while this was going on, Elizabeth noted that Miss Russell's eyes lingered on her.

Most of these here, Elizabeth thought, were from families that were quite wealthy. Clara and Fiona's fathers were gentlemen whose estates yielded in excess of five thousand a year, with Miss Campbell's family standing just below, and Miss Allen's family somewhat above their stations. Miss Russell's behavior was interesting, as other than Olivia, her family was the lowest in consequence, though Elizabeth had heard some talk of an inheritance from an elderly relation which had increased her dowry. It was likely this that provoked an increase in haughtiness.

After the conversation about the season had wound down a little, Miss Russell spoke again, apparently unaffected by being thwarted earlier. "Excuse me, Miss Bennet, how long will you be staying in the area?"

"The length of my stay has not been determined. But I believe that I will be here at least until the end of summer."

"I have heard that you have become quite close with Miss Georgiana Darcy," said Miss Campbell. What little Elizabeth could garner from Miss Campbell's tone suggested that the woman was no more pleased with Elizabeth's presence than was her friend.

"She is my closest friend!" exclaimed Olivia.

"Is she, indeed?" asked Miss Russell, an eyebrow raised in skepticism.

"Yes!" replied Olivia, clearly not understanding the other ladies' displeasure. "We have many interests in common, and she is ever so amiable."

"She is quite amiable, indeed, though I have not spoken to her often," said Miss Campbell. "You are quite . . . fortunate to have come to her notice."

"It is shocking," said Miss Russell casually, as if saying nothing of greater import than she expected it to rain, "that some young ladies are intent upon forwarding their interests by imposing themselves upon timid young ladies who, coincidentally, are connected to men of high standing in society."

"Indeed, it is a mean art," added Miss Campbell. "But if forced to stand on their own merits, their ambitions will not be realized, so their reliance on such subterfuge is not surprising."

"What is next?" asked Miss Russell tittering behind her hand. "Perhaps a compromise, or a fortunate meeting in a deserted hall?"

"I feel for the young lady. To have her earnest offers of friendship repaid in such a way would be very hard, indeed."

The spiteful comments between the two women were exchanged with such rapidity that no one else could insert a word while they were speaking. By the time Miss Campbell fired her parting shot, Clara was so livid that her fingers on the arm of the chair in which she sat were white with the force she was exerting on them. Fiona's eyes blazed, Miss Grant watched the two cats with sardonic disdain, while Miss Allen, who was known to be close to them, looked on, her eyes wide with shock.

Knowing that Clara was about to respond with a disparaging comment which would only provoke an argument, Elizabeth put her hand on her arm and turned to the two ladies.

"That would, indeed, be a shame, Miss Russell, for their hospitality to be repaid in such a fashion. Of course, it is a reprehensible art to show friendship for the sake of ingratiating. Fortunately, I think most gentlemen are intelligent enough to see avarice for what it is, and I have no doubt that those who befriend wonderful ladies such as Georgiana Darcy do so for no more reason than to be acquainted with such a wonderful young girl.

"Of course," added Elizabeth in an offhand manner, "attacking others for nothing more than jealousy and spite is at least as mean an art as that which you described. It shows a lack of confidence in oneself, for if one is content with one's situation and the content of one's character, such devices would become quite unnecessary. Do you not agree?"

Though Miss Russell's gaze bored into her and Elizabeth had no doubt she would have been impaled if Miss Russell could have managed it, she seemed to know enough not to say anything further. As a result, she did not make a response.

The visit continued for some time, though the words exchanged were strained, no doubt due to the mean-spirited attack. Elizabeth affected a nonchalance and endeavored to speak with her friends much the same as she ever had. Clara continued to glare at Miss

Russell and Miss Campbell, and for their parts, Miss Russell's aura of disdain for Elizabeth never diminished, though Miss Campbell had the sense to hide her feelings from the group.

At length, the two ladies whose presence had become unwelcome rose to depart, leaving behind six relieved women. No sooner were they out of the room than Clara vented her displeasure.

"Those odious chits!" exclaimed she. "How dare they come into my house and attack my friends!"

"Do not concern yourself, Clara," said Elizabeth. "I was uninjured by their barbs. The only thing they accomplished was to make themselves appear more than a little ridiculous."

"They are not usually this spiteful," said Miss Allen softly. "I am usually happy to be in their company, but at times they speak when they would best remain silent."

Miss Grant snorted, her disdain evident. "The only reason you do not hear more of their vitriol is because they are often circumspect in your presence. They know you do not appreciate it, so they restrain themselves."

Miss Allen appeared to be more contemplative than surprised.

"Apparently, they did not feel the need to do so today," said Fiona.

"Or their worse natures got the better of them," responded Clara. "It will be some time before I invite either of them into my house again, I assure you."

"Their behavior was reprehensible, of course," said Miss Grant, turning her gaze on Elizabeth. "But I am curious. It is said that Mr. Darcy is courting you, Miss Bennet. I understand if you do not wish to confirm or deny, but his behavior is enough to set tongues wagging, as he has always been most circumspect in showing attention to *any* young lady."

Elizabeth could feel her cheeks blooming, a problem exacerbated even more when Olivia, who had fallen silent when she recognized the hostility in the room, blurted: "Of course he is! He likes her very much and can hardly take his eyes off her when he calls!"

"Olivia!" exclaimed Elizabeth. The other ladies only laughed, though it was with true mirth, rather than any spite.

"Oh, come, Elizabeth," said Clara, true amusement flowing off her. "We have all witnessed his attentions and heard of his calls to Kingsdown. You must allow us our curiosity, though we will attempt to restrain our jealousy."

"I assure you that I am not being courted," replied Elizabeth. "You may lay your envy aside."

"Having only met Mr. Darcy," said Fiona, "you cannot understand his previous behavior or his legendary reticence. Though we are teasing, nothing we say is not the absolute truth."

"And you must understand the jealousy," added Miss Grant. "Though we are not gauche enough to behave as those two harpies did, still we all feel it, at least a little. Can we be blamed? Mr. Darcy is handsome," Miss Grant began to tick the points off on her fingers, "kind, he possesses a great estate and a mighty fortune—which is rumored to be only part of his wealth—and we have all dreamed of claiming his attention for our own. But you come to Derbyshire, an unknown relation of a minor landowner—I am sorry, Miss Drummond, but it is the truth—and steal all his attention away from us. Of course, we are jealous!"

The other ladies laughed, but they all nodded their agreement, including the restrained Miss Allen.

"In fact," continued Miss Grant, humor and playfulness in her manner, "we have all wondered if perhaps there is some peer to whom you have a connection, or some elderly relation who will soon die and leave you fabulously wealthy which makes you so irresistible to Mr. Darcy."

"I assure you," said Elizabeth, desperate to end this mortifying conversation, "that I have none of these virtues to my name. I am naught but Miss Elizabeth Bennet, a country girl from a small estate in Hertfordshire."

"Which makes it all that much more puzzling," said Miss Grant.

Elizabeth decided at that moment she liked Miss Grant very well, indeed, though she had not truly known the woman previously. She wished that she would cease her teasing, but she thought that in essentials they were much alike, though Miss Grant appeared to be somewhat more cynical and much more vocal.

"I think it is because Miss Bennet does not behave any differently to Mr. Darcy than she does to anyone else," opined Miss Allen quietly. "Mr. Darcy has no doubt had his share of fawning ladies, looking to garner his attention and, though Hillary stated it ineloquently, praising his sister, for nothing more than *his* benefit. But Miss Bennet treats everyone the same and does not give him any undue attention or flattery."

The room was silent for a moment, as they all considered Miss Allen's words. Then Clara said: "I believe Miss Allen might have the right of it."

"It makes sense," added Miss Grant, looking at Elizabeth with open speculation. "Most young ladies look at Mr. Darcy akin to how a starving man gazes on a fatted calf."

Elizabeth could only laugh. "Including you?"

Miss Grant only waved her off. "My father was a close friend of Mr. Darcy's, so I have known him for years. Neither Mr. Darcy nor myself sees the other in such a way."

"I did not know," replied Elizabeth. "I have not seen you at Pemberley, or speaking with Mr. Darcy, for that matter."

A shrug was followed by: "We do not speak much. Since Mr. Darcy's father died, we have been at Pemberley but rarely. We do exchange some words on occasion, but as I said, we do not really interest each other."

"Not like our Elizabeth interests Mr. Darcy," said Clara with a sly look at Elizabeth.

It was time to put an end to this talk. "I would remind you all that there is nothing between Mr. Darcy and myself. There is no courtship, and he has not approached my uncle. Please do not create rumors, for I am certain there are more Miss Russells in the district, and I would not wish to give them a reason to despise me."

"I suppose we should end our teasing," said Fiona, though her look clearly showed that she enjoyed it. "But you must excuse us if we continue to envy."

The laughter produced by this statement lured Elizabeth into responding in like fashion. By the time Elizabeth and Olivia left Heath Hill, she was on a first name basis with all the ladies present. But the incident taught Elizabeth an important lesson. There would be detractors—particularly should Mr. Darcy's intentions continue or even intensify—and she would need to have her entire arsenal of wit and composure with her to deflect their jealousy.

CHAPTER XVI

$\mathscr{A}$ more idyllic spring Elizabeth had never passed, and though she missed her family, she was quite content to be in Derbyshire. There was something magical about the place, she decided, and though she knew she would be required to return to her father's home eventually, she thought she would be quite happy to remain in Derbyshire for the rest of her life, if the opportunity presented itself.

Her father, never a great correspondent, exerted himself to write on occasion, though his letters were long overdue and shorter than Elizabeth might have wished, as was his custom. She did not receive anything from Jane, whose absence Elizabeth still felt keenly, or Mary, from whom she had not expected to receive anything, but Kitty and Lydia's letters were full of comments about the officers, parties, dances, and other such frivolities, and her mother's were often nothing more than ill-concealed attempts to induce Elizabeth to inform her if she had found a man willing to propose to her. Elizabeth still enjoyed them, regardless of how frustrating they sometimes were.

But though there was always work to be done at Kingsdown and her aunt continued to be distant and disapproving, there was still more than enough society for Elizabeth's taste. Her friendships with the young ladies of the area were becoming closer the longer she lingered at her uncle's home, and she thought they were friendships she would keep for the rest of her life, even after she returned to her father's home.

She and Olivia were also becoming very close to Georgiana Darcy, who was a sweet and angelic soul, and who often reminded Elizabeth of Jane. The three young ladies often visited each other at their homes, Georgiana even gathering the courage to visit Kingsdown on occasion. As her aunt was still a source of frustration, Elizabeth and her cousin preferred it that way, as they did not wish to subject the young woman to the bitter elder woman.

Mr. Darcy's attentions, however, grew apace, and soon he could be found at Kingsdown several times a week. He was agreeable to them all, but it was clear—even to Elizabeth's eyes, determined, as she was, to avoid hoping unreasonably—that he came to see her. He would sit with her, speaking of literature, music, or any other subject which crossed their minds, or they would walk out on the pathways of the estate. Olivia was usually claimed as their chaperone, and the girl was happy enough for Elizabeth that she was pleased to provide this service for them. It was especially surprising to Elizabeth that Mr. Darcy did not simply walk and allow her to tail behind them—rather, he would often speak to her and ask her opinion. The first time this happened, Olivia was almost overcome with awe and shock.

"What say you, Miss Drummond?" asked Mr. Darcy.

It was clear Olivia had been caught by surprise. Elizabeth herself wondered what was happening, for she had not thought that Mr. Darcy had truly even noticed Olivia's presence, so focused he had been on Elizabeth.

"I-I beg your pardon?" Olivia managed to stammer in reply.

"Miss Bennet and I were just speaking of my offer to teach her—and you—to ride, and I suggested we begin next week. Will that be agreeable to you?"

It was quite clear that Olivia had expected to be ignored. For her part, Elizabeth was not certain if she should be pleased that Mr. Darcy was thoughtful enough to include her young cousin in their conversation or annoyed that her suitor's attention was not fixed solely on her.

"I am happy with whatever Lizzy decides," said Olivia, after a long pause.

"Have you much experience?" asked Mr. Darcy, his tone soft and kindly, designed to persuade her to speak. "Your cousin informs me that she has some experience, though she will likely need practice before she is proficient."

"I have only ridden once or twice, Mr. Darcy," replied Olivia, the beginning of a shy smile appearing on her face. "I am afraid I will be a much more difficult pupil than my cousin. She is capable of anything; I do not have her courage, I am afraid."

"You do not deserve such censure, and I do not deserve such praise," said Elizabeth, wondering why her cheeks suddenly felt so hot. "You are capable of a great deal, Olivia. You simply need to have confidence in your own abilities."

Mr. Darcy watched her gravely. "In fact, I am of the same mind as you, Miss Drummond, though I also agree with Miss Bennet. She *is* capable of anything to which she puts her mind." He turned to Olivia. "But I am certain that you are capable of great fortitude as well."

Elizabeth was certain they presented an amusing picture at that moment, for the man had prompted them both to blush at the same time!

"Come, Miss Bennet," said Mr. Darcy, gathering her hand again and placing it on the crook of his arm, "let us speak more of this. Then you may help me as to the best method of teaching your cousin."

"I have already owned to a lack of skill, Mr. Darcy," said Elizabeth. "I cannot think how *I* would be in a position to advise you."

"I am sure you are more than adequate, Miss Bennet," replied Mr. Darcy. "You *are*, after all, capable of accomplishing anything, are you not?"

The teasing glint in the man's eye forced Elizabeth to re-evaluate him. He was laughing at her.

"For shame, Mr. Darcy!" cried Elizabeth. "You are aware what you just caused, and you *meant* to do it!"

"I was reasonably assured of my ability with Miss Drummond," replied Mr. Darcy. Elizabeth was annoyed to see that the man was positively smug. "*You*, however, are a much more difficult target, for your self-assurance is much more developed than Miss Drummond's."

This was not the only time Mr. Darcy spoke with Olivia during their walks. He would often speak with her, asking her opinion on various matters, asking her more of herself, of the things that brought her pleasure and little details of her life. Often, he also asked about Elizabeth, though Elizabeth wondered why the man did not ask her himself. Then she realized that he enjoyed hearing about her from another's perspective. It prompted Elizabeth to ask of Georgiana for stories of her brother, but though Georgiana readily obliged, nothing she said could induce the man to respond with anything other than an indulgent smile.

The exception to this was, of course, his cousin, Colonel Fitzwilliam. It was apparent the men had been close for many years, and that there was much undiscovered information to be gleaned from his stories of his cousin. It was also fortunate that Colonel Fitzwilliam was more than happy to oblige Elizabeth's curiosity.

"You may not believe it, Miss Bennet," said Colonel Fitzwilliam when Elizabeth asked, "but my cousin was actually quite a mischievous scamp when we were young."

"Please, Fitzwilliam, I do not believe that Miss Bennet and Miss Drummond are interested in hearing of our escapades."

"If she did not wish to hear, she would not have asked," replied Colonel Fitzwilliam, and from his smirk Elizabeth knew he had no intention of obliging his cousin by remaining silent.

"Of course, I wish to hear," said Elizabeth, directing a teasing grin at Mr. Darcy. At her side, Olivia and Georgiana watched with amusement, entirely unsuccessful in controlling their laughter.

"You should know, Miss Bennet," said Mr. Darcy with an entirely straight face, "that Fitzwilliam is not to be trusted. He is known throughout our family as the bearer of tall tales. We have all learned to ignore him completely."

"I'll have you know that I *never* embellish," replied Colonel Fitzwilliam with mock affront. Then he turned and winked at Georgiana and Olivia, prompting their giggles yet again. "At least not *much*, and never when it comes to stories of my youth. If I say that Darcy and I let loose a grass snake in the dining room of Pemberley, it is nothing more than the absolute truth!"

Mr. Darcy only glared at his cousin. "That was at *your* instigation. You were the one to receive a thrashing, as I recall."

"That is only because you managed to convince your father that you were not involved. I seem to remember you actually catching the creature and then running when I began to put the plan into motion."

"We should ask James the next time he is here. He would remember the sequence of events as I do."

Colonel Fitzwilliam only waved his hand. "You cannot trust James. After all, he is naught but a viscount."

"Snakes?" squeaked Olivia. Elizabeth had watched as she had listened to the conversation with growing horror, her eyes darting around the room nervously.

"Ah, you should not worry, Miss Drummond," replied Colonel Fitzwilliam with evident amusement. "Darcy has long outgrown such childish pranks. Why, I do not believe he has brought a snake into the house in the last several weeks at least!"

Eyes round with fright, Olivia stared at him. Mr. Darcy, however, took pity on her, and after impaling his cousin with a withering glance, said: "Fitzwilliam is, as always, fond of a good yarn, Miss Drummond. There are no snakes in the house."

"But do not go out by the lake," said Georgiana with a laugh. "They seem to consider it their own particular domain."

"You have snakes at Pemberley?" asked Olivia, aghast at what she was hearing.

"I believe snakes are found in many places," said Elizabeth, grasping Olivia's hand and squeezing it fondly. "Grass snakes are not harmful and will be more afraid of you than you are of them. Surely you have seen snakes about your father's estate."

"I have," said Olivia, shuddering uncontrollably. "But I always give them a wide berth."

"Then you must do the same here." Elizabeth turned back to Colonel Fitzwilliam—who was grinning at them as if he had never seen anything more diverting—and said: "For shame, sir. Bringing snakes into a house where young ladies might be frightened by them."

But far from being repentant, Colonel Fitzwilliam only laughed. "As I recall, the thrashing I received was made worse by the fact that it was Darcy's mother who discovered it. I never saw anyone jump so high as she did."

"And you telling her that snakes could climb the chair she stood on to escape it did not help matters either," said Mr. Darcy.

They all burst into laughter, even Olivia, though hers was hesitant. Colonel Fitzwilliam, however, was thoughtful. "I had forgotten about that. I thought Aunt Darcy would expire right on the spot."

Colonel Fitzwilliam then turned to Elizabeth. "I must own to being intrigued, Miss Bennet. Our own Georgiana is quite used to snakes, though she will not go near them, and Miss Drummond appears to have quite the fear of them. But you do not seem to share your cousin's aversion."

"Snakes are *not* pleasant creatures, I will own," said Elizabeth. "But I do not fear them, though I have a healthy respect for adders and other dangerous creatures. But the choice to use a snake of all things was quite poorly done, Colonel Fitzwilliam. Quite clumsy, in fact."

It was clear Colonel Fitzwilliam did not quite know what to make of her assertion, but he gamely continued. "Your comments become more fascinating all the time. Do you have another opinion of the proper way to execute a good prank?"

"I have always preferred frogs, sir," replied Elizabeth with exaggerated unconcern. "Frogs are even slipperier than snakes, and though ladies view them with revulsion, they do not fear for their lives."

Colonel Fitzwilliam stared at her for a moment and then burst out laughing. "I suppose you have experience in the matter of using frogs for pranks?"

"Of course, I do, sir. My father, having had no sons, found in me a kindred spirit, and he taught me the proper way to do things. I would never do anything so uncouth as to use a snake."

They all joined into the laughter, and Colonel Fitzwilliam laughed the hardest. "Then I shall be guided by you, should I have the opportunity to prank again. I had not known you had such an expert in your sitting-room, Darcy. Miss Bennet is a lady of uncommon talents, it would seem."

"Well do I know it," replied Mr. Darcy. His gaze upon her never wavered, and Elizabeth felt her cheeks heat up in response. But rather than make her feel uncomfortable, his scrutiny made Elizabeth feel warm all over. He nodded to her, and they both turned their attentions back to the conversation.

By the time the date for the return engagement to dinner at Pemberley arrived, Miss Drummond and Miss Bennet were regular visitors to Pemberley. When they led their family into the room, Darcy noted that they did so with ease and no pretensions, which was further exhibited by their easy greetings to Fitzwilliam and Georgiana. It was so unlike Bingley's sister, thought Darcy as he bowed to the Drummonds and welcomed them to his home—though Miss Bingley was not so crass as to act as if she were already Pemberley's mistress, her coveting gaze would roam over every detail, every item in the room, and then her gaze would alight on him. Darcy would then be able to detect the cunning, feel the determination to have him at all costs. She was one of the few people in the world he forced himself to abide—others of her ilk were firmly rejected. It was only due to his friendship with Bingley that he associated with her at all.

"Pemberley is quite a grand estate," said Edward Drummond as they sat down to visit while waiting for dinner to be announced. "I have heard my father speak of it, but I could not have imagined that it was this fine."

It was clear that the young man was awed, not avaricious. "My sister and I only think of it as our home, Mr. Drummond. I would be happy if you would feel welcome, not overwhelmed."

"Thank you, Mr. Darcy," said the young man, relaxing a little. "I can see that it is a beloved home in every detail."

"That is the work of my dearly departed mother. Relatively little has been changed since she was mistress of this house."

The conversation proceeded from there, Drummond sharing his memories of Darcy's mother and father, and Darcy responding with some of his own observations. Such subjects could not continue without becoming maudlin, and after a few moments they began to speak of other things.

When they were called in to dinner a few moments later, Darcy escorted Mrs. Drummond as the highest ranking female guest, but though the woman took his arm with no comment other than a quietly spoken thanks, he rather wished that he had been able to escort Miss Bennet to the table. He was fortunate in that the table was small enough that he could look down and see her smiling countenance, witness the sparkling joy in her eyes as she conversed with his sister and his cousin, though he was not close enough to speak with her himself. Mrs. Drummond was not voluble herself, so Darcy's main source of conversation was Miss Drummond, who he found to be a pleasant girl, though not utterly captivating like her elder cousin.

When dinner had been eaten and the appropriate thanks and compliments had been given, Georgiana led the ladies from the dining room, leaving Darcy alone with the other three men. There were no important conversations or questions regarding his intentions like there had been during the dinner at Kingsdown, and Darcy was happy to enjoy pleasant conversation until it was time to rejoin the ladies.

When they arrived back in the music room, to where Georgiana had led them after dinner, it was to see the younger ladies in earnest conversation, the subject of which was the upcoming event the Darcys had decided to host.

"You shall be the hostess for your first event, Georgiana," Miss Bennet was saying as the gentlemen entered the room. "What a fine thing, indeed!"

As was her wont, Georgiana looked at her friend, her timidity shining through the additional confidence she had gained of late. "Mistress? I am not sure . . ."

"Nonsense, my dear," said Miss Bennet, grasping her hand. "You are your brother's sister, and even if you are not out, there is nothing wrong with acting as the hostess in your own home."

"Especially as this will be an informal event," added Darcy. He turned his attention to Miss Bennet. "I see Georgiana has informed you of our tentative plans."

"She did, and I believe it is a marvelous plan, sir." Miss Bennet turned her expressive gaze on Edward. "You enjoy fishing, do you not? The gentlemen are to fish, while the ladies are to enjoy games on Pemberley's lawn."

"I would very much like to attend," said Edward. He paused and looked at Mr. Darcy apologetically. "If I can be spared from the farm, of course."

"We will wait for your invitation, Mr. Darcy," said Drummond. "I am certain Edward would be happy to attend."

Edward beamed at his father's words and looked at him with gratitude, while Mrs. Drummond rolled her eyes in exasperation. She did not say anything, however, for which Darcy was grateful.

"Perhaps you and Miss Olivia would like to assist my sister in the preparations?" asked Darcy of Miss Bennet.

"I am certain what she has planned will be lovely, sir," said Miss Bennet.

"Oh, I would so appreciate your assistance, Lizzy!" exclaimed Georgiana, her expression pleading. "I have never planned anything like this before."

"And you suppose I have?" asked Miss Bennet, fixing an arch look on his sister. "I believe you have me mistaken for someone with years of experience."

"Of course not," replied Georgiana. "But I believe you may do anything you set out to do."

"Do you not remember our conversation already, Miss Bennet?" asked Fitzwilliam in a teasing tone.

"Very well," said Miss Bennet. "I would be happy to help."

"And perhaps you would also agree to perform a duet with me?" asked Georgiana slyly. "I could play while you sing?"

Darcy was shocked. Never would he have thought his sister would suggest that she perform in front of an audience. In fact, the last time she had been in Miss Bingley's company, the lady had attempted to induce her to do so, but Georgiana had resisted, other than a short piece. Miss Bingley had praised it to the heavens, nonetheless, never seeing how uncomfortable she made Georgiana with such excessive flattery.

"Very well," said Miss Bennet with a laugh. She turned an amused eye on Darcy. "I can see that your sister likes to have her own way, sir."

Could this be a trait common to your family?"

"I believe we all prefer to have our way, Miss Bennet."

"Perhaps. But there is something about you Darcys which seems to ensure you have *yours* more often than most others."

"That may be so. But as long as my sister is happy—and I believe your generosity in assisting her makes her happy—I can have no cause to repine. I am quite eager to make certain Georgiana is as happy as I can make her."

"You make me quite envious, sir. I have no brothers to look after my interests in such a manner."

"I cannot imagine your family is any less adept at ensuring your pleasure, Miss Bennet."

For a moment, there was no one else in the room other than they two. Darcy fancied that he could hear something in her voice which suggested that she too wished for the protection of another and to guard his heart in return. Darcy's feelings were becoming clearer every moment. He was becoming convinced that should he know of the sublimity of her love, it would make his life complete. Then she would be convinced to agree to obtain the protection of a *lover and husband* and no longer repine that absence of a brother.

"Then let us choose a piece of music," said Georgiana, breaking the spell.

She rose and led Miss Bennet to the pianoforte, Miss Drummond following close behind. Darcy was left to watch them as they spoke among themselves, laughing and discussing the merits of this piece or that. Darcy found himself insensible to the rest of those in the room, so focused was he on the person of Miss Elizabeth Bennet. Something significant had passed between them, and Darcy contemplated it much of the remaining time their guests were present.

As the planned event at Pemberley was only a few days away, Elizabeth and Olivia found themselves at Pemberley often, ostensibly assisting Georgiana in her preparations for her guests, but in reality, they only provided moral support—Georgiana had matters well in hand. In addition, they spent some time practicing the song they had chosen, and though Elizabeth had no fear of Georgiana's abilities, the practice assured Elizabeth that she would not embarrass herself before the guests.

As always, Elizabeth was happy to see her friend as often as their schedule at Kingsdown would allow. Her uncle, eager as he was to see them accepted by their neighbors, ensured that they were able to attend Georgiana as often as possible and, seeing that his eldest son was becoming more interested in society, cheerfully shouldered his son's work so that he could also experience more freedom.

Perhaps the most surprising development, however, was the men sent by Mr. Darcy to ease her uncle's burden. These men were, Elizabeth discovered, young men whose fathers farmed Pemberley's land, but were largely idle due to an abundance of available labor. Mr. Drummond had, predictably, in Elizabeth's opinion, protested that he had no need of Mr. Darcy's charity, but a discussion between the two men had resulted in his acceptance and the lessening of his burdens. Elizabeth was happy for her uncle, knowing how hard he worked. She also admired Mr. Darcy for his compassion and kindness. The gentleman was rising in her estimation.

And so it happened that Elizabeth and Olivia were at Pemberley the day before the event, once again practicing for the following day. They had just completed the song when the door to the music room opened and the housekeeper, Mrs. Reynolds, entered the room, leading Lady Emily.

Lady Emily started as the housekeeper announced her, but she quickly recovered and stepped forward to greet them all. "Miss Darcy, Miss Bennet, Miss Drummond. I am sorry for intruding."

"You are always welcome, Lady Emily," said Georgiana. "Please sit with us. I shall ring for tea."

Lady Emily smiled and did as she was bid. While Georgiana was attending to a request for tea, Lady Emily turned her attention to Elizabeth and Olivia. "I am sorry, Miss Bennet, but I did not expect to find you here today."

Feeling a little hesitant, considering her impression of Lady Emily's state of mind the last time they had met, Elizabeth nevertheless answered. "Miss Darcy is quickly becoming a dear friend."

"Oh, Lizzy!" exclaimed Georgiana, as she approached. "You do have a gift for understatement. Miss Drummond, Miss Bennet, and I have become the best of friends."

"Is that so?" asked the lady, seemingly interested in her assertion. "I was not aware you had become so intimate. I am also surprised I have not seen you here before."

"I am very happy that we have," replied Georgiana. "I suppose it *is* a surprise, considering how often they visit. A pair of better friends one could not find. In fact, Elizabeth was just practicing a duet we have planned for tomorrow. I am so happy that she has consented to perform with me, for it gives me so much confidence in my abilities."

"I hope that someday I am able to perform like Lizzy and Georgiana," said Olivia. "I have only been practicing for a short time."

"I am certain you will be a delightful performer," said Lady Emily, sharing a smile with the girl. "You simply require a little confidence. And, of course, lots of practice!"

Olivia beamed, no doubt as much due to *who* had praised her as what had been said. As for Lady Emily, though she had just complimented Olivia, her smile soon faded from her face and she watched the interaction. As was usual with her, Elizabeth could not quite make out whether the woman was pleased with what she was seeing, or if she viewed them all with severity and disapproval. They spoke for some little time, Lady Emily and Georgiana—surprisingly—carrying the conversation while Olivia inserted a few opinions on occasion. Elizabeth observed them, saying little herself, wondering at the woman's behavior.

They had been situated in this attitude for only a few moments when the gentlemen entered the room, Mr. Darcy following Colonel Fitzwilliam. They greeted the company pleasantly and joined them, and Elizabeth was surprised to see Colonel Fitzwilliam sit close to Lady Emily, though Mr. Darcy's approach to Elizabeth was nothing out of the ordinary.

"Miss Bennet," said he as he bowed and sat close by, "I am happy Fitzwilliam and I returned before you and your cousin departed."

"Come, Mr. Darcy," replied Elizabeth, slipping into her teasing without thought, "one might have thought you were eager to see me."

Mr. Darcy grinned. "If I was not quite so transparent, I might have thought you were adept at reading my intentions."

Before Elizabeth could reply with another teasing reply, she caught sight of Lady Emily, who was watching them, and though she was as inscrutable as usual, Elizabeth thought she notice a hardening around the woman's mouth and an iciness in her gaze.

It was fortunate that Mr. Darcy did not notice her sudden silence, for Elizabeth did not wish to explain what she saw, especially when she did not know for certain she had seen anything at all. She did her best to respond to Mr. Darcy's conversation with her usual liveliness, and she thought she must have been successful, for he gave no indication of sensing anything amiss. But Elizabeth's mind was quite divided, for though Colonel Fitzwilliam seemed to be paying rather close attention to Lady Emily, the lady's eyes seemed to be firmly fixed on Elizabeth and Mr. Darcy. And for the first time, she wondered if the lady was looking on them with a friendly eye.

CHAPTER XVII

*T*he deliberations which dominated Elizabeth's mind during the visit to the Darcys' continued with her throughout the evening at Kingsdown and again the next day before they were to return to Pemberley. She attempted to distract herself with the doings of the estate, but inevitably her mind would return to the mystery.

In all fairness to Lady Emily, Elizabeth was not certain of what her eyes were telling her, and even if she was correct in detecting the woman's disapproval, there was more than one explanation of why. It was possible that Lady Emily admired Mr. Darcy and was offended that she, a woman from a different neighborhood, had come into their lives and stolen the attention of the most eligible man. It was uncomfortably like Miss Russell and her ilk, but it *was* possible.

But Lady Emily's behavior in all other ways seemed to give a lie to that assumption. Lady Emily never, in Elizabeth's sight, behaved as if she admired Mr. Darcy. She was polite but distant, and there was nothing which suggested esteem or possessiveness. In fact, Elizabeth could not tell that Lady Emily behaved any differently with Mr. Darcy than she did with Colonel Fitzwilliam.

The more she thought about it, the more she realized that continuing to obsess about it was doing no good. Even if Lady Emily *was* expecting Mr. Darcy's attention, the fact was that Elizabeth was the one who was receiving it. There was nothing the woman could do, but attempt to redirect him, which Elizabeth thought was as likely as the sun not rising the following morning. Either that or she could attempt a compromise, a thought which made Elizabeth shake her head. She could not imagine the woman engineering such a situation—it was completely ludicrous. Thus, Elizabeth put it out of her mind.

When Elizabeth and Olivia, in Edward's company, arrived at Pemberley that day, they were welcomed by their hosts and led into the house. There were already several guests in attendance, and additional guests continued to arrive for some time after. In all, the Darcys had invited approximately twenty people, about half of whom were ladies, half gentlemen, and among their number were included not only Elizabeth's new circle of friends and Lady Emily, but also Misses Russell and Campbell. Elizabeth would prefer not to be forced to endure their presence, but she was not about to tell her hosts whom they could invite, and she had no desire to inform them of what had happened with the two ladies. Their greetings were given perfunctorily, which suited Elizabeth, as hers were no friendlier.

Soon, when all the guests were gathered, the Darcys led them from the interior of the estate out toward the lake, where the fishing rods and tackle awaited the gentlemen and games of different sorts were gathered for the ladies.

"Lizzy!" exclaimed Georgiana as they stepped outside. "Might I claim you as a partner for horseshoes? I am certain you must be very skilled at the game."

"And why do you think that?" asked Elizabeth, entertained by her friend's enthusiasm. "I might be the worst player you have ever seen."

"Yes, indeed, she is correct," said Miss Russell. Georgiana and Elizabeth turned as one to see the woman approaching with Miss Campbell in tow. "Perhaps you should partner with me, instead."

"Perhaps we could play against you," said Georgiana, completely missing the disdain in Miss Russell's voice. "You and Miss Campbell could partner against Lizzy and I."

Though frustrated by Georgiana's insistence on pairing with Elizabeth, Miss Russell readily agreed, seconded by Miss Campbell. The ladies took their places in front of the stake and grasped their horseshoes, two each, and proceeded to play. Miss Campbell, who threw first, completely missed the target by several feet, showing that she, at least, had rarely played.

"I understand that you quite fancy yourself a friend of Miss Bennet," said Miss Russell as Elizabeth was taking her position. Elizabeth, who expected something like this, shook her head with exasperation, wishing that the woman would not involve Georgiana in this dispute.

"Oh, we certainly *are* good friends," replied Georgiana with unmistakable enthusiasm. "Very good friends, in fact. Lizzy has been ever so kind to me, and I simply adore Olivia too."

"And so soon after Miss Bennet's arrival!" cried Miss Russell as Elizabeth threw her horseshoe, missing the target, but coming much closer than Miss Campbell's had been.

"The length of time is not relevant, Miss Russell," said Georgiana as Miss Russell stepped forward to take her first throw. "Elizabeth is genuine and friendly, and I felt like I knew her for months within days of meeting her."

The perturbation of spirit Miss Russell obviously felt was reflected in her poor toss, which sailed far beyond the target, almost hitting Fiona where she stood observing the game. She exchanged a glance with Elizabeth, and they both rolled their eyes as one, almost descending into giggles at the sight of the same reaction in the other.

"I am certain you did, Miss Darcy," said Miss Russell. "There are some who project an ease of conversation and effortless friendship wherever they go, and I do not doubt they are adept at capturing others' attention. I dare say Miss Bennet is counted among their number."

Georgiana took her place at the line and hefted her horseshoe, her toss flying through the air and coming to rest within inches of the stake, though it did not actually strike it.

"Your assessment may be quite true, Miss Russell. Indeed, I cannot imagine anyone not being immediately charmed by Miss Bennet's manners, for they are as engaging as she is remarkable."

She stepped back from the line to allow Miss Campbell to step forward for her second toss. The woman threw a look at her companion, one of warning, Elizabeth thought, but Miss Russell either did not see it, or she completely ignored it, so intent was she on making her point.

"There is much to be said for acquaintances from your own district whom you have known all your life. I am happy to extend the further hand of friendship with you. Perhaps if you have others of your own station upon whom to rely, you will not feel the need to befriend those of whom you have no actual knowledge."

Miss Campbell's throw went far wide of the mark, and she grimaced, though Elizabeth was not certain if it was due to her unskilled throw, or because of Miss Russell's continuing determination to make a fool of herself. Not wishing to belabor this already interminable game any longer, Elizabeth stepped to the line and made her toss, which went wide of her earlier throw. As long as the game finished quickly, Elizabeth would be happy.

"I am quite happy to be your friend, Miss Russell," said Georgiana as the other woman stepped up for her throw. "But it does not follow that I cannot also be Miss Bennet's friend. Indeed, I doubt there is anything which could induce me to give up her friendship, for we have become as close as sisters."

It was with tolerable composure that Miss Russell took her next shot, throwing the horseshoe to within a few inches of the stake. She nodded with satisfaction and turned to Georgiana. "I am very happy to mentor you, Miss Darcy. In the future, I would recommend you take care in bestowing your friendship. You have your reputation to uphold, after all, and it would not do to allow the infatuation of the moment to compromise your future prospects."

Without saying a word, Georgiana stepped forward and, after swinging her arm a few times to gauge the distance and the force of her throw, she proceeded with the toss. The horseshoe, glittering in the light of the sun, flew in a perfect arc, to clang against the stake and spin around it once before it spun to the ground, still circling the stake.

"That was a marvelous throw, my dear Georgiana!" exclaimed Miss Russell. "You are truly skilled." Then Miss Russell stepped forward, throwing an insolent glance at Elizabeth. "I hope to hear from you later today, as I have heard that your talent on the pianoforte is exquisite. It is a gift we share in common!"

"That is gratifying to hear," replied Georgiana. Elizabeth was shocked for she could detect a wryness in Georgiana's voice the likes of which she had not heard before. "Elizabeth and I will perform a duet today, and though my skill at the pianoforte is, I hope, adequate, you shall hear the voice of an angel. Miss Bennet almost brought me to tears several times as we were practicing it."

The smile ran away from Miss Russell's face as new evidence of their intimacy was almost thrown in her face. But Miss Darcy was not finished and not about to allow Miss Russell to respond.

"As for the character of those new to the neighborhood, I am quite satisfied with what I have learned." Georgiana's countenance became positively frosty. "Furthermore, I am convinced that my brother also approves, for he thinks as I do. Your concern is admirable, but completely unwarranted."

It was a clear dismissal and a warning not to speak in such a way again, and Elizabeth could not be prouder of Georgiana's intrepidity and fortitude. Miss Russell gaped at her for several moments, anger descending over her. Elizabeth was certain the woman was about to say something impolitic when Miss Campbell touched her arm in warning, proving that of the pair, she was by far the more rational. Miss Russell subsided, though not without a glare at Elizabeth. She turned back to Georgiana and attempted a sickly sort of smile.

"I see you are intent upon it, and I salute your courage. Not all are willing to give consequence to others of a different station."

Unfortunately, Miss Campbell had not been completely successful in deflecting her friend's rashness, and Georgiana returned a brittle look in response.

"Come now, Miss Russell—we are all of the same station here. Perhaps there are differences in fortune and situation, but we are all daughters of gentlemen. The only one among us who might be considered of a higher sphere is Lady Emily, who is the daughter of an earl."

"Of course," said Miss Russell. Then she curtseyed and moved away in the company of Miss Campbell. Elizabeth did not miss the whispered conversation between them and the fact that Miss Campbell appeared to be admonishing the other woman.

"I do not believe I have ever encountered such insolence," said Georgiana, though she did a creditable job of refraining from glaring at Miss Russell's retreating back. "She is naught but the daughter of a man whose estate yields less than three thousand a year!"

"As am I, if you recall," replied Elizabeth gently.

"That is what I mean! Even if she has inherited a further five thousand from an uncle, it does not allow her to act like the daughter of a duke. She has no reason to consider herself above you, when you are her superior in every way that matters."

"No, it does not," replied Elizabeth, ignoring Georgiana's praise. "But, unfortunately, there are many of her ilk among society, and there is little to be done about it."

Georgiana snorted. "I never knew that *she* was one of them, though I have met others before."

Elizabeth and Georgiana exchanged a glance and burst into laughter—Elizabeth was certain they had both been thinking of Miss Bingley, but they both possessed enough manners to resist censuring

192 ~ Jann Rowland

the woman when she was not present.

"If she cannot behave herself, I will ensure she is not invited to Pemberley again."

"I cannot say I would repine the loss of her company."

"I am sure you will not," said Georgiana. "*She* may not realize it, but I would much prefer to have *you* as a sister."

With those last words and a wink at Elizabeth, Georgiana turned and walked away, calling out to some of the other ladies, inquiring after their comfort and offering to engage them in some of the activities.

"More trouble with Hillary?" asked a voice close behind.

Turning, Elizabeth greeted Clara. "The same as before." Elizabeth stifled a laugh. "She was put in her place, though, from a most unexpected quarter."

"It seems our Georgiana is benefiting by the acquaintance with your more outspoken character. I do not know her well, but she has always seemed more than a little shy to me—almost mousey."

"She is maturing rapidly," replied Elizabeth. "I have no doubt that Mr. Darcy will be required to use a large stick to keep the gentlemen away before long."

With a laugh, Clara pulled Elizabeth away to engage in one of the other games scattered about the lawn. Elizabeth went willingly—there were so many agreeable young ladies that she did not mean to exasperate herself over one who was not.

Though Darcy was superficially hosting the men of the party as they fished in Pemberley's stream, the feminine laughter emanating from the lawn no more than a stone's throw away caught his attention frequently, and he found himself gazing over toward the house more often than not. Though the voices were indistinct and Miss Bennet's could not be differentiated from them, he thought it likely that hers was among them, so joyful and open in company was she. Though he wished to go there, he knew his duty and attempted to focus on it.

"If you do not stop looking toward the house," said his cousin in a soft voice, "everyone will know you cannot keep your eyes off Miss Bennet."

"I believe that much is already evident," said Smallwood, a gentleman of an estate of some size said from where he stood by their side. "The area is abuzz with the pretty young miss from the south having captured the elusive Mr. Darcy's attention."

"Abuzz?" asked Darcy, turning a frown on Smallwood.

"Perhaps Smallwood overstates the matter," interjected Fordham, another man of the area. "But it is well known that you have been calling on her."

"And why should he not?" asked Smallwood. "I have heard it said that she has not much dowry, but one would give much to be able to gaze into those eyes of hers every day."

Fordham shrugged. "She is a little too impertinent for my taste, though I will grant you that she has pretty eyes."

"Some men prefer an impertinent wife," said Fitzwilliam. "Better that than a dull wife who will bore you into a stupor on a daily basis."

"I believe a little placidity would go a long way in a wife," said Wainwright, joining the conversation.

"I prefer the term 'lively' to 'impertinent,'" said Darcy. "There is nothing improper about Miss Bennet, and impertinence suggests less than proper behavior. As for placidity, I prefer a woman with whom I can speak on an equal level. Placid might be fine, but I expect it would become tedious quite quickly."

"Your preference for *liveliness* is quite clear, Darcy," said Smallwood, laughing. "And I commend you for seeing her worth and snapping her up so quickly. Had I been more observant when she came, I might have given you some competition."

Darcy turned to look at Smallwood, wondering if there was a hidden meaning in his words.

The man only laughed. "You have nothing to fear from me. Anyone who has seen you in company these past weeks knows which way the wind blows. I would not attempt to turn her from you, even if I possessed the lure of a larger income. And whereas you are independent with an estate of your own, any lady I court will be required to contend with my father for a goodly number of years yet."

"Only be certain that it *is* your person which has attracted her and not your pocketbook," said Wainwright. "A young lady in her reputed circumstances would give much to be the recipient of the addresses of a man of your situation."

"I doubt Miss Bennet is such a woman," said Smallwood.

"It is difficult to tell," rejoined Fordham. "A woman may hide much in her heart while in pursuit of a man's fortune."

"Anyone who has the pleasure of Miss Bennet's acquaintance can have no thoughts of her being mercenary," averred Fitzwilliam.

"Such beliefs are a recipe for disaster," said Fordham.

"She is not a fortune hunter," said Darcy, feeling obliged to defend her, though he was not certain she wished her private matters to be bandied about. "I have it on good authority that she refused a very eligible offer only last autumn."

"Better and better," said Smallwood.

"Were you given the reason for her actions?" asked Wainwright.

"And is your authority anyone other than the woman herself?" added Fordham.

"She claimed incompatibility with the man," said Darcy. "As he is the heir to her father's entailed estate—a distant cousin, as I understand—it was an eligible match. And yes, my friend, Bingley, who is married to her elder sister, has corroborated the story."

"Refused her father's heir?" asked Wainwright with a frown. "I might think her a simpleton were I not already acquainted with her."

"I also understand this man is our Aunt Catherine's parson," said Fitzwilliam. "Given what I know of the obsequious oafs with whom she prefers to surround herself, I cannot think Miss Bennet anything other than completely sensible!"

There was a murmuring of commiseration for Fitzwilliam's words. The previous year, Lady Catherine and her daughter had descended on Pemberley without warning, and as Darcy had been hosting many of the gentlemen of the nearby estates at the time—and all three had been present—they had all had a firsthand taste of what the woman was like.

"If this is true, then she is everything she appears to be," said Wainwright, albeit a little grudgingly. "In your situation, you need not care whether she has a healthy dowry, unlike some of this company."

"Some will wonder at your decision, if she brings so little to a marriage."

The content of the conversation amused Darcy, and he was not afraid to show it. "That presupposes the thought of society's disapprobation will give me a moment's hesitation."

"Perhaps you do not care," said Fordham. "But what of your wife? She will need some familiarity with London society, some acceptance from them or her time in London will be difficult."

"My mother will support her," declared Fitzwilliam. "She will be so happy that Darcy is marrying—especially considering my single state and that of my brother—she will not care from whence the girl came, as long as she is a gentleman's daughter."

"I doubt many will care to disparage her to her face anyway," said Darcy with a nod of thanks to his cousin. "I have some standing in society, and the Darcy name is not to be trifled with."

"You are correct, indeed," said Smallwood, clapping Darcy on the back. "I, for one, wish you well in it."

"I am not engaged," replied Darcy, feeling he should pull back on this conversation a little.

"No, but I have little doubt you soon will be," replied Smallwood.

At that moment, a tug on Fordham's line indicated the presence of a fish, and the gentlemen's attention was captured by the struggle between man and beast. Throughout the course of that morning, the gentlemen succeeded in catching several beautiful trout, which were to be sent to the kitchens to be prepared with cook's special recipe and served at a late lunch. Darcy was relieved to have the conversation redirected—if the talk was becoming as prevalent as the others were saying, his honor might soon be engaged, and he had not yet decided.

In the deep recesses of his heart, though, a small sibilant voice whispered to him that he had already made a choice. He was only waiting for his mind to catch up to his heart.

When the gentlemen had finished their sport for the day, they returned to where the ladies were still engaged in their games, and that was when the tenor of the event changed a little. Since Darcy had begun to pay attention to Miss Bennet, he had noticed a lessening of the notice he received from the ladies of the neighborhood. Until that day he had not truly thought of the matter, though now he wondered if he were witless to have missed it. Or perhaps he had just been too absorbed in the charms of Miss Bennet. Either way, it had been some time since he had been forced to fend off the attentions of all but the most determined flirts. Unfortunately, Miss Russell was one of those.

"Mr. Darcy," said she, showing him a coquettish smile as he approached with the other men. "Shall you play against me at bowls?"

The sight of his sister, who was standing not far away, an expression of annoyance with Miss Russell etched upon her face, caught him off guard. But Georgiana only noted his look and looked skyward before turning her attention back to Miss Drummond, with whom she was speaking.

"Of course, Miss Russell," his sense of polite behavior overcoming his aversion for her company. "Please allow me a moment to see to the disposition of the fish we have caught, and I will be at your disposal."

The girl beamed at him and Darcy stepped away to speak with a nearby footman. When he returned, they stood nearby to where a game was already in progress, and Darcy noted with an admiring glance that Miss Bennet was quite skilled. She was playing against Miss Grant, whose character Darcy had always thought Miss Bennet resembled.

"It seems you have caught many fish, Mr. Darcy," said Miss Russell, bringing his attention back to her. "I knew you would. I do not know any other man who would have done as well as you."

It was an outrageous statement, though nothing Darcy had not heard before. He gave her some answer, though he was so intent upon Miss Bennet that he was not even certain what he said, but he was certain it was as silly as her own comment had been. Miss Russell did not seem to notice his incivility, for she continued to chatter on. Darcy heard little of what she said, though he was certain that it consisted of mostly praises of himself and his sister.

She was not unattractive, Darcy decided, looking absently between Miss Russell and Miss Bennet. Miss Russell was taller, but she was willowy, not unlike Georgiana's form, whereas Miss Bennet was more diminutive and while still slender, was possessed of a curvier figure. The ladies' looks were also quite different, as Miss Russell had reddish hair framing fair and pleasant, though not precisely pretty, features. On the other hand, Miss Bennet was exquisite, with mahogany locks, and while she was also fair, her skin was slightly darkened by the time she spent in the sun, lending her the aura of health and vigor.

Where they differed was in their eyes. Miss Russell's were light blue, but there was nothing extraordinary in them, in Darcy's opinion. By contrast, Miss Bennet's were dark and mysterious, gloriously framed by long, luscious lashes. Her eyes also changed with her moods, sparkling like a spring brook when amused, or flashing like the strike of lightning when offended. They were her true claim to beauty, and Darcy could not imagine anyone finding them anything other than entrancing.

At length, the game before them finished, and Darcy and Miss Russell stepped forward to play their own. Darcy graciously motioned for her to throw the jack, resisting the urge to sigh and roll his eyes when she giggled and obliged him. The jack rolled to a stop several feet away, and Darcy threw his first ball, stood aside while she threw hers, and then threw his second. It was when she stepped forward to throw her second that she began to speak again and the conversation became objectionable.

"I must say, Mr. Darcy," said she as she stepped up to the line and hefted her ball, "I was surprised at the society those of the neighborhood have been keeping lately."

Darcy regarded her. Clearly the woman thought she was being clever by not mentioning any names, but it was clear of whom she was speaking.

"I rather think that new additions to society cannot be anything but welcome," replied Darcy as he stepped forward to take his turn. "The presence of beloved friends who are known to us is agreeable, but is there not something admirable to discover in new acquaintances?"

"If those new acquaintances are of estimable characters," said Miss Russell, a hint of annoyance seeping into her voice.

"There is no one who could be considered new in our society who is not of an estimable character, Miss Russell," said Darcy.

As she had thrown, Darcy stepped up to take his final throw, and when he had delivered it, he turned and bowed to her. "Thank you for this game, Miss Russell. If you will excuse me."

Bowing, Darcy turned and walked away toward Miss Bennet, who, noticing his approach, greeted him with pleasure. They began to speak, and though their conversation was about nothing important, Darcy felt that it was the most stimulating in which he had ever participated. But that was the influence of Miss Bennet. She had that talent.

Contrary to the attempts of such women as Miss Russell, Fitzwilliam saw Lady Emily as a true threat to Darcy's happiness and intentions to woo Miss Bennet. Fitzwilliam was aware that if pressed, Darcy would deny any such intention, but his cousin's feelings were as clear to him as if he had taken the time to write them out on a piece of paper. And though Miss Russell simpered and threw herself in his path, hoping to garner his attention, and made veiled—but obvious—disparaging statements concerning *other* ladies whom she deemed her rivals, Darcy handled her with aplomb. But Lady Emily . . . That lady was no less determined to have him for herself, though her methods were different.

That was not quite true, mused Fitzwilliam. Though he was certain Lady Emily was no friend of Darcy's pursuit of Miss Bennet, she did not behave as a woman who wished to steal a man's attentions for herself. Or at least she did not behave like most other ladies of her ilk would. From Fitzwilliam's observations and a few carefully oblique questions he had asked of Darcy, it did not appear like the lady threw herself in his path. Rather, she watched and considered and unless he missed his guess, she plotted. The endeavor to capture a man's eye was usually undertaken by the lady putting herself in his path, drawing attention to herself. But Lady Emily did none of those things—or if she did, she did them so subtly that Darcy did not even recognize them. Even Fitzwilliam, who was watching for them, was hard pressed to identify them.

Still, Fitzwilliam was ever dutiful and determined to see that his cousin was not interrupted, and he played his part to the best of his abilities. When luncheon was served—consisting of the trout the gentlemen had caught, accompanied by various fruits of the season and a selection of salads—Darcy was obliged to escort Lady Emily into the room as the highest-ranking lady present. It was then that Fitzwilliam saw the first indication of her interest in him.

"I thank you for inviting me today, Mr. Darcy," said she as they entered the dining room.

"You are welcome, Lady Emily. Our families have been friends for many years. I would not wish to exclude you."

The woman turned a level look on him, but Darcy, who was now seated at the head of the table, was already distracted by the sight of Miss Bennet, who was seated several places down the table next to Smallwood. Fitzwilliam chuckled into his hand—there would be no trouble from Smallwood, he was certain, regardless of the man's stated interest in Miss Bennet. Darcy did not know it himself, but Smallwood had always been intimidated by his tall and imposing cousin.

"I would hope that you would include me in your invitation because you wish for my company, not due to any obligation for our family's association."

It appeared Darcy was caught off guard by her words, though Fitzwilliam did not know how he could have been otherwise, given the lack of attention directed at the lady. "Of course not, Lady Emily. My sister and I are quite happy to see you at any time. You bring much to our company."

"I am happy to hear it, Mr. Darcy. I hope that our intimacy continues to grow, for Pemberley has always been our closest neighbor."

"I agree," replied Darcy, though his mind was clearly already back on Miss Bennet.

A spasm of annoyance flashed over her face, though it was gone in an instant. "It seems we are dinner partners, Mr. Darcy. What shall we discuss?"

Thus began the game of cat and mouse, though in this instance the mouse was not even aware of the cat stalking him. Lady Emily would make some attempt at conversation, and though it was obviously not Darcy's intention to slight his guest, he would often respond with naught but banal comments, quite different from the result Lady Emily intended. Fitzwilliam, seated as he was to Darcy's right, saw that his eyes did not often stray from the person of Miss Bennet. Before long, it was evident that Lady Emily was becoming more than a little perturbed.

"I understand that your father has purchased a new stallion for his breeding program," said Fitzwilliam, drawing the lady's attention to himself. "Shall you tell me about it?"

Lady Emily turned a long level look at Fitzwilliam, and for a moment he thought she would rebuff him. It might be considered an inappropriate topic of conversation, but Fitzwilliam knew that she was as proud of the horses her estate produced as was her father, and after a quick glance at Mr. Darcy, noting his continued observation of Miss Bennet, she sighed and responded. They discussed the subject until the end of the meal, and Fitzwilliam found that he quite enjoyed it, though Lady Emily's enjoyment was debatable. If Darcy had not been so intent upon Miss Bennet, he could have done a lot worse than to marry her, for she was intelligent and would be the mother of a future earl.

After luncheon, the company retired to the music room where they were treated to the talents of several ladies' efforts on the pianoforte, not the least of which was Georgiana playing while Miss Bennet sang. Fitzwilliam did not consider himself a good judge of talent, but she sang like an angel, he thought, and he could find no flaws in her performance. Darcy was apparently of the same mind, for Fitzwilliam did not think his eyes left her the whole time she sang.

"What is your purpose in deflecting me, Colonel Fitzwilliam?"

The quietly spoken words were almost an accusation, though Lady Emily betrayed no outward emotion. Her eyes, however, flashed as he turned to respond to her.

"Deflecting you?" asked Fitzwilliam. "I have no notion of your meaning."

"I believe you do. You were careful in keeping me from conversing with Mr. Darcy at luncheon."

"Actually, I believe Darcy was managing that task rather splendidly himself."

Her brows furrowed, which indicated to Fitzwilliam that she would have been scowling had they not been in company.

"I do wonder," said Fitzwilliam, speaking before the lady could respond. "Why do you dislike Miss Bennet?"

"I do not dislike Miss Bennet. She is an interesting sort of woman, though perhaps possessing a level impertinence usual for one of her status."

Fitzwilliam laughed quietly, prompting a level look from the lady.

"Darcy prefers to refer to her manners as lively."

Lady Emily's eyes darted to Miss Bennet's face and then just as quickly back to Fitzwilliam. "That is one way to describe her."

"Let me be clear, Lady Emily," said Fitzwilliam, "Darcy will not be coerced. I am certain you are intelligent enough to see where his affections lie. I would ask you to give up this doomed pursuit of him."

Her gaze never wavered. "What makes you think that I wish to pursue him?"

"You have been quite transparent."

A hint of exasperation crossed her features and was as quickly extinguished. "You have no need to fear, Colonel Fitzwilliam. I am no danger to Miss Bennet."

And Lady Emily turned away to listen to the rest of the song. But Fitzwilliam did not miss the glances she threw between Miss Bennet and Darcy, nor did he miss the expression of absolute adoration on Darcy's face as he watched her sing. Neither did Lady Emily, and though her countenance was as closed as ever, her displeasure was clear.

Lady Emily would require continued scrutiny.

When the time had come to depart, Elizabeth noted how Mr. Darcy approached her and bowed, offering his arm with a warm smile. "Shall I walk you to the carriage, Miss Bennet?"

"Thank you, sir," replied Elizabeth, resting her hand on his arm, though with no more pressure than a feather.

"I wished to thank you for the assistance you rendered to my sister in preparation for this day."

"She had no need of it," replied Miss Bennet. "She had everything quite well in hand. But what assistance I was able to provide, I was happy to do it."

"I think you underestimate your own contributions." Mr. Darcy paused and seemed to be thinking intently on something. At length, his eyes once again found hers. "You would not be aware of it, Miss Bennet, but this is the first time since my mother died that we have hosted any sort of event at Pemberley." He smiled. "Of course, my family has visited and I have hosted the gentlemen for hunting or fishing, but an event to which we have invited those of the neighborhood at large has not been held at Pemberley in over fifteen years."

"No, I was not aware," was all Elizabeth could think to say.

"Thus, you can understand why Georgiana was more than a little nervous, wishing to make a good impression on our neighbors. I have the fullest confidence in her abilities, but that little extra encouragement you provided, even if you did nothing more, was worth more than any encouragement *I* could have given her. And for that I thank you."

They had reached the waiting coach, and Darcy stopped and turned to look at her. "So, again, I say thank you, Miss Bennet. I appreciate, more than I can say, the friendship you and Miss Drummond have offered my sister. I am so grateful you have come into our lives."

"Thank you for your returning friendship," said Elizabeth. "It is partly due to your actions that I have felt so welcome in Derbyshire."

"Until next time, then."

Mr. Darcy extended his hand and helped her up and soon they were off. But Elizabeth looked back at him, noting his constant gaze at her as the carriage moved away. And she could not help but think that his regard was now clear as a bright summer day.

Chapter XVIII

The next few days saw a return to a more sedate pace in the neighborhood. Elizabeth did not mind the change—she was at home in society and enjoyed it, but if the situation demanded that she stay closer to home, she was happy to do that as well. There was much to do at Kingsdown, and she set to it with the rest of the family with a will. The fields had been sown and the green shoots of their crops were showing themselves, a promise of what was certain to be a fine autumn bounty. And though the men Mr. Darcy had sent continued to provide their assistance, there was still much work to be done on the estate and around the house.

Mr. Darcy was still a regular visitor in those days and it was becoming clearer on every visit that his attentions were becoming ever more ardent. He continued to walk with her around the pathways of the estate with the faithful Olivia following behind, giving them time and space to become more truly acquainted. Elizabeth esteemed him greatly by this time, and though she was not certain he would ever be induced to propose to her, she was coming to understand that she would welcome a proposal should he choose to make it.

The situation at Kingsdown was much the same as it ever was. Mr. Drummond was industrious and kind, his wife disapproving, the elder children hopeful, and the younger, growing and learning. The two younger boys still tried the adults' patience with their antics, while Leah continued to become closer to Elizabeth, charming her with her innocence and childish intelligence.

"I have mentioned this before, Lizzy," said her uncle one morning after breakfast, "but I am quite happy you have come to Derbyshire."

"I am happy you invited me," replied Elizabeth.

Her uncle directed a long look at her. "You were not in the best of spirits when you came. Can I assume, from what I am seeing now, that you have recovered?"

Elizabeth smiled. "I have, Uncle. Many of the things weighing down on my mind when I was in Hertfordshire have faded to the back of my mind, and though I know they still exist, I believe I have learned to accept them. And the welcome I have received—not the least of all from you, Olivia, and Leah—has restored my equanimity."

"I am glad to hear it. It is clear to me that I made the right choice, for your ability to move in society has assisted my daughter to be more confident herself. I do not know what the future holds for Olivia, but I am hopeful she will find contentment and joy in life, however she chooses to live it."

"Olivia is a sweet girl. I am happy to have come to know her."

In this manner Elizabeth was gratified that her uncle thought so well of her, and she assured him that she had no thought whatsoever of leaving Derbyshire at present. That would be required eventually, but for now she was content to stay where she was happy.

The other member of the family who seemed to have grown was Edward. He had struck her as taciturn and angry when she had come, but his outlook on life seemed to have matured and he now went about his tasks with a more hopeful demeanor, his cheerful expression infectious, making them all glad. Elizabeth thought it was, to a large extent, due to the friendship offered by Mr. Darcy and Colonel Fitzwilliam, and she could not be more grateful to them.

"I believe I told you once before that I had some thought of whether we might be compatible," said he to Elizabeth one day when the family was together after dinner. His words were quietly spoken, but his countenance was no less earnest for that fact.

"You did, but we agreed it was for the best we did not pursue such thoughts."

"We did," replied Edward. "I have been thinking on it for some time now, and I have concluded that I have erred greatly, Cousin. It has become clear to me that you will make an excellent wife."

He must have noticed a hint of the consternation Elizabeth felt upon hearing him speak in such a way, for he laughed and shook his head. "My intention was not to make you uncomfortable or to press my suit."

"Then what do you mean by it?"

"Only to inform you that I think much more highly of you now than I did when you came." The wry smile with which he favored her was returned by Elizabeth, though with less enthusiasm. "I have come to see you as a rare gem, Cousin, but I shall not attempt to gain your affections. It is more than clear where they lie, and I know any chance I had has vanished."

Elizabeth could not help the warmth which spread over her cheeks.

"Do not attempt to deny it," said Edward, waving away any protests she had yet to make. "I cannot imagine anyone who would make you a better husband than Darcy, and for his part, it seems to me he could search high and low and not find a woman better suited to him than you. I just wished to say that I believe you will do well together, should he choose to offer for you, which I am almost certain he will. I find that I am happy with the prospect that you will stay close by, for I have come to enjoy your company."

"Thank you, Edward," replied Elizabeth. "I have also grown fond of you and your entire family. I could not be happier that I have come into Derbyshire."

It was a conversation she could not have imagined having with Edward, so discontented had he appeared when she had come. It was the wonders of the friendship of a pair of good men which made it so, Elizabeth was certain, and she was certain to thank Mr. Darcy once again the next day he came.

But Mr. Darcy had a more serious subject he wished to discuss. Elizabeth supposed she should not have been surprised—she had been in Derbyshire for some time, and as he had become an intimate of her family, some mention of her situation in Hertfordshire must have reached his ears. When he brought the subject up with Elizabeth, he did so with the greatest gentleness, for which she was grateful, as she was not quite certain how she felt about his news.

As was their custom, they had stepped out of the house to walk, but they confined their steps to the lawn, eschewing any of the longer paths due to Mr. Darcy's statement that he was unable to stay long that day.

"You did not need to come if you are occupied with other matters," said Elizabeth.

Mr. Darcy smiled. "And give up a chance to converse with you, Miss Bennet?"

Elizabeth blushed but Mr. Darcy only chuckled. "I will own that the lure of your society is part of the reason which has drawn me hither, but it is not the only reason. In fact, I bring tidings which will be of interest to you."

"Oh?" asked Elizabeth. "I hope everything is well at Pemberley."

"Yes, we are all well. The news I bring has to do with *your* family. You see, I have been corresponding with Bingley, and we confirmed that he and his family will visit Pemberley."

The situation with Jane had been pushed to the back of Elizabeth's mind of a purpose, as she had not wished to make herself unhappy. As a result, she had not even thought of Jane's visit to the neighborhood in recent weeks and found herself unable to immediately reply to Mr. Darcy's words.

"It is possible that I am incorrect," replied Mr. Darcy. The concerned look he directed at her suggested that his jovial tone was affected to pull her mind from gloomy thoughts. "Bingley's handwriting is perhaps the worst I have ever seen—he leaves out words and blots the rest, and sometimes I wonder if I should have some key to decipher his code."

Elizabeth laughed. "I have seen Mr. Bingley's hand before, Mr. Darcy, and I am quite in agreement."

"He claims it is due to the rapidity of his thoughts and their eagerness to escape his mind in favor of being expressed on the paper, but I suspect it is only because he cannot take the trouble to attempt neatness."

"I do not disagree, Mr. Darcy," said Elizabeth. It was a faithful portrayal of Jane's husband, and it only endeared him to her all that much more. He was a delightful man, his worth not lessened by his inability to write in a way that anyone could read it.

"They will come in early July, though the exact date has not yet been determined," said Mr. Darcy, his pleased smile suggesting satisfaction with the effort to redirect her melancholy, "and though the length of their stay has not yet been determined, I believe they are likely to remain for at least six weeks."

Elizabeth digested this bit of news, wondering how she should feel about the imminent arrival of her sister. Though she had hope that Jane would be changed from the distant woman she had become, in her heart she knew it was unlikely. Even if her letters from her family had not referenced the continued distance between Netherfield and Longbourn, the feelings of Elizabeth's heart would have given lie to the hope.

"And the Hursts?" said Elizabeth, realizing she had been silent for some time and sensing Mr. Darcy's concern. "Are you to be gratified in your desire to avoid their society?"

With a laugh, Mr. Darcy said: "Indeed, we are to be blessed. Bingley has informed me that his eldest sister is with child and will not be traveling for some time, so we are spared their company, though I had not planned to invite them regardless."

"Indeed?" said Elizabeth. "There was some talk of it when I was last in Hertfordshire. I am happy for them, though I do wonder what either Mr. or Mrs. Hurst will do with a child."

Mr. Darcy nodded. "They have been married for some years and neither seemed to repine the lack. If it is a son, I do not doubt that Hurst will set about corrupting him as soon as he is able to toddle about on his own feet. If a girl, I doubt he will give her any real notice, though I am not certain Mrs. Hurst will be much better."

Though unable to withhold her laughter, Elizabeth still attempted to glare at her companion. "It is very unkind of you to say so, sir. I am certain that Mr. Hurst wishes for an heir, as would any man, and perhaps Mrs. Hurst will surprise you."

"Perhaps she will," said Mr. Darcy, though his expression suggested he did not hold much hope, and his tone was not at all apologetic. "Regardless, I am happy to escape their company, so the news is welcome.

"I hope you will be happy to see your family again, Miss Bennet. I know Bingley is quite eager to join us, and I suspect he wishes to look for an estate in the area while he is here."

"And I will be happy to see him again," replied Elizabeth, choosing to push thoughts of Jane residing in the neighborhood to the side. "I am not surprised he wishes to purchase an estate in a different county. My mother can be . . . Let us just say that she considers it her duty to advise Jane on all matters, and I do not doubt that Mr. Bingley is eager to put some distance between himself and Longbourn."

"A typical mother, then, unable to let go of her eldest child."

"Perhaps."

"And your sister?" Mr. Darcy stopped walking and turned to face her. "Though I cannot imagine you eager to be in company with Miss Bingley again, I hope the prospect of meeting your sister again brings you pleasure."

Elizabeth thought her pause was the briefest in nature, but the worry which creased Mr. Darcy's forehead showed that he had noticed it. Elizabeth was uncertain what to say. She knew he had some knowledge, but she thought he was not acquainted with the true facts of the situation. To demure and proclaim herself eager to see Jane would be seen through, and the lie would be evident when she arrived. So, Elizabeth responded in the only way she knew how.

"My sister . . . Let us only say that marriage seems to have altered her. I *will* be happy to see her, but I know not if that sentiment will be returned."

For a moment Elizabeth thought Mr. Darcy would inquire further into the situation between Elizabeth and her sister. But though a question appeared to be on the tip of his tongue and his lips parted, he thought better of it and allowed it to remain unspoken. Instead, he gathered his thoughts and then said:

"Then I hope matters have changed, for I understand that you were once very close."

"I hope so too, Mr. Darcy," said Elizabeth, though she wondered if he could even hear her.

They continued to walk for some time after, though mostly in silence, both lost in their respective thoughts. Elizabeth was consumed with thoughts of her sister and her upcoming arrival, but that did not mean she was unaware of the silence between them. Although she had often observed that two people with little to say to each other often led to an uncomfortable situation, there was no such feeling that day with Mr. Darcy. On the contrary, she recognized the man's solid presence, akin to the feeling of the warmth of the sunshine on her face or a good book and a crackling fire on a cold winter day. And she was comforted by it.

When Mr. Darcy excused himself to leave, Elizabeth stayed in the gardens for some time thinking. In truth, she could understand very little of her thoughts herself, for they seemed to jump in some random pattern from Jane to Mr. Darcy to her time in Derbyshire to what she left behind in Hertfordshire and to various other subjects. Olivia, dear girl that she was, sensed that Elizabeth was out of sorts and needed to think, and she absented herself, presumably returning to the house. Elizabeth was grateful for her forbearance, for she knew that she was not good company in her present state.

But one cannot stay in such an attitude for long without it adversely affecting one's state of mind. It was a little later when Elizabeth first began feeling the initial hints of a headache, no doubt brought on by the combination of her jumbled thoughts and the bright sunshine which continued to shine down on her. She reached up and rubbed her temples, wincing at the pain. It would not be long, she thought, before it would be as a hammer beating on her head in time with the beating of her heart.

With a sigh, Elizabeth rose to her feet, intending to return to her room and lie down for a time, only to be arrested by the sight of Mrs. Drummond watching her. The woman's customary sneer was present, as was the barely concealed hostility with which she usually greeted the world. But there was something else in her manner which Elizabeth could not quite define, but which suggested that her silence of the past weeks was about to be broken.

"You have been sitting in that attitude for too long," said the woman. "Perhaps it would be best to see to your tasks for the day."

"I completed those before Mr. Darcy came," replied Elizabeth, not wishing to provoke an argument with her aunt. "If you will excuse me, I believe I will lie down for a time, for I have a headache."

"So typical of a gentlewoman," said Mrs. Drummond, almost spitting the last word out like it was an offensive taste in her mouth. "I told you when you came here that we had little room for your airs and fainting spells. This is a farm and you will do as you are asked or be sent home."

"I have done everything that has been asked of me without complaint," said Elizabeth. Wishing to avoid an argument was one thing, but Elizabeth was not about to put up with the woman's slander. "I know of nothing of which you have cause to criticize."

"I criticize your coming here. I did not wish for your presence."

"I am sorry to hear that, Aunt. I have good relations with every other member of your family; I wish we could put this animosity behind us and behave with civility, if not friendship."

"Your friendship is not required."

The venom with which the woman spoke informed Elizabeth that a bridge would not be built that day. The only help for the situation would be to absent herself immediately, which Elizabeth determined to do.

"If you will excuse me," said she, and dropping into a shallow curtsey, she made to depart.

"It seems your pursuit of Mr. Darcy is bearing fruit." The contempt in Mrs. Drummond's voice startled Elizabeth, so virulent was it. "I believe you are now secure in the hope that he will propose to you."

"I am no such thing. Mr. Darcy is a very good man, and should he propose to me, I would be honored, indeed."

"He is nothing more than a proud rich man."

"It is clear you do not know him if you think that."

Mrs. Drummond took no notice of Elizabeth's short tone. "I know enough of his ilk to know what kind of man he is. But I expect he will disappoint you in the end. Gentlemen of his station do not deign to pay attention to you women of *yours* for any reason but one. The question is, whether you will reject him when he asks."

"Do not say anything else!" cried Elizabeth. "I will listen to no more of your poison!"

"It seems the truth is a difficult thing to face."

Elizabeth would not deign to give such a ridiculous statement the benefit of her attention.

"I would ask what this unreasoning enmity you have for me and my family is, if I expected a sensible response."

"I have every reason to despise your family." The words were spoken quietly and without the force of the woman's usual pronouncements, though Elizabeth was certain it was not because of a lack of confidence in the rightness of her position, whatever that was. Certain she was on the cusp of learning of her aunt's long-held grudge, Elizabeth pressed her further.

"I cannot imagine what it could possibly be. We have not seen you in many years, so if you have hated us, you have hated us from afar. Is that not more than a little childish?"

"You do not know anything!" rasped Mrs. Drummond, her affront robbing her voice of its usual strident tones. "Of course, you would not understand—considering the creature who gave you birth."

"My mother?" asked Elizabeth, wondering what the woman was going on about. "What has she to do with anything?"

"She has *everything* to do with it." Mrs. Drummond walked away, her shoulders heaving, drawing great breaths of air which seemed to do nothing to calm her.

"You are aware of your mother's origins, are you not," said Mrs. Drummond at length, though the strain in her voice made her difficult to understand. "I would not put it past her to try to pass herself off as a gentlewoman, little though she deserves the appellation."

"I am aware of my mother's background," replied Elizabeth. "Her father was the solicitor in Meryton, he the grandson of a gentleman whose estate was further to the north."

"Then you are aware she is no gentlewoman."

"I know she was not born to that estate," replied Elizabeth carefully. "But she is *now*, given she has married a gentleman."

Mrs. Drummond's snort told Elizabeth exactly what the woman thought of that assertion. "In name, perhaps. But she will never be anything other than an uncouth, loud, social climber. Your manners are somewhat acceptable, so I do not doubt you have seen the deficiencies in your mother."

Though Elizabeth had most certainly seen her mother's faults, she was not about to confess them to this woman. "You object to my mother."

"Of course, I do!" cried Mrs. Drummond, spinning to face Elizabeth. "I knew her when she was a young woman, knew her as she entered society and set about attempting to entrap my brother. I always knew her for what she was, knew what kind of a grasping, artful shrew she was. I cannot imagine she has improved over the years.

"But my brother, enamored as he was by her *beauty* and *liveliness,* allowed himself to be caught by the woman, forever tainting our line. The Bennets have never been high on society's ladder, but we have long been the masters of Longbourn, long been a respectable family. Your father threw that away in a moment of infatuation, when he married his empty-headed solicitor's daughter. How I despised him for being so weak!"

"But what can it be to you?" asked Elizabeth. "It was *his* choice. What possible effect could it have on *you?*"

"It seems you are not nearly so intelligent as you want others to think," spat Mrs. Drummond. "Do you not see that his marrying so unsuitable a woman tainted me? I was painted by the same brush as his strumpet of a wife. I had a suitor—a good man who, though he was not high in society himself, was a gentleman of some means and property. But when your father married the daughter of a country solicitor, my suitor decided that he did not wish to gain such connections and ended our courtship. It was your father's fault, brought on by the fact that he could not control himself when confronted by a pretty face with no more intelligence than a sow!"

A harsh bark of laughter escaped the woman's lips. "As a result, I was forced to settle for your uncle, a man who is a gentleman in name only. In raising herself, your mother has managed to lower *me* to this state, a state which I despise. I was meant to be a gentlewoman. I was born to be a gentlewoman! But now I am nothing more than the wife of a farmer, forced to be mother to his brats. And this estate, so erroneously named 'Kingsdown'—it is a bitter irony that such a low shell of an estate should have such a grandiose name. If it was my choice, I would rename it to something much more appropriate to indicate the squalor in which we live!"

Mrs. Drummond's breast was heaving by the time she finished her diatribe, and Elizabeth could not have been more shocked. Yes, her mother was not born a gentlewoman and Elizabeth had often been embarrassed by her ways, but she had never thought such vitriol would exist. Her mother was improper at times, but she was nothing like Mrs. Drummond described.

"Perhaps what you say is true, Aunt," said Elizabeth, her own frame shaking with anger at this unjustified attack. "But consider this: my mother, for all her faults and limitations, is a good woman who loves her children and does the best to fill a role she was not born to. By contrast, you are a hard, unfeeling woman who torments the children to whom she gave birth and a husband who is a good and industrious man, no matter what is his position in life. You have become nothing but a bitter, twisted, shell of a woman, one who blames her misfortunes in life on another. I think it would be best if you looked at yourself in the mirror and asked the person you see there why you are so discontented in your life. If you are honest with yourself, I am certain you will not like the answer."

Elizabeth turned and marched away from the woman, wishing to end this confrontation. She expected Mrs. Drummond to follow her, to take offense to Elizabeth's words and demand she leave Kingsdown immediately. But she appeared rooted to the spot where Elizabeth had left her.

A few moments later Elizabeth reached the sanctuary of her room, and she stormed inside, leaving the outside world behind. She sat herself on her bed, brooding about the scene that had just played out, her disgust with her aunt in the forefront of her mind. But as she thought, her mind kept going back to the bitter woman, and the more she thought of it, the more she wondered if she had been told everything. Surely her aunt's account of the matter alone was not one to be believed explicitly. There must be something she was unwilling to say or did not consider in her bitterness.

Elizabeth knew she could approach her uncle and he would explain to her as best he could, but she knew her uncle suffered because of his wife's behavior and did not wish to add to his burdens. There was one other to whom she could turn, though. And Elizabeth intended to ask him.

Thus decided, Elizabeth went to the small desk in the room and began to compose a letter.

CHAPTER XIX

$\mathcal{I}$f it was not thoughts of Lady Emily's behavior, it was reflections of Mrs. Drummond's words which dominated Elizabeth's contemplations. While Elizabeth had not seen much of Lady Emily in recent days, Mrs. Drummond was, of course, a constant presence. She said little to Elizabeth, though her eyes often followed Elizabeth's movements, and Elizabeth could not determine what the woman was thinking. But her manners betrayed a hesitant quality, an uncertainty which had not been there before. Elizabeth could not imagine her aunt would suddenly become a loving, happy woman due to nothing more than Elizabeth's admonishments, but she hoped that at least she might be less eager to criticize.

Of her aunt's assertions Elizabeth was not able to gain any true perspective. At the very least, she thought Aunt Drummond *believed* what she said to be the literal truth. But Elizabeth had long known that truth and perception are sometimes strangers, and in this instance, she thought there must be more to the story; Aunt Drummond's words concerning a suitor choosing to throw her over because of whom her brother married did not sound right. It was possible—perhaps even probable—had the Bennets been higher in society, but lower level families were usually much less concerned about rank, especially when the undesirable relation would be nothing more than a sister-in-law.

As for her mother, Elizabeth was forced to own that most of what Mrs. Drummond said was true, though not to the degree she had asserted. The embarrassment of being the daughter to Maggie Bennet when she spoke without thinking or brazenly put her daughters forward to any single man had told Elizabeth many years ago that her mother's manners were not fashionable. But Elizabeth's opinion of her mother was also correct—she loved her daughters and wanted the best for them, and though Elizabeth could not agree with her idea of what was best, she had never been in doubt of her mother's love.

In the end, Elizabeth decided to force the matter from her mind, for though she was still confused, there was no hope of relief at present. Her father, though he was a negligent correspondent, would respond eventually, and Elizabeth hoped he would address the matter with at least a partial explanation.

There was a little more society in those days—often consisting of teas or lunches, but nothing on the scale of the games at Pemberley or the picnic at Teasdale Manor—but it was more than enough to satisfy Elizabeth. She and Olivia were often at Pemberley, and at times Georgiana would return their visits by coming to Kingsdown. Mr. Darcy was ever present, and his attentions seemed to grow more ardent as time progressed. It was becoming clear that it was not a matter of whether he would offer for her, but when. Elizabeth often found herself breathless with anticipation, only to remind herself to wait and be patient. He was a deliberate and careful man, and he would propose at a time of his own choosing, when he was convinced of not only *his* feelings, but *hers*.

It was evident that whatever Lady Emily's intentions were, she had not given up on them, for she often appeared at Pemberley when Elizabeth and Olivia were there—and likely when they were not, Elizabeth suspected, though Georgiana did not confirm that suspicion. But her purpose was still opaque, and she remained as maddeningly inscrutable as ever.

"Hello, Lady Emily," said Georgiana cheerfully when she called on them one day. "How nice it is to see you again."

Elizabeth smiled fondly at her young friend—Georgiana was growing in confidence by leaps and bounds, and Elizabeth could not be happier for her. She also seemed to be completely unaware of the possibility of ulterior motives in Lady Emily's visits, welcoming and conversing with her with the same friendliness she displayed to

Elizabeth or Olivia.

"Miss Darcy," said Lady Emily in response. "Miss Bennet, Miss Drummond. How do you do today?"

"Very well," replied Elizabeth, which Olivia echoed.

The ladies settled down to speak, and for a time all was well, and Elizabeth had noticed a pattern in this. When they first came together, Lady Emily was amiable and pleasant, conversing with them all with little animation, but with perfect civility. That day was no different.

"How is your practice of the new sonata, Miss Darcy?" asked Lady Emily, turning the subject to one in which they could all participate.

"I am making progress," said Georgiana. "There are a few passages which still give me a little trouble, but I am improving. Lizzy plays it beautifully, though."

"Not very beautifully at all!" exclaimed Elizabeth. "You know you are much more technically proficient than I. I can muddle my way through, but your playing is superior."

"It seems to me this conversation is one which has been repeated often," said Lady Emily. Though she did not often display her emotions on her face, on this occasion her mirth was unmistakable.

"Yes, it is," said Olivia. "They constantly argue about which of them is the more accomplished."

"We do not argue, Olivia, for there is nothing to dispute," said Elizabeth. "It is clear Georgiana has a greater technical proficiency than I possess."

"And you play with greater feeling," rejoined Georgiana.

They laughed together, Lady Emily watching with the indulgence of an older sister. "Perhaps you should allow me to judge. If you both play the same sonata, I might be able to give some advice or lay to rest your dispute altogether."

"It is not a dispute!" said Elizabeth and Georgiana together. Then they giggled at their own silliness and were joined by the other two ladies.

Thereafter they moved to the pianoforte, and there they enjoyed themselves without reserve. Lady Emily confirmed Elizabeth's opinion that Georgiana was the greater proficient, but she stubbornly agreed with Georgiana that Elizabeth played with greater feeling. When Lady Emily took her own turn, it became quickly clear that *she* was the one who took both qualities and mixed them together. Her playing truly was exquisite and clearly closer to what Georgiana was aspiring in her own.

"I wonder that we have not heard you play more often, Lady

Emily," said Elizabeth as the final notes of the sonata faded away. "I have rarely heard someone with as much talent as you."

"I simply have more experience," replied Lady Emily, though she appeared truly pleased with the praise. "I believe you all have the same potential, should you dedicate yourselves to it."

"And that is where I tend to fail!" exclaimed Elizabeth. "There are far too many activities which bring me pleasure to sit and do scales in front of the pianoforte all day long."

"Only an hour or two is required, Lizzy," replied Georgiana. "I believe your playing has improved since you came to Derbyshire, so perhaps you are finding more opportunity to practice here?"

"I believe I have. But I still will never be your equal."

The door opened and in walked the two gentlemen in residence, with Edward, who had accompanied them that day, in tow. "Ladies," said Mr. Darcy with a bow, mimicked by his cousin and friend. "How do you do today?"

And that was when the transformation of Lady Emily's manners usually took place. When the gentlemen entered the room, the lady seemed to have little time to speak to the other women, choosing instead to focus her attention on the approaching men. But though Elizabeth thought that Edward had developed a hint of infatuation for her, and Colonel Fitzwilliam looked at her as if he was privy to some joke, Mr. Darcy's attention was fixed on Elizabeth as usual when in her company. Elizabeth was gratified by it, though she was concerned at the way Lady Emily's contentment would erode.

The ladies removed from the pianoforte and sat on the sofas nearby with the gentlemen, and for a time all was well. The conversation was carried by the more vocal of those present—meaning Elizabeth, Colonel Fitzwilliam, and Olivia, to a certain extent—but all were able to express their opinions and contribute. The largest change in Lady Emily's demeanor came when the activity changed.

"Shall we not all walk in the gardens?" asked Georgiana. "It is such a fine day—I believe we would all benefit from the exercise."

Elizabeth, to whom this last comment was directed, laughed. "I shall certainly not dispute your words. If everyone agrees, I would be happy to go as well."

It was decided and they all rose to follow their hosts through the house and out through the back doors into the garden. Pemberley's gardens were as fine as anything Elizabeth had ever seen. There was a hedge maze, though it was not very large, and delightful pathways filled with flowers of all kinds, a lovely rose garden which had been the pride and joy of Lady Anne Darcy, and even a few topiaries. But it was also not too large, and much of the park had been left to its original wildness, a circumstance which Elizabeth appreciated greatly. The hands of man could never compete with the wonders of nature, in her opinion.

When they stepped out, Elizabeth hung back, walking with Georgiana and Olivia, with Edward watching over them with indulgent pleasure. Ahead of them, Elizabeth could see Mr. Darcy escorting Lady Emily with Colonel Fitzwilliam at her other side. The partners were a little fluid, as the walkers changed positions as they went, and Mr. Darcy and Georgiana pointed out interesting sights or explained what they knew of certain flowers which bloomed at the sides of the paths.

But while Elizabeth did not walk next to Mr. Darcy for the first part of their excursion, she could often feel his eyes upon her, though as her eyes were on him nearly as much, she supposed they were equal in that regard. The others also saw the same thing, for Elizabeth heard many stifled giggles and knowing looks. But from Lady Emily's part, she saw what she took to be a growing exasperation, for though she kept her position beside Mr. Darcy, she could see his eyes often turn to Elizabeth as much as any of the others. And, thus, the transformation took place.

"I also tend to the rose gardens at Teasdale Manor," said she, as they walked. Elizabeth, who at that time was close behind them, could hear every word they spoke.

"And lovely gardens they are," replied Mr. Darcy. "I understand you have added certain additional varieties to your collection."

If it had been any other woman—and certainly Miss Bingley—Elizabeth would have thought her to be preening at the praise. "Yes. My father acquired a cutting from an acquaintance in Shropshire and he brought it back to me. His acquaintance had it from a friend in Cornwall. I was concerned that it might not thrive in our colder climate, but it has grown wonderfully."

"No doubt because you have lovingly tended it," said Mr. Darcy.

Lady Emily nodded graciously, apparently pleased with how the conversation had proceeded. Her complacency was not to last, however, for Mr. Darcy turned and spoke to Elizabeth.

"You have also mentioned the rose garden at your home, Miss Bennet. Do you have many varieties there?"

"We have several," replied Elizabeth, noting as the smile ran away from Lady Emily's face. Mr. Darcy remained oblivious. "Before her marriage, my elder sister often tended to them, though I often helped. Now that we are both gone, I believe our gardener has taken over their primary care. My younger sisters are not interested in botany, you understand."

"Neither is Georgiana," said Mr. Darcy with a laugh.

"I love to look at them, but I have little skill in caring for them," interjected Georgiana.

"You simply need a little practice," replied Lady Emily, Elizabeth thought in an attempt to regain control of the conversation. "If you speak with your gardener, I am certain he would be able to instruct you. I would also be happy to come at any time and share whatever I know with you."

"Thank you, Lady Emily," replied Georgiana. "But I believe for the time being I will content myself with simply admiring them."

"To be honest, I much prefer admiring them myself," said Elizabeth. "It is my sister who is the true gardener of the family, though I assisted her."

At that moment, their positions changed, and had Elizabeth not known better, she might almost have thought it was choreographed. Mr. Darcy dropped back to where Elizabeth was walking, prompting Georgiana and Olivia, with Edward in attendance, to pull back themselves. At the same time, Colonel Fitzwilliam stepped toward Lady Emily and directed her attention to some view down the valley behind the house. And all this happened as if they were actors in an opera, having practiced the steps innumerable times.

"Do you miss your home, Miss Bennet?" asked Mr. Darcy, preventing Elizabeth from considering the situation any further.

"Perhaps a little," replied Elizabeth. "When I left I was quite ready for a change in my life, so I have not repined my time here. But I have longed for my family on occasion, especially my father, with whom I have always been close."

"I believe you have spoken of him at times," said Mr. Darcy. "I understand he is a bibliophile?"

Elizabeth laughed. "Ah, yes, Papa would be miserable without his beloved books. I believe you may have difficulty ejecting him from your library, should he ever see it."

"I am happy to host him at any time."

"You may wish to reconsider that, Mr. Darcy. I was not exaggerating."

The look Mr. Darcy bestowed on her took her breath away, in its tenderness and depth of feeling. "I believe nothing you say will change my mind, Miss Bennet. I am happy when you are here, for you bring such a lightness to our lives and happiness to our hearts. You, your father, and anyone else in your family are welcome at Pemberley at any time."

It could not have been clearer had he stated his love for her. As it was, the look in his eyes, the way he leaned over slightly, speaking directly to her, the caress of his free hand on hers, which rested on his arm—all these things shouted his regard for all to see. And it was clear that no one else in the party missed it.

"What a wonderful place this is!" interrupted a voice.

Though neither Elizabeth nor Darcy had been behaving inappropriately, they jerked apart as if they had been caught in a compromising position, and startled, Elizabeth looked up to see Lady Emily watching them. Though she still put forward the veneer of complacency, her gaze boring into Elizabeth and her slightly bared teeth spoke to her displeasure.

"You have a heavenly estate, Mr. Darcy," continued she, her gaze sliding from Elizabeth to rest upon Mr. Darcy, possessive and determined. "Though my father's estate adjoins it, I believe you have the superior beauty inherent in Pemberley."

"Thank you, Lady Emily," replied Mr. Darcy. "Teasdale Manor— and, indeed, all of the estates in this vicinity—are not devoid of their own beauty."

"Yes, but there is something about Pemberley which defies all description."

"I must agree with Mr. Darcy," interjected Elizabeth. By this time, she was almost amused, though the lady's obvious displeasure tempered it. But such obvious flattery, accompanied by her flirtatious tone was something Elizabeth might almost have expected from Miss Bingley. "Teasdale Manor *is* beautiful. I must also agree that Pemberley is one of the finest estates I have ever seen."

Lady Emily's eyes fell on Elizabeth like a branch falling from a tree, and Elizabeth decided it might be best to simply be silent. Mr. Darcy, however, appeared not to see the woman's annoyance, for he turned back to Elizabeth.

"Your home also has many beauties, I imagine? Bingley has written to me several times about how agreeable he finds the neighborhood."

"Yes, I do find it beautiful," replied Elizabeth, keeping a wary eye on Lady Emily. "But that is not precisely surprising, given it is my home and the place I know best."

"It will not be your home forever," inserted Georgiana, throwing more fuel on the conflagration that was Lady Emily's temper. "I believe I would like you to stay in Derbyshire forever. You once told me you would be happy to do so."

Feeling the heat of Lady Emily's contempt upon her, Elizabeth only forced a smile at the girl and said: "That was said in jest, Georgiana. Though I have come to love Derbyshire and enjoy the company here, I know that eventually I will need to return to my father's home."

"Mayhap you will," said Georgiana. "But I doubt you will be there long."

Then she began to walk again, forging ahead of the rest of the group with Olivia by her side, the two girls giggling between themselves and shooting looks back over their shoulders at Elizabeth and Darcy. Elizabeth was mortified—the girl's words had made her appear mercenary to Lady Emily, a circumstance she wished to avoid at all costs.

Mr. Darcy watched the girls walk away, Edward once again in tow, and he turned a grin on Elizabeth. "It seems my sister has acquired a hint of impertinence in her manner, Miss Bennet. I will own to some surprise, for she has always been shy and hesitant to speak up, even with her family."

"Perhaps it is the company she keeps," said Lady Emily, though in a soft tone.

Colonel Fitzwilliam immediately directed her away, though it appeared like Mr. Darcy did not hear or had ignored her comment, for he looked at Elizabeth, expectation in his gaze and a slight upturn to his lips.

"You agree with Lady Emily?" asked Elizabeth, attempting to determine whether he had noticed the lady's comment.

"I do," replied Mr. Darcy. "She has seen to the core of the situation. Before you and Olivia came into Georgiana's life, she was exactly as I described. Your friendship has been invaluable. I cannot be happier with how you have influenced her."

And there it was. Elizabeth had always known that Mr. Darcy approved of her and appreciated her friendship with his sister, but in that short statement, he had turned Lady Emily's criticism into a compliment.

"As I have said before myself, Mr. Darcy, I do not consider befriending your sister to be a virtue. She is a lovely young woman, and Olivia and I have been fortunate to make her acquaintance."

"Then all have benefited, myself included."

Mr. Darcy took her hand and placed it on his arm, and he began walking after the others. Georgiana, Olivia, and Edward were already some distance ahead of them, and Lady Emily and Colonel Fitzwilliam had gone some distance as well. A glance at Lady Emily's form showed her back stiff and her head high, and though Colonel Fitzwilliam appeared to be speaking to her in an attempt at distraction, Elizabeth doubted it was successful.

They continued walking and Mr. Darcy kept making comments, to which Elizabeth responded, but her mind was not truly on his words. Lady Emily had made her displeasure with his attentions to Elizabeth clear, but it seemed that Mr. Darcy had not truly noted it. She was flattered that he was so firmly fixed upon her that he could not see how Lady Emily tried to insert herself into his notice. But she could not help but think that one day the lady's frustrations would boil over, leading to a scene none of them wished to witness.

Elizabeth thought of pointing it out to Mr. Darcy, but she rejected the notion out of hand. It was not proper to do so, after all, and she had not the slightest notion of how to go about it. Hopefully, even when that explosion occurred, Lady Emily would retain enough of her reason and dignity to avoid making a terrible scene.

CHAPTER XX

Though he supposed he should not find the situation so diverting, in truth Fitzwilliam was enjoying himself immensely. It was a farce, pure and simple, something Shakespeare himself might have designed for a comedy to be presented on stage. Fitzwilliam watched carefully, ready to insert himself at any moment, but the urge to laugh was nigh overpowering at times.

Darcy, for all his keen intellect and power of observation, was utterly ignorant of Lady Emily's efforts in his direction, though the woman had almost thrown her interest in his face. And Lady Emily, for all her own intelligence and superior breeding as the daughter of an earl, had begun to throw flirtatious comments at the man like a common barmaid on the hunt for a man to warm her bed at night. Georgiana and Olivia were oblivious, which Fitzwilliam could only count a blessing; should Georgiana become aware of Lady Emily's designs on her brother, it might induce her to say something she ought not. She was clearly determined to have Miss Bennet as a sister.

It seemed to Fitzwilliam that Miss Bennet was the only one who recognized the situation for what it was, and he could only admire her restraint as Lady Emily's behavior became more overt. Several times he had seen Miss Elizabeth watching Lady Emily, clearly afraid that her composure might be overcome. She did everything she could to defuse any potentially volatile situations, often taking herself out of Darcy's company in order to prevent it, though it was also clear to Fitzwilliam that she desired his presence as much as he desired hers. And Darcy, far from being discouraged from her propensity to seek the society of others, appeared perfectly content to watch her from afar when the occasion demanded it.

So matters continued until a day in which there was again a large gathering of society in the area. There were enough of the younger generation that there were often separate amusements for them alone, apart from their elders. On this particular day, it had been proposed that they visit the ruins of an old roman fort which sat some distance north of Pemberley. Those who were to attend gathered at Pemberley as the closest estate to the ruin and proceeded there in a line of carriages, with several of those attending having brought baskets for a large picnic lunch once they had reached the area.

The departure from Pemberley proceeded without any issue, and soon they had reached their destination. Having visited it before, Fitzwilliam was not much interested in the site—it was little but a small clearing on top of a low hill, foliage surrounding it, a few low walls covered with moss and lichen, slowly being swallowed up by the surrounding forest. A road ran within a few hundred feet of the fort, which was there the carriages stopped, and they alighted, walking the final distance.

Miss Bennet, Fitzwilliam saw, was surrounded by the close friends she had made in Derbyshire, and they chattered gaily as they walked. By contrast, Lady Emily had immediately attached herself to Darcy, reminding Fitzwilliam of Miss Bingley's propensity to clutch his arm as if she never meant to let go. Fitzwilliam kept himself near to Darcy to be of assistance, should it be required.

They stopped in a large open area near the top of the summit, and the baskets were laid down while those present began to explore the ruin. As Fitzwilliam walked with the others, he was privy to their conversation, though he remained attentive and silent. Lady Emily was still attached to Darcy's arm, but they were also close enough to Miss Bennet that they were able to converse easily.

"I will own that I had not expected there to be a Roman ruin in such an out of the way place," said Miss Bennet, her interest and curiosity lighting her face, making her appear uncommonly pretty.

"Though many have tried to explain it, its purpose is unknown," replied Darcy. "It is thought it was the stronghold of some minor lord or something of that nature. There is not much left of it, as much of the stone has been carried away for use in other buildings."

"Is that so?" asked Miss Bennet, her customary archness coming to the fore. "And does some of the stone of this fort reside in the walls of Pemberley?"

Darcy laughed—even while Lady Emily frowned—and said: "No, though that would be a fine thing, indeed, do you not think? In fact, the stone that makes up the walls of Pemberley comes from a quarry some miles to the west."

"I should have known, for the stone does not look at all alike."

"Have you become an expert in rocks?" asked Lady Emily. Though the woman attempted to rein in her annoyance, it was still clear in her tone. Miss Bennet also recognized it.

"I am not, though it is evident that the coloration of the rocks is quite different from Pemberley."

"Come, Mr. Darcy," said Lady Emily, steering Darcy toward the west site of the structure, "shall you not tell me what you know of the history of this place?"

Though Darcy's eyes strayed back to Miss Bennet, he went along. His voice floated back, saying: "You have visited this place before, have you not, Lady Emily? I would have thought you were well acquainted with what is known."

They passed out of earshot and Fitzwilliam debated going after them, but for the moment he decided against it. Darcy did not need him to play nursemaid, though Fitzwilliam wondered at times, given his obtuseness. Fitzwilliam turned back and he caught the eye of Miss Bennet, noting her contemplation of the pair who had just walked away.

"Her actions are not precisely hidden, are they?"

Though a little startled by his observation, Miss Bennet rolled her eyes. "It appears they are to Mr. Darcy."

Fitzwilliam nodded agreeably. "He appears to have a bit of a blind spot, though he is usually adept at seeing this type of behavior. I would not have you worry, however, for he has no interest in her."

"Why should I be concerned?" asked Miss Bennet. "I have no claim on Mr. Darcy."

"Perhaps you have no claim on *Darcy*, but it is clear you have a claim on his attention, for he can hardly turn away, it seems." Miss Bennet blushed and Fitzwilliam gleefully twisted the knife a little further. "And I do not doubt you will soon have a firm claim on Darcy himself, Miss Bennet. And I am convinced he will be happy to be caught."

With a roguish grin, Fitzwilliam stepped away from her, noting the progress of Lady Emily and Darcy as they walked the perimeter of the fort. Fitzwilliam did not think the woman to be the type who would attempt a compromise, and with the rest of the party walking among the ruins, he did not concern himself regardless. Miss Bennet was joined by her friends, and they inspected every inch of the ruin, laughing and talking amongst themselves.

Soon they all gathered near the side of the ruin and baskets and blankets were produced, their lunch spread out before them, and the company set out to partake of it. As so many of their number had contributed to their lunch, there was a wide variety of food, and far more than they could ever eat. For a time, all unpleasantness was forgotten as they ate. In time, however, Lady Emily's displeasure soon made a reappearance, as Darcy and Miss Bennet took the opportunity to sit close together to eat. And as soon as it was eaten, they rose and excused themselves to walk to the far side of the ruin.

Fitzwilliam watched carefully as Lady Emily's eyes followed them, and as soon as she rose herself, Fitzwilliam was by her side, claiming her hand to escort her. The flashing of her eyes and thinness of her lips spoke to her displeasure, but Fitzwilliam did not care for it.

"To what do I owe the pleasure of your company, Colonel Fitzwilliam?" said she when they had stepped sufficiently away from the rest of the company to assure they would not be overheard.

"Does a man require a reason to wish to escort a lovely young lady, other than the desire to bask in the brightness of her company?"

The glare she shot him informed him she was not impressed by his flattery. "If I thought admiration to be the only motive for your interference, I might give credence to your words. But I cannot, for your actions have been too marked to be mistaken."

"And yours have not?" asked Fitzwilliam. His pointed look failed to make her blush; she only appeared to be more exasperated. "Unfortunately, it appears you have not been as blatant as necessary, for the object of your actions has missed your meaning entirely."

Lady Emily's eyes darted to where Darcy and Miss Bennet now stood, speaking earnestly some distance away. A quick glance at the remainder of their party revealed that though some had begun to walk again, having finished eating, several who remained at the blankets were watching the couple and speaking amongst themselves. Georgiana and Miss Drummond were giggling together, no doubt expecting an announcement of an engagement before long.

"It is only a matter of time," replied Lady Emily, her eyes never leaving the couple.

"You may think that, Lady Emily. Perhaps believing it will make it true, though I doubt it very much."

"I have much more to offer him than Miss Bennet does," replied she. Obstinacy, it appeared, was one of her failings.

"You do?" asked Fitzwilliam. "Does Darcy love you, cherish you, bestow every bit of his attention on you as if you were the most important person in the world?"

A glare met his statement. "I am the heir to my father's earldom. Whoever marries me will sire the next earl of Chesterfield, will see his consequence and influence grow. Do you think Mr. Darcy will put love ahead of such considerations?"

"Do you think he will not?" rejoined Fitzwilliam.

When she did not reply, Fitzwilliam continued: "Watch them, Lady Emily. Observe their behavior with each other, without the clouding lens of your own scheming, without any prejudice for her situation, and without any bias, and tell me you do not see a young couple completely devoted to each other. Almost from the first moment of their acquaintance, their regard for each other, their attention for each other, everything in their behavior, and those little signals which I believe they are both ignorant of in themselves have told me how their relationship will end. They are becoming more and more devoted to each other, and there is nothing you or I could ever do to separate them."

For a moment the woman watched them, her brow furrowed and her air pensive, and he thought she was truly taking his words into account. For a moment, Fitzwilliam thought he had reached her, had induced her to give up this doomed pursuit. But the moment did not last long.

"He shows some infatuation with her. But I do not believe he loves her. In the end, he will see the benefits of an alliance with me and come to his senses."

"If you will not be turned from this course, then so be it. Only take care to protect your heart, if you truly have feelings for him, for I do not doubt you will ultimately fail. Darcy has had his share of heartache and sorrow, and he has also endured his share of ladies trying to attach themselves to him. His closest friend, Mr. Bingley, has a sister who has been determined to become Mrs. Darcy, and has not succeeded, though she has tried for more than three years."

"From what I understand of the Bingleys, they are new money," replied Lady Emily. Her words were said as a fact, with no malice or contempt, as so many of her circle might have spoken them. "The situations are completely different."

"Maybe they are. I only mention it as an illustration of my point. Darcy is not a man to be coerced. I believe he has decided that he wants Miss Bennet as a wife, and if he has, he will allow nothing to stand in his way. He deserves his happiness, Lady Emily. Please do nothing to make it harder for him to obtain it."

With those final words, Fitzwilliam turned and walked away. Lady Emily, for her part, stayed where she was, contemplating the couple who had begun to walk the ruin again, with no seeming destination in mind. Fitzwilliam hoped he had done enough. But he could not help but think it would take something more before she would surrender to the inevitable.

The feeling of being on Mr. Darcy's arm, having him point out various locations of interest, the feeling that they two were alone in the world, was sublime. Elizabeth felt all her cares fall away as they walked, Lady Emily and her actions faded to the background as the sound of Mr. Darcy's rich baritone worked its way into her consciousness. It was quite the most wonderful feeling she had ever felt.

They walked along the outside wall of the fort, and Elizabeth took it all in, noting the richness of the soil on which it rested, the verdant greens of the plant life which had sprung up between the stones strewn about the ground, or resting on top of one another. In one location, a hardy tree had taken root among the stones at the base of the wall, pushing them aside in its desire to reach for the sun high above. The dull murmur of the conversation of their party faded into the distance, and the buzz of winging insects took over, accompanied by the rustle of the wind in leaves of the trees overhead.

When they had reached the base of the far wall of the fort, Mr. Darcy turned to Elizabeth, his manner serious, his gaze searching. For a moment he did not speak, and Elizabeth wondered at his hesitance, even as she shied away from the possible explanation for it.

"I did wonder, Miss Bennet," said he at length, "when we were at Pemberley, you spoke of your need to return home. Do you plan to do so soon?"

"It *is* my home, Mr. Darcy," replied Elizabeth gently. "My uncle has been very kind in his invitation, and I have enjoyed the weeks I have spent here, but inevitably my steps must return me to Hertfordshire.

"But I do not think I will return soon. I believe that I am settled here at least until the end of the summer. His original purpose in requesting my visit was to assist Olivia in society, and I believe she grows ever more confident. She will do well, I think, and will not need my constant attendance, though I will be happy to return again in the future."

"It is clear to me," replied Mr. Darcy, "that it is due to your careful guidance that she has become more confident. You have had a great influence on us all, I think, and I believe I am not the only one loath to be deprived of your company."

Elizabeth blushed, but she could not look away from his eyes. They pierced her, staring into her very soul, making all her secrets bare before his searching gaze. And Elizabeth wished to know all *his* secrets in turn, to hold and cherish them, to prop him up in times of need and hardship, and to accept his support in turn. She began to feel lightheaded, almost drunk on the feelings which coursed through her.

"If it were possible for you to stay in Derbyshire, would you take that chance? I know you must long for your family, and I am certain you will see them again often, but I cannot think of your leaving without the greatest distress."

Elizabeth's heart began to pound, the blood to flood through her veins, a rushing sound in her ears. This was the greatest declaration of his regard she had heard yet, and she wondered if it was all nothing more than a dream.

"I believe, Mr. Darcy," said she, speaking in a halting fashion, "that should the opportunity present itself, I would be happy to stay in Derbyshire forever."

Though Elizabeth could hardly believe that she had been so audacious to speak such blatant words, it appeared like her companion was not at all displeased by her declaration. Quite the opposite in fact. Mr. Darcy's eyes positively burned with intensity, and she felt she might be caught in their depths, scorched to cinders and blown away on the wind.

"I am happy to hear it, Miss Bennet," replied he, though in a voice only slightly above a whisper. When he spoke again, his strength appeared to have returned. "If I might impose, Miss Bennet, I think I would like to call on you tomorrow. I believe you and I have important matters of which to speak and our current surroundings, however agreeable, will not be conducive for such."

Elizabeth was required to force herself not to start, for it was the first time she had considered where they were in some time. "You are welcome to call at any time, Mr. Darcy," said she, refusing to look back at the rest of the company, who were almost certainly watching them, enjoying the performance. "I am willing to speak on any subject you deem necessary."

"Thank you, Miss Bennet," said Darcy. He had apparently understood her meaning, despite her rather inelegant way of speaking.

With an excess of tenderness, Mr. Darcy reached out and took her hand once again. He bowed over it, pressing a kiss to its back. Then he placed it in the crook of his arm and began to lead her back to the rest of the company, though Elizabeth's mind could not withstand such mundane discussions when compared with the import of what had just occurred. She desperately wished to return to Kingsdown, there to seclude herself in her room to think about what the morrow would bring. It was fortunate for her that the party soon broke up, and the company made their way back toward the carriages for the return trip to their estates.

"You will join my sister and your cousin in the carriage?" asked Mr. Darcy as they were walking. "Will you stay at Pemberley for a time?"

"I believe Olivia and I should return to Kingsdown," replied Elizabeth. "But I will certainly ride with Georgiana."

"Very well," replied Darcy. "I will ride on ahead with Fitzwilliam, for there is a matter which requires my attention on the estate. I will see you tomorrow."

Elizabeth acquiesced, and they soon reached the road where the carriages waited. Mr. Darcy and his cousin saw them situated, and as he was handing Elizabeth up, she could not refrain from teasing him. "But, Mr. Darcy, should we come across a vicious patch of mud, intent upon devouring us, what shall we do without you to beat it back?"

With a grin, Mr. Darcy replied: "I am certain you would be more than a match for it. But I have ensured there are no other mud monsters to be had, Fitzwilliam and I having chased them all away some days previously."

"Then I will rest easily, knowing that our intrepid knights have cared for us so faithfully."

With a grin and another kiss to her hand, Mr. Darcy departed with Colonel Fitzwilliam in tow, but not before the genial man bowed to her, a grin plastered on his face. After they had departed, there was some delay of the carriages, for one of those in front of them was not quite prepared to depart. It was while they were waiting that they received a visitor at the carriage.

"Miss Bennet," said Lady Emily, appearing in the window, "would you consider riding in my carriage? I would greatly appreciate the opportunity to speak with you."

The wariness she had felt with Lady Emily over the past days materialized in Elizabeth's mind, and though the woman appeared to be pleasant, she thought she detected a hardness in the other woman's eyes. Elizabeth opened her mouth to decline when Georgiana spoke first.

"You may ride with Lady Emily if you like, Elizabeth. Olivia and I will be very well together." Then Georgiana turned to the lady as if the decision had already been made. "We were to go to Pemberley first, before our carriage was to convey Elizabeth and Olivia back to Kingsdown. Will you join us at Pemberley, or take Elizabeth directly to Kingsdown?"

"I am happy to take her directly back to her uncle's house," replied Lady Emily.

"Then it is settled," replied Georgiana. She turned a teasing look on Elizabeth. "I am certain you have much of which to speak and many secrets to exchange. I will see you the next time you visit."

Though Elizabeth could hardly understand how it happened, it seemed like she was now to ride back to Kingsdown with Lady Emily, a woman she was not sure appreciated Mr. Darcy's attentions to her. Carefully suppressing a sigh, Elizabeth alighted from the vehicle and made her way back down the line to Lady Emily's conveyance. It was, perhaps, for the best that this discussion take place as soon as possible, though Elizabeth was not anticipating it in the least. She expected that Lady Emily wished to make her sentiments known, or perhaps only to satisfy herself that Elizabeth was acting with the purest possible motives. Why the lady would concern herself with such things, Elizabeth could not say, but at this point it truly did not matter.

By the time they reached Lady Emily's carriage, whatever problem had held up the departure of the first carriages—Lady Emily's was the last one in the line—had not been resolved. They ascended and sat on opposite seats, Elizabeth taking the rear facing seat, and for some moments there was no conversation between them; Lady Emily appeared content to simply study Elizabeth, and Elizabeth was willing to allow the lady to have her say if it avoided unpleasantness.

At length, however, the line of carriages began to move, and they were soon under way. Even then, it was some moments before Lady Emily could be induced to speak. The silence between them was uncomfortable, not at all like that which on occasion existed between Elizabeth and Mr. Darcy. The thought of the man, coupled with Lady

Emily's unexpected silence, caused Elizabeth's mind to wander, and she spent some agreeable few moments thinking of what had just passed between herself and Mr. Darcy.

"You have had an eventful time in Derbyshire, Miss Bennet," said Lady Emily.

Having sat for so long in silence, Elizabeth was caught off guard by the lady's sudden words, but she rallied herself quickly.

"It is different from my home. The society there is closer, less varying than what I have seen here."

"Yes, I can imagine." Lady Emily paused for a moment, and then looked Elizabeth in the eye. "I do wonder, Miss Bennet. I have heard you say that you will eventually be required to return to your father's estate. How long do you expect to stay?"

All manner of responses crossed Elizabeth's mind at that moment, and many of them would have been acceptable, and likely would not have provoked the response which followed. She might have restated that she was here at her uncle's request and had no knowledge of how long he wished her to say. She could have said that she was enjoying her cousins' company and did not wish to leave for some time. She might even have just repeated what she had told many others since her arrival, that she expected to stay until the end of summer, and return to Hertfordshire soon after.

Unfortunately, none of these safe answers found their way past her lips. When Lady Emily asked her of her intentions, Elizabeth found herself offended by the woman's impertinence, wondering why she should not be allowed to have her happiness, and why this woman would claim Mr. Darcy for her own against his will. Though she had rarely suffered from the affliction of a loose tongue in the past, on this occasion she found that her tongue had loosened significantly.

"There may be a reason for me to stay much longer than I had originally anticipated, though I will almost certainly return home for at least some time."

Whatever else Lady Emily was—and Elizabeth was not quite certain *what* she was—the lady was no fool. As soon as the words left Elizabeth's mouth, she hazarded a glance up at Lady Emily's face, and what she saw there was true fury. Elizabeth had never seen its like before in the normally closed young woman. Her response was beyond anything Elizabeth could comprehend.

After glaring at Elizabeth for a moment, the woman reached up and banged on the top of her coach, yelling for the driver to hear: "Stop the coach!"

The conveyance stopped, though even Elizabeth could sense the reluctance in the way it rolled slowly to a stop. They sat for a few moments, Lady Emily's icy cold gaze boring into Elizabeth, Elizabeth wondering what the woman was about.

"I believe, Miss Bennet, that this is where we must part."

Elizabeth gasped in surprise. "Here?" asked she, though her voice caught a little in her consternation.

"Yes, *here*," said the lady, an implacable sort of resentment coloring her voice. "I find that I have tired of you and your presumption. You may make your own way to your uncle's estate." Lady Emily lifted a hand and pointed past Elizabeth down the road. "Lambton is that way."

"Lady Emily," said Elizabeth, her voice shaking ever so slightly, "you cannot think to simply abandon me on the side of the road."

"I can and I will," grated the woman. "Now, if you will kindly leave me the use of my carriage, I would be much obliged. You had best start walking if you wish to make Lambton before sundown."

Aghast at the woman's behavior, Elizabeth could only gape at her. A moment was all it took to realize Lady Emily was in earnest. With nothing else to do, Elizabeth reached over and grasped the handle, opened the door, and stepped out, landing a little heavily due to the distance to the ground. The driver and the two footmen standing at the back of the coach, looked at her with astonishment, clearly never having witnessed anything like what was currently occurring. Elizabeth had not ever herself and could do nothing but look away.

"Drive on," commanded Lady Emily, speaking to the driver through the open door.

Though reluctance sang from the man's posture, he turned to look at the lady, and said: "But Lady Emily, are you certain—?"

"Yes, I am certain. Drive on."

Elizabeth grimaced, but she gave the man a sickly smile and nodded at him. But when he still hesitated, Lady Emily barked: "Now!"

With a shake of his head and a wince of his own, the man turned and clucked to the horses, goading them into motion. They began to walk again, though very slowly. As the carriage pulled away, the door through which Lady Emily had given her commands closed, and she disappeared inside. Elizabeth saw one of the footman turning and looking at her, and for a moment she wondered if he would alight and escort her back to town. In the end, he did nothing, and soon the carriage turned a corner and moved from Elizabeth's sight. All the other carriages had already gone on ahead.

Still feeling the shock of being so unceremoniously abandoned, Elizabeth turned and looked down the road behind her, and then cast her gaze up to where Lady Emily's coach had disappeared. The road was straight for a stretch, the towering lengths of trees nestled up against it, huddling around it as if wishing for the comfort of civilization. No one was in evidence. Elizabeth was well and truly alone.

CHAPTER XXI

*T*he shock of being left to her own devices on an unfamiliar road so far from her home soon gave way to anger and disgust. She could hardly fathom what would provoke a woman to force a guest from her carriage and leave her in such a situation—even Caroline Bingley, whom Elizabeth detested, would not act in such a reprehensible manner!

The righteous anger, however, soon gave way to the realities of Elizabeth's situation. Derbyshire was a wilder country than what she was used to in Hertfordshire. Her father often jested about how dull a section of the kingdom hosted his estate. At this moment, however, Elizabeth longed for the safety of the area, the lack of any form of brigandry or other dangers. Elizabeth had no real knowledge of the safety of Derbyshire's roads, and had seen little to give her cause for alarm, but the possibility of highwaymen was real, and she knew it would go ill for her should men of their ilk find her.

Elizabeth was well used to walking. She had walked the pathways of her father's estate since her earliest memories, venturing further from the house once she had gained maturity, and from the time she had been thirteen years of age, she had often ranged beyond his estate. Even so, the longest walk she had ever attempted was to Oakham

Mount which, to walk to and then return to Longbourn, was only about four miles. She was not certain, but she suspected that Lambton was further from her present location, as she thought the ruin was closer to ten from the town. She did not think they had traveled far from the ruins before she had been unceremoniously removed from the coach.

There appeared to be nothing to be done but walk, so walk Elizabeth did. At least the road, a gravel track which, though wide, was free of holes or bumps, appeared well maintained, allowing her to walk swiftly and without fear of falling.

Of course, no one could experience what she had without her thoughts constantly turning to what had just happened. She wondered at Lady Emily's reaction. Her attentions to Mr. Darcy, though increasing of late, had always struck Elizabeth as lukewarm. Did the woman covet him and his wealth for herself, or was there something else at work here? She could not crave Mr. Darcy's position in society, as her own was higher.

Though the matter clutched on the edges of her consciousness with the iron grip of a falcon's talons, Elizabeth could not understand what had happened. All she knew was that leaving a young gentlewoman stranded on the side of the road in an area with which she was unfamiliar was such a breach of proper behavior that should it become known, Lady Emily would almost certainly suffer the consequences of gossip, not to mention the disapproval of local society. Her position as daughter to an earl would undoubtedly protect her to some extent, but she would not emerge unscathed.

What it would do to Elizabeth's reputation, she was uncertain. Society being what it was, and gossips being what they were, it was equally likely that she would be looked on with pity as she would bear the censure of being all alone on a deserted road and having who knew what happen to her, despite her lack of culpability in the matter. Her only hope was to reach Lambton without anyone being the wiser, make her way to the inn, and send a note to Mr. Drummond, acquainting him with her situation. It seemed best that the entire incident be kept from the ears of as many people as possible.

So intent was Elizabeth on her ruminations that she almost missed the sound of a horse's canter, and she realized that she had come to a section of the road where it meandered this way and that, around small hills and across bubbling brooks, she could not see who was approaching her. The thought of highwaymen and what would happen should an unscrupulous man find her entered Elizabeth's mind, and she became frightened, looking wildly this way and that for a place to hide. The woods had never looked so inviting, and she hiked up her skirt to make a mad dash for the tree line and its dubious safety. And then the rider came around the corner.

Elizabeth barely had time to see the tall dark man sitting in the saddle, before the man kicked the horse into motion and he approached Elizabeth at a run, vaulting from the saddle when he drew close to her.

"Miss Bennet! Why in the blazes are you alone, walking in this god forsaken place?"

Elizabeth almost wilted with relief as she recognized the sound of Mr. Darcy's voice, and for a moment she almost felt like swooning. She found herself encircled by strong arms, her head pulled to rest against his broad chest, and she allowed herself to lean heavily against him. Though the day was warm, and the exertion of her walk had caused her to perspire, she found herself shivering against him. It was improper, indeed, but Mr. Darcy's hand went to her back and he caressed her tenderly, though he did not attempt to take any further liberties. For the comfort he was imparting, Elizabeth could forgive him these little lapses, especially when the tension in her limbs was bleeding away due to his ministrations. In a short time, she felt almost lethargic.

"It appears that you are overcome, Miss Bennet," the deep voice of her rescuer broke her reverie.

Elizabeth drew away a little and attempted to fix him with an impish smile. "Do you not know, Mr. Darcy? I am an excellent walker."

"Miss Bennet," said Mr. Darcy, the gravity in his tone and demeanor telling Elizabeth her attempt at levity had been an abject failure, "this walk to which you have set yourself is still above six miles to Lambton, to say nothing of the additional distance to your uncle's estate. Surely even that is too much for you, especially considering our earlier exertions."

"It was not by choice, sir," replied Elizabeth.

He frowned at her quiet reply, but though he seemed on the verge of asking for additional clarification, he thought better of it for the moment.

"Then we should ensure you are returned to your uncle's house as soon as may be. If you will allow me, I will place you on my horse and then sit behind you."

Though she hesitated, Mr. Darcy cut into her ruminations: "If I was to walk the horse with you situated on its back, it would take much longer for us to reach our destination. I know of a path which will prevent us from being observed so that we may preserve our reputations."

Knowing he was correct, Elizabeth assented. He picked her up and deposited her on the back of his tall horse with no greater effort than he would have expended had he lifted a child, and after he had scrambled up behind her, he grasped the reins in one hand and urged the horse forward. Soon they were cantering down the road, though before much longer, he turned his mount toward a barely visible path to the right, and they began to make their way through the trees.

"This trail will lead across country toward your uncle's estate," said Mr. Darcy in response to Elizabeth's unspoken question. "We will traverse a southern section of Pemberley and come out near the edge of Mr. Drummond's estate, down the long valley where our properties meet."

Elizabeth turned to face him. "I was not aware that I was walking along Pemberley's border."

"The ruin is just north of my estate. If Pemberley extended a little further northward, it would be within my boundaries. You might recall that Pemberley lies to the west of Lambton, and Kingsdown to the south of Pemberley. That is why we passed through Lambton on the way to the ruin this morning. Your walk, had you continued on in this direction, would have been in excess of ten miles, as you would have come to Lambton, and then would have been obliged to continue to the south and then west to come to Kingsdown."

"I had thought to go to the inn in Lambton and send word to my uncle of my predicament," murmured Elizabeth. "I knew I was still some distance from Lambton, and I did not wish to be caught by darkness before I reached Kingsdown."

Mr. Darcy chuckled. "Nightfall is quite late now, Miss Bennet. Given what I know of your abilities, I doubt you would have been so long on the road that you would not have arrived before then. But your uncle would certainly have worried for you long before you returned to his home. It would have been a sensible plan."

"Would I have needed to worry about bandits?" asked Elizabeth.

"Not here, though one can never be certain. There is a stretch of road fifty miles north of Pemberley that is notorious for them, but this district is largely peaceful."

Though the worry was no longer present with the coming of Mr. Darcy, Elizabeth still found herself almost overwhelmed with relief.

They would not have any difficulties that he could not handle, then.

"Now, Miss Bennet," said Mr. Darcy, his tone firm but questioning, "you have stated that your predicament was not your own doing, but I still do not have any indication of what happened. The last time I saw you, you were in my carriage with my sister and your cousin. Shall you not inform me what happened?"

Elizabeth would have desired to avoid thinking of the matter altogether, but something in the man's voice told her he was not in humor to be put off. For a moment, she wondered if married life to him would consist of nothing more than his taking charge and compelling her compliance. But then she realized that he had been his own master for some years, and he was likely used to managing things without considering the opinions of others. She would almost certainly need to show him that she was capable and desirous of her own opinion being heard, but for now, there was no need to make such a fuss. He had asked, and it was incumbent upon her to provide him an explanation, especially after he had rescued her from a long walk.

"I was abandoned by the side of the road," said she, however reluctantly.

"Georgiana would never have done such a thing!" exclaimed he. His arm, holding her steady on the horse tightened around her in his agitation.

"It was not Georgiana," said Elizabeth quickly, wondering where her wits had gone. "I am very aware she would not, as she is the sweetest young lady I have ever met."

"Then who?" asked Mr. Darcy, a hint of exasperation creeping into his tone.

"Lady Emily," replied Elizabeth, though softly. She proceeded to relate to him all that had passed, focusing on the facts of the matter and eschewing any conjecture around Lady Emily's motivations for her behavior. In the end, however, it did not matter, as Mr. Darcy was as angry as Elizabeth had ever seen him when she finished her recitation.

"What could have possessed her to do such a thing?" demanded a seething Mr. Darcy when Elizabeth had finished her tale. "It is completely beyond the pale! You could have been put in serious jeopardy by her unthinking, heinous actions. What was she thinking?"

"I rather think she has disapproved of your attentions to me," replied Elizabeth.

That brought Mr. Darcy up short. "Disapproved? I have noticed no such disapproval."

Elizabeth sighed. "Your single-minded devotion to *me* has been all I have ever hoped from in a suitor, Mr. Darcy. But it seems in this instance you have not recognized that Lady Emily is not a friend of your attentions to me."

"It is none of her concern," snapped Mr. Darcy. "She has no more control over my actions than does my aunt."

Elizabeth turned to look up at him. "Then there is truth to Mr. Collins's assertion that your aunt expects you to marry her daughter?"

It hardly seemed like Mr. Darcy's countenance could become even more forbidding, but he managed it all the same. "Your cousin was spreading such things when he does not even know me?"

"No, Mr. Darcy," replied Elizabeth. "My cousin is eager to speak of any and all concerns with respect to Lady Catherine. He did not spread that intelligence around the neighborhood. Mr. Bingley chanced to mention your name, after which Mr. Collins only mentioned your engagement in passing." Elizabeth pierced him with an arch smile. "I might wonder, sir, to what end your attentions to me portends, given your long engagement to the daughter of house de Bourgh."

The exasperation with his aunt and Mr. Collins appeared to be tempered by Elizabeth's teasing tone. "Lady Catherine is eager to state her expectations of me with respect to her daughter, but I am in no way bound to my cousin. She attempts to say that it was my mother's favorite wish and that they agreed on it when we were young. I have confirmation from my mother, however—a sweet, reticent lady, who was not accustomed to standing up to her sister—that she never agreed to it. Moreover, my father did not take any steps to seal the agreement, so there is little Lady Catherine can do."

"And your cousin?" asked Elizabeth, feeling a curiosity toward this young woman who had been described in such glowing terms as Mr. Collins's. "Is she in agreement with your aunt?"

"Anne is of a sickly constitution and has never truly been well. Since she is required to live with her mother, she prefers to avoid provoking her mother's ire by disputing her words. But Anne had no intention of ever marrying, least of all me."

It appeared that Mr. Darcy was, indeed, free to do as he wished, though Elizabeth had never doubted it.

"But we have been distracted from our original discussion," said Mr. Darcy. "You say you have seen Lady Emily's disapproval when we have been together?"

"It has been difficult to understand anything of lady's opinions, as she is quite the most inscrutable lady I have ever met. Almost as enigmatic as a certain gentleman." Elizabeth raised an eyebrow at him, but he only responded in like fashion. "But, yes, I have seen her displeasure at times, but I have never been able to discern whether she wishes to have your attentions for herself or merely believes you should not be so attentive to a woman who is not of your station."

"Then she is incorrect," was Mr. Darcy's short reply. "But that is not at issue here. I could never have expected her to behave in such a manner. To offer to take you to your uncle's house and then leave you by the side of the road no more than two miles from where you started? I cannot imagine such disgusting behavior. You could have been injured, or worse. Her father will be most seriously displeased to hear of her reprehensible actions."

"Oh, Mr. Darcy," said Elizabeth, "I would prefer that this does not reach the ears of society. Perhaps it would be better to simply allow the matter to rest?"

"I assure you, no," said he. "Though I would agree with you to keep it from wagging tongues, his lordship must be informed. He is a good man, and he will not be happy with his daughter's actions. I would never dream of keeping this from him, and I assure you, neither would your uncle. It is he who is responsible for your safety while you are here."

"I suppose you are correct," said Elizabeth, though grudgingly.

"There is no doubt I am," replied Mr. Darcy. "I shudder to think of what might have happened had I not come upon you when I did. Though you may have made your way to Lambton and Kingsdown without incident, it is also possible something dreadful might have happened."

"Why are you here?" asked Elizabeth. "I had not expected to see you returning to such a place so soon after leaving it."

"I was not returning to the ruin. As I mentioned, this land is part of my estate. I had business with one of my tenants, and this is the quickest way to reach his lands."

"You have my apologies, Mr. Darcy. Should you not return to meet with your tenant before you convey me to Kingsdown?"

"Definitely not," replied Mr. Darcy, his tone allowing for no dissent. "Your safety is the paramount concern, Miss Bennet, and I will see you safely to Kingsdown before I take care of that other matter. Mr. Davies was not expecting me at any specific time, and the matter is one that may wait until tomorrow."

"Very well," said Elizabeth, knowing he would not be dissuaded. In fact, she was not even certain she wished to make the attempt.

They rode on in silence for some minutes, Elizabeth maintaining it because she suspected that Mr. Darcy was attempting to rein in his temper. For her part, Elizabeth was simply grateful he had happened upon her and that she would be returned to her uncle's house long before she might have expected.

It was a pleasant land through which they traveled, largely forested, and though sections of it were the thick, heavy jumble of trees Elizabeth might have expected to find in a land only tenuously tamed, Mr. Darcy seemed to know instinctually of where to guide his horse to take advantage of the easiest route. They crossed bubbling streams more than once, their murmured babblings a soft counterpoint to the sounds of birdsong and insects buzzing lazily past. Off to her right, Elizabeth could see through the trees to what looked like a series of wide open fields which appeared to be cultivated, though she could not make out their composition—it was too early in the season, and they were too distant for her to see them with the requisite clarity.

It was clear the man's estate was intimately known to him, a well-respected friend. He was part of the land he cared for, a solid dependable head to the estate's body. He was one with it, as it was with him, in a manner so profound that Elizabeth thought it would take her years of study to understand. It was something she doubted Miss Bingley ever would, for to her, he was nothing more than a ticket to a life of wealth and indulgence, the gateway to the higher echelons of society. That he did not care for them in the way *she* did would matter not at all to the woman.

"Will you not share your thoughts, Miss Bennet?" asked Mr. Darcy, interrupting her reverie.

A glance at the man told Elizabeth that he had either mastered his pique, or she had misinterpreted his silence. He was watching her with his usual intensity, and Elizabeth could hardly control her hand, which wanted to rise of its own accord and touch his cheek.

"I was thinking of how you belong in this place, Mr. Darcy," said Elizabeth with all honesty. "Your estate becomes you, I think, for it is impossible to see one without the other."

"It may just be because you have never met me anywhere else."

"Perhaps. But I think it is something more than that."

"I *am* most comfortable when I am here. I was taught by my father to respect it, to manage it as if it is a friend and partner, rather than a source of wealth. So many of Pemberley's people depend on the good management of the master. It is a responsibility I never thought to have so soon as I did, but I have always striven to uphold my father's confidence in me."

"I am certain he cannot be anything but pleased with how you have performed your duties." Mr. Darcy appeared pleased by her praise, but sensing that he was becoming embarrassed, Elizabeth changed the subject. "Is that the long valley of which you spoke to the west?"

"It is. I had thought to keep to the woods until we reach your uncle's lands. We are less likely to be observed here, and I would not wish to injure your reputation."

"You think your tenants will gossip?"

Mr. Darcy rolled his eyes and grinned. "While they are not mean-spirited, news has a way of making its way about the district. To be honest, I sometimes think the men are worse than the women!"

Elizabeth laughed. "You are very severe on my sex, Mr. Darcy, to be so surprised at such a thing. Will we reach my uncle's estate soon?"

"We will before too much longer. Do you wish to escape my company so quickly?"

"I must. I fear your contempt oversetting my sensibilities."

Mr. Darcy laughed, and Elizabeth soon joined with him. The trail they traveled was, by this time, almost indistinguishable, and Mr. Darcy soon turned toward the east, finding the open ground at the end of the valley, after which they climbed a little rise and approached a fence, which Elizabeth presumed marked the boundary between Pemberley and Kingsdown. It gave the impression of being a new construction, and it contained a gate, which Mr. Darcy dismounted to open and close once he had led his horse through. Though they had approached it from an unfamiliar angle, Elizabeth soon realized that she had seen that place before.

"Why, this is where Olivia, Leah, and I picnicked not long after I came to Derbyshire."

"Yes, I remember."

Elizabeth turned to face the man, noting that he appeared a little embarrassed. "You remember it? I do not believe you were present."

The raised eyebrow she directed at him prompted a grin in response. "Fitzwilliam and I were riding the estate that day, and we happened to see you from a distance. As I recall, it was the second time I saw you."

"And you did not make yourself known?" asked Elizabeth.

"At the time, we were not introduced. We were doing some surveys down toward the lands of one of my tenants, and we did not truly have the time to stop and visit. Regardless, the three of you appeared to be enjoying yourselves, and we did not wish to interrupt."

"Do you always spy on young ladies who are unknown to you?"

Mr. Darcy laughed delightedly. "Only you, Miss Bennet. I have never spied on another woman, known or unknown to me."

There was little to say to that. Elizabeth had never met a man who was so adept at turning her teasing back on her, and she was delighted, even while she was feeling more than a little shy about prompting him to make such a statement.

"Miss Bennet," said he, all levity gone from his voice, "I had asked to call on you tomorrow, if you recall."

"I do," replied Elizabeth, though quietly, her heart speeding up in anticipation.

"Since we are now together, it appears to be a propitious time to discuss what I wished to say to you, if you agree."

Nothing could have been more agreeable to Elizabeth, and she managed to convey that to him in a manner which he could understand, though she thought it was a near thing.

"In fact," said Mr. Darcy, his manner contemplative, "I am not certain precisely what I wished to say." He blushed a little. "You must understand, Miss Bennet, that I am not a loquacious man, and I tend to stumble when speaking to certain individuals and at certain times, and in university I often found it helpful to write my comments beforehand, so that I might be able to make myself clearly understood."

"You do not know what you wished to say?" asked Elizabeth, feeling a little crestfallen.

Mr. Darcy chuckled—making Elizabeth wonder if she should feel offended—and then spoke in a soothing tone. "There! You see? I tend to say things which might be misunderstood when I speak without rehearsing in advance. What I meant to say is that I asked for an audience with you, not knowing *which question* I meant to ask. I thought to offer a courtship, but now I am not so certain. You see, it is on my mind, having you on my horse, situated so delightfully in front of me, that my feelings render a courtship completely unnecessary."

"Oh," replied Elizabeth, feeling a little dazed at his words. Then the full import of them hit her, and she breathed: "*Oh!*"

"Exactly. You see, Miss Bennet, I can be quite deliberate in forming my opinion, but once it is formed, it is as immovable as a mountain. I have come to a conclusion, but the true determining factor is yours."

"Mine?" asked Elizabeth.

"Yes, yours. I have an important question to ask, but you will determine which one I will ask. If you require a courtship, then I am happy to oblige and to continue to pay my attentions to you before all the neighborhood. If, on the other hand, you feel you are ready for more—as I am myself—then I will ask you a more permanent question. The decision is entirely yours."

Elizabeth gazed at him wide-eyed, wondering if she heard him correctly. "That is highly irregular, Mr. Darcy."

"It is, is it not?" It was not a question, and to emphasize his point, Mr. Darcy winked at her, causing Elizabeth to giggle. But he did not speak; instead, he continued to watch her, an expectant air prompting her to consider his words. She had the power to elicit a proposal! How many ladies could say the same?

But as she looked up at him, experienced the sensation of his arms surrounding her, sat cradled to his breast, a powerful feeling of belonging crept over her. She had been expecting an offer of courtship. But now Elizabeth knew exactly how she felt and what she wanted.

"I believe you may proceed in whatever way you feel fit, sir," whispered Elizabeth.

The delight which settled over him became him exceedingly, and he wasted no time.

"In that case, Miss Bennet, I must tell you that I feel an ardent passion and love for you and humbly request that you accept my hand in marriage."

Elizabeth laughed, and this time she did reach up to cup his cheek. "After all that, your proposal was rather perfunctory in nature."

"As I said, I am not an eloquent man, Miss Bennet."

"Oh, I believe you are, sir—with the right inducement. I was not complaining—indeed, your proposal contained everything necessary to convince me that you are in earnest. And I am happy to accept, for I wish for nothing more than to stay with you forever in the wilds of Derbyshire."

"You are certainly the right inducement, Miss Bennet," replied Mr. Darcy. And he leaned forward to press his lips against hers. It was sweet and sublime, kissing her newly betrothed, and though Mr. Darcy did not press his breach of propriety any further, it was enough for Elizabeth. It carried the promise of so much more.

CHAPTER XXII

$\mathcal{D}$arcy had kept his temper admirably. Though his first instinct upon finding Miss Bennet alone and abandoned on that lonely country road had been to go directly to Teasdale Manor and confront Lady Emily, he had recognized the necessity of ensuring Miss Bennet arrived home safely first. The ride through the woods of his estate and on to Kingsdown had allowed him an unparalleled opportunity to secure her hand, and he could not feel more blessed that he had been able to do so. She was a wonderful woman, and he did not doubt his days would be happy with her by his side.

But this time, so dearly bought, was coming to an end. As the house at Kingsdown appeared in the distance, Darcy was loath to relinquish her company back to her relations, though he knew it to be necessary. Soon, she would not be required to leave him again.

"Mr. Darcy, perhaps we should dismount?" asked Miss Bennet, her cheeks flushed with a most fetching blush, no doubt embarrassed to be found atop a horse with a man.

"There is little to be done about it now," replied Darcy. "I must speak with your uncle, not only to acquaint him with what has happened, but also to solicit his conditional approval for our engagement."

"I assume you mean to speak with my father?"

"Of course. Your uncle is your surrogate guardian, but it is your father who must approve an engagement."

Miss Bennet nodded, though slowly. "Then I would request that we keep our engagement between us at present. I would not wish to have our actions scrutinized, to become the subject of gossip."

Though Darcy was initially taken aback by her request, he soon began to see the sense in it. "Are you suggesting that I speak to your father when you return to your home?"

"I am, Mr. Darcy. Furthermore, my sister is to visit soon, and I am not sure how she will behave when she comes. If possible, it seems better to keep this matter from her ears until I can understand how she will react."

Darcy frowned. "You think that she will not approve?"

"It is not that specifically, sir. I am sure she can have nothing to say on the matter. Let us simply say jealousy is a possible reaction to the news of our engagement."

"But she will be forced to accept it sooner or later."

"She will," replied Miss Bennet. "But she has been told by my mother that she is the most beautiful, the best of her daughters since she was a child. You are a gentleman of much more consequence than Mr. Bingley. It might be difficult for her to accept my marriage to a gentleman of higher standing."

It was difficult to know what to think of the new Mrs. Bingley. Darcy did not think he had heard all there was to hear of the matter which lay between Miss Bennet and her sister, but this new account of the woman did not reflect well on her. To resent another sibling because of whom she married spoke of a mercenary attitude which was quite beyond anything Darcy would have expected in the sister of an exceptional woman such as Miss Bennet.

Miss Bennet apparently sensed his confusion and moved to reassure him, though they had not much time before they arrived at the house.

"I will explain as much as I am able the next time we are together. For now, please trust what I have informed you of my sister. We were always very close, but her marriage has changed her, and I do not know what to think. Unless you are set on announcing our engagement to the neighborhood, I would ask that it be kept from anyone other than ourselves and my uncle."

"It cannot be announced until I speak to your father and obtain his consent. All you are asking me to do is refrain from riding to

Hertfordshire on the morrow to speak with him."

Miss Bennet smiled at him. "That is exactly it, sir."

"Then I have no objection, as long as I am granted leave to inform Georgiana and Fitzwilliam. They will surely badger me on the matter, and since you visit so often, it would be difficult to keep it from them."

"Agreed. For my part, I shall inform Olivia for the same reasons."

They emerged from behind a small copse and the house stood in front of them. Reining the horse to a stop, Darcy dismounted, and then held his hands up to help Miss Bennet from the top of the horse. He was already feeling bereft due to the absence of her in his arms, and he wondered how he would manage until the day when he was able to make her his in every way.

When they were both standing on the ground, he offered her his arm and stepped forward, intending to go around the house to the drive at the front. Before they could reach that objective, however, Mr. Drummond emerged from that direction and hurried around the corner, concern evident in the way he searched Elizabeth's eyes.

"Elizabeth!" exclaimed he. "We were beginning to become worried for you."

"I have much to tell you, Uncle."

"I believe it would be best if I was to make this communication, Miss Bennet," interjected Darcy. "Will you allow me the honor of speaking for you in this matter?"

With slow deliberation Miss Bennet nodded, and he knew that she had quickly understood his meaning. Though he knew he could not claim to be her protector until they married, in allowing her to speak for him, she was allowing him to make a statement of intent. Darcy did not think that Mr. Drummond missed the inference, given the searching looks he was directing at both of them.

"You were both riding on Mr. Darcy's horse," said he. It was a statement of fact, and contained no overtones of accusation, though Darcy detected substantial curiosity.

"That is, in part, why I need to speak to you, sir. There are reasons why I felt it necessary to travel in such a way. We encountered no one on our journey, so there should be no repercussions."

Not that the thought of being forced to marry Miss Bennet much sooner would be onerous to me!

"Then let us retire to my study," said Mr. Drummond.

They made their way inside the house, Darcy declining an offer to stable his mount, preferring instead to tie him up for what he intended to be an imminent departure. Miss Bennet took her leave of him, retreating to her room, while Darcy followed Mr. Drummond to his library.

"Has your daughter returned yet?" asked Darcy as they entered the room.

"We received a message not long ago that your sister had invited her to stay the night at Pemberley. It was the lack of any mention of Elizabeth that concerned me. I cannot imagine how she came to be with you, on horse, of all things, rather than at Pemberley with her cousin."

"I could not have imagined it myself, Mr. Drummond," said Darcy, the memory of the rage he had felt when he had found her once again welling up in his breast. There was no reason, however, to surrender to such passions, and every reason to stay calm, not the least of which was the need to prevent Mr. Drummond from jumping up and riding to Teasdale Manor to confront Lady Emily himself.

Thus, Darcy related what had happened that afternoon, describing in full what Miss Bennet had told him regarding Lady Emily's actions, how she had come to be in the lady's carriage in the first place, and how he had found her and returned her home. He kept any mention of an engagement to himself for the moment, knowing there would be ample time after the fact to acquaint the man with the new state of affairs. By the time he had finished, Mr. Drummond's ire had matched that which Darcy had felt when he had first found Miss Bennet on the side of that road.

"What could she have been thinking?" demanded Drummond after Darcy had finished his explanation. The man jumped to his feet and began pacing, his agitation visible in his curt hand gestures and quick pace. "How could I have faced Elizabeth's father had some harm befallen her?"

"I hardly think Mr. Bennet would have held you responsible, Mr. Drummond. But it *is* fortunate I happened along and no damage has been done."

"No damage has been done, but there must be a response to this. I care not if Lady Emily were the queen herself — this betrayal is beyond comprehension!"

"I do not disagree," replied Darcy, thinking this was an excellent opportunity to move to the other topic of his interest. "But I would ask you to cede the right of response to me."

That stopped Drummond up short, and he turned to peer at Darcy. "Why would I do so? I am her guardian while she is in Derbyshire. Despite how grateful I am you intervened, the right of response is mine."

"Because there has been a development of which you are not aware."

"There has?" asked Drummond in a tone which suggested that Darcy had best explain himself."

"Yes, sir. You see, I had spoken with Miss Bennet during our outing today, asking to be allowed to call on her."

"You have been calling on her for weeks."

"I have. But today I wished to call for a specific purpose."

Drummond released a bark of laughter. "So, having her alone for ten miles on your horse, you took the opportunity which presented itself."

"You have the right of it, sir."

"And now you wish for my approval?"

"I do. As you stated, I have been calling on your niece for some time, and I have developed an affection for her which cannot be denied. Today, she confirmed the strength of her returning feelings by accepting my offer of marriage. I request that you give her consent in her father's stead until I am able to journey thither to ask for his permission in person."

"An engagement? I had thought it likely you would ask for a formal courtship."

"That was my first thought, sir. But as we were riding and speaking together, I realized that a courtship is not required. It is nothing more than an opportunity to come to know a woman better, to determine if she is compatible, and allow her the same opportunity. In my situation, I have always wished to find a true meeting of minds and hearts, and I have no doubt that I have found that with Miss Bennet. She is kind, thoughtful, intelligent, happy, loves life, she loves my sister, and will be a wonderful mistress of Pemberley. I do not need the additional period of a courtship to know my feelings. I know them now."

By the time Darcy finished speaking, Drummond was favoring him with a true smile of delight. He approached Darcy, his hand extended, which Darcy took gratefully. "I cannot tell you how pleased I am. I was hoping Lizzy would find a man to love her while she was here, as I consider her to be a jewel of the first order. But I never would have imagined it would be you."

"I cannot but agree with you, sir," said Darcy. "She *is* a jewel, and I will do my utmost to ensure she is happy all the days of her life."

"I know you will." Drummond sat behind his desk and frowned. "But I am not certain that I agree with your request to leave the response in your hands. Yes, you are engaged, dependent on my brother Bennet's consent, but I am still her guardian while she is here. I believe I should take an active hand in the coming unpleasantness."

"I understand your feelings, sir, and will not gainsay you if you decide to join me at Teasdale Manor. But I will still advise you to allow me to take the first steps. I believe that Lady Emily's actions were the result of a sudden anger and, moreover, that they were as much directed at me as at Miss Bennet. The earl will not be pleased and am certain he will insist she come to Kingsdown and deliver an apology in person."

Drummond paused to think, and when he spoke his words were slow and hesitant. "Though every feeling revolts against it, perhaps you are correct. There is nothing I would like better than to storm the walls of Teasdale Manor and demand satisfaction, but it would be better if this matter were not known to society in general. And as I have little reason to visit the earl . . . ."

"Exactly."

"And may I suppose that you will not be announcing your engagement at present?"

"Your niece does not wish it," replied Darcy, feeling a little rueful at his agreement to conceal their understanding. "As her father is more than two days distant and she will return home at the end of summer, she prefers that I travel to Hertfordshire then and approach him, at which time the engagement may be announced."

"Though I am certain you would wish to proclaim it from the rooftops long before then," replied Drummond with a laugh.

"I will not say you do not have the right of it," replied Darcy. "I understand she also wishes to keep it from her sister when she comes."

Drummond sobered immediately. "I am not surprised. The girl I knew would be nothing more than happy for a most beloved sister, but given what Elizabeth and her father have told me of Jane's behavior, I am not certain what to think. If she has become proud because of her marriage, it may be that she will wish to restore her relationship with her sister due to Elizabeth's rise in status upon becoming your wife."

The same though had occurred to Darcy, and he was hard-pressed to refrain from reacting with disdain. "I will, of course, never prevent Miss Bennet from maintaining any relationships she wishes. But if that be the case, I do not think she will wish to keep up the connection—at least not a close connection like that they previously shared."

"I agree," replied Drummond. "Will that affect your friendship with Mr. Bingley?"

"I do not know," replied Darcy. "I cannot imagine Bingley would appreciate his wife's behavior any more than Miss Bennet does. He is about the least pretentious man I have ever met. I suspect he is as baffled by his wife's behavior as Miss Bennet is."

"Very well," said Drummond, rising and extending his hand. "I will wait to hear the results of your conversation with Lady Emily. Please do not leave me in suspense."

"I will not," replied Darcy, gripping the other man's hand in his own. "Tomorrow, I will return Miss Drummond to your house, and I believe my sister and cousin will accompany me for a visit. We can speak at that time."

"Then you had best be on your way if you wish to confront Lady Emily today."

Darcy was, indeed, on his way soon after, and as Pemberley was not far out of his way to Teasdale Manor, he decided to stop there and change from his dusty clothes first before proceeding to the coming confrontation. He quickly confirmed that Miss Drummond was present and, as subtly as he could, pulled the story of Miss Bennet's departure from the Darcy carriage early that afternoon from his sister. Fortunately, neither young lady seemed to have any suspicion of the reason for his questions.

"I assume Lizzy returned to Kingsdown?" asked his sister after she told him what had happened.

"Yes, she did," replied Darcy. "I saw her earlier."

"It is unfortunate that she was invited by Lady Emily to ride with her. I had intended to invite her along with Olivia to stay."

Darcy smiled at this evidence of his sister's approval, though she did not yet know of his proposal. He would inform her later and allow Miss Drummond to be informed by Miss Bennet herself.

"I am certain she would have accepted with pleasure. But she is at Kingsdown now, and I think it is best that she stays there tonight. There will be other opportunities for her to stay with us."

A lifetime, said Darcy in the confines of his own mind.

Soon he excused himself, saying he had a matter of business, leaving the two young ladies behind. But he was not able to make his escape without first coming across his cousin. Fitzwilliam, who had been able to read his moods since they were children, was not long in realizing that Darcy was out of sorts.

"What is wrong?" demanded Darcy, the anger at the way his

fiancée was most infamously treated bubbling up from where he had kept it locked up. "I shall tell you." He leaned in close, mindful of any servants nearby, and said: "After we left this morning, Lady Emily invited Miss Bennet to ride with her in her carriage, and she left Miss Bennet by the side of the road to make her own way home."

"What?" There was no mistaking Fitzwilliam's surprise or his quickly rising ire. "Are you certain?"

"Of course, I am certain," replied Darcy. He beckoned Fitzwilliam to follow him and began to walk down the corridor toward the entrance. "If you recall, you and I parted when we came to Lambton. I had a small matter of business to attend to, after which I returned along that same road to visit with one of my tenants, when I came upon Miss Bennet quite alone. You can imagine my surprise. She informed me of what had happened, though she was more than a little reluctant. I do not know what prompted it, but Lady Emily became angry at something Miss Bennet said and stopped the coach, forcing her to disembark, and then driving off, leaving her behind."

"So, you intend to go to Teasdale Manor?" guessed Fitzwilliam. It was one of the things Darcy liked most about his cousin—Fitzwilliam was not prone to obvious exclamations or drawn out clarifications. He moved to the crux of the matter with the unerring aim of an arrow pointed at the center of a target.

"This cannot go unanswered," replied Darcy. "If the earl does not know, I will inform him of what has happened."

"I agree. I am astonished, Darcy. I could not have imagined her capable of this."

Darcy stopped abruptly and turned to his cousin. "Miss Bennet has informed me of Lady Emily's behavior of late, and she's of the opinion that the lady is not a friend of my attentions to her."

"She is a discerning lady," replied Fitzwilliam. "In fact, I am surprised that you did not recognize it yourself, given how adept you are at avoiding such women. I, myself have had to interfere with her machinations, as I knew you were not cognizant of them."

Darcy felt as if his head had been encased in stone these last weeks. It seemed he had been blind on many occasions.

"Do not distress yourself, Darcy. She has been very subtle in her actions. Your attention was fixed on your young lady, as it ought to be."

"I should have seen it," said Darcy, disgusted with himself for his lack of comprehension. "Had I recognized it, I might have informed her of my feelings and avoided this situation altogether." Darcy shook his head. "When I think of what might have happened . . . ."

"Nothing happened and Miss Bennet is well." Fitzwilliam turned a shrewd eye on his cousin. "And, I suspect, you are further along on your road of courtship than you were previously."

His mind was so full of righteous indignation that Darcy had no time to be embarrassed by his cousin's teasing. "You would be correct. I have asked for, and received, Miss Bennet's hand in marriage. You see before you an engaged man."

"Excellent!" Fitzwilliam beamed and slapped Darcy on the back. "I am happy for you, Darcy. I knew you had an interest in her, but I thought it would take you longer to come to the point."

"It almost did," replied Darcy. They reached the entrance and stepped through into the mid-afternoon sunlight. "I will tell you as we ride."

Darcy's horse was already waiting for him, and it was only the work of a moment to have Fitzwilliam's brought out. Soon they were mounted, cantering toward Teasdale Manor. For all his qualities as a campaigner and his growing expertise as a land owner, Fitzwilliam was one of the worst gossips Darcy had ever met. He promised to keep the news of Darcy's engagement in confidence, but he was thorough in extracting every piece of information from Darcy concerning what had happened, the proposal, and the discussion with Mr. Drummond after. He was only content as Teasdale Manor rose before them in the distance.

It seemed, however, that there was already some uproar in the house. The earl's voice, usually so moderate and kind, was raised such that they could hear him as soon as the butler opened the door. They asked to see the master of the house, and contrary to what Darcy might have expected, they were admitted immediately. The earl's voice became louder, the closer they came to the sitting-room, and it was clear that he was not happy about something. Darcy hoped that his ire was raised toward his daughter, though he soon felt shamed by such an uncharitable thought, regardless of how deserved it might be.

"Mr. Darcy," said the butler as he led them to the earl, "might I assume your presence means the young miss has been recovered?"

"Yes, she has," replied Darcy, not surprised he had knowledge of the matter. "She was returned to her uncle's home more than an hour ago."

"Very good, sir."

When they entered the room, they were greeted by the sight of the earl standing, his face red with anger, while Lady Emily sat in a chair, clearly the target of her father's ire. The lady's countenance was distressed, though Darcy was not certain if that was due to remorse or simply her father's censure. When they were announced, the earl stopped his pacing and drew himself up to his full height, greeting them in a perfunctory manner.

"Darcy, Fitzwilliam," said he. "I suppose I should not be surprised to see you here, though I will own I had expected to receive Mr. Drummond."

"I have come from Kingsdown myself, your lordship," replied Darcy. "We decided that it would be best if Mr. Drummond did not visit you, though he sorely wished to do so."

The earl grunted. "I must thank him for that. The events of the day would not reflect well on my daughter, were they ever to become known to the neighborhood."

Lady Emily had the grace to blush at his words. Darcy, who had been watching her, was loath to give the woman any credit, but was able to acknowledge that she at least appeared to regret her actions.

"So, you are aware of what occurred today?" asked Darcy, wishing to come directly to the point and then leave.

"I am," replied the earl, "though I will own to some surprise that *you* are aware."

"I came across Miss Bennet as she was walking along that road toward Lambton," replied Darcy.

"There is the answer to your riddle, Emily," said the earl. "By the time you returned to look for her, Miss Bennet had already been rescued."

Lady Emily appeared relieved, but there was a tightness around her eyes which suggested displeasure. Though Darcy thought to call her on it, Fitzwilliam, apparently seeing the same thing, spoke first, likely to prevent any unpleasantness.

"You returned to look for her?"

"She realized what a foolish thing she had done," replied the earl for his daughter, prompting an annoyed glance from Lady Emily. "But when she returned, Miss Bennet was nowhere to be found. Though she has an imprecise notion of how long Miss Bennet was left alone, my driver suggests that it was at least twenty minutes, perhaps thirty. When Miss Bennet could not be found, Emily returned here and informed me of the matter, and I mounted a search with every man I could find. I was just about to join them myself."

The matter having been brought back to his mind, the earl pulled the bell and summoned his butler to have the search called off. His butler, however, responded that it had already been done, based on the intelligence Darcy had given him.

"Good man, Gates," said Lord Chesterfield when his butler had departed. Then he addressed Darcy and Fitzwilliam again. "You may be assured that this matter is not closed. I am ashamed of my daughter's behavior, and though she is too old to put across my knee, I cannot countenance such behavior. I have also informed my drivers that regardless of their mistress's instructions, no one riding in one of my carriages will ever be left on the side of the road again."

Lady Emily once again flushed at her father's words, but she did not say anything, seeming to understand there was nothing she *could* say. While the revelations they had heard since they arrived mollified Darcy a little—he had expected to arrive to a woman completely unmoved by the distress in which she had left a young woman who had never done her any harm—he still wished for nothing more than to be gone from this place.

"There appears to have been certain . . . expectations held by your daughter, Lord Chesterfield, and I feel I must address them now."

The look the earl bestowed on Darcy was unreadable, but he had already turned to Lady Emily. "It appears you have harbored some hope for a union with me, Lady Emily, which may, in part, have led to today's unpleasantness. Let me state unequivocally so there is no misunderstanding: that which you desire will never be. While I am sensible of the advantages you would bring as a wife, there will be no alliance between Pemberley and Teasdale. I apologize if this brings you pain, but I believe it is best that it be clearly understood."

Though Lady Emily appeared annoyed with Darcy's declaration, he could detect no hint of sorrow he would expect to see in a woman rejected by a man from whom she wished to receive a proposal. Whatever the lady's reasons had been, he was almost certain they had been dispassionate. In the end, she replied with dignity.

"I understand, Mr. Darcy."

"Then I shall depart," said Darcy, not wishing to stay there any longer.

"Darcy," called the earl as he stepped out of the room. "A moment of your time, if you will."

Darcy assented and as he waited for the older gentleman to approach, he could feel the weight of the earl studying him.

"May I assume the reason you will not pursue my daughter is due to Miss Bennet?"

"That is not the only reason," said Darcy. "I have never considered

Lady Emily as a possible bride. I believe in essentials we are too much alike, and though I understand the benefits of marrying her, I do not care for her the way a man should a woman he is considering making his bride."

"It is likely for the best, though I would have liked to have you as a son-in-law." Earl Chesterfield paused for a moment, then he continued: "I assume you have thought of the repercussions of an alliance with Miss Bennet?"

Darcy was about to respond angrily when the earl shook his head. "I mean no slight against the lady. She seems to be an intelligent, estimable sort of girl, and I know no ill of her. But from what I have heard, her portion is small and her connections are insignificant. Your father, God rest his soul, was one of my closest friends, and I would be serving his memory ill if I did not attempt to advise you in this matter, one which will be the most important decision of your life. I know you are too young to remember the countess, but she was my other half, Darcy, and I was devastated when I lost her, much as your father was when Lady Anne passed. I would not wish for anything less than what I or your father shared with our wives for you, and I know your father and mother would have felt the same way."

"Thank you, sir," said Darcy, the irritation fading away. There was no reason to deny his interest now, not with the earl who had often counselled him in his father's stead. "I know my parents would have come to love Miss Bennet, even though they would not have been happy with her situation. But her worth is above the price of any of my worldly possessions. I am wealthy enough to make her lack of dowry insignificant, and I have more connections to repulsive members of society than I know what to do with."

The earl barked with laughter and shook his head. "I have no doubt you do. I cannot blame you for wishing to find a wife untainted by that cesspool. I wish you the best of it. I hope, in time, all will be forgiven, and we may resume our previous closeness."

Darcy nodded. "I hope so too, sir. But it will depend on your daughter's good behavior and on Miss Bennet's generosity. Since I have no doubt of the latter, and I hope the former has learned her lesson, we should be able come to some accommodation."

"Then go to it, son. You may count on my support."

With a word of thanks and a shaken hand, Darcy turned to depart. Soon he was on his horse, cantering back toward Pemberley. He was not certain why Fitzwilliam had chosen to stay with Lady Emily, but he was certain his cousin would return before long. For now, he wished to return to his estate.

"You are fortunate no harm came to Miss Bennet," said Fitzwilliam when his cousin and the earl left the room.

Though the lady's lips tightened to a thin line, she did not respond, angering him all that much more.

"What were you thinking?" demanded he. "How could you possibly have taken leave of your senses sufficient to leave a young lady to shift for herself in such circumstances? I would say your father taught you better, but it should be obvious that such an action cannot be considered; I should not have thought anyone needed to be told."

Lady Emily mumbled something, but Fitzwilliam was not about to allow her escape with such a non-reply.

"I am sorry, Lady Emily, but I could not hear you. May I request that you repeat yourself?"

"I said, I believe I was not thinking at all," replied Lady Emily finally, turning a glare upon him.

"That much is evident, madam, but it does not excuse your actions."

"I did not claim it did."

Fitzwilliam nodded curtly. "At least you see that clearly. Why did you do it?"

"The woman made me angry!" cried she. "I did not even stop to consider my actions. I merely wished her out of my sight as quickly as possible."

"And what could she have said that was so offensive that you decided to abandon her?"

Though it was clear Lady Emily would prefer not to answer, she looked away and replied, and though her voice was soft, it was easy for Fitzwilliam to hear. "She all but declared her interest in Mr. Darcy. I became angry because I knew in my heart that she was correct. She had beaten me and I knew it."

Surprised that she would confess as much, Fitzwilliam said: "If you will pardon my saying so, Lady Emily, though I noticed your interest in Darcy from the beginning, I did not witness any great endeavor from yourself to turn his attention to you. Your efforts appeared lukewarm to me."

"I cannot explain it," replied Lady Emily. "I have always esteemed him—who would not? I thought . . . He never paid any attention to any young woman until Miss Bennet arrived, and then she—a woman he has known less than two months—appeared and drew all his attention. I will own that it . . . offended me."

"Lady Emily," said Fitzwilliam, "it is clear to me that your downfall has been jealousy. It is not laudable, but you are not the first."

"I suppose it is," replied the lady with a sigh.

"You owe her an apology. She deserves that much from you, even if you do not ever intend to speak with her again."

"Of course, she does."

Fitzwilliam turned to see the earl had stepped into the room, and though he had not spoken, Fitzwilliam had the impression he had been there for some time.

"The apology will be offered tomorrow. We should both be grateful that Miss Bennet has not chosen to embarrass us. Is that not correct, Emily?"

"It is, Father," said Lady Emily softly. Fitzwilliam had never seen her so humble as she was now.

"Darcy has departed?" asked Fitzwilliam.

"He has."

"Then I shall take my leave. I hope we shall meet again under better circumstances."

"You may depend on it. Thank you for coming and speaking to me of this matter, Fitzwilliam. You and your cousin are welcome at Teasdale Manor at any time, and if what I suspect should come to pass, Miss Bennet is welcome to come too."

Fitzwilliam bowed and departed, leaving the disgraced woman with her father. He was content—Darcy had secured the woman who would make him happy in life, and he could wish for no greater boon for his cousin. But though he would have preferred to forget about it, Fitzwilliam found the situation with Lady Emily spinning about, collecting his thoughts as it careened through his mind. She would escape any public censure, but it would be some time before relations were easy between Pemberley and Teasdale Manor. Why that should bother him, Fitzwilliam did not quite know.

CHAPTER XXIII

$\mathcal{I}$t was much later that evening when Elizabeth had the opportunity to once again speak with her uncle. Upon returning to Kingsdown, she had left them, though unwillingly, given the wonder of her new understanding with the gentleman. The chief of the afternoon had been spent resting in her room, and though she had slept a little, most of it was spent in contemplation of all that had happened that eventful day. With Olivia at Pemberley for the night, Elizabeth felt little desire for company.

Furthermore, after she did emerge from her room, she noted Mr. Drummond's barely concealed distraction and evident annoyance, and expecting it to be a result of Lady Emily's actions toward herself, she allowed him time with his own thoughts. Dinner was a quiet affair, more so than usual, with Olivia's absence and her uncle's distraction. The younger children were as they ever were—Elizabeth did sit with Leah and take her sister's place as the girl's confidant—but Mrs. Drummond and Edward both seemed to sense that something had happened. But as they had both been engaged in other activities when she had returned, they were, therefore, ignorant of the event. Elizabeth was quite happy to leave them in suspense, not wishing to discuss the matter.

After dinner, however, that changed. Mr. Drummond shook off his prior mood and approached Elizabeth, seating himself beside her. When he spoke, it was in a quiet tone, as he understood that his wife was watching them through suspicious eyes.

"I am happy you were returned safely to us, Lizzy." He paused and a hint of pain seemed to come over him. "I understand the bond between your father and yourself, and I shudder to think of his reaction had something happened to you."

"There is no reason to think on it any further, Uncle. It is in the past. I am well."

"Indeed, you are. There is also reason to congratulate you, or so Mr. Darcy informs me."

"I should hope so," said Elizabeth. "He was to ask for your consent."

"That he did. But you are aware that nothing is official until your father gives his consent."

"At present, perhaps," replied Elizabeth. She grinned at him. "You forget that I shall be one and twenty next month and of age. Mr. Darcy will not journey to Hertfordshire until I am to return home, so at that time, if Papa withholds his consent, I may ignore his dictates."

Her uncle laughed. "I confess I *had* forgotten it. Not that I could imagine your father denying you anything you desired or refusing a man such as Mr. Darcy. I believe he will be content with your happiness, though he might regret losing you from his home."

"I see you are well acquainted with my father's ways."

"Indeed, I am."

Mr. Drummond paused and darted a look around the room. Edward had taken up a book and the three younger children were playing some game on the floor. Mrs. Drummond, however, was watching them while chewing her lower lip in thought. She was too far distant to hear their whispered words, however, so Elizabeth did not care for the woman's scrutiny.

"Mr. Darcy mentioned your desire to keep your engagement from Jane's knowledge." Elizabeth nodded, sudden emotion causing her to choke up and stifling her response. "Can I also assume you wish to keep it from your aunt and the rest of my family?"

"I will tell Olivia," replied Elizabeth. "I cannot imagine keeping it from her, especially since Mr. Darcy means to tell Miss Darcy. But for the rest of the family, yes, I prefer they did not know. I will not be writing to Papa."

"Very well," replied Mr. Drummond. "I cannot say that I blame you. I will keep your confidence."

"Thank you, Uncle."

Mr. Drummond grinned. "I am quite happy at how this has all turned out. It was in my mind that you might find a husband here, but that you have attracted Mr. Darcy's attentions is more than I could ever have hoped for. And I am not insensible to the benefits to my family to be gained by having my niece installed as the mistress of the neighboring estate—Olivia, in particular, will have the privilege of your continuing society, which can only be to her benefit."

"I have been very happy to come to know her, Uncle," said Elizabeth, feeling the embarrassment of his praise. "That I will not be leaving the neighborhood is a boon I had not thought to receive."

"It will occasion some sorrow at being so far distant from your family, though."

Elizabeth sighed. "I suppose it will. My father will find it hard. My mother will, no doubt, insist upon my introducing all my sisters to society in hopes of their catching wealthy husbands themselves. She will expect Lydia to marry nothing less than an earl!"

"Mayhap you should turn her toward Colonel Fitzwilliam," replied her uncle, a twinkle in his eye. "I have heard of her predilection for red coats."

They laughed together, and Elizabeth agreed that it was so. "But I would never impose upon poor Colonel Fitzwilliam in such a way. Surely he does not deserve my sister."

Their spirited discussion continued for some little time, after which her uncle excused himself to go to his study to complete some work on his books. Edward went along with him to assist, leaving Elizabeth alone with the three children and Mrs. Drummond. The woman studied her, and several times Elizabeth thought she might speak. But she held her silence until it was time for Elizabeth to take the children upstairs and see them in their beds.

The next day, the Darcy party arrived at Kingsdown with Olivia in tow just after the family partook of their luncheon. Anticipating this visit and all which would likely transpire because of it, Elizabeth was certain to awake early that morning and complete her daily tasks so there would be no interruptions and no reason for Mrs. Drummond to insist she attend to other matters.

When the visitors arrived, Georgiana and Olivia entered the room first, followed by the gentlemen, and it was clear from their demeanors that one had been told the news, while the other had not. Georgiana was alive with excitement, shining eyes, searching for Elizabeth, while

Olivia watched her friend with evident confusion. As soon as Georgiana caught sight of her, she released a girlish laugh, disengaged from Olivia, and fairly skipped toward Elizabeth, throwing her arms around her in delight.

"Oh, Lizzy!" said she, though in a low voice, proving she had been told of the need to be circumspect. It was, of course, ruined to a certain extent by her present behavior. "I am so happy. You shall stay in Derbyshire after all!"

"I believe I shall, Georgiana," replied Elizabeth. "But please be circumspect at present, for your brother has not yet sought my father's consent."

"I will. But I am so happy, I could burst. Olivia is positively alive with curiosity." Georgiana giggled. "It was so diverting watching her this morning!"

Elizabeth directed a look over at her cousin, who was watching them, her brow furrowed in confusion. With a smile and a nod, Elizabeth mouthed "later" to her cousin. Olivia nodded and seemed to sense she should not make an issue of it at present.

"It seems your brother has been teasing my cousin. He should have simply informed you both!"

"I believe he wished to give you the pleasure of it yourself."

As soon as he had moved into the room and while Georgiana was accosting Elizabeth, Mr. Darcy had approached Mr. Drummond and was now speaking with him intently. After a moment of this, Mr. Drummond nodded to him and thanked him, after which Mr. Darcy greeted the room and Elizabeth in particular. For a moment, Elizabeth wondered what it might be like to be able to receive Mr. Darcy as her fiancé openly, before she shook off such thoughts, knowing she would know that pleasure soon enough.

"I have some intelligence for you," said Mr. Darcy as soon as he had sat by her side. Mr. Drummond had welcomed his other guests into the house and invited them to sit, then had started up a conversation with Colonel Fitzwilliam, apparently knowing that Elizabeth and Mr. Darcy needed to speak unobtrusively.

"Of Lady Emily?"

Mr. Darcy's countenance was overset with an expression of distaste. "I visited Teasdale Manor yesterday in Fitzwilliam's company."

"Your cousin accompanied you?"

"Indeed. It seems that he also saw Lady Emily's behavior for what it was and took it upon himself to interfere with her actions, though I wonder why he did not inform me."

Elizabeth was certain she knew exactly why Colonel Fitzwilliam had not informed his cousin, but she held her tongue, as Mr. Darcy continued to speak.

"It seems that Lady Emily did, at least, recognize the foolishness of her actions, and she returned to the road to try to locate you. By then I had already found you, and we had left the road behind. When she could not find you, she returned to her father and confessed all, leading him to launch a search for you."

In some obscure way, Mr. Darcy's account of Lady Emily's belated conscience was comforting, though Elizabeth was still not sanguine about the matter. Perhaps the friendship they previously shared might be repaired, though it would be some time before she was willing to listen to the woman's overtures. Then Elizabeth realized that she was not even certain that Lady Emily had *ever* been a true friend to her, and was thus uncertain if there was anything to restore.

"Regardless," Mr. Darcy continued speaking, "she has confessed herself to be completely in the wrong and has agreed to make her apology. If that is acceptable to you, of course."

"Had your account been different, I might have been otherwise inclined," said Elizabeth.

"And I would not have blamed you."

"As it is, however, if she will make one, I will listen to her. I do not think I will trust her for some time, but I will accept her apology."

Mr. Darcy nodded. "In addition to this, it seems she has had some expectation that we might come to an agreement." Elizabeth was not at all surprised by this. "I have informed her of the fact that I have no intention of offering for her, and that she should not expect any attentions to be forthcoming."

"You did not inform her of our engagement?"

"I did not. But the earl guessed our developing relationship, and he spoke to me about it."

Elizabeth arched an eyebrow. "To warn you away from the penniless daughter of a minor landowner in favor of his daughter?"

A chuckle was his response. "You are far too erudite for your own good, Miss Bennet, but you also do him a disservice. His lordship was a close friend of my father's. Along with my uncle, he provided a great deal of assistance in the days after my father passed. He did mention those things, but only to be certain that I had considered them myself. When I informed him of my intentions, he supported me, and he specifically praised you."

"Then I owe him an apology," said Elizabeth with a shake of her head. "My father has sometimes told me that I am much too quick to make judgments, and this appears to be one of those times."

"Perhaps," replied Mr. Darcy. "But you can hardly be blamed for them."

Elizabeth shook her head, but she allowed the comment to pass. They joined the general conversation in the room, and for a time it was carried on with the effortless ease of those who have long been comfortable in one another's company. There was an indefinable quality in what Elizabeth was witnessing before her, as if those who were aware of the engagement had imparted their excitement to those who were not without even realizing it. This would be the scene of many family gatherings in the future, Elizabeth was certain, and she could only anticipate such events and inviting her family to her new home in turn.

It was not long, however, before another party arrived, and the earl and his daughter stepped into the room. Earl Chesterfield held his head high and betrayed no hint of trepidation concerning the upcoming meeting, but the same could not be said of his daughter. For the first time in her acquaintance with Lady Emily, Elizabeth sensed her hesitation.

They were welcomed and invited to sit, and they did, exchanging pleasantries. During this brief period, Elizabeth watched Lady Emily, attempting to take the lady's measure anew. The woman darted several glances at her, and she appeared to not know what to make of Elizabeth's silence, as if she expected Elizabeth to denounce her the moment she entered the room. There was nary a display of haughtiness or unwillingness—though it would not be unexpected, given the circumstances—leading Elizabeth to believe that her forthcoming apology was to be offered willingly. It made her feel a little better.

"Miss Bennet," said Lady Emily during a lull in the conversation, "I wonder if I might have a word with you."

"Perhaps we should retire to the other parlor?" said Elizabeth, speaking as much to her uncle as Lady Emily. "This is a private matter, after all."

The reactions of both Lady Emily and the earl bespoke their gratitude. Elizabeth had no desire to publicly humiliate anyone and wished for this episode to be behind her as soon as may be. The best way to do that was to accept her apology without witnesses.

"I believe that would be best, Lizzy," said her uncle, and he rose to lead them from the room.

Mrs. Drummond, Edward, and Olivia's eyes were all alight with curiosity, but Colonel Fitzwilliam immediately began to speak, distracting them. For her part, Georgiana looked at Elizabeth, but Elizabeth only smiled and shook her head, and the girl responded by nodding. Mr. Darcy and the earl both rose to accompany the principals of the situation, along with Mr. Drummond, from the room, and they repaired to the second parlor. It was a smallish sort of room, the furnishings old, but remarkably well-preserved, given the lack of use it received. They would not be disturbed here.

"I thank you for your restraint, Miss Bennet," said the earl.

"I have no desire for this incident to be known to any more people than necessary. Only the five of us, your servants, and Colonel Fitzwilliam will ever know."

"Thank you, Miss Bennet," said Lady Emily quietly. "I wish you to know that I am aware of how badly I behaved yesterday. It was wrong of me, and I confess it without hesitation. Great harm could have befallen you due to my actions, and I am heartily sorry for putting you in such danger. I humbly beg your forgiveness."

"I appreciate your apology, Lady Emily," replied Elizabeth. "Though I will confess I was taken aback at what happened and could not understand it, no harm has been done and I offer my forgiveness readily. Let us put this incident behind us and think of it no more."

"You are very good," replied Lady Emily. "I hope that in the future we may become friends again. I understand that it will be some time before I will be able to gain your trust, but I am willing to work to earn it."

"I hope so too," said Elizabeth. It cost her nothing to say it, though she was not certain it was possible at present. But as Lady Emily lived just to the north of Pemberley and would be her neighbor for many years she hoped it would be. She well understood how important it was to have good relations with one's neighbors.

"And I add my sentiments to my daughter's," said Lord Chesterfield. "Though I know you only a little, I have been impressed with you, Miss Bennet. Your coming to Derbyshire has been accepted by all, especially the Darcys, and I do not wish you to think we are any exception."

"I am not naïve enough to think that I am universally liked, your lordship. But I have felt quite welcome and have made many friends. This is a wonderful corner of the kingdom, and I could not be happier that I have come."

"Excellent! Then we shall work to restore your trust and build our relationship again. I believe there are many years of association ahead of us."

The knowing look the earl directed at her confirmed his good information of at least the attraction between Elizabeth and Mr. Darcy, if not the full scope of their current situation. Elizabeth was forced to smile—he was not what Elizabeth might have thought to find in a peer of the realm, being both friendly and unpretentious. Elizabeth thought she might like knowing him better.

The apology having been offered and accepted, they soon returned to the sitting-room where the others awaited them. The Teasdales sat with them for another quarter of an hour before they excused themselves, leaving the Darcy party behind. Mr. Darcy suggested a walk, to which Elizabeth immediately agreed, and Olivia, Georgiana, Colonel Fitzwilliam, and Edward all indicated their willingness to accompany them. Mr. Drummond waved them out with a smile and they left to prepare.

But as Elizabeth was attempting to leave, she was arrested by the presence of her aunt, who was looking at her with curiosity, and for once, without disdain.

"It is not every day an earl and his daughter visit my home and ask to speak with my niece. It is even rarer that she directs them from the room to speak in private. Do you care to explain?"

"My apologies, Aunt," replied Elizabeth. "But I cannot satisfy your curiosity. Lady Emily wished to speak to me of a private matter. It must remain between us."

"Your uncle and Mr. Darcy accompanied you," replied her aunt. "And for that matter, the earl went as well."

"That is because they were all aware of the contents of our discussion, Aunt. There is nothing underhanded happening. But what was discussed must remain confidential."

Mrs. Drummond nodded slowly. "I suppose I must be content, then. Are you certain you did nothing to offend Lady Emily?"

"No, Aunt." *Quite the opposite, in fact.* "It was a trifling matter."

"Very well." Her aunt's haughty mask once again slipped into place. "I suppose you had best join your friends before they depart without you."

The woman turned and walked away, leaving Elizabeth to watch, bemused, at her sudden mood shifts. She exited the house to where the others were waiting, and they turned toward the back park, walking as a group, speaking animatedly amongst themselves. Elizabeth felt herself to be happy—she had known none of these people only three months earlier, but now she felt as if she had been acquainted with them all her life. And she would marry one of them. It still felt surreal to think of herself as an engaged woman, but there it was.

As they entered a path through the trees, the path narrowed so that they were forced to walk two abreast, but that worked well for Elizabeth, as she wished to make the communication to Olivia concerning her good fortune. Colonel Fitzwilliam understood what was about to happen, and he distracted Edward by speaking to him and walking down the path quickly, leaving the others to walk more slowly as they spoke. Olivia was not blind to the colonel's actions, and as soon as she saw he was leading her brother away, she turned to Elizabeth.

"Will you all now explain what has happened? I am quite confused by Georgiana's behavior, and now by Elizabeth's need to speak in private with Lady Emily."

"The two are not related, Olivia," replied Elizabeth. She turned to her cousin, fairly bursting to tell her the news. "In fact, something of significance has happened, and I would like you to know."

"Then what is it?" asked Olivia. The girl's eyes were alight with curiosity and anticipation.

"Yesterday, Mr. Darcy made me an offer of marriage, and I have accepted. I am to live in Derbyshire forever, after all."

The shock in Olivia's countenance left her speechless for several moments, but soon she let out a squeal and flew at Elizabeth, laughing and crying at the same time. "Is it true, Lizzy? Are you to stay in Derbyshire?"

"It is," said Elizabeth, crying right along with her cousin. "Though I will return home when the summer is complete like I always intended, Mr. Darcy will speak to Father at that time, and then I shall return as a married woman."

"Oh, I am so happy, Lizzy! Not only shall I continue to have your society, but you shall also be married to such a wealthy man!"

The sight of Olivia covering her mouth in consternation brought giggles to Elizabeth's lips, and she was joined by Georgiana, who was obviously enjoying her friend's antics.

"I am sorry!" squeaked Olivia. "I did not mean that how it sounded."

"We know you did not, dearest," replied Elizabeth. "Only remember, for sometimes we say things which may be misconstrued, if we do not take the trouble to check our thoughts, so that our mouths do not ramble ahead of us."

"Georgiana and I did not take any offense," added Mr. Darcy. "I know your genuine feelings of happiness for your cousin."

"I *am* happy, Mr. Darcy," said Olivia, her initial shyness concerning Mr. Darcy returning. "Elizabeth has become a dear friend in addition to being a wonderful cousin. I am so happy for her. But I cannot be more ecstatic that she will continue to be here, that I may see her so often."

"No more than I will be, Olivia," said Georgiana. "I shall be gaining a wonderful sister, and we shall both have our friend and mentor present always."

"Perhaps we can arrange invitations to town," said Mr. Darcy. "Georgiana loves the theater, concerts, the menagerie, Kew Gardens, and many other attractions which can be found in London. I have no doubt that you will enjoy them and provide Georgiana company, for she will undoubtedly be bored living with two such old married people."

Georgiana and Olivia laughed together. "I would be very grateful for any such invitations," said Olivia.

"It will be so much fun!" exclaimed Georgiana.

"Then you will have something to anticipate," said Mr. Darcy. "Now, unless I am very much mistaken, Fitzwilliam and Edward will wonder what has become of us if we do not hurry to catch them. If you girls will go on ahead, I have something of which to speak with Miss Bennet."

Clearly the girls imagined some clandestine and highly improper actions between the engaged couple, for they giggled together and turned to walk down the path. Mr. Darcy watched them go with affection, before he turned to Elizabeth and offered his arm. She accepted, and soon they were walking behind the girls, the object of their scrutiny, as they several times looked back and laughed as they whispered together.

"I believe I have said it before, Miss Bennet," said Mr. Darcy, "but your friendship and that of Miss Drummond has been good for my sister."

"And hers has been good for us. Georgiana was the first young lady who accepted me when I came to Derbyshire. She is a delightful girl."

Darcy turned his attention toward Elizabeth. "I am happy to see you so well. I know many young ladies who would have been distressed by yesterday's events even now."

"I like to think I am resilient, Mr. Darcy. I will not allow such poor memories to rule me."

"Exactly as I would have expected." Mr. Darcy then sobered a little and turned his attentions to other matters. "I have a little more news to relate to you. Bingley and I have settled on a date for their arrival."

"I see," said Elizabeth, that familiar blend of trepidation and anticipation welling up in her heart. "Can I assume it will be soon?"

"Next week, Miss Bennet. They will arrive on Monday next, only three days after your birthday."

Elizabeth shot him a surprised smile. "How did you know of my birthday?"

"Come, Miss Bennet—you did not think I would be complacent about such an important date. Should your father see fit to reject my proposal that is the first date when you will be free to accept me without his consent. Of course, I would wish to be cognizant of it."

A laugh met his declaration, and Elizabeth brought her fee hand up to place over his hand. "Are you certain that is all?"

"Well, Georgiana might have mentioned it to me—it seems you told her some time ago?"

"Only in passing. And it must have been several weeks ago."

"I believe it was. Georgiana has been planning to invite you to a special event that day, complete with a birthday cake. Our cook, you understand, makes heavenly creations on our birthdays and is eager to display his talents whenever the opportunity presents itself."

"Then I shall anticipate his masterpiece keenly, sir. Should I hold my peace about this matter? Has Georgiana intended to surprise me with it?"

Mr. Darcy shook his head. "No, I believe one of her purposes today was to extend the invitation. It is, of course, open to Miss Drummond, and any of her family who wish to attend."

"Then let us keep it to just Olivia and me, and perhaps Edward," said Elizabeth slowly. "A more intimate setting would be preferable."

"Then let us make a picnic of it. We can ride to a location I have wished to show you and eat our luncheon there."

Elizabeth laughed. "Will you not destroy your cook's wonderful creation?"

"We will return to Pemberley to partake of the cake," replied Mr. Darcy.

"And the state of my riding skills? I recall someone promising to teach me to ride, yet I have remained uninstructed."

Mr. Darcy chuckled and shook his head. "Of course, we must remedy that lack, Miss Bennet. I will ensure Georgiana invites you in the next week so that we can attend to it."

"Then I accept, sir."

"Excellent!"

And they continued to walk and talk together. If Georgiana and Olivia still giggled and looked at them from time to time, Elizabeth could cheerfully ignore them. After all, she was walking with the best man she had ever known, and she was increasingly loath to turn her attention away from him.

CHAPTER **XXIV**

$\mathcal{T}$he days between Lady Emily's apology to Miss Bennet and the coming of her sister were spent in an agreeable fashion. Darcy continued to call on her often, and those days when he did not, she could be found at Pemberley with Georgiana. It was clear she was more distracted, no doubt due to the imminent arrival of the Bingleys, but Darcy could not blame her.

It was the day after the apology that he became aware of the true state of affairs which existed between Miss Bennet and her sister, and he could not be more confused. The reports she had given him of her sister's character in no way suggested her to be a woman who would throw her family over due to an increase in wealth, nor did he think it likely that Bingley could be so deficient in understanding as to be entrapped by such a woman. He was easily led, at times, but Darcy knew he was not at all lacking in intelligence.

But Darcy did not doubt Miss Bennet's account either. The one thing of which he was wary of was the instinct to think poorly of Mrs. Bingley before he had ever met her for no more reason than the pain she had caused to Darcy's beloved. It would not be useful to pre-judge her, for there may be some explanation for her behavior which did not result in his damning her character.

The one item of which Darcy was curious was canvassed while she was a visitor at Pemberley. Georgiana and Miss Drummond were amusing each other, and Fitzwilliam was away somewhere, which allowed Darcy to speak with his betrothed alone, and he lost no time in asking her opinion.

"Miss Bennet," said he carefully, as they were walking in Pemberley's gardens, "I wish to ask your opinion on a matter of which I spoke with your uncle."

Miss Bennet nodded. "Of course."

"Mr. Drummond raised the possibility that your own change in status when we marry will prompt your sister to again alter her behavior toward you. I wished to know your thoughts about it."

A faraway look descended over Miss Bennet's countenance, and for some few moments she was silent. At length, however, she turned toward him, her glorious eyes filled with a depth of pain he had never before beheld in them.

"*If* she is behaving the way she is because of pride in her new situation that would not be unreasonable to expect." Her voice was quiet and Darcy was forced to strain to hear her. "I *hope* that is not the case. I am not confident of it, however."

"And what will you do if it is proven true?"

A sigh escaped her lips. "I do not wish to believe it of my dearest, angelic sister. But you are correct to suggest it. I suppose I do not know what I shall do. There is not only my relationship with my sister to consider, but also your friendship with Mr. Bingley which, I have heard, is quite close."

Darcy smiled at her resilience expressed in the lightness of her tone, however forced. "Yes, it is, indeed."

"If she does so, then I suppose I will accept it, in the name of family unity and your friendship with Mr. Bingley, of whom I also think highly. But I cannot imagine it will ever be the same between us should that be the case."

"I am afraid I do not know what to think," replied Darcy.

"Nor do I," replied Miss Bennet. "Think of it in this fashion, Mr. Darcy: what would you think if Georgiana suddenly began to behave in like fashion because she married a man who was of greater consequence than you?"

Darcy frowned. "I cannot imagine her doing that."

"I could not have imagined it in my sister until I witnessed her behavior myself," replied Miss Bennet. "In essentials, Georgiana and Jane are quite similar. Both are quiet and reticent, and both are possessed of an obliging, pleasing disposition. Jane attempts to see the best in others, no matter the situation, and though I have always thought it naïve of her, it was a counter to my own cynicism, a viewpoint I treasured. Mr. Bingley has often referred to her has an angel, a sentiment with which I cannot disagree."

"And yet the angel has become less estimable than you could have imagined."

"Exactly," said Miss Bennet. "I am hoping her behavior will have changed since I saw her last. Mr. Bingley suggested she needs time to adjust to her new situation."

"Discomfort with one's position would lead to an increased desire for the intimacy of those dear to one's heart, I should think."

"I do not disagree. But in Jane, the opposite seems to be true. We shall see when she arrives. At present, I have hope, but little confidence."

Miss Bennet then turned the conversation to other matters, and though she spoke willingly and at times with her usual vivacity, still he could tell her heart was not in it. The upcoming visit of her sister weighed on her mind. It was only with the greatest of will that Darcy kept his own council—he knew enough of her by now to know she would approach him if she wished for his opinion or the comfort of his assurances, but that she consulted her own feelings and came to her own conclusions before she would ask for his.

As the day for Miss Bennet's picnic approached, Darcy gave her the promised riding instruction and was delighted at her aptitude.

"You informed me you were not much of a rider, Miss Bennet," said he as he led her around the fenced yard in which they trained horses and riders. "But I see little to criticize in your technique."

"Then I must be a quick study," said Miss Bennet with her typical impudence. "I have not been on a horse in a year at least."

"You are more than qualified to join us on the picnic, Lizzy," said Georgiana. The two girls stood nearby behind the fence, Georgiana observing and making amusing comments while Olivia awaited her turn.

"Then perhaps it would be best to allow Olivia to gain more confidence," said Miss Bennet. "She has not as much experience as I."

They quickly agreed and Miss Drummond took her cousin's place on the back of the placid mare they had been using for their practice. Darcy found that she, too, possessed some natural aptitude, and though she would not be jumping fences in the near future, he was happy to inform her that she was competent enough to accompany them when they went on the picnic.

When Friday finally came, they gathered together at Pemberley to set out, six in the group, as it included Fitzwilliam and Edward. The location to which Darcy intended to guide them was some miles distant, and it passed through the rougher parts of his estate, not to mention several streams, all of which Darcy was certain Miss Bennet would delight in. It was a beautiful day, the sun shining brightly, prompting the ladies to pull down their bonnets to cover their eyes, the warmth of the day such that even such mild exertion of a walk raised a sheen of perspiration on the horses' backs. It was wonderful to be alive in such a time and place, and Darcy envisioned many more such opportunities with his beautiful bride in the years to come.

Miss Bennet and Miss Olivia stayed close to Georgiana, the three of them laughing and talking as they rode, while Darcy and Fitzwilliam rode ahead and Edward brought up the rear, watching the ladies carefully and casting around for any hint of trouble.

"It is a sight to move any man, is it not Darcy?" asked Fitzwilliam, glancing back at the ladies as they rode. "Such fair maidens all gathered together in one place is rarely to be seen."

"You will receive no argument from me, Cousin," replied Darcy. Miss Bennet laughed at something his sister said, and for a moment she seemed to have shed the specter of Mrs. Bingley's coming and returned to her usual self.

"In some ways I envy you, Cousin. You recognized a jewel and determined to have her, and you let nothing stand in your way."

"There is nothing preventing you from doing the same."

"Except for the lack of a similar jewel."

"You will find her. And when you do, I believe you will act in the same manner I have."

Fitzwilliam replied with a noncommittal shrug and the subject was dropped.

"I saw Chesterfield yesterday," said Fitzwilliam after they had ridden on for several more moments.

"I trust he is well?"

"He is. The topic of our discussion was Lady Emily. The earl is concerned for her, as she has largely withdrawn into herself."

Darcy snorted; he had little sympathy for Lady Emily, not after her behavior with Miss Bennet. "I am certain she will recover. Her infamy was kept from society, so she will have no consequences to bear on that front. I hope she will learn from this episode."

"I am certain she will. I told the earl I thought she was revaluating much of what she believed and, in the end, will come away better for the experience."

Darcy nodded. "Then I wish her luck. For my part, it will be long before I can meet her as an agreeable acquaintance. You know of my resentful temper—my good opinion will take time to restore."

"Perhaps that is so," replied Fitzwilliam, turned to Darcy, spearing him with a glare, "but for you to say you have a resentful temper is patently absurd. What of George Wickham and all the chances he was given over the years? If anything, I think you tend to be too forgiving at times."

"I know my own temper, Cousin. I will do my best to extend Lady Emily the balm of forgiveness as Miss Bennet has, but do not hold out hope it will happen soon."

"For my part I believe that she may be changed. There is something . . . estimable about her, though her jealousy over your attentions to Miss Bennet was reprehensible. I believe this experience will make her into a new woman."

Darcy nodded but he did not reply. The wound was still too new, too raw, for him to consider whatever good qualities Lady Emily might have. It was unfair, perhaps, but there it was, nonetheless.

It was not many more minutes before they arrived at the site Darcy had designated for the picnic. It was a grassy section beside a stream, happily rumbling and tumbling over rocks and little depressions. The woods were close around three sides, while on the fourth side rose a low hill which overlooked the long valley that contained much of Pemberley's lands. It was deep within the boundaries of Pemberley, some distance from the lands Darcy's tenants farmed, a location which was not suitable for farming, though Darcy knew that at times the herds of sheep might be led hither to drink from the stream or eat of the hearty grass which covered the ground.

"What a delightful place this is!" exclaimed Miss Bennet as the horses filed into the glen.

"I knew you would enjoy it," replied Darcy. "This place could have been made for you specifically, so tailored is it to your tastes."

Miss Bennet turned and regarded him. "Has my character suddenly become easily understood, Mr. Darcy? I had always prided myself on its intricacy."

Darcy returned her grin. "It is simply because I have undertaken a study of your preferences, Miss Bennet. How else was I to ensure you accepted our friendship?"

"You might have simply showed me this place and saved yourself the trouble!" Miss Bennet laughed, and Georgiana and Olivia, listening to their banter, joined them in their humor.

"Perhaps you should wait until I have shown you the second vista. I believe you will be even more impressed."

"That may wait until later!" cried Georgiana. "I am hungry. You shall need to wait until after we eat our luncheon!"

The others all agreed with Georgiana's claim, and though Miss Bennet grumbled in a teasing fashion, they all agreed to eat before they undertook any further exploration.

Luncheon was excellent, nothing less than he would have expected from Pemberley's kitchen, and as the company was good, laughter and lively conversation reigned. It was about an hour later that they had finished eating and set about exploring. Eager as he was to have Miss Bennet to himself, Darcy guided her a little way down the stream to a low waterfall. Miss Bennet came along with pleasure, though she did not resist the temptation to tease him.

"Not that I am complaining, but I believe you mentioned something about a view from the top of that hill. Have you suddenly changed your mind, Mr. Darcy?"

"I have not. But at the moment, I believe it is more important to have you to myself than to show you the view. We can attend to that after."

Miss Bennet looked over to the hill to see their four companions climbing toward the top, talking and laughing as they went. Darcy's gaze followed hers and it was easy to see the glances they were drawing and to note the laughter was directed at them. It did not bother him, for it was he who was in this wonderful creature's company and no one else. He hoped they were circumspect enough not to speak with too much openness, as Edward still did not know of their engagement. Then again, Darcy was certain he could trust the young man to keep the confidence should he discover it.

"There is one boon I would request, though." Miss Bennet turned to face him. "I would wish, now that we are almost officially engaged, for you to call me by my given name and to be afforded the same privilege."

"But if I do that, I shall confuse you with your cousin," replied Miss Bennet.

Darcy grinned. "We could not have that, could we? Georgiana has always called me William, and I would find it very agreeable if you would do likewise."

"Very well," replied Miss Bennet, a shyness descending over her like the onset of night.

"So, what is your opinion, Elizabeth?" said he, relishing the sound of her name on his lips for the first time. "Do you approve of Pemberley?"

"Is there anyone who does not?" was her reply.

"My aunt, Lady Catherine de Bourgh. Though she has not visited in several years, preferring *us* attend *her* in Kent, every time she has visited she has complained about the wildness and castigated us for leaving it the way it is."

The laughter his words prompted spoke to a knowledge of the woman which could only have been gained by listening to her toady of a cousin's accounts. "I am not surprised, sir. I am convinced that at Rosings Park everything is maintained to Lady Catherine's exacting standards and not even a blade of grass would dare be out of place."

Darcy joined her in laughing heartily. "You are not that far from the mark, Elizabeth. Lady Catherine insists that there be formal gardens aplenty with all of society's ideas of truly modern gardens incorporated. It is beautiful and pleasant and so very sterile."

"I much prefer this," said Elizabeth. "It is as nature intended it to be."

"It is," said Darcy, though his gaze was fixed upon her, enchanted by her beautiful form amongst the flora of his home.

They wandered for some time, speaking of very little of consequence, though there was no deficit of words between them. At each new scene, each new sight of the beauties of Pemberley, she exclaimed anew, lighting her countenance like the sun could never accomplish. At one point they saw a deer in the distance, grazing on the soft grasses below its feet, and Elizabeth watched it for some moments, marveling in the abundant wildlife which also permeated Pemberley.

"Come, Elizabeth," said Darcy at length. "Let us go to the top of the hill so I may show you what lies beyond.

Elizabeth turned to look, noting that Georgiana and Fitzwilliam had led their guests to another location, leaving the hilltop bare of occupants. "Of course, William," said she as she took his hand and allowed him to guide her as they climbed. The slope was shallow, rising to a gentle crest amid strands of trees, but at the very top it was bare, allowing those at its peak a view down into the valley below.

When they had reached the top, Darcy turned to Elizabeth, noting the utter delight with which she gazed down into the valley. The land just below them started as a narrow passage, with trees pressing down on all sides. But as it sloped downward, it opened, a wide avenue of fields, showing their early summer bounty, the promise of the harvest to come. And down in the center, in the distance shining like a jewel set there by the hand of god, sat Pemberley.

"Oh, how lovely!" cried Elizabeth, clapping her hands in joy. "I have never seen such a wonderful sight, William. I could not have imagined we would be in sight of the house from here, though I will own it does look like a child's toy from this distance."

"We journeyed through the woods, climbing as we came," said Darcy, pointing to the line of trees which gradually fell off to the right. "On the left, the wide valley is bounded by that other line of trees, which provides much of Pemberley's production. In among those trees, however, are other fields which cannot be seen, and woods where lumber is produced, and areas to herd sheep. If you look down the valley far past the house, you just might be able to make out where it curves toward the right."

"I believe I can see it," said Elizabeth. She was gazing down the valley, one hand shielding her eyes and giving her a clearer view of the long valley.

"The end to the valley in that direction is the edge of your uncle's property."

"Oh!" said Elizabeth. "That is where we passed by when you returned me to Kingsdown and where Olivia, Leah, and I picnicking not long after I arrived."

"Exactly," replied Darcy. "This valley is the main part of Pemberley's land, though there is more to be found on all sides. But much of what we produce can be found down this broad avenue."

"What are your primary crops?"

Pleased that Elizabeth would be interested in such things, Darcy said: "Wheat and barley, though we do adhere to modern practices of crop rotation, so it varies. I also have cattle on the western edge of the estate, we have already spoken of sheep, and there is a coal mine at the very north of the property. In fact, if we went a little north we would come on that mine, and then a little further would take us to the ruin we visited."

"A diverse and complex estate, then."

"It is," replied Darcy. "But I would not have it any other way. Not only has Pemberley been in my family's possession since the time of William the Conqueror, but a diverse operation, though more challenging, is more resistant to changing prices and the failure of certain crops. For example, in times past, Pemberley has been converted almost entirely to cattle, when the prices of certain grains fell so low as to harm our levels of profit. It is very much like an investment which must be watched carefully and adapted as needed."

"You are an excellent master, William. I am certain your father would be proud of how you have performed your stewardship of your land."

Nothing Elizabeth could have said would have brought more pleasure into Darcy's heart than her praise. Without thought, he gathered her to him, kissing her head and pressing her slight form against his own, heedless of anyone watching.

"Thank you, Elizabeth," said he. "I can truthfully tell you that you belong at Pemberley as much as I ever did. You will be the perfect mistress, and our heirs will be blessed for having you as their mother."

Elizabeth pulled away from him and favored him with an arched eyebrow. "Are you not concerned that I shall only produce girls? My mother birthed a succession of five, you know."

"No, Elizabeth," said Darcy, kissing her once again. "Pemberley is not entailed, and any of our children may inherit. As long as her husband is willing to take on my name, any girl of our blood may inherit.

"And I am far from objecting to a gaggle of little girls with their mother's eyes and liveliness. Should we have twelve such, I will never repine."

"Then perhaps *you* should birth them!" said Elizabeth, in that teasing tone he so loved. "I believe twelve might be a little excessive."

Darcy was a little surprised that Elizabeth would know so much on the matter, and he asked her with more than a little curiosity. "Are you familiar with the process?"

"I was raised on a farm, Mr. Darcy. I have seen animals mating and have even witnessed horses birthing foals. I have always assumed it to be similar."

"True," said Darcy. "Then how many children would Miss Elizabeth Bennet consider to be ideal?"

Elizabeth laughed. "Perhaps four or five. I have not thought of it, to be honest, and I am not certain one can determine how many children one is to have."

This was not a subject on which Darcy wished to speak in any detail, for even if she *had* seen animals reproduce, she was still a young lady of her times, albeit an uncommonly intelligent one.

"You are one and twenty today, Elizabeth. This is the day I know without a doubt you will marry me, as your father cannot stop you any longer."

"He never would, William. He cares too much for my happiness to deny me what I truly want."

"Do you think you will be happy here?"

His quiet question seemed to take Elizabeth by surprise, and she turned to him, a question written on her brow. Darcy was uncertain why he had voiced it. It was perhaps an echo of his old distrust of any woman or maybe a lingering fear that he would not be able to make the woman he loved happy, despite the advantages he possessed. It might be nothing more than a simple request to be reassured that she loved him as much as he loved her. Darcy was unable to articulate exactly what he meant, for he did not understand himself.

She sensed this and approached him, reaching out to grasp his hands in hers, and she looked deeply into his eyes, trying to understand him, or trying to reassure him.

"William," said she, "looking at all this, I cannot imagine *any* woman would be discontented with her situation."

"But you are not a woman who is moved by mere possessions."

"I am not," agreed she. "But from the standpoint of nothing more than that, a woman could be nothing but well pleased to be mistress of Pemberley. I will own to a little trepidation, as your holdings are so vast, but I have never allowed anything to intimidate me in the past, and I will not do so in the future."

"There is also the house in town, and three secondary estates to consider," said Darcy, throwing her a teasing grin.

Elizabeth laughed. "That is most certainly not helping."

"You will be fine."

"I am certain I will." Elizabeth paused, and her gaze became more penetrating. "But as you know, I consider the needs of wealth to be less important than those of the heart. When we were girls, Jane and I were the daily witnesses to a couple who were not happy in their marriage. We vowed to each other that only the deepest love would introduce us to matrimony.

"As we grew older, we began to understand that my parents were not as unhappy as we thought. When they can be bothered to make the attempt, they share a good and loving relationship. But my mother is intent upon her nerves and her worries for the future, though that has eased to some extent with my sister's marriage to the next master of Longbourn, and my father loves to amuse himself by teasing my mother and provoking her nerves. Jane and I both decided we could never live that way."

The steady gaze that bored into Darcy's eyes took his breath away, and he was captivated by those beautiful, deep, glorious pools of dark brown, which seemed to go on forever.

"What I am trying to say, Mr. Darcy, is that I love you with my every breath. I would not have accepted you if I did not. I know there will be vexations, we will disagree and argue, but if we treat each other with respect and remember our love, we will be happy, despite our trials. I love you, William. There is nothing which will make me happier than to become your wife. There is nothing more I require to make me happy."

Overwhelmed, Darcy drew her to him and held her there, a tenderness for this woman welling up within him beyond anything he had ever felt. He had already known she loved him, though she had not said the words. They would be well. They would start a family, the next generation of the Darcys of Pemberley. They would be happy for the rest of their lives. Nothing would stop them.

CHAPTER XXV

Three days later, Darcy found himself on the front steps of Pemberley, watching as a carriage approached. In it were the Bingleys, and while Darcy was anticipating meeting his friend again and witnessing the changes that marriage had wrought in him, he was not anticipating the meeting with Miss Bingley and, to a lesser extent, Mrs. Bingley. The latter, of course, he had never met, and he could own to a little curiosity, but if the woman had maintained her previous behavior, he was not certain he could stand idly by and watch his beloved Elizabeth experience the pain of an indifferent sister.

The conveyance rumbled along the low drive, its approach startling a large flock of ducks on the lake which flew off, squawking their indignation, only to alight on its surface again once the disturbance had passed by. The other parts of the estate continued, unconcerned with the arrival of those who had the potential to throw the master and future mistress into such confusion. Darcy wished Elizabeth were here—but she had declined, mentioning a previous engagement with some friends, and reminding him that she was not yet the hostess to his visitors. Darcy was forced to own that she was correct, though he would have preferred her presence.

"I wish you had not invited Miss Bingley," said Georgiana. She was standing by his side, eying the carriage as it approached as if it were some harbinger of doom.

"Why ever not, Georgiana?" asked Fitzwilliam, the cutting edge of satire sharpening his voice. "Do you not anticipate the arrival of your dear friend? Is the pleasure of Miss Bingley's conversation, replete with compliments and innuendo, not enough to make you swoon with delight?"

"Have a care, Fitzwilliam, Georgiana," said Darcy. The carriage was only moments from arriving, and regardless of his personal feelings for the woman, he did not wish to insult her, though it may bring about some relief if she finally understood his lack of interest in her. Then again, she would likely convince herself that she had misunderstood, and her attentions would continue unabated.

"You are both aware why I could not exclude her. She is a guest and should be treated as one."

"As long as she does not try to order Mrs. Reynolds," said Georgiana, a dark look, rarely seen, fixed on the carriage.

"You must think of better things, Georgiana," replied Fitzwilliam. "When Miss Bingley is grating on your nerves, just remember the pleasure you will receive when she learns of Darcy's engagement with Miss Bennet. The look on her face alone would be worth capturing on a canvass and preserving for posterity."

Georgiana giggled and Darcy himself could not hold in a snort. His thoughts on the subject were nearly identical to his relations'. Hopefully they would make it through this visit unscathed.

Their banter was brought to a close as the coach stopped before the stairs and the footman on the back hopped down, placed a step beside the vehicle, and opened the door. Soon the familiar form of his closest friend emerged and turned to help the ladies down.

"Bingley, my friend," said Darcy, stepping forward and offering his hand, a gesture which was accepted with his friend's typical enthusiasm. "Welcome to Pemberley. I am very happy to see you."

"It is good to be in your company again," replied Bingley.

"Oh, there is no question of our acceptance of your kind invitation, Mr. Darcy," Miss Bingley's strident tones assaulted their ears. "After the months we have spent in the savage society of my brother's *leased* estate, coming to Pemberley is a balm to our souls."

"Miss Bingley," said Darcy, bowing, but not taking the hand she offered. "Welcome. I trust your journey was agreeable."

"Very long and tiring, Mr. Darcy. The roads were abominable, the inns barely tolerable, and I could hardly wait for it to end. I have told

Charles that he needs to purchase his estate in a more sophisticated location, but we are still stuck in Hertfordshire for the present."

"It is a good estate, and it provides me with the experience necessary before I embark on the next challenge, Caroline," said Bingley, censure coloring his voice. "I have not yet decided what I wish to do, though I do hope we can speak of it while we are here. I would value your advice on the matter, Darcy."

"Of course," replied Darcy. "But we seem to have forgotten our manners. Shall you not introduce your wife to us, Bingley?"

"How silly of me to have forgotten," said Bingley, though his glance at his sister told the story of his exasperation with her for monopolizing the conversation.

The woman who had been standing a little behind her husband and sister-in-law stepped forward at Bingley's gesture, her hand finding his. She was tall—taller by several inches than Elizabeth, fair of both countenance and hair, with a pleasing, willowy figure and a calm, careful demeanor. Darcy could immediately understand why Elizabeth had maintained that her sister was the beauty of the family, for she was one of the prettiest women he had ever seen. In in the shape of their chins and the high cheekbones, Darcy could see a distinct close connection between the two sisters.

"Please allow me to introduce my wife, Mrs. Jane Bingley," said Bingley with obvious pride. "Jane, this is one of my oldest friends, Fitzwilliam Darcy, his sister, Georgiana Darcy, and his cousin, Colonel Anthony Fitzwilliam."

"Simply 'Mr. Fitzwilliam' now, Bingley," said Fitzwilliam, throwing Bingley a grin. "I would prefer you did not mention the colonel business, as I have left the army behind and am now naught but a country gentleman."

Bingley laughed. "I cannot think of you as anything but a colonel. In fact, I am anticipating the day when you are introduced to my youngest sisters-in-law, for they adore a man in a red coat."

"Oh, Charles!" said Caroline. "Let us not speak of such objectionable subjects. I doubt very much that Mr. Darcy and the colonel will ever have the opportunity to meet Catherine and Lydia Bennet."

Though Darcy could not quite be certain, he thought he heard her say under her breath "And for that we can all be grateful." Even if he had not had Elizabeth's accounts of Miss Bingley's behavior in Hertfordshire, he could not have imagined the woman actually embracing such people as she no doubt considered to be beneath her.

"You can never know, Miss Bingley," said Fitzwilliam, his eyes darting knowingly to Darcy. Darcy shot him a glare and shook his head, Fitzwilliam only grinned and extended his arm to Mrs. Bingley. "Shall we proceed into the house? My cousins have ordered some refreshments, after which I am certain you will wish to rest in your room."

It was clear that Mrs. Bingley did not quite know what to make of Fitzwilliam's gallantry, but she readily took his arm. Darcy glared at his cousin's back as he led her away—by offering to escort Mrs. Bingley and usurping his position as host, he all but ensured Darcy would be required to escort Miss Bingley, a necessity which was made certain when Bingley offered his arm to Georgiana. Having no other choice, Darcy allowed Miss Bingley's talons to wrap around his arm as he led her into the house.

"Well, what do you think, Mr. Darcy?" asked she before they had gone three steps.

It was too much to ask that the woman control her vitriol and wait to make some disparaging remark, which he was certain was forthcoming. Darcy only kept his eyes on those walking in front of them and said: "I do not understand on what subject you are soliciting my opinion."

An unattractive sound emanated from Miss Bingley's throat. "Why, my brother's countrified wife." Miss Bennet's eyes bored into the woman's back. "And she is by far the best of her family."

"She seems like a lovely woman," said Darcy, ignoring his own reservations about her in the face of Miss Bingley's rudeness.

"You do not need to speak circumspectly to me, Mr. Darcy. I quite comprehend your feelings, as I am certain that they mirror my own. I only wish you had been in Hertfordshire with us—you might have been able to put a stop to this infatuation before it ever reached this point."

It was one of the traits this woman possessed which annoyed Darcy more than anything else—her certainty that his opinions matched hers when, in fact, they were rarely in agreement.

"But I suppose there is naught to be done on the matter now," continued she. "Jane is, by herself, tolerable, I suppose, but she is certainly not what I would have wished for my brother."

"She is a gentleman's daughter, is she not?"

Another snort told Darcy the woman's opinion, as if he did not already know. "*If* you can refer to Mr. Bennet as a gentleman, then I suppose she is. But as the family is uncouth and improper, my brother's marriage does nothing to raise our standing. I suppose I must be thankful they never go to town—I should never be able to hold my head up high if I was seen in society attached to such people."

Darcy had little doubt that Miss Bingley was well able to hold her head high in any situation. It was fortunate for Darcy's equanimity that they reached the parlor soon after, and he managed to disengage his arm from the woman's vice grip. Their guests were invited to sit, which they did—though Miss Bingley attempted to wait for him to sit so she could choose a seat next to him, no doubt—and Georgiana began to serve tea and cakes.

"How wonderful it is to be at Pemberley again!" said Miss Bingley when they had all been served.

"You are all very welcome," replied Darcy. "We have anticipated your coming."

"Thank you, Mr. Darcy," simpered Miss Bingley, as if she thought his words were spoken for her benefit alone. "Derbyshire is so lovely, I am certain I could spend the rest of my life here."

Darcy almost gaped at her. The woman had never been subtle, but he had not ever known her to be so unconcealed in her attempts to induce him to offer for her. Bingley also appeared surprised, for he frowned at her. It was obvious that he had taken her aside—again—and informed her of his sure knowledge that Darcy would not offer for her. It was equally evident that the woman had not paid him any heed. After years of pursuing and failing to entrap him, it may be that Miss Bingley was becoming desperate. Darcy did not *think* she would be so crass as to attempt a compromise, but he would have to be on his guard.

The company sat together for some few minutes, making trivial conversation. As they sat, Darcy tried to study Mrs. Bingley without making it obvious that he was doing so. The woman was serene—there was no other way to describe her. But at the same time, Darcy thought he detected a hint of strain about her, a tightness around her mouth and a wariness in her eyes. On several occasions, she looked toward Miss Bingley, as if attempting to determine how she should act. Darcy did not quite know what to make of it. Mrs. Bingley was an enigma.

A few moments later, Darcy's attention was caught by Georgiana, who had been speaking with Mrs. Bingley, though he did not think their words had concerned any subject of consequence.

"You are aware that your sister is visiting your relations here in Derbyshire?" asked Georgiana.

Mrs. Bingley responded she was aware, but though she seemed like she was about to say something else, she subsided. Instead, Miss Bingley stepped into the conversation.

"Oh, yes, Eliza was to come here," said she, her voice colored with an exaggerated level of languor. "Has she acquitted herself well in Derbyshire?" The sneer on her face was unmistakable. "I dare say she traipses from here to there with no thought of her petticoats or the state of her boots. She can be quite wild when she puts her mind to it."

Watching Mrs. Bingley as he was, Darcy noted the tightening around her eyes at Miss Bingley's criticism, but it was Georgiana who responded.

"Actually, Miss Bingley, Elizabeth has become a very good friend. I would be quite bereft if I was denied her company."

Mrs. Bingley positively started at this bit of information and looked to Miss Bingley, while Miss Bingley looked at Georgiana through narrowed eyes. "Eliza is often at Pemberley?"

"She is, indeed, Miss Bingley," said Georgiana, seemingly unconcerned about the woman's displeasure. "Your cousin, Olivia," continued Georgiana, looking at Mrs. Bingley, "has also become a dear friend. I look forward to our continued acquaintance for many years to come."

The smile which appeared on Mrs. Bingley's face was tentative, but Darcy thought it to be genuine. "I am happy to hear it, Miss Darcy. I am . . . eager to see my sister again."

"We are all grateful that you have taken our Eliza into your home," said Miss Bingley, though her tone told a different story. "As a friend, however, I would advise you not to emulate her, Georgiana. She possesses some habits which are not at all fashionable and would not be received well in higher society."

"There is nothing wrong with Elizabeth's manners," said Bingley, a warning note in his voice. "I, for one, anticipate being in her company again." Bingley turned to Georgiana. "When do you expect her to visit?"

"She is visiting with friends today, a longstanding engagement as I understand. I shall send a note around, inviting her to come on the morrow so that she may greet you all."

"An excellent idea," said Darcy, forestalling whatever Miss Bingley was going to say. The woman subsided with a huff.

Before long, the Bingleys were shown to their rooms to rest and prepare for dinner. As they were walking out of the room, Darcy saw Miss Bingley step close to Mrs. Bingley's side and begin talking to her in earnest. What she was saying, Darcy could not fathom, but she did not cease the whole time they were within Darcy's sight.

"Miss Bingley truly is an admirable creature," said Fitzwilliam once they were gone. "If I ever wished to be reminded of how those of high society behave, I have only to watch her. I am then reminded what I am not missing when I am not in London."

"I wanted to remind her of her origins when she disparaged Lizzy," said Georgiana with a huff of annoyance. "How I wish we were not required to endure her."

"I understand she has a healthy dowry," replied Fitzwilliam. "Perhaps I will attempt to woo her — an extra twenty thousand pounds would be useful to improve Thorndell."

"Do not even joke about such things, Cousin."

"I suppose I should not." Then Fitzwilliam turned a devilish grin on Darcy. "It would not work, regardless, for there is no man in the world for her other than our dear Mr. Darcy."

These final words were spoken in a breathy falsetto imitation of Miss Bingley, and even Darcy was forced to laugh. He was no less desirous of Miss Bingley's absence than his relations, but there was nothing to be done. The woman must be tolerated. There was no other option.

Though it was nothing less than the truth that Elizabeth had been invited to Clara's home for the day, she had grasped the invitation as an excuse to absent herself from Pemberley when her sister arrived. It was unusual, she thought, that she should be so bereft of courage, but she found that as the time approached for Jane to arrive, she was uneasy and unwilling to face the possibility of her sister's continuing indifference. Thus, she had accepted, and spent the day with her friends.

She had not been good company, however, a fact which was made clear in the odd looks she received from them and in some few of the comments they made. None of these ladies were aware of Elizabeth's troubles with her sister, and she was not about to enlighten them concerning such a delicate subject. But that did not mean she did not receive several comments concerning her dullness that day.

"My word, I have never seen our Elizabeth so unlike myself," said Deborah. "Usually you vie with me for the title of who can speak with the most impertinence."

Erica Allen, who had distanced herself from Misses Russell and Campbell and could often be found in company with Elizabeth and her friends, said: "How you do go on, Deborah. Elizabeth is a little quieter, but I have never found your comments impertinent."

"That is because you are sweet and patient with us, not because of any virtue that *we* possess."

The ladies laughed at her jest, but Clara, who had been watching Elizabeth since her arrival, was quick to agree with Deborah. "I have noticed your quietude myself, Elizabeth. Is there some weighty subject in your mind?"

"I am well," replied Elizabeth. "I have merely been contemplating my weeks in Derbyshire. My sister will soon come to Pemberley, and my time here grows short, I believe. It *is* July, after all."

"We would not wish you to depart!" exclaimed Fiona. "But if you must, we must have you back next year. Perhaps I shall ask my father if I may extend an invitation to you next summer. I am certain he and Mama would be happy to have you."

"And perhaps you can stay at Heath Hill for a time," added Clara.

"Thank you all," said Elizabeth, feeling emotional at the evidence of having made so many good friends. "If the opportunity should be available, I would be happy to visit."

Later, when she returned to her uncle's house, Elizabeth could not help but pace the sitting-room, her restless energy rendering it impossible to sit in one attitude. As it was already late in the afternoon, she knew that it was likely the Bingleys had already arrived at Pemberley, and the nervousness which had been building was reaching a fever pitch. How she longed to go to Pemberley and throw herself in Jane's arms! But how she dreaded her sisters' rejection.

"Do not worry, Lizzy," said Olivia. "I am certain your family will arrive at Pemberley safely."

"How the Darcys must anticipate their coming," said Mrs. Drummond. "I do not doubt they long for yet another of Maggie Bennet's daughters to be in their midst."

It was not worth Elizabeth's effort to correct her aunt, so she ignored her. Mrs. Drummond's remarks of late had lost much of their bite, and Elizabeth had begun to wonder if the woman was still making them due to nothing more than the force of habit.

"I do not worry for their safety," said Elizabeth, smiling at Olivia. "I have not seen my sister in some time, and I find the anticipation almost unbearable."

Olivia, who had not been informed of the trouble between the sisters, only smiled. Mr. Drummond, however, seeing that Elizabeth was discomposed, invited her into his study. "I have received a letter from your father I would like to ask you about."

Grateful for the distraction, Elizabeth agreed, and she followed him thither. But when they entered and sat down, he only smiled at her.

"I did receive a letter from your father, but I do not need your opinion on it. I thought you required a respite from the parlor."

"Thank you, Uncle," replied Elizabeth, grateful for his subterfuge.

Mr. Drummond peered at her for several moments before he spoke again. "It is clear that you are looking on your sister's arrival with trepidation, rather than anticipation. I would never attempt to force your confidence, but you have said enough to inform me that not all is well with Jane. I have often found it beneficial to speak of my troubles to another, for I will often gain another perspective on the matter. Will you not share yours with me?"

Though reluctant, Elizabeth decided that he was right, and that, furthermore, he would learn of it before long anyway, since Jane would be staying not far distant and her behavior was unlikely to be unmarked. Thus, she told him what she had witnessed in her sister, and what others, especially her parents, had observed. Mr. Drummond made no response during her comments, listening intently. And when Elizabeth's words finally tapered off, he sat there, his attention obviously far away, considering her assertions.

Finally, he sighed and turned to her. "I cannot say that I am surprised, given what I have understood from both you and your father. Since Jane has chosen to cut your family from her life, I doubt that I should expect her to behave any differently with mine."

"No, I would not suppose so. She has always been the soul of politeness, even after she changed, but I doubt she will attempt anything more than civility."

"It does not sound like her at all. I have not seen any of you in many years, but I remember Jane as a quiet, though affectionate child."

"Until she left for her wedding tour, she was exactly how you described," replied Elizabeth quietly. "It was only after she returned that she was changed."

"Did they return to Hertfordshire directly from their wedding tour?"

"No. They were in London after their tour. They were only in Hertfordshire for about a month before I came to Derbyshire."

"Then it is possible she heard something in London which unsettled her. I would caution you not to lose all hope. She may simply not know how to behave, having married into a world which is so different from the one in which she was raised."

"The Jane I knew would not have changed, regardless," grumbled

Elizabeth.

"You have the right to be angry. You have the right to feel resentful. You have the right to rail at your sister and demand she explain herself. But that will not bridge the distance which has sprung up between you."

Mr. Drummond stood and circled the desk, stopping to rest a hand on her shoulder. "You will regret it later in life if you do not do everything in your power to reconcile with your sister now, Elizabeth. I suspect, in this instance, the responsibility will rest with you. Have patience. It may yet be that you are able to reach her."

Having said those words, Mr. Drummond departed, leaving Elizabeth to her thoughts. She sat there for some time her uncle's words ringing through her mind, and for the first time in months, she felt that which was most precious of all: hope.

It was not that much later that Olivia came searching for her. They had received a note from Pemberley, inviting them for tea the following day.

Chapter XXVI

With almost debilitating trepidation, Elizabeth made her way to Pemberley, her concerns for Jane's attitude holding her in a tight grip of anxiety. Her uncle's advice the previous day was still winding its way through her thoughts. It was good advice—she knew this—but it was difficult to hold to in the face of Jane's indifference.

Beside her in the carriage, Olivia chattered away about her eagerness to meet Elizabeth's sister, and Elizabeth did not have the heart to tell her how it was unlikely that Jane would respond with any pleasure. Elizabeth was grateful to her uncle for arranging for only Olivia and Elizabeth to go that day and in the Drummond carriage, over Mrs. Drummond's protestations. Elizabeth did not know if it would be any easier without the rest of the family present, but their absence would mean less distraction, so she was grateful nonetheless.

When they pulled into Pemberley's drive, the carriage stopped before the massive doors and only Georgiana was there to greet them. Elizabeth was uncertain whether to consider this a good omen, but she welcomed the few extra moments she was afforded to compose herself.

"Our guests are waiting for us in the sitting-room," said Georgiana as they stepped down. She grasped their hands and pulled them into the house. "Come, Lizzy, they have expressed an eagerness to see you."

If they have, they might have *come to the door to greet me,* thought Elizabeth, her cynicism overwhelming her determination to wait and see how Jane would react.

Out loud, she only said: "All of them? I would have thought that Miss Bingley would wish me miles away."

Olivia started. "Is she not Jane's new sister?"

Her nose wrinkled with distaste, Georgiana said: "Miss Bingley is a different breed altogether. She is a tradesman's daughter, but she is as haughty as a duchess and gives herself airs that would be excessive in the queen."

"She particularly does not like me, Olivia," said Elizabeth, wondering if she had kept the girl ill-prepared by keeping this all from her. "I am neither sophisticated enough for her, nor am I high enough on society's ladder, and I am altogether too impertinent."

Georgiana sniffed with disdain. "In her own mind, she is the perfect mistress for my brother's estate."

Eyes widening in surprise, Olivia could only squeak: "But what of Lizzy? You are already engaged to Mr. Darcy!"

"Please do not say anything of that," said Elizabeth. "Mr. Darcy has not approached my father, and I do not wish to become an even greater target of Miss Bingley's vitriol."

"She will eventually learn of my brother's attentions to you," said Georgiana, "even if the neighborhood does not know of the engagement. There is to be an assembly next week, and I am certain she will not miss the gossip."

"There is nothing to be done about that," replied Elizabeth with a shrug. "For the present, however, I believe it is best to say nothing."

Olivia nodded, though reluctantly, and Georgiana began to pull them once again toward the sitting-room. "We may discuss it later. For now, they are waiting for us."

Far too soon for Elizabeth's liking, they arrived at the sitting-room, and with Georgiana's quick gesture to one of the footmen, the door was opened, and Georgiana led them in. In that first jumble of moments in which Elizabeth's eyes darted about the room, she could hardly make sense of what she was seeing. William and Mr. Bingley were nearby, and Elizabeth appreciated the encouraging smile the former directed at her. Miss Bingley was seated on a nearby sofa, her sneer clear for all to see, but Georgiana was blocking Elizabeth's view of the woman beside her, so Elizabeth could not see her sister clearly.

"Really, Georgiana dear," said Miss Bingley, rising to her feet and approaching them, "I was shocked to see you scamper off in such a way. Could Mrs. Reynolds not have guided your *guests* to this room?"

"Lizzy is my dear friend, Miss Bingley," replied Georgiana, brushing off the woman's words. "I wished to greet her as soon as possible."

Miss Bingley turned her judgmental eyes on Elizabeth. "I see you have come, Eliza. I see you are none the worse for wear."

"I am quite well, indeed, Caroline," said Elizabeth, impatient to push past the unpleasant woman and greet her sister. It was odd, but there it was—though she had been reluctant to greet Jane, now that she was in the room she could not wait.

"How have you found your uncle's house? Is it everything you would have expected?"

"Everything and more," replied Elizabeth, ignoring the woman's tone. "I have been made to feel welcome in Derbyshire, and have enjoyed my months here immensely."

"I doubt you could fail to be welcome," said Mr. Bingley. He approached and bowed to her, an irrepressible grin greeting her. "I see you are very well, indeed, Lizzy. I cannot tell you how good it is to see you again. We have been quite bereft at your absence."

"I am pleased to see you too, Mr. Bingley. How is Netherfield?"

"The weather is fine, and I believe we shall have an abundant harvest this year. And I have my dearest Jane, so all is well in my world."

At the mention of his wife, the woman herself suddenly appeared. Jane looked well. The joys of being a wife to a good man had infused her with a kind of healthy vitality which was somehow more than she had possessed when she had been nothing more than Miss Jane Bennet. But the eyes which looked back at her, that clear blue gaze which had always looked on her as if she was the most important person in the world had been replaced by clouds tossed about in a gale.

"Lizzy," said Jane, though quietly. "It is good to see you again."

Hurt at her sister's lack of a more familiar greeting, Elizabeth turned and presented Olivia, introducing her to all three Bingleys. Their reactions were entirely predictable, as Miss Bingley sneered, Mr. Bingley greeted her with all the enthusiasm Elizabeth would have expected, and Jane greeted her with restraint and asked after her family.

After this had been completed, Jane turned with Miss Bingley holding her arm, and returned to the sofa where she seated herself. Elizabeth was crushed. Her sister had not returned. This stranger remained.

A hand touched her arm, and Elizabeth turned to see Georgiana looking at her, some measure of confusion evident. Georgiana guided Elizabeth and Olivia to a nearby sofa where they all sat together, and for a moment Elizabeth gathered herself for the coming ordeal. It was an effort, but Elizabeth looked up at her sister, noting that Jane was peering into the distance at something only she could see, her serenity gathered about her like a cloak. To her side, Miss Bingley was watching the room with the eyes of a predator, which turned positively menacing when they alighted on Elizabeth.

For a time, nothing more than banal conversation was exchanged by the company. They spoke of what the weather had been like in Derbyshire, the journey of the Bingley party to Derbyshire—Mr. Bingley assured them it was agreeable, while Miss Bingley had never passed such a wretched time—and some little doings of the area. Elizabeth asked for news of her family and the people of Hertfordshire, and though it might be expected that her sister, who had known them the longest, would respond, it was Mr. Bingley who did most of the speaking.

"They are all very well, I believe. In fact, I have been charged to bring you the particular regards of your friend, Charlotte Lucas, who, I believe, is quite desolate without you."

The mention of her friend brought a little spark back to Elizabeth. "I have not received a letter from Charlotte in some weeks. I had begun to think she had abandoned any attempt at correspondence."

Mr. Bingley laughed, but before he could speak, Miss Bingley interjected: "I dare say that is impossible. I have always observed you to be thick as thieves, though I suppose you both have nothing to recommend you, so your friendship is to be expected."

The glare Mr. Bingley directed at his sister demanded silence, though Elizabeth did not think it would last long. She had a talent for insulting with little subtlety, though Elizabeth was certain the woman thought herself the soul of restraint. Then Jane directed a look of irritation at her and leaned away a little, and Elizabeth felt her spirits rising.

"In fact, I believe Miss Lucas has been busy of late," said Mr. Bingley. "You see, she has had a caller in recent weeks, and I believe that has taken up much of her time and attention."

"Charlotte has a caller?" asked Elizabeth, clapping her hands in delight. "I am so very happy for her! Is it anyone I know?"

"A gentleman from an estate close to Stevenage, I understand. I have never actually met him, myself, but I have heard it said that he is a widower with two small children."

"Then Charlotte would be an excellent choice. She is caring and would be a good mother to them."

"I have a letter from her I have been charged to deliver to you. I will retrieve it before you leave."

Elizabeth thanked him with grateful anticipation. She did not wonder at her mother and sisters neglecting to mention this piece of information—Mrs. Bennet would likely be annoyed, though as she already had two daughters married, she could hardly be envious, while Kitty and Lydia would find such news beneath their notice. Her father's continued silence, however, was beginning to make Elizabeth wonder. He had not responded since she had sent the letter asking about her aunt's assertions, and she had begun to question if he would ever respond.

As the company continued to visit, Elizabeth snuck looks at her sister, trying to make her out. To a casual observer, she appeared as she ever did—quiet, reticent, and little affected by any emotion. At times Elizabeth had been required to defend her sister from naysayers who had deemed her to be little affected by *anything*. Elizabeth knew her sister better—she was simply disinclined to display her feelings to anyone, even to a most beloved sister.

On this day, however, Elizabeth thought she sensed more than a little tension in her sister's manners. One could only repress her feelings for so long without experiencing an explosion, and though Elizabeth could not determine her sister's current state of mind, she wondered if Jane was happy. Apparently, Mr. Bingley was uncertain of his wife's contentment as well, for he also watched her with a gravity which was not part of his usual character.

When they had been there for some time, Olivia, who had been silent and watchful for the most part since being introduce, spoke up.

"My mother and father have instructed me to invite you all to dinner at Kingsdown. Would Tuesday next be convenient?"

While she was pleased with the composed way Olivia presented the invitation, Elizabeth quickly noted Miss Bingley's foul expression, as if some revolting scent had just wafted past her nose.

"Surely we will be engaged that day?" said she. Then she turned to William and fixed him with a coquettish simper. "I am eager to once again be in company with all your charming neighbors, Mr. Darcy. The last time we stayed at Pemberley we met several I liked very well, indeed."

The woman would fit in well with Misses Campbell and Russell, thought Elizabeth cynically, though Miss Bingley would almost certainly consider Miss Russell to be beneath her. William ignored her, however, and turned a questioning glance on Mr. Bingley.

"I know of no engagements that day. What say you, Bingley?"

"I will be delighted to attend and meet the relations of my wife," replied the amiable gentleman.

"It is proper, I suppose," said Miss Bingley, "to greet one's relations. Perhaps an invitation to Pemberley would be more appropriate? They can then witness the splendor of your estate."

"On the contrary," said Mr. Darcy, his tone leading Elizabeth to believe that he was nearing the end of his patience, "we have had the Drummonds to dinner at Pemberley, and our families have grown much closer of late, especially since Miss Bennet came to Derbyshire. We have also dined at Kingsdown."

The tightness of the woman's countenance spoke to Miss Bingley's displeasure, but the glare directed at her by her brother convinced her to be silent. She did not do it with any grace, of course, but Elizabeth did not care to examine her any further. Instead, she was caught by the sight of her sister, watching the interaction around her intently. Jane was as reticent as ever, and she did not display her emotions for all to see, but Elizabeth was certain that Jane was confused. Perhaps she had been told the Darcys would never associate with those beneath them. If so, Miss Bingley did not understand her hosts nearly as well as she thought she did.

"Then it is settled," said William, granting Olivia a warm smile. "You may tell your parents that we are happy to attend."

"Thank you, Mr. Darcy, I shall," replied Olivia.

They stayed in this attitude for some minutes longer before Elizabeth and Olivia rose to leave. Their leaving was not, however, unopposed.

"Can you not stay longer?" asked Georgiana. "I would appreciate your presence, for I so value your company."

"I apologize, Georgiana," said Elizabeth, "but today we must leave. We will be happy to return tomorrow and stay as long as you desire."

"You may not understand this, Eliza, but the proper length of a visit is thirty minutes."

Elizabeth turned a glare on Miss Bingley. "You may not understand this, Miss Bingley, but where an invitation is given, a visit may be as long or short as the hostess deems appropriate."

"Besides," said Georgiana, adding her annoyance to Elizabeth's, "Lizzy and Olivia are my particular friends. I do not stand on such ceremony as to require them to leave after a mere thirty minutes. In fact, I would be very pleased if they would stay forever."

Miss Bingley's eyes widened to be spoken to in such a fashion, but Georgiana turned away, denying her the opportunity to respond. Jane, for her part, looked between Miss Bingley and Georgiana, as if attempting to puzzle out some particularly difficult mystery. Elizabeth decided it was now time to leave to review what had happened and prepare herself for further time in her sister's company. On the morrow they would, indeed, stay longer.

"We would be happy to return, Georgiana, but today we must leave."

"Oh, very well," said Georgiana. She appeared glum and Elizabeth understood her consternation—anyone would be thus afflicted to be stuck with the company of so objectionable a woman, and as Jane was as reticent as Georgiana, the two ladies would have difficulty coming to any kind of understanding of each other.

They said their farewells to the room, and then Elizabeth and Olivia left, accompanied by Georgiana and William. The two younger girls walked on ahead, their heads together as they whispered urgently between them. For a few moments, therefore, Elizabeth was left alone with William.

"Are you well, Elizabeth?" asked he, concern infused in his voice.

"I shall be," answered Elizabeth, forcing a smile onto her face. "Though Jane still refuses to speak much and it is as difficult as ever to understand her thoughts, I believe I saw enough to give me hope."

William was silent for a few moments before saying: "I shall trust your judgment. I do not know your sister, so it would be presumptuous of me to suggest I know better than you do."

A smile—the first in what felt like quite some time—spread over Elizabeth's face, and she looked up at her fiancé with devotion. "You are so good to me, William. But I will remind you that I do not need protection, especially from indifferent sisters. It will work out between us or it will not. I shall accept it either way."

"You have a wonderfully positive outlook on life, Elizabeth," said William.

They arrived at the entrance, and William handed the two young ladies into the carriage, but not until he had kissed Elizabeth's hand with a reverence which set her heart to fluttering. The carriage lurched into motion and began rolling down the drive to return to Kingsdown, and when Elizabeth turned back, she could see William watching as they wound their way away from Pemberley. Elizabeth could not help but feel that she was leaving her heart behind. Soon, she thought — soon she would not be required to leave at all. She could hardly wait for that day.

As his heart receded in the distance, Darcy watched until he could no longer see the carriage. He never could have fathomed such feelings only a few short months ago, but Elizabeth's coming had changed everything. He had hope, now — hope he had scarcely allowed himself to feel before. A happy life was waiting for him, and though he knew it was necessary, he was loath to wait much longer.

Though perhaps it might have been proper for him to return to the sitting-room and his guests, the thought of once again being the target of Miss Bingley's schemes after her horrid behavior toward Elizabeth filled him with revulsion. As a result, he took himself toward the privacy of his study, thinking he could always use the excuse of business to explain his absence. Georgiana was not exactly happy with his subterfuge, but she waved him off, likely knowing he required distance from Miss Bingley, before turning her steps in the direction of her waiting guests.

Unfortunately, Darcy was not able to do any work, not that he had intended to, regardless. The planting was done and the growing season was progressing, and from all the reports from his tenants and steward, everything was proceeding as it ought. Summer was typically a time when there was little which needed to be done, and Darcy had often countered the feeling of ennui by riding his horse or finding a book to read. But thoughts of Miss Bennet rendered such mundane activities impossible.

Furthermore, thoughts of what had just happened in his sitting-room preyed on his mind, leaving him unable to concentrate on anything else. Elizabeth's words concerning the similarity between his sister and hers had been proven correct, but now that he had seen a little of Mrs. Bingley's aloofness toward her sister, he could see why she was so troubled, especially if they had previously been close. The distress he could see in his beloved's countenance ensured that his opinion of Mrs. Bingley remained low.

He did not know what to do. Though he wished to repair everything for her, ensure she never had cause to feel pain and sorrow again, there was nothing he *could* do. As she said, she would either reconcile with her sister or she would not—she had accepted that, and he would too, though reluctantly.

After Darcy had sat in this attitude for some time, a soft knock on his door startled him from his reverie. He sat himself at his desk, hoping to appear busy, and called out permission to enter. For a moment, he wondered if he had made a mistake, and if Miss Bingley was on the other side, intent on finally forcing his hand. But the door opened, and Bingley appeared instead.

"I thought you might retreat here," said the man by way of greeting. "Do you mind if I join you?"

"Not at all, Bingley," said Darcy, gesturing his friend toward one of the chairs in front of the fireplace, taking the one next to it himself.

Bingley entered and sat on the indicated chair, but while he did so, he did not say anything, a matter of some interest. Bingley was a splendid fellow and a true friend, but he did not often descend into serious thoughts or introspection. The Bingley before him appeared to be disturbed, indeed.

"I am sorry for my sister's behavior, my friend," said he finally. "I have told her several times—including again just before we departed Hertfordshire—that you have no intention of offering for her. I do not doubt you have seen the results of those discussions. She has remained impervious to anything I say to her, and I doubt anything but your marriage will dissuade her."

"That was very much evident, Bingley," replied Darcy. "I was, however, surprised by the level of antipathy she seems to possess for your new sister by marriage."

Bingley grimaced and looked about him, espying a decanter on a side board. "It could be deemed to be too early in the day, but I require a little fortification. Do you mind?"

Darcy waved him to proceed, refusing a portion himself when Bingley asked. After pouring himself two fingers' widths, Bingley returned to his chair, sipping the amber liquid, distracted by his thoughts.

"It has ever been thus," said Bingley at length. "Caroline and Elizabeth met at an assembly for the first time, and though Caroline appeared to take to Jane immediately, Elizabeth overheard her making some disparaging remarks and was not shy in letting her know how inappropriate her words were."

A smile fell over Darcy's face as he imagined his courageous and outspoken fiancé coming to the defense of her friends and family.

"Of course," continued Bingley, "Caroline amply displayed her feelings for my wife when she assiduously argued against my offering for her, giving lie to her first overtures of friendship. Since my marriage, however, they have seemed to grow close, for which I suppose I must be grateful, if for no other reason than the promotion of harmony in my home.

"But Caroline and Elizabeth have never worked past that initial dislike, and I suppose I should not be surprised." Bingley grimaced. "I am not blinded by affection for my sister. I know she is mean, shrewish, arrogant, and entirely too confident in her position in the world. Lizzy, by contrast, is a lovely woman, amiable, open, engaging, loving, and friendly to all. At times, I have wondered why I was cursed with such a woman for a sister instead of a woman like Elizabeth."

"And your wife?"

Perhaps Darcy should have been a little more circumspect, but he needed to know what Bingley saw in his wife's behavior. Though she was perfectly proper, and Darcy thought he had enough of her measure to know that she would never descend to such malicious behavior as Miss Bingley, he still felt the responsibility for Elizabeth's wellbeing, though he was not yet officially engaged to her.

The sour face Bingley made at the question told Darcy much of what he needed to know. "I was initially attracted to Jane Bennet because of her beauty." He shot a wry smile at Darcy. "I am certain you know enough of my predilections to be unsurprised by such intelligence.

"But it was not long before I came to understand her true worth. She is kind to all, unpretentious, displays a pleasing delicacy which is manifest in a modest comportment and attention to all, and she cannot be induced to think poorly of anyone, even when they deserve it. You know my impetuosity—Jane nicely balances that with her calm rationality. I believe I have become a better man because of it."

"And yet I have heard something of her behavior to her family," said Darcy. "That does not reflect well on her, my friend."

Bingley looked up with surprise. "I never would have imagined you were that well acquainted with Elizabeth."

"I will explain in a moment, Bingley," replied Darcy. "First, I would like to hear your thoughts on the matter."

Though for a moment Darcy thought his friend would resist, Bingley eventually shook his head. "I do not know what to think. I have tried to induce Jane to speak to me, but she will not. She has only said that she requires time to settle into her new position. I do not think she has changed enough to hold her family in contempt, but I have no explanation for her continued aloofness." Bingley paused and colored. "Certain characters in her family *are* a little . . . rough around the edges, if you take my meaning. But there is not a mean-spirited one among them. I know they have been hurt by Jane's distance—Lizzy most of all. She is polite and civil, but the detachment is striking. She has not even visited Longbourn—her family estate—since Elizabeth came away to Derbyshire."

"And yet in all other ways she is the same woman you married?"

"She is," said Bingley slowly. "She is as gentle and pleasant as she ever was. I have begun to notice a certain . . . strain about her recently, however, that I had not noticed before. With me she is as she ever was, but I almost wonder if she was dreading this visit."

It was then Darcy decided his friend deserved to know all. They were to stay here for some time and had not come to any conclusions about why Mrs. Bingley was behaving the way she was. Bingley needed to be forewarned, not only due to his wife's behavior, but also because of his sister's. Though Darcy could look on the prospect of Miss Bingley's reaction to the news of his engagement with a certain level of savage glee, the woman's sure knowledge of his engagement would no doubt lead to difficulties, and Bingley would need to know it to attempt to control her.

"There is a matter of which I believe I should inform you, Bingley. It is one that may affect your wife's relationship with her sister even more and will certain cause your sister misery."

"Oh?" asked Bingley. "Have you ruined Caroline's hopes of happiness and become engaged?"

It was typical of Bingley to miss the first part of Darcy's statement and focus on the second. When Darcy only looked at him, Bingley sat up straighter.

"You have!"

"I have," replied Darcy. "In fact, I am now engaged to the woman your sister apparently despises."

"Elizabeth?" asked Bingley, befuddled.

"Yes. It is not official yet because I have not spoken with Mr. Bennet, but I have asked, she has accepted, and her uncle has given his conditional approval in her father's stead."

A beaming smile of utter delight came over Bingley's countenance and he surged from his chair and caught Darcy, who had stood in response, in a jubilant embrace.

"Well done, Darcy! Well done, indeed! You know, I had considered the possibility that she would do well for you last autumn when I met her, so I am feeling unusually perspicacious. She is a beautiful girl! I know you shall be very happy with her!"

"Thank you, Bingley," said Darcy. "She is everything I ever hoped to find in a wife. I cannot wait to join you in your happy state."

The final words Darcy spoke seemed to remind Bingley of his own state with his wife. He sank back into his previous chair, though all traces of his distraction were absent.

"You have not announced your engagement yet."

"We have not," replied Darcy. "I mean to seek Mr. Bennet's approval when Elizabeth returns home."

"As I recall, she has recently turned one and twenty. You do not need her father's approval."

"That is correct," replied Darcy. "But I wish for it all the same. Elizabeth's relationship with her father is so profound that I would never consider anything else."

Bingley paused, his manner troubled. "Does she mean to inform Jane?"

This was the crux of the matter, and the most likely to offend Bingley, if he was of mind to be offended. "I do not know for certain, but I expect not, at least at present."

Bingley winced. "Last autumn, such an unshared confidence would be unfathomable. I have it on good authority that Elizabeth was the first person Jane told of her engagement to me, even before I approached her father."

"You will excuse me for saying it, but this distance is entirely due to Mrs. Bingley's actions."

"I know," said Bingley, resting his head in one hand while the other he raised to Darcy in a gesture of surrender.

Darcy paused, not knowing whether he should say so, but Bingley's continued troubled countenance informed him that it was best to ensure the entirety of the matter was understood.

"It has been suggested that your wife has changed because she now considers her family beneath her due to her marriage. If that is the case, Elizabeth's marriage to me might induce her to rethink that distance."

Surprised, Bingley gaped at Darcy for several moments. Then he shook his head and said: "No, I cannot believe it."

"But you acknowledge it is a fair assessment."

"If Jane's reserve is as you suggest, then yes. But I cannot believe that of her, and to be honest, I am surprised Elizabeth does as well."

"I do not believe she does," replied Darcy quietly. "But she has been hurt terribly and does not know what to think. You cannot blame her."

"I cannot," conceded Bingley. "But I do not believe it of Jane. There may be reasons to distance herself from the rest of the family, but never from Elizabeth. I cannot believe she would throw off her family because she has married me. I am certain there is something else at work."

"That may be the case, Bingley. But until Elizabeth feels she can trust Jane again, I would ask you to keep this confidence."

"Of course, I will. But I shall not cease my attempts to discover what has happened to my wife."

"Nor would I expect you to."

They sat in silence for several moments, and Bingley resumed sipping his previously forgotten drink. For his part, Darcy did not know what to think. His primary goal was to ensure that Elizabeth was protected and suffered as little as possible, but he understood Bingley's wishes as well. It was a difficult situation, indeed.

"I presume your earlier words concerning Caroline were also with respect to your engagement to Lizzy," said Bingley at last.

"You are aware of her hopes with respect to me," replied Darcy. "Now that slight hope which might have existed for her must be extinguished. While I sympathize with her disappointment, she has been told repeatedly that I will not consider offering for her.

"She was not even tolerable this morning, Bingley," continued Darcy, speaking quietly. "Her behavior toward Elizabeth bordered on hateful, and I would not see a guest in my home treated so poorly, even were she not my fiancée."

"It has always been thus," replied Bingley, "but I do not disagree with you. I will speak to Caroline and warn her to curb her tongue. I suppose if all else fails I can send her to my aunt in Scarborough. She will not like it, but as she cannot go to the Hursts, it is the only place left for her." Bingley paused and grinned. "The threat of it might be enough to tame her, as long as she believes me to be in earnest. To be banished from Pemberley would be a blow to her vanity she would never tolerate."

"Then go to it."

In the end, the friends spent some hours together in the study, speaking of nothing of consequence. It was good to have Bingley back, Darcy reflected. Bingley was his closest friend for a reason, and Darcy would not wish to give him up.

CHAPTER XXVII

*T*hough Colonel Fitzwilliam might have wished to be at Pemberley to witness the scene which had played out there, he was absent, having decided to call on Lady Emily. Thus, when Miss Bennet and Miss Drummond were stepping out of the carriage on the steps of Pemberley, Fitzwilliam was riding down the drive toward the house at Teasdale Manor.

He dismounted in front of the house, passed his horse off to the care of a groom, and mounted the steps. The door was opened a few moments after he rapped on it by the butler, who was familiar with him by that time.

"I am sorry, Colonel," said Gates, "but Lady Emily is not home this morning. She is calling on some friends."

"I see," said Fitzwilliam.

"But the earl has indicated a desire to speak with you. May I lead you to him?"

Fitzwilliam was of two minds about the earl's wish, but he readily agreed and was led into the house. As he walked behind Gates, Fitzwilliam thought of what had brought him to this house. It was, unfortunately, a mystery, even to Fitzwilliam, and something he knew he would never be able to explain to anyone else. He had interfered with Lady Emily's attempts to hinder Darcy and Miss Bennet's courtship, but he had seen her several times since. Often, he had simply served as a willing ear, giving the woman support as she determined her own reasons for her actions, while at times they had spoken of many different subjects.

But why did he do it? Was it for the joy of her company? In fact, he found that he did enjoy speaking with Lady Emily. She was intelligent and articulate, and she was certainly attractive. Or was it simply the fact that he felt sorry for the woman? He did not think so, though it was possible. Whatever it was, he was now on his way to meet with her father, who would likely wish to know what his purpose was, and unfortunately, Fitzwilliam did not think he could answer the question with any confidence.

Though he might have expected to be led to the earl's study, it was to the sitting-room Fitzwilliam was directed, and when they entered, the earl looked up from where he was sitting on a chair, a letter held in his hand.

"Ah, Colonel Fitzwilliam," said the earl, rising at his entrance. "I thought you might visit us today. Please, have a seat."

Fitzwilliam did as he was bid, waiting while the earl ordered some refreshments. When the butler left, the earl settled back onto his chair, studying him in a manner Fitzwilliam did not quite like.

"It seems to me you have been here several times in the past days," said the earl after a moment.

"I have," replied Fitzwilliam, though he was determined not to give anything away until the man asked.

"A man might wonder if a single man who visits so often possesses intentions toward his daughter."

"I assure you I have only honorable intentions," said Fitzwilliam.

The earl looked at him for a moment before he looked away. "You do not need to fear anything from me, Fitzwilliam. I am aware of your character, and I have no suspicion of anything underhanded. I would, however, wish to fully understand your motivation for coming here. My daughter, as you know, recently suffered a disappointment with your cousin, though I do not know to what extent she wished for his attentions as she will not tell me. I do not think she was overly affected, but she is still recovering, and I am protective of her."

"I understand your concern," said Fitzwilliam, speaking with great care, as he did not wish the earl to misconstrue his words. "I find . . ." He stopped, uncertain of what to say. When he saw the other man watching him carefully, Fitzwilliam sighed and put out his hands. "I believe you are aware that initially, my intentions were to obstruct your daughter's machinations with respect to Darcy and Miss Bennet."

"Oh?" asked the earl, though the knowing glint in his eye suggested this was not surprising.

"I knew of Darcy's interest in Miss Bennet, indeed, long before Darcy himself was even aware of it. I could also see Lady Emily fixed on him, and I determined that she would not keep Darcy from the object of his affections."

The earl laughed. "A loyal man! There are few traits which would garner my approval more quickly than loyalty. I am curious, however—your cousin has been, by all accounts, a target on the marriage mart for some time. I would have thought he would be able to handle his own concerns."

"He usually is. But for some reason, he was blinded by Lady Emily's behavior and had no real indication that she wished for his attentions. He is adept at spotting a fortune hunter, but Lady Emily is not in need of a fortune."

"And why did you not tell him before?"

"Because I was not certain myself," replied Fitzwilliam honestly. "At first, I had only suspicions, and by the time those were confirmed, I chose to distract her away from him by means of engaging myself."

The earl gave him a steady look. "It seems to me, sir, that your decision suggests you wished to be in her company rather than simply wishing to keep her away from your cousin."

It was a possibility Fitzwilliam had not considered. This line of questioning had made him a little nervous—the earl could have charged that Fitzwilliam had made her ultimate humiliation worse by not telling Darcy, and Fitzwilliam could not have denied the possibility. It was another interpretation of his behavior that he had not even thought of himself.

"Fitzwilliam," said the earl, "I do not hold your failure to inform your cousin against you." The earl paused and chuckled. "I know my daughter. She is headstrong and stubborn, and she possesses more than a little of her mother's haughtiness. For all this, she is a good woman, loyal—like yourself—clever, confident, and I believe she is not at all ill-favored."

"No, sir," replied Fitzwilliam quietly. "Quite the opposite, in fact."

"I am not surprised you would feel so," murmured the earl. Then he spoke again in his usual tone. "What I am trying to say is she is not a perfect woman, by any means—of this, I am aware. But there are many things in her favor for a man looking for a wife, and as she will be mother to my heir, there are many who wish to win her hand."

"Yet she remains unmarried," said Fitzwilliam.

The earl only shook his head. "She has not favored any of the men who have vied for her hand, and I have not attempted to persuade her. We have an agreement, she and I: she knows that she must marry and bear children and has accepted that duty, but she does not wish for me to push anyone on her or choose her husband. I have agreed to allow her the power of choice, and in return she has agreed that she *will* marry, and she will do it soon."

A gravity settled over Fitzwilliam. "Do you think this is what prompted her to set her sights on Darcy?"

"I do not know." The earl paused, and when he spoke again, he was contemplative. "It is possible, though I cannot say for certain. Your cousin is an excellent man, and she has known him all her life. As I said before, I do not think her heart was in any way engaged with Darcy, but I am certain she thought she knew enough of him to know he would be a good husband and father of her children, regardless of whether he was emotionally attached to her."

"I am certain he would," replied Fitzwilliam. "But Darcy has always wished to make a love match. You knew his parents, and you know how they felt about each other."

"It was the same as what I had with her mother," replied the earl, subdued and thoughtful. "But Emily does not remember her mother, and though she knows of our felicity, she never experienced what it was like to live in a home with parents who were devoted to each other. Thus, though I believe she would like to find such a connection, I do not think she would repine if she could only find a good man who would care for her."

Fitzwilliam paused to consider what he was being told. It was clear the earl wished to move his daughter's search for a suitor along if he possibly could, and the way the conversation had proceeded, he was thinking of Fitzwilliam himself as a potential suitor. What Fitzwilliam was unable to fathom at that moment was whether he wished to be considered for the role. He did esteem the woman, but he was uncertain if he could love her. He and Darcy had been close all their lives, and when they were young, it had been Darcy who had looked to emulate Fitzwilliam, who was the elder. But more as they aged and Fitzwilliam came to see what a fine man his cousin had become, their roles had reversed, and one of the things he wished for was what his cousin would have with Miss Bennet. He was not certain if he could find that with Lady Emily.

"Let us speak of your situation, Fitzwilliam," said the earl, capturing his attention once again. "From the standpoint of nothing more than eligibility, I believe you and my daughter would make a good match. You are the son of an earl and she is the daughter of one, so your positions in society are equal. Furthermore, though I know you are independent, your life as the father of a future earl would be one of much greater consequence than your current estate would support. I understand it yields about three thousand five hundred pounds?"

"Closer to four thousand," said Fitzwilliam, wondering at the earl's good information. "Darcy and I have talked about purchasing more land, with him investing in my estate and being paid back over time from the extra yields."

"A prudent plan," said the earl. "With the funds of the earldom, however, you would not need to partner with Darcy—you could do it with some of the moneys my estates yield."

"I could never—"

"Of course, you could," said the earl, interrupting him. "You and Emily, if you marry, may live on the estate in the future when my grandson assumes his birthright, and I would wish for my daughter to be as comfortable as possible in that eventuality. There is also the possibility of a second son to consider.

"Now, I do not support this simply in terms of financial and societal considerations, though they *are* important. I do believe, however, that you may be compatible. I believe you could have the same felicity as my wife and I shared, and I wish that for my daughter. If that is the case, then there is no other consideration as important."

Fitzwilliam paused, considering all his options. "With all due respect, I am not certain Lady Emily and I would develop that level of affection. I have been thinking on it of late, but the question remains unanswered, and I would not wish to lead her on."

The earl nodded, approval written on his brow. "I appreciate that. I am not suggesting a formal courtship or an engagement, but if you were to continue to call on her, perhaps with greater frequency than you have thitherto done, I believe the question would resolve itself quickly, either yea or nay. What say you?"

There was only one response to make. "Then I will call on her with your permission."

"Excellent! To that end, will you join us for dinner Tuesday next?"

"I would be delighted, sir."

That settled, the earl invited Fitzwilliam to a game of chess, and they sat down to it with a will. They were on their third game much later in the morning when Lady Emily returned. She seemed more annoyed than surprised that he was sitting with her father and had been most of the morning, but a look passed between father and daughter and she relaxed. The message had been received. Fitzwilliam thought she would still require reassurance that his interest in her was not predicated on pecuniary advantages, but that was something he could ensure she knew as he continued to call on her.

Though he had come thither without truly understanding the reason for it, Fitzwilliam now had a sense of purpose, which helped clarify matters. He still did not know how it would end, but he thought the woman estimable and worthy of his attention. As the earl said, it would all work out.

When Fitzwilliam returned to Pemberley and joined Darcy and Bingley in the study, they had already been there for several hours. Bingley greeted the new arrival expansively, but Darcy just watched him, wondering at Fitzwilliam's absence. He was certain that Fitzwilliam had gone to visit Lady Emily, but he was not yet able to fathom his purpose. Darcy was still annoyed with the woman, but the hot edge of his anger had cooled, and he was able to look at the matter objectively. Fitzwilliam had, by his own admission, engaged the woman to distract her from Darcy, but had that purpose turned to an interest in her? Darcy did not know, but he meant to discover it.

"Have you two been hiding in here from the ladies all day?" asked Fitzwilliam as he poured himself a glass of Darcy's brandy. He took his glass and sat on the sofa near the two chairs Darcy and Bingley were using.

"You have two sisters, I understand," said Bingley.

"Indeed, I do. But if you are suggesting they do not cause as much trouble as yours, I should inform you that my sisters and I have experienced some rather fantastic arguments. Charity, in particular, is known to be short-tempered and selfish. You would be surprised at how vindictive she can be."

"But I doubt she is purposefully cruel," replied Bingley. "Mine often is, and after her performance this morning, neither Darcy nor I had any desire to be in her company."

"She does not appreciate Miss Bennet's charms?" asked Fitzwilliam, highly amused.

"Water and hot oil," replied Bingley. "She was not best pleased to learn that Lizzy has become such an intimate of Georgiana's."

"Then . . ." Fitzwilliam paused, looking at Darcy, and he felt obliged to answer.

"Bingley knows. Mrs. Bingley and Miss Bingley have not been informed."

Fitzwilliam's raised eyebrow spoke volumes. "Miss Bennet did not inform her sister of her engagement? Is the situation between them that poor?"

"My wife has . . . changed with respect to her family since our marriage," said Bingley. "At present, I do not know the reason for it. Lizzy has, unfortunately, little reason to trust Jane at present."

"I knew there was some trouble there, but I did not know the extent of it," replied Fitzwilliam. He seemed to think his words to be inadequate, and Darcy could not disagree. But as none of them knew what to say, he could not fault his cousin.

"We are to go to Kingsdown on Tuesday next for dinner," said Darcy, wishing to change the subject. "You are invited, of course."

"Ah, but that evening the Earl of Chesterfield has invited me to dine with them. I am afraid I shall be forced to decline."

"Truly?" asked Darcy, now more than ever intent upon learning of his cousin's intentions.

Fitzwilliam only nodded and sipped his drink. "I visited this morning. We spoke for some time, and the invitation was extended."

"That is unfortunate," said Bingley, unaware of the import of what Fitzwilliam was telling them. "The company, I have no doubt, will be excellent. Then again, with Caroline and Elizabeth in attendance together, it might be best that you are absent. You do tend to throw fuel on the fire, old boy."

A bark of laughter met Bingley's tease. "Someone must take on the responsibility. It would be dull otherwise."

"If you had Caroline for a sister, you would agree a little dullness is more than welcome."

Unsure, Darcy looked at his friend, wondering at his behavior. Though Bingley had made comments concerning his sister in the past, he had rarely been as critical of her as he was now.

Bingley apparently saw Darcy's look, and he waved him off with an un-Bingley-like burst of irritation. "She has been difficult to tolerate of late, Darcy. From her objections to my wife, to her continuous arrogance toward Lizzy, to her constant complaints on the way to Pemberley, as if it was not the place in the world she most wished to go."

The smile Bingley flashed at his last point was returned by Darcy's grimace. But Bingley was not finished his teasing.

"Are you certain you do not wish to take her off my hands, old man? I would be willing to augment her dowry if you would."

"I am an engaged man, Bingley," replied Darcy.

"Ah, the man hides behind his engagement, which has not yet even been announced. I had high hopes for you, Darcy." Bingley's eyes swung lazily to Fitzwilliam, but before he could speak, Fitzwilliam demurred.

"I am sorry, Bingley, but you could augment her dowry with your entire fortune and I would still refuse."

"You see?" asked Bingley, regarding them both with mock annoyance. "I cannot even give her away to Fitzwilliam, and he is more in need of her dowry than you. How am I to ever find a man willing to marry her if her dowry is not inducement enough?"

Darcy winced at Bingley's less than kind assertion of his sister's caustic personality, though he agreed without reservation. Fitzwilliam, however, only snorted with laughter.

"You are severe on your sister."

"I know I should not speak so," replied Bingley. "But it is not unwarranted."

"It seems to me the first task should be to get Darcy married off to Miss Bennet. With him removed from consideration, your sister will be forced to turn her attention to some other man."

Bingley sighed. "She has had marriage proposals from perfectly acceptable men but has rejected them in hopes of capturing Darcy. She sets her sights too high."

"But if Darcy is not available, then the truth of the matter might become clear to her. She is, what, three and twenty now?"

"Four and twenty, actually," replied Bingley absently.

"The fear of becoming an old maid might make her more reasonable."

"It is possible." Bingley turned to Darcy. "I do not suppose I could convince you and Lizzy to announce your engagement now?"

"I am bound to follow Lizzy's wishes," replied Darcy, shaking his head.

"She is of age."

"And yet she wishes to wait. You know her reasons. I will not insist."

"Either way," interjected Fitzwilliam, "you know that nothing less than Darcy's marriage will induce her to surrender. You should be pushing him to make for Gretna Green.

Bingley brightened and looked at Darcy, who just shook his head.

Fitzwilliam burst out in laughter, and though Darcy thought the discussion was highly inappropriate, he and Bingley soon joined him.

"Ah, well, it was worth asking," said Bingley.

The discussion descended to ennui after that, nothing more than a comment here and there of little import. Darcy watched his cousin as they talked, noting Fitzwilliam was his usual lighthearted self. Nothing he said indicated what he had been doing at Teasdale Manor, and Darcy's curiosity increased the longer they sat there.

Finally, Bingley excused himself to return to his room and Darcy was afforded the opportunity to quiz his cousin. The answers, however, were not to his liking.

"You seem to have been engaged often at Teasdale Manor lately. I am surprised you have been there so often of late."

Fitzwilliam's eyes swung to Darcy. "She is not a bad woman, Darcy."

"I have never considered her to be so, regardless of her behavior with Elizabeth. But I do wonder about your intentions."

"As do I, Darcy," replied Fitzwilliam quietly. "The earl has taken an interest in me, and I cannot fault him. I will be calling on Lady Emily, but I do not know how it will end."

"That is an interesting development. How did it all come about?"

Fitzwilliam spent the next several minutes explaining his conversation with the earl, of the earl's wishes for his daughter, Fitzwilliam's agreement to call on her, his confusion of whether she was what he wished for, and the possible motives for her actions toward Darcy and Elizabeth. In the end, Darcy was forced to agree that Fitzwilliam's information did explain quite a lot.

"I still do not exonerate her for leaving Elizabeth to fend for herself," said Darcy after his cousin had completed his recitation.

"Nor should you," replied Fitzwilliam. "I am inclined to think of it as losing her temper in a moment of anger. It was not right, and she will need to prove herself in that regard. She will need to regain my trust, as well as yours."

Darcy grunted, but did not respond.

"The earl's arguments were persuasive, but I want more than simply to father the next Earl of Chesterfield. The coming days and weeks will reveal my future path. I will say that I am not opposed to an alliance with Lady Emily, only that I wish to have a connection with her before I move forward."

"Then I wish you the best of luck, Cousin," replied Darcy. "I know what this could mean for you, beyond finding a woman you can love.

I hope it all works out in the end."

And Darcy did. Though a few short days ago, the notion of a connection with the lady might have been abhorrent, he had had time to think about it. She *was* and would continue to be his neighbor, and it was important to maintain good relations with her and her father. If Fitzwilliam married her, Darcy had no doubt their relations would return to what they were before. It was equally obvious that Fitzwilliam would be a good master of the estates and would be a good husband and check on her, if her behavior toward Elizabeth was not simply an isolated incident.

Chapter XXVIII

$\mathcal{E}$ lizabeth spent the rest of the day moping—there was no other way to describe it. The hope for her sister's change back to the person she knew had been tempered by the realistic expectation that nothing had, indeed, changed, but that did not make the blow any less severe.

It was fortunate, then, that Elizabeth was not made for melancholy, and furthermore, had relations who were not about to allow her to wallow in self-pity. In particular, it was Olivia who took it upon herself to raise Elizabeth's spirits.

"I was surprised by your new sister by marriage, Lizzy," said Olivia.

"Oh?" asked Elizabeth. "In what way?"

"Why, from all the hints you have given me of her character, I expected her to be much more prideful than she was. She only sneered at *me* once, though she made a much better showing to you. How can you account for such a lackluster performance?"

Olivia's tease was so surprising that Elizabeth almost choked on her tongue. Then she had no choice but to burst into laughter. "I am sorry to inform you, dearest, but I believe she felt you beneath her notice. If she had considered you more, I am certain she would have made a better showing."

A superior sniff, so reminiscent of the woman at whose expense they were laughing, was Olivia's response. "I suppose I shall have to wait and see, then. But if she does not respond appropriately, I will be forced to consider your words an exaggeration."

"You may do so if you like," said Elizabeth.

They bantered on for some time, speaking at Miss Bingley's expense, and though Elizabeth knew that she should moderate Olivia's words and her own amusement at the woman's conceit, she decided she had little desire to do so. The lady was eminently deserving of it. For the rest of the evening, therefore, Elizabeth found herself in much better spirits, and she allowed herself to forget her troubles for a time.

The next day brought a shock which Elizabeth had not been expecting. It happened in the morning, as Elizabeth and Olivia were preparing to once again go to Pemberley in the Edward's company. They were in Olivia's room changing into appropriate clothing and making certain they were presentable when the sound of a carriage was heard on the drive.

"Was Mr. Darcy to come today, Lizzy?" asked Olivia.

Elizabeth frowned. "I do not think so, though I suppose it is possible."

As Elizabeth was still looking in the mirror, ensuring her hair was in place, Olivia took herself to the window, which overlooked the front drive of the house, and pulled aside the curtains to afford herself a better view.

"It is not one of the Darcy carriages," said she. "It is much smaller, in fact."

Curious, Elizabeth followed her cousin to the window and looked out. The carriage was familiar to Elizabeth. Very familiar.

"Papa!" gasped she, and she turned and ran out the door, the sound of Olivia's startled exclamations following her down the stairs.

By the time Elizabeth had reached the outer door, her father was already alighting from the carriage and her uncle was greeting him.

"Lizzy!" said Mr. Bennet, as Elizabeth flew into his embrace. "I have missed you, my darling daughter."

"I have missed you too, Father, but I am shocked to see you." She turned a look on her uncle. "Did you know Father was to come?"

"He did, but you may reserve your displeasure for me alone. I asked him not to inform you."

Elizabeth looked on her father, wondering at his meaning, but he was already turning to supervise the unloading of his trunks and seeing to the disposition of the carriage driver. Soon these tasks were complete, and Mr. Bennet came into the house with the rest of them. He was greeted by all, Mrs. Drummond greeting her brother with more than a little asperity, and settled in to speak to them.

"What brings you here, Father?" asked Elizabeth.

Elizabeth did not miss the glance he shot at Mrs. Drummond, and she was aware of his dissembling when he responded. "I have received some interesting news of late, Lizzy, and I thought it would be best if I came to deal with it personally."

There were two interpretations to his statement. His wish to keep the reason for his coming from his sister might have applied to either reason. Elizabeth did not think he was aware of the engagement and did not think he would have come for nothing more than the knowledge that a man was paying attention to her. But she did not think he would have come for the other reason either.

Regardless, she did not wish to speak with him with her aunt listening intently to their every word, so she suggested a walk around the back park, to which he readily agreed.

"Shall I send a note to Pemberley, Lizzy?" asked Olivia. "It seems like we will not be going there today."

"I see no reason why we should not, Olivia," replied Mr. Bennet. "If you will allow me to speak with Lizzy for a few moments, we may depart soon after. I believe I will enjoy meeting these people of whom I have heard so much."

"And Jane is there," said Olivia.

"She is, indeed, though I did see her only days before she departed Hertfordshire. Still, I would be happy to go with you if you will wait patiently."

Olivia nodded happily and father rose to escort his daughter from the room, Mrs. Drummond looking on, her countenance more than usually unreadable.

They walked in silence for some few minutes, Elizabeth waiting — albeit with impatience — for her father to tell her why he had taken the trouble to visit Derbyshire *again* when she knew how much he loathed to travel. But Mr. Bennet appeared less than inclined to speak. His manner was contemplative, his mien thoughtful.

Finally, Elizabeth could stand the silence no longer. "I must own to some confusion and concern, Papa. I cannot account for your being here. Was it wise to leave Kitty and Lydia at home with Mama? You know she will indulge them without anyone to check her."

"You speak of the matter as if *I* have ever taken the trouble to check her, Lizzy."

Elizabeth, confused, could not immediately respond, and Mr. Bennet chuckled. "In fact, I believe you would be proud of me of late, Lizzy. You are correct that the girls should not be left to their own devices, but they are not alone. Your Aunt Gardiner has come to Longbourn for the summer with her children, and it is she who has the care of your sisters."

"I thought aunt and uncle were to journey to the lakes."

"Their plans were altered because of your uncle's business," replied her father. "It seems he is not able to travel after all this summer, so they made arrangements for your aunt to have a holiday of her own in Hertfordshire, though I cannot imagine it will be at all restful for her."

"Oh," said Elizabeth. "And what of Mama? You know that she is not happy if anyone gainsays her with respect to Kitty and Lydia."

"That is another matter that has changed. I presume you are aware of the militia's removal to Brighton for the summer?"

Elizabeth rolled her eyes. "Lydia has written of little else, though rumors were circulating before I came to Derbyshire."

"Well, they have since departed," replied Mr. Bennet. "Before they left, Lydia received an invitation from the colonel's wife to accompany her there."

Elizabeth looked at her father with consternation. Since he spoke of Lydia's presence at Longbourn, Elizabeth was reassured that he had not allowed her to go. But the mere thought of Lydia in Brighton, where she could flirt and carry on and ruin them all with naught but the colonel's wife to check her—a woman as silly and ungovernable as Lydia herself—was enough to fill her with disquiet.

"I see from your expression that you are horrified by the mere thought," said her father with a chuckle. "I will own that my first instinct was to allow it."

"Oh, Papa!" exclaimed Elizabeth, but her father only chuckled.

"As you will have guessed, I did *not* allow it, and I resisted all of Lydia's tantrums and wailings. Not only would her behavior have been beyond redemption among all those soldiers, but I thought I detected a hint of interest from Wickham in your sister, and it made me uncomfortable. Had Lydia gone, Kitty would have been left to her own devices, and with no other sisters to remain with her, I did not think it was fair for Lydia to have fun while Kitty was left alone." Her father paused. "I did not inform Lydia of the role Kitty played in my decision, for I am certain you will apprehend Kitty would have received the bulk of the blame."

"I am sure that is an understatement," murmured Elizabeth.

"Your sister, needless to say, did not agree with me. It was her constant complaints and outbursts which convinced me that she has no business being out of the schoolroom."

"And Mama?" asked Elizabeth. "I cannot think that she was sanguine about your decision either."

"She was not, at first. But I took her aside and spoke with her quite firmly about the reality of Lydia's behavior. Furthermore, I spoke of our connection with the Bingleys and your sister's distance since her marriage. Though I do not know all of Jane's reasons, the thought of two unruly and undisciplined sisters and how they might embarrass her in public may be part of her thoughts. If nothing else, I am certain Miss Bingley understands and does not appreciate the connection.

"I explained these things to your mother and spoke of how Lydia and Kitty must improve before they can be introduced to any of Mr. Bingley's rich friends." Mr. Bennet laughed. "Your mother has high hopes of marrying Lydia and Kitty off to wealthy men, introduced to them by your new brother."

Elizabeth rolled her eyes. "Did Mama not make those same comments at Mr. Bingley's ball, in a loud voice no one could possibly have missed?"

"Indeed, she did. I also informed her that her words were not appreciated and that she should be more circumspect in the future. When she wailed about her actions possibly being what has driven Jane away from the family, I pointed out to her that was precisely the behavior someone of high society would find objectionable. She was very thoughtful for the rest of the day.

"So, you see, the changes we have instituted in Lydia's life have not been against your mother's wishes—quite the opposite, in fact, once she understood the need for them."

"And how is Lydia taking them?" asked Elizabeth."

"About as well as you might expect," replied her father. "But I will own that I have noticed some small improvements in the days before I left, though I do not expect that such changes will be wrought overnight. Kitty is a little better, especially once I pointed out to her that she would do better emulating you or Jane, or even her Aunt Gardiner."

Elizabeth sighed. "I will not say that I am not happy that you have made these changes, though Lydia's improvement will be slow. I pity Aunt Gardiner for being forced to put up with her ill humors while you are away."

Though Elizabeth would have expected commiseration, Mr. Bennet only chuckled again. "You do not think I would have left your aunt if I expected Lydia to give her any trouble, do you? In fact, Lydia has always been more than a little intimidated by your aunt, and she listens to *her* better than she listens to *me*."

Surprised by his assertion, Elizabeth giggled at the thought of fearless Lydia being cowed by her mild-mannered aunt. But then she thought of the woman in question, and she remembered that Mrs. Gardiner was capable of being stern when required. More than that, however, Elizabeth suspected that Lydia was intimidated by her aunt's comportment, which was beyond reproach.

"Then perhaps some good will come of it," said Elizabeth. "If she had gone on in that manner much longer, she might have ruined us all."

"When I left, your aunt was speaking to her of London society, and the delights she might savor there. For the first time in her life, Lydia is being forced to think of something beyond her immediate gratification. There is some hope yet."

The conversation had been exhausted, and though Elizabeth was happy to hear that her sisters had been taken in hand and taught to behave, of more immediate concern was the reason for her father's presence, and she did not mean to allow him to put it off any longer.

"I can see you are impatient," said Mr. Bennet before she could say anything. "I suppose my coming must have been a shock."

"It is, Papa, and I can hardly account for it. Surely you did not mean to come here to inform me of the changes you made at Longbourn."

"No, you are correct." Mr. Bennet stopped walking and turned to speak directly to her. "In fact, my reasons for coming here are twofold. First, you told me enough of your doings here to provoke my interest, particularly your friendship with a young man of the area and his sister?"

Her father's raised eyebrow prompted a blush. Mr. Bennet chuckled. "I thought so. In fact, given what you have said of him, I expect he has, at the least, already asked for a courtship. Am I correct?"

"You are," replied Elizabeth quietly, feeling unequal to answering her father's teasing.

"And?" It appeared her father was not about to let her get away so easily.

"He has proposed, Papa. And I have accepted him."

It was clear she had caught him by surprise, for he fairly gaped at her. Then he burst out laughing. "Well, well, I had not expected *this*. If he can see your worth so quickly, then I must think him an intelligent man, indeed! I anticipate meeting him very much!"

"Papa!" chided Elizabeth.

"You must allow your old papa the pride of his favorite daughter, Lizzy. Any man who is clever enough to see your worth so quickly must be acceptable in my opinion."

Embarrassed, Elizabeth changed the subject. "You mentioned another reason for your journey here?"

Though it was clear Mr. Bennet was loath to leave off his teasing he soon sobered and began to walk again. "It was your questions about your aunt which played the other part in my decision to come, Lizzy. You were not explicit, but I suspect she did not relate the full of the matter, or what she said favored her own viewpoint, but I could only guess."

"That is correct," replied Elizabeth. Then she proceeded to relate the matter to her father, explaining what her aunt had told her. As expected, Mr. Bennet's view of what had happened was quite different from his sister's, though he listened to her intently to ensure he understood the charges which were laid at his door. When she had finished her explanation, he sighed and stared off into the distance for several moments before he spoke.

"As you have surmised," said he at length, "your aunt's account is accurate to a certain extent, but it is, nevertheless, colored by her own perceptions."

"In what way, Papa?"

Mr. Bennet turned back to her. "You are aware of your mother's origins, so I shall not delve into that subject. Your aunt was, indeed, dismayed when I announced my intention to marry your mother. My father had already passed on by then, so I was master of Longbourn, and though my mother was alive, she made no objection to my choice, declaring that I was my own master and capable of managing my own affairs.

"In fact, your mother and my mother got on famously. My mother taught her as much of managing the house of a gentleman as she could before her death, which unfortunately occurred less than a year after our marriage. Your mother was devastated at the death of my mother and took many months to recover."

"I did not know," said Elizabeth quietly. "You have not spoken of my grandparents much."

"There did not seem to be any reason to do so, other than to acquaint you all with the history of the Bennets, which I have attempted to do. For some time, speaking of her mentor was painful to your mother, so I avoided the topic. After a time, it became a habit, one which we have kept to this day."

"And Aunt Claire?"

"Unlike your grandmother, your aunt railed against my choice and was not afraid to let your mother know it. While Claire continued to live with us until her marriage—which was not until after your grandmother's death—it was quite uncomfortable at Longbourn. Your aunt did everything she could to undermine your mother, even after I explicitly told her she would not be welcome at my estate if she did not cease her objectionable behavior." Mr. Bennet snorted. "Claire only laughed at me, saying there was nowhere else for her to go. The Collinses were our only living relations, and she knew I would never send her there.

"As for this matter of a suitor, your aunt is correct that the man decided against proposing, but she is wrong as to the reason. In fact, her suitor—a man who lived north of Stevenage—decided against her because of her behavior after my marriage. He came himself to inform me of his decision, confessing his worries concerning her behavior. If she was so objectionable to me and my wife, he was concerned for how she would act after she became his wife.

"Of course, Claire blamed your mother and her 'common origins' for the loss of her suitor, and though I attempted to tell her the true reason for his retreat, she would not listen to me."

"How did she become known to Uncle Drummond?"

"He was a friend of one of my friends," said Mr. Bennet. "By the time your uncle had inherited Kingsdown, the estate had been reduced to a fraction of its former size and income. Your uncle wished to marry a woman of dowry, but at the time, no one of the neighborhood would commit their daughters to him for fear he would be the same as his father. My friend vouched for his industry and the goodness of his nature, and Claire and I met him. With nary a hesitation, your aunt declared that she would marry him, and though I was shocked, nothing I said could talk her out of it."

"But did you not wish her to marry?"

"Wish her to marry, yes, but not in such circumstances. I wanted her to be courted. To learn more about him, and for him to learn of her. I tried speaking to your uncle, to inform him of what her behavior had been, but at the time he was desperate for the funds, so he proposed, she accepted, and they were married soon after.

"Before she left for her new home, however, she informed me that she married for the sole reason of removing herself from my home and what she considered the tainting of our family legacy. She blamed everything on me—her failed courtship, her fall from what she thought she could expect in life, how she was *forced* to marry an unsuitable man. She made it clear that she was the one to suffer from my disgrace, and left in the bitterest of spirits."

"I can hardly take this all in," said Elizabeth. "I never knew any of it."

"It was never intended that you should know of it." Mr. Bennet stopped and looked at her seriously. "I know this tale does not reflect well on your aunt, and I did not wish your perception of her to be colored by it. I could not have imagined she would tell you as much as she did."

"I assume you wish my sisters to remain ignorant of it?"

"That would be for the best," confirmed her father. "What good is there in their knowing? None of you have met her since you were small children, and though the connection will become closer again with your marriage, I cannot think that she will wish it to become known. I believe that deep down Claire knows that she was wrong, though I do not think she will ever own to it. There is nothing to be done but leave it in the past. If she had not spoken of it to you, we would not be having this conversation.

"Now, I have a desire to meet this man who has had the temerity to propose to my favorite daughter." Mr. Bennet's tease brought a blush to Elizabeth's face again. "If you will finish your preparations, we may go directly."

"Very well, Papa. I shan't be long."

As he watched his favorite daughter walk back to the house, Bennet was struck with a sense of melancholy. She was the bright light in his life, his companion, his debate partner, and his happiness all rolled into one package, complete with bright eyes and a sunny disposition. He would miss her, now that she was to live in Derbyshire with her young man.

On the other hand, unburdening himself to her proved to be a cathartic experience. There were others who were aware of the history, of course; Drummond himself, Gardiner—who still wished to have no contact with Claire due to how she had treated his sister, regardless of his esteem for Drummond—and even the Phillipses had some knowledge of the matter. But speaking of it to Elizabeth, one who had possessed no knowledge and could provide a new perspective, helped relieve the burden on Bennet's shoulders, one of which he had not even been aware.

Bennet knew his sister had not been completely incorrect as to the reasons for his marriage and her objection to Maggie in particular. Bennet *had* proposed to her in a moment of infatuation, blinded by her happy disposition and beauty to her lack of sense and irritable nature. Still, he liked to think that he and Maggie did well enough together, though the infatuation had long since died. His mother's death had come at an unfortunate time—had she had another year to work with Maggie, he thought his mother might have been able to mold her into a respectable gentlewoman. That he himself had not done enough was a fact of which Bennet was not unaware, but in his defense, his mother's death had affected him severely as well. And nothing he had taught her would have ameliorated the situation brought about by the succession of five daughters born without a son.

Regardless, it had not been Claire's place to act as she had. Her disappointments in life were her own doing.

"Are you telling tales, Brother?"

Bennet turned to see his sister standing nearby, staring at him with her usual contempt. "I have not the pleasure of understanding you, Claire."

"I assume you came to poison that daughter of yours against me by pushing the blame of your disgrace away from where it rightly belongs."

"Had I desired to do that, I could have done it before she came so as to save myself the annoyance of another long journey." Bennet dared her to respond, and when she did not, he added: "It was not I who dredged the river of old wrongs and brought it to light again. I have not spoken of the matter to any of my children before today, but I could not allow Elizabeth to be misinformed."

"Misinformed!" Claire's tone was dripping with resentment. "Do you deny you married an unsuitable woman and sullied our line? Even my *husband* has done his duty by fathering three boys. Your wife could not even manage that much."

"There is much about life we do not understand, Claire," replied Bennet. "But I do not believe a woman has any control over the sex of her offspring, any more than the man possesses.

"But though *you* do not approve of my wife, she has settled into her role as mistress of my estate with tolerable ease, and has given me five beautiful daughters. I find that I have, on the whole, no cause to repine."

Claire did not respond, though her lips thinned in anger. Looking at her, Bennet was struck by a notion, one he had not considered before, but which seemed likelier the longer he thought of it. This woman, who had once been his sister, still seemed to wish to be proven correct about his wife. In fact, she burned with the desire to be acknowledged correct. It was unfortunate for her that Bennet was not about to gratify that desire.

"A word of advice for you, Claire," said Bennet. "I suggest you forget your pride and resign yourself to be as happy as you can in your life. And most of all, you should descend from your high horse. Your continued anger at life is doing no one, least of all yourself, any good."

With those words, Bennet turned and walked toward the house. He had no time for a bitter woman when there were many other things of more importance on which to focus.

Chapter XXIX

Although the carriage ride to Pemberley was not long, it seemed interminable to Elizabeth. Elizabeth could not imagine what her sister's reaction to seeing her father again would be, and except from some second-hand accounts of Jane's rarely seeing her family since Elizabeth's departure, she was not certain how Mr. Bennet's relations with his eldest daughter stood. The only one of them who was truly excited for the upcoming visit was Olivia.

"What a shock Jane will get!" exclaimed Olivia as the carriage rolled along the road. "You did not tell her of your coming to Derbyshire, did you, Uncle?"

"No, Olivia," said Mr. Bennet with a smile for the young girl. "When Jane left Hertfordshire, I had not yet made the decision to come and had not even conceived of the idea yet."

"It was a surprise to see you. You did not tell Lizzy you were to come?"

"I did not. By the time I decided to come, I was off, so there was no time to inform her, though I did send an express to your father."

"How strange Papa did not mention it, even to Lizzy."

"I asked him not to. I was hoping to surprise your cousin."

Olivia clapped her hands with glee. "Then you were successful!

Lizzy had no notion you would come, though if you had been ten minutes later, you would have missed us altogether."

"Oh?" asked Mr. Bennet, raising an eyebrow at Elizabeth.

"Yes, for we were about to go to Pemberley ourselves."

In this manner, the girl continued to chatter, and though Mr. Bennet only gave her banal replies, Elizabeth could readily understand that they were designed to persuade the girl to reveal stories of Elizabeth's activities in Derbyshire. Thus, much of what had happened had soon been prompted from the girl's mouth—their outings with those of the area, Lady Emily's visits, William's attentions, and his sister's friendship. Though Elizabeth did not think she had done anything particularly noteworthy, certainly nothing to provoke embarrassment, still she found herself uncomfortable by what Olivia revealed. Was it possible to be mortified beyond all endurance by nothing more than receiving a good man's attentions? She would not have thought so before.

When the carriage stopped at Pemberley, Elizabeth was eager to disembark, and they did so and made their way inside. From the looks Mr. Bennet was giving their surroundings, he was impressed by what he was seeing. Mrs. Reynolds was curious about the man's presence, but like any experienced servant, she did not ask questions.

The door to the sitting-room was opened, and Elizabeth led her father into the room, to the surprise of more than one of the inhabitants.

"Papa!" exclaimed Jane upon seeing her father. "What are you doing here?"

Mr. Bennet chuckled and greeted his eldest daughter. "I found I had business with your sister. My coming was unannounced, though I hope I will be welcome nonetheless."

"Of course, you are," said William, standing and approaching them. He turned to Elizabeth with a broad grin—which seemed to suggest pleasure that he would be able to ask her father's permission long before he might otherwise have been able to—and requested an introduction.

Elizabeth obliged readily, including Colonel Fitzwilliam and Georgiana in her introductions. When that had been completed, Mr. Bingley stepped forward and greeted his father-in-law with a vigorous handshake.

"Mr. Bennet, I am surprised to see you here. I had no idea you were contemplating following us to Derbyshire."

"I had no notion of it myself, Bingley," replied Mr. Bennet. "But I found I needed to speak with Elizabeth, and once I had made that determination, I wasted no time in setting out."

Mr. Bingley laughed. "That is much like I would do it. I have always said that should I decide to leave a place, I should do it on a moment's thought."

"I never would have guessed," was Mr. Bennet's dry reply.

"You are very welcome here, Mr. Bennet," said William. "In fact, your presence is quite serendipitous."

"I rather thought so myself, Mr. Darcy."

"Are my mother and sisters well, Papa?" asked Jane, though she hesitated first.

"They are. Your Aunt Gardiner is visiting, and I do not doubt that between them they have the estate well in hand."

"I hope the journey from *Gracechurch Street* was not too taxing for your aunt," interjected Miss Bingley. "I understand she has several children of her own to care for."

Though Miss Bingley's words were solicitous in tone, anyone who knew her—and most likely those who did not—were aware of the contempt in her voice. Mr. Bennet regarded her with a steady look, but the woman, likely aware of his understanding of her meaning, possessed no shame, her returning gaze all innocence.

"Mrs. Gardiner has made the journey many times, Miss Bingley," was Mr. Bennet's reply. "And she employs a governess to help care for her children."

"That is well then," said Miss Bingley, nodding cheerfully. "Since she must also care for your daughters, I would not wish her strength to be taxed unduly."

Mr. Bennet bestowed a faint smile on the woman. "As I said previously, I am certain they have matters in hand. My wife knows what must be done, and Mrs. Gardiner is there to assist. They have both been mothers for some years, and have cared for their children in an exemplary fashion. Someday *if* you have children of your own, you will no doubt understand."

Miss Bingley sucked in a breath, offended by Mr. Bennet's words, but Mr. Bingley quickly interjected, with a stern look at his sister. "I do not doubt the competence of Mrs. Bennet or Mrs. Gardiner. I was quite impressed with the Gardiners when we met them in London. Very genteel, amiable folk, indeed."

They sat down with the existing company, but Elizabeth did not miss the look Mr. Bingley shot at his sister, warning her to lock her tongue away. Miss Bingley, though she appeared like she had drunk vinegar, nevertheless stayed silent for the most part, though she and Jane carried on a whispered conversation between them. For Jane's part, though her surprise at seeing her father had been evident when he had arrived, it had faded to a confusion which appeared to be even greater than that Elizabeth had witnessed only the day before. The façade she had shown upon her return from her wedding tour had begun to crack, though Elizabeth could not determine what was behind it. Would it be the true Jane, or would it be something even more objectionable than before?

"Miss Bennet," asked William in a quiet tone as he took a seat beside her. The action drew the attention of Miss Bingley, and it was easy to see the woman did not appreciate his attention to Elizabeth. "Does your father know?"

"He does," replied Elizabeth.

"Then I shall find a pretense to speak with him alone."

"Are you so impatient, sir?" asked Elizabeth, fixing him with a playful smile.

"I have been given the opportunity to secure your hand long before I might otherwise have expected," replied William, showing her not a hint of a tease. "Of course, I am impatient."

"Then offer to show him your library. The only issue I see is that you might not be able to remove him from the room once he is inside, and you might not be able to hold his attention for long enough to ask."

"I believe I will take that chance. Before I excuse myself, however, I would like to take the opportunity of securing your hand for the first dance at the assembly next week. Is that agreeable to you?"

Elizabeth feigned offense. "*Only* the first dance, sir?"

"I am certain there will be other opportunities to secure other dances that night. But since I cannot claim you for *all* the dances, I believe I will settle for the first, if you please."

"Of course, William. I would be happy to."

William grinned and nodded to her. "Now, if you will excuse me, I believe I would like to know my future father-in-law better."

And with that, he rose and approached Elizabeth's father, where he was speaking with Colonel Fitzwilliam. They three men were joined by Mr. Bingley soon after, and they stood there speaking with some animation. Though Elizabeth was not close enough to overhear all their words, she thought she heard mention of a hunting party, as well as William's commentary on his fishing stream. Though her father was not the angler her uncle boasted of being, he seemed agreeable to William's suggestion of a fishing party in the next few days.

Soon after, William, following Elizabeth's suggestion, offered to show the library to her father, which was accepted with alacrity. Mr. Bingley and Colonel Fitzwilliam begged off—each being quite familiar with the room—and the two men left together. Elizabeth could not hope for anything more than good relations between her father and her future husband. She hoped the business would be completed quickly and they would return—she could hardly wait, though she still did not mean to make it known due to her uncertainty over Jane.

"You should not read too much into Mr. Darcy's attentions to your father, Eliza."

Startled from her reverie, Elizabeth looked up to see Miss Bingley looming over her. When she had approached, Elizabeth was not certain, but given the offense she was displaying, not to mention the ever-present contempt, the woman was not happy with what she had been seeing.

"Mr. Darcy, you see," continued she, "is attentive to all those duties as a host with guests in his home. I have no doubt his civility is prompted by nothing more than the desire to maintain good relations with Charles. They are such close friends, you understand, and Mr. Darcy will do anything for my brother, even accepting those with whom he would not usually associate."

"You need not fear for me, Miss Bingley," said Elizabeth, ignoring the woman's insinuations. "I have no desire to interpret Mr. Darcy's actions."

Especially since I already know why he asked to speak with my father.

"It is well then, for only heartache can come of such expectations."

"Of what expectations do you speak?" asked Elizabeth, though inside she wished she could put this woman in her place.

Miss Bingley only sneered. "The expectations nearly *all* young ladies have of Mr. Darcy when they meet him. But his are the highest, most discerning tastes, and I have no doubt his destiny lies in a place unlike that which you inhabit."

"That of a gentleman's daughter?" asked Elizabeth mildly.

The lines of her mouth tightened and Miss Bingley chose not to answer. Elizabeth was more than willing to oblige her by speaking again.

"I assume it is marriage of which you speak. I suppose you mean that he will likely marry a noble's daughter, if he is not to marry the daughter of a mere gentleman, for I hardly think you would suggest he would marry a woman who was not at least his equal."

"My words were nothing more than friendly advice to one who is, after all, related by marriage," said Miss Bingley, ignoring Elizabeth's rejoinder. "I suggest you do not forget this, Eliza, for if you do, you will surely be disappointed in the end."

The woman than turned and walked away, returning to the sofa on which Jane sat. Again, Elizabeth watched her sister, noting the way there was once again a crack in the veneer of her behavior, though this time it consisted of annoyance with Miss Bingley. It was a feeling Elizabeth could well understand — she, herself, was almost perpetually annoyed by Jane's new sister.

As for the woman herself, though Elizabeth longed to inform her of her new status, she forced herself to practice patience. Though it would be gratifying to see Miss Bingley's countenance when she discovered Elizabeth's understanding with William, the anticipation would make the event that much sweeter. She should not enjoy another's consternation so much, but for such a specimen as Miss Bingley, Elizabeth was willing to make an exception.

"You have a fine estate, sir."

"Thank you, Mr. Bennet," said Darcy, nodding to the man's praise. "It has been in the family many generations, and I am proud of it."

"There seems to be much to be proud of. Bingley has given you a rather flaming character, but I can see the care and attention you have put into Pemberley, and, I expect, into every facet of your life. It seems, therefore, the praise was not exaggerated."

Darcy, as ever, was uncomfortable speaking of himself, nevertheless he took pains to speak with the man he was hoping would approve of his marriage to Elizabeth. They exchanged some few words as they walked through the halls of Pemberley, Darcy noting some of the history of the place to Bennet, who listened and asked questions with interest unfeigned.

When they arrived at the library, Elizabeth's prediction of her father's reaction to the room was proven correct, and even more to Darcy's amusement, it mirrored his daughter's rather closely. Mr. Bennet stepped into the room, his eyes widening in awe as he took in the sight of so many bookshelves stuffed with the bounty accumulated by so many generations of the Darcy family. For a moment, he wandered about, looking at this title, or pulling a volume out, reading the cover and taking in the beauty of the written word.

"I think you have made a tactical error, Mr. Darcy," said Mr. Bennet after he had wandered about the room for several moments. "I may never wish to leave this room, for I do not doubt that it would take me more years than I have left to make my way through such an abundance of books."

Darcy laughed. "I can see that you are, indeed, Miss Bennet's father. She predicted your reaction to the letter, and even suggested that I might face a difficult time of evicting you."

"Ah, my Lizzy. Yes, she knows me quite well." Mr. Bennet pulled out another book and inspected it. Then he turned and gestured with it before setting it back in its place on the shelf. "I can see that your collection is of longstanding, sir, for this volume is much older than I am."

"I cannot take credit for most of this, though my father, my grandfather, and I have added a great many volumes as books have become cheaper to produce and more readily available. The house itself is over a century old, and several times modifications or additions have been made to it. This particular room was remodeled by my grandfather when the old room in which the library resided became too small for our collection."

"And how much longer will it be before this collection outgrows its home?" asked Mr. Bennet, looking about the room. It was an astute observation, as there was very little room left on the shelves which was not already dedicated to existing volumes.

"I have already drawn up some preliminary plans to expand," replied Darcy. "We could use the small rooms to either side and join them to this one by removing walls, or we could build an addition out from the house to accommodate our needs. The most intriguing option, however, is building up."

Mr. Bennet turned, his countenance alight with interest. "Building up?"

"The architect suggested that we could remove the ceiling from this room and convert the rooms situated above for additional space. Above us is the guest wing, including a pair of suites which are hardly ever used. If we removed the floor in between, left a balcony around the edge to walk on, installed a railing and a stairway, we would double our available space."

"Then you could go about spending your annual income purchasing more books to fill the empty space."

"Exactly."

The two men shared a grin. "I would love to see your plans, if you are willing to share them. As Lizzy has already told you, collecting books is a hobby of mine as well. Since she is the only one of my daughters who truly appreciates the written word, I have arranged in my will that she will receive my book collection."

"None of them are tied to the estate?"

"Some few volumes, yes," replied Mr. Bennet. "But most are the personal additions contributed by myself and my father. They are nothing compared to your collection, but I have some first editions, books which Elizabeth will remember fondly."

"I am certain she will treasure them."

"Yes, she shall." Mr. Bennet paused, and then said: "I must suppose that showing me your library was not your only reason for inviting me here, Mr. Darcy. Shall we proceed to that discussion before I lose myself in your treasure of books?"

"Certainly, sir. Shall we go to my study? It is just through this door."

With Mr. Bennet following—though a little unwillingly, Darcy noted with amusement—Darcy led him through the door at side the of the room to his study and invited him to sit in one of the chairs before the fireplace. Darcy himself remained standing, leaning on the fireplace mantle while he marshalled his thoughts. He was grateful to Bennet for allowing this time to gather himself, though the man did show a little amusement at his predicament. Darcy supposed it was not unusual for men to display such feelings upon being confronted by a suitor for their daughter, and a large part of it must be the remembrance of their own experience on the other side of the equation.

"Miss Bennet has told me that you know of my proposal."

"Yes, she did inform me."

It appeared the man was not about to make this ordeal any easier. "It was not many days after meeting Miss Bennet that I understood her worth. Her capabilities are extensive, and she complements me perfectly, her joy in life and ability to be easy in company pulls me from my sometimes more dour temperament and awkwardness. I respect and love her, and have her assurance that she loves me in return. I ask for your permission and your blessing to marry her, sir."

"You have said the words any father wishes to hear, particularly when the woman in question is most like him in temperament and cherished accordingly." Mr. Bennet paused. "I have seen your estate and I know you can support her in comfort, so that is not an issue. Are you also aware that Elizabeth possesses little dowry and little in the way of connections?"

"Not the specifics, no. Mr. Drummond has told me that she does not have a large fortune of her own, and he has told me something of your heir and your wife's brother in London. In fact, we share an odd sort of coincidental connection, for your cousin is parson to my aunt, Lady Catherine de Bourgh."

Mr. Bennet laughed. "Indeed! I apologize, sir, but I have often wondered about your aunt, and I have suspected she is not a sensible woman. Any woman who would offer a living to my cousin, one of the most foolish men I have ever met, must be out of her wits."

"So Miss Bennet has informed me, sir," said Darcy, chuckling along with him. "I must own that I am curious to meet this man of whom both you and your daughter have spoken so glibly. He must be an interesting specimen, indeed."

"That he is, Mr. Darcy."

"As for my aunt," continued Darcy, "though she is my dearly departed mother's sister, they were nothing alike. Lady Catherine is a force unto herself, and I only see her once a year. Given how often she exceeds her income and the excessive interest she takes in the lives of those around her, I can only concur that she is not the most sensible woman, though she herself would not agree."

"So I have gathered. Then are you the cousin Mr. Collins has so generously told us is destined for Miss de Bourgh? For that matter, how would the rest of your illustrious family view your marriage to my daughter?"

"Miss Bennet mentioned something about having heard that rumor," said Darcy.

"In Mr. Collins's defense, I do not believe he related it to all and sundry. But as Elizabeth's father, the matter is one of some concern."

"Then let me put your mind at ease. This supposed cradle engagement is nothing more than a fabrication of my aunt's. My mother never spoke of it, and though my aunt began to speak of it after my mother's passing, my father openly disparaged such a report. It is only since his passing that Lady Catherine has begun to speak of the matter in detail. I pay little attention to her."

"And Miss de Bourgh's wishes?"

"I avoid much contact with her," confessed Darcy. "If I pay her even the slightest hint of attention, my aunt assumes I am about to propose. But though I do not know my cousin's wishes on the matter, it is my thought that she does not wish to marry, as her health is poor. Regardless, as Lady Catherine's schemes require my participation and consent, it is of little matter, for I will not yield.

"As for your questions regarding the rest of my family, I have no Darcy relations close enough to solicit their opinions, and my uncle's family—Lady Catherine's brother—though close, will not object. The earl is proud of his situation, but he knows he cannot direct me. Colonel Fitzwilliam you have already met, and he esteems your daughter highly. His brother and sisters and the countess will all accept her, some more readily than others, it is true. But their support will go far in smoothing Miss Bennet's way in society."

"And her lack of dowry?"

"Does not concern me in the slightest. Pemberley is not my only holding, and I have a diverse set of investments which make the lack of a dowry irrelevant. I have enough wealth to provide for her and twelve children, if necessary.

"I am fortunate enough to possess the means to marry wherever I like." Darcy gazed into the other man's eyes, speaking frankly so he was clearly understood. "All the wealth in the world means nothing if I do not use it to secure my happiness. Miss Bennet complements me in every way. There is nothing I would not do to be granted her presence in my life."

"Then there is nothing left to be said," replied Mr. Bennet. "Though you do not need my consent, I grant it anyway, in addition to my blessing. I could not have wished for more for her than to see her married to a man who will respect and cherish her."

"Thank you, sir," said Darcy, extending his hand to his soon-to-be father-in-law.

"Now," said Mr. Bennet, rubbing his hands together, "if I might be allowed to sample some of your excellent library, I think I will be very well pleased."

"Of course, sir," replied Darcy, grinning with delight. "I shall arrange to have you called for luncheon."

He led the way back into the library, showed Mr. Bennet where the port could be found and took his leave. Before he could, however, Mr. Bennet's amused voice stopped him.

"Surely you must know that I shall be inclined to visit frequently after you are married, Mr. Darcy."

"And you shall be quite welcome, sir. I would expect nothing less, given your close relationship with Miss Bennet. I am certain the library has nothing to do with it."

Bennet chuckled and turned to the book he had already chosen, and Darcy left the room. Though the outcome had never been in doubt, he knew Elizabeth would be thrilled to hear the results of their conversation.

Chapter XXX

*T*he official nature of Elizabeth's engagement did wonders for her happiness, and she could often be found humming to herself, or smiling at the oddest times. It did a world of good to Bennet's heart to see his daughter in such high spirits; he would miss her, it was certain, but he could not have asked for a better man to be her husband. The decision to send her to Derbyshire had turned out spectacularly well, far better than Bennet had ever expected. And he was certain to let his host know of his gratitude.

"Thank you for the invitation, Drummond," said he to his brother one day when they were ensconced in the man's study. "I could not have imagined a better outcome for my Lizzy than she has found here in Derbyshire."

"You are quite welcome, Bennet," said his brother. "I have enjoyed having her, and I know my daughters have had as much benefit from her presence as she has derived from being here."

They raised their glasses and sipped from them, Bennet already lost in thought. "She was not happy in Hertfordshire," said Bennet quietly. "I have never seen her so affected, from Jane's marriage and subsequent distance to what she considered to be the monotony of life in her home. She has always been so happy and resilient. It was difficult to witness it."

"I noted some of the same when she first arrived, but with new acquaintances and the company of my daughters, I could quickly see the resilience you have mentioned. She has a unique ability to adapt."

"I dare say she does." Bennet snorted. "I believe she would have even been able to adapt to marriage to my fool of a cousin, though she never would have been happy with him. I have always struggled to imagine a man who was worthy of her, who would appreciate her for what she would bring to a marriage beyond the obvious concerns with which society is so enamored. It is fortunate that such a man existed so close to your borders."

"She would have met him eventually," said Drummond. "Darcy's closest friend *is* married to your eldest."

"True," said Bennet, wondering if it would have come to pass, considering Jane's distance.

Those days were filled with more society than Bennet usually wished for, though he surprised himself by enjoying it thoroughly. There was the promised fishing expedition at Pemberley, visits there and to some of the other friends Elizabeth had made in the district. The spoils from the fishing expedition were sent to Kingsdown with Darcy's compliments, to be used at the dinner to which the Drummonds had invited those at Pemberley. Of course, there was much ridiculous behavior to savor, primarily perpetrated by Miss Bingley, whose head Bennet had always known was far too big for her bonnet. The woman seemed to sense something had changed between Elizabeth and Darcy, and though their engagement had not been announced, she seemed to sense the danger to her schemes, redoubling her efforts accordingly. Bennet watched her flailing with great relish and amusement, though Darcy appeared to appreciate it much less.

When the day arrived for the Darcy party to join them at Kingsdown for dinner, Bennet anticipated it with his usual eagerness for amusement, for there was much to be had. They arrived and entered the estate, and Bennet could have predicted their responses in advance, had he cared to think on the matter. Bingley entered with a jovial smile and an eagerness for his company, while Miss Bingley appeared like some foul odor had wafted past her upturned nose. Darcy and his sister entered with eyes for no one but Elizabeth, whom they joined with alacrity upon entering the room, further souring Miss Bingley's disposition.

The one for whom Bennet possessed some concern was Jane. The past few days in her company told Bennet that her troubles were at the very least being exacerbated by Miss Bingley's poisonous presence. The two women were always together, when Miss Bingley was not attempting to put herself in Mr. Darcy's lap, and there were many whispered conversations to be had between them. Jane appeared confused during those days, as if nothing was as she had expected and she was having trouble accepting it. Thus, when Miss Bingley appeared preoccupied by Darcy's attentions to Elizabeth, Bennet took the opportunity to approach his daughter.

"How are you enjoying your visit to Pemberley, my dear?" said Bennet as he sat beside her.

"It is a lovely estate," replied Jane with her usual reticence.

"I assume you will be visiting many times over the years, your husband being so close to Darcy."

"I am sure we shall."

"Then you might take the opportunity to come to know your cousins better. They are intimates with the Darcys, it seems, so you shall be in their company frequently."

Jane appeared unsure, and she hesitated before responding. "But the Darcys are much higher in society than my uncle and his family."

"I suspect societal standing means little to Darcy. He is all friendliness and ease with your uncle, and Lizzy has become a close friend to his sister."

When Jane did not respond, Bennet turned to her and eyed her, annoyance such as he had rarely felt for his eldest welling up within his breast. "Jane, I do not know the reason for your recent detachment, but let me give you a piece of advice. If you wish to maintain your relationships with your family—particularly with Elizabeth—I suggest you make more of an effort."

And with that, he rose to join Bingley and Drummond, who were speaking together in animated tones. Throughout the evening Bennet watched Jane, and though she remained as reticent as ever, there appeared to be a hint of thoughtfulness in her manner which he had not seen recently. And more alarming, he thought he detected a hint of fear in her eyes. There was something he was missing—he was certain of it. But he could not determine what it was.

When the company was called in to dinner, William escorted Mrs. Drummond, but he was also quick to put Elizabeth's hand on his arm and claim her for his partner for dinner by the simple expedient of sitting himself between the two ladies. Elizabeth was far from being opposed to his solicitous behavior, though it did provoke suspicious stares from both Mrs. Drummond and Miss Bingley. As the engagement was already sanctioned, Elizabeth did not care for their opinions. In fact, she was beginning to wonder why she had not already agreed to have it announced. Jane would act how she would act and there was nothing Elizabeth could do on the matter. Miss Bingley's opinion concerned her not a wit.

As usual, the food was good, and the gentlemen laughingly boasted of their prowess in catching the fish. It was prepared well by the Drummonds' cook, and Elizabeth thought everyone enjoyed the dinner.

A chance comment from Olivia brought to mind the upcoming assembly, and Elizabeth could not resist teasing her fiancé once again.

"Shall you rescue any travelers in distress this time, Mr. Darcy?" asked she playfully. "If there is no rain, you may be required to scour the countryside for someone to assist in some other manner."

"I do not believe I have heard this tale," interjected her father. "Mr. Darcy makes it a habit to roam around the countryside helping unfortunate travelers?"

"Indeed, he does," replied Elizabeth, throwing a smirk at William. "I shall tell you the tale, Papa, for you shall be amazed by Mr. Darcy's prowess."

True to her threat, Elizabeth proceeded to regale them with the tale of Mr. Darcy's rescue the night of the first assembly in Lambton, complete with all the requisite embellishments, wondering and thankful maidens, and impossible feats, much as she had to Georgiana some weeks earlier. By the end of her tale most of the company was in stitches, though there were a few expected curmudgeons present.

"Not that I would doubt my daughter's honesty," said her father to Mr. Drummond, "but is that truly the way it happened?"

"More or less," replied he. "I will own that I do not recall being set upon by desperate brigands, but it is a fine story nonetheless."

"What is a good story without a little embellishment?" asked Elizabeth, fixing her father with an impish smile.

"I find a story that cannot be related exactly as it happened to be intolerable," huffed Miss Bingley.

Elizabeth and her father caught each other's eye and burst out laughing. Miss Bingley only glared at them.

"Your comment concerning embellishment is one my cousin subscribes to," said William. "He has never heard a story he did not think needed a rash of details added to it. They add spice, he claims."

"I shall have to ask after his experiences then," said Mr. Bennet. "I love a good yarn."

"A yarn is what you would get from my cousin. Whether it is good, I am afraid I cannot say."

Dinner was consumed with this banter and after dinner was over, the ladies returned to the sitting-room, leaving the gentlemen to their port. Though Elizabeth might have expected Miss Bingley to display her usual ill breeding, she might have thought Mrs. Drummond would make her own mark on the company. Her aunt, however, surprised her.

The conversation appeared to go smoothly for a time, though the bulk of it was carried by Elizabeth, Georgiana, and Olivia. Miss Bingley sat beside Jane, who watched them all as if they were the pieces to a puzzle which did not quite fit together. Aunt Drummond added very little to the conversation, contenting herself with a few remarks occasionally inserted at different times. As they sat, Miss Bingley attempted to interject her opinion by speaking to Georgiana, but as Georgiana only listened politely, made a brief response to Miss Bingley, and then turned her attention back to Elizabeth and Olivia, it was clear that Miss Bingley was becoming frustrated. Then Miss Bingley tried to change tack.

"Miss Drummond," said she, her manner all insolent superiority, "it seems you have had the good fortune to become close to dear Georgiana these past weeks."

"Yes, she has become a good friend. I could not be happier."

"Nor could I," interjected Georgiana before Miss Bingley could respond. "Lizzy and Olivia becoming my friends is one of the best things that could have happened to me."

"I am certain you believe so," replied Miss Bingley, in a tone which suggested she believed anything but. Miss Bingley then turned back to Olivia. "Did your mother follow the country practice of bringing you out into society when you were but fifteen? I dare say you are a veteran of the drawing rooms in the neighborhood."

"In fact, I have only started to participate in society since Lizzy came to join us," replied Olivia. "I am indebted to her, for she has helped me become accustomed to society and provided the support I needed."

"And you did not instruct your daughter?" asked Miss Bingley, turning to Mrs. Drummond.

"Of course, I did," said Mrs. Drummond. "But I am frequently busy, and since the girls are of age, my husband and I decided to extend the invitation to Elizabeth, knowing she would be a good example."

It was a bald-faced lie, Elizabeth knew, but she did not challenge her aunt on the matter, as there was little point, and she did not wish to give Miss Bingley any fuel for her caustic tongue.

"I did not know you had come to Derbyshire to be a companion to your cousin, Eliza," chortled Miss Bingley. "If you are interested, I have an acquaintance who is looking for a companion. I could put in a good word for you, if you like."

"That will not be necessary, Miss Bingley," said Elizabeth. "I came to mentor Olivia, but I am not in need of a position."

"Perhaps you should give it greater thought," replied the woman. The spite in her words lashed out at Elizabeth. "You have naught to recommend yourself and as your father can give you little, I do not doubt you will end in such a position. If you can find someone to take you on, given your lack of education."

"I believe you have said enough, Miss Bingley," said Mrs. Drummond. "Whatever Elizabeth's future might be, I would appreciate a little more tact and a little less venom when you are speaking in my sitting-room."

"I apologize for my words," said Miss Bingley, her tone oozing insincerity. "I mean only to give my sister by marriage some advice. I had not known that the sitting-room of a farmhouse was so fine as to make such subjects objectionable."

Mrs. Drummond directed a faint smile at Miss Bingley. "You are excused, Miss Bingley. Given the fact that you are naught but the daughter of a tradesman, we could not expect you to understand the finer points of polite behavior."

It was fortunate that the door opened at that moment and the gentlemen rejoined them. Miss Bingley's reddish locks seemed to be connected to her skin, for all the color seemed to leech out of them and into her face, which soon turned as red as a ripe tomato. She almost certainly would have said something unforgivable if not interrupted, and so Elizabeth was grateful no further unpleasantness could occur. That was not to say that the woman was finished speaking her piece.

"What a charming family you have, Mr. Drummond," said she not long after the gentlemen had returned. "I cannot remember a time when I was so . . . entertained during an evening engagement."

"I thank you, Miss Bingley," said Mr. Drummond. Elizabeth was certain he understood Miss Bingley's meaning perfectly, but he refrained from exacerbating the situation further and said nothing else.

And when Miss Bingley saw that she would not be successful in provoking a reaction, she sat in sulky silence for the rest of the evening. Elizabeth could not speak for the rest of the company, but she could quite cheerfully accept the woman's lack of contribution to further discussion.

"Did something happen while we were away?" asked William some moments later. He had, again, joined her without delay, an action which was surely fueling Miss Bingley's resentment.

"Nothing more than a simple disagreement," replied Elizabeth.

"Have you all been sworn to secrecy, or will you share it with me?"

Elizabeth laughed and laid a hand on his arm. "Miss Bingley was attempting to introduce me to a friend who is looking for a companion, since I obviously did wonders with Olivia, and when Mrs. Drummond objected to her lack of tact, Miss Bingley responded by informing us she did not think those who live in *farmhouses* were so easily offended."

A wince was William's answer, and he said: "I doubt Mrs. Drummond appreciated such sentiments."

"No, but the final comment was hers, for you returned immediately after. She commented that Miss Bingley, as a *tradesman's daughter* could not be expected to understand how those in polite society behaved."

William's response was a burst of air from his lips, which normally would have preceded laughter. But he admirably gained control over himself, though his eyes spoke to the mirth which was fighting for release. The glance in Miss Bingley's direction did not help his composure, though it arguably was a greater detriment to *hers*. She watched them, the hammers of suspicion raining down on them—especially on Elizabeth. As she did not care for the woman's concerns, Elizabeth chose to simply ignore her.

"That is a rather . . . blunt assessment of the situation," said William, when he felt he could speak without his laughter escaping.

Elizabeth only grinned. "Miss Bingley seems to have lost whatever discretion she might once have possessed, for her barbs have been obvious and not veiled under a cloak of civility as they were in Hertfordshire."

"Perhaps the air in Derbyshire does not agree with her?"

"I rather think her desperation is to blame, not the air," replied Elizabeth, attempting to control her own amusement. "If the air here does not agree with her, it would be terribly sad, do you not think? Her ambitions being what they are . . ."

"I suppose she shall have to retreat to another county to entrap . . . I mean secure a husband," replied William, his eyes dancing. "Perhaps

Norfolk would be much more to her tastes."

"Personally, I would prefer the Orkneys," said Elizabeth. "The further the better."

This time William did laugh, though he indulged in only a low chuckle. "Though we are perhaps not to be commended for making sport of another, I cannot but anticipate the coming years of our marriage, my dear. If this is to be the example of our future felicity, I dare say we shall be anything but bored."

"I believe you are correct, William," said Elizabeth. "But do not despair, should it ever become monotonous. I promise I will start an argument to liven things up."

They laughed together again and turned their conversation to other subjects. So involved were they in the discussion that they hardly noticed the scrutiny of others. Had Elizabeth known of it, she would have realized that their secret was no longer a secret, though there was one in particular who continued to deny what she saw.

By contrast to what the Darcy company was experiencing at Kingsdown, Fitzwilliam found his time at Teasdale Manor to be both enjoyable and somewhat more tranquil. There were no Caroline Bingleys or Claire Drummonds to make the rest of those present uncomfortable—it was nothing more than dinner with the earl and his daughter.

Quickly, however, Fitzwilliam noted that while the earl was his usual conversational self, his daughter did not participate. Fitzwilliam had seen her several times in the preceding days, and he had noted her quietude was more pronounced than he had seen from her in the past. Though she did not seem averse to his company, Fitzwilliam thought Lady Emily was still uncertain as to her interest in his attentions.

It was not until after dinner when they were able to come to at least something of an understanding. The earl, using a tactic Fitzwilliam might have expected from a society mother, rather pointedly shot them a look and retired to the far side of the room with a book in hand. That did not stop him from looking up at them periodically. Fitzwilliam was certain he noticed less of the earl's scrutiny than was actually there.

"Well, Colonel?" asked Lady Emily after she directed a pointed look at her father. "What is it to be? Shall you propose to me now, so that we may avoid the tedious business of courtship?"

Fitzwilliam was surprised at the venom in the lady's voice and paused for a moment, taking care in his answer. "I do not believe you wish for such a thing, any more than I do."

The long look the lady directed at him made Fitzwilliam wonder if his abbreviated courtship was about to end without a whimper. "Is my opinion of any concern?"

"Have you forgotten your agreement with your father?"

Her eyes darted to the other side of the room and then back at Fitzwilliam. "You spoke to him of that?"

"Perhaps we should be completely frank with each other," replied Fitzwilliam.

Another long look ensued before she agreed. "Please."

"You are aware of the initial reason for my attentions to you, are you not?"

A shadow passed over her countenance. "If you refer to your intention to prevent me from interfering with Mr. Darcy and Miss Bennet, then, yes."

"After the . . . incident with Miss Bennet, I thought I had protected Darcy's interests enough, and there was no further reason to seek your company. And yet, I found myself drawn here, though at the time I did not understand it. The day you returned here to find me with your father the picture became clearer for me, though not yet completely in focus."

"May I assume my father asked after your intentions?"

"Yes."

"And what did he say?"

"Only that he considered me a worthy candidate, but had no intention of brokering a marriage for you. I was still confused about my own feelings, but I felt that to continue calling on you would bring them further into focus."

"And now?"

It was maddening, but Fitzwilliam could reach no conclusion as to the woman's feelings on the subject. Though Fitzwilliam had known of her interest in Darcy from the very start, he now understood what Miss Elizabeth had said about her inscrutable countenance. She was Darcy's equal in that sense. Thus, he decided it was best to be completely open with her.

"It has only been a week, Lady Emily. I have always found you to be an estimable woman, but for any further feelings on both our parts, I believe we may need time together to sort those out. Do you not agree?"

"What of my position as my father's heir and the advantages which would be yours by marrying me?"

Fitzwilliam frowned. "You know those will be a consideration for any man who contemplates marriage to you."

"I am aware of that. I wished to know *your* thoughts on the subject."

"Then yes, they *are* a consideration, but I hope they are not the *only* consideration. As you know, I am independent myself, and though my estate will not make me a wealthy man, it does make me comfortable. It may be difficult for you to believe, but I too wish for what Darcy will share with Miss Bennet."

The mention of Darcy was deliberate. Though she had shown no tendency toward continuing to bedevil Darcy and his betrothed, Fitzwilliam was not at all certain of what her feelings for his cousin consisted, not even considering Miss Bennet, the woman she had so callously left at the side of a lonely country road. But he was destined to be disappointed, as she did not even batt an eyelash at his mention of the two for whom she might harbor resentment.

"Then what do you propose?"

"I thought it was clear," replied Fitzwilliam. "I have been calling on you, speaking, sharing of myself, and seeking to understand you better in turn. Is that not the purpose of these courting rituals? The fact that I have your father's blessing truly only smooths my way and in no way sets the matter in stone."

"And if you propose and I reject your suit?"

"Then I believe we will have nothing further to discuss." Fitzwilliam returned her steady look. "Really, Lady Emily, I would have thought this much would be evident. Your father is not trying to force you into anything with me, nor am I. You are an estimable young woman—of that I am aware. What I do not know is if we are compatible. That is what I hope to discover. The question is, whether you wish it. If you do not, then I will not bother you again."

Lady Emily sighed and turned away, her gaze far away. Her father looked up at that moment and caught Fitzwilliam's eye, and though Fitzwilliam could see some concern in the older gentleman, he shook his head, asking him not to intervene. The earl gave him an almost imperceptible shrug and turned back to his book, though he remained watchful.

"My behavior has not been the best," said Lady Emily. "I acknowledge that. I have been engaged in much reflection these past days, and I have discovered things about myself I do not like."

"We are all less than perfect, Lady Emily," said Fitzwilliam. "We all fall short of the mark."

"But we will never improve if we do not reflect and strive to do better."

"That I cannot deny. But I did not speak to you to demand your improvement or to shame you in any way. You are already an estimable woman, and I think highly of you."

Lady Emily turned to him and regarded him for several moments before speaking. He thought she seemed a little annoyed, though whether it was his presence, her father's presumption, or something else which was promoting it, he could not be certain. She did not seem to be opposed to his attentions, but Fitzwilliam could not determine it. But if she did not wish for him to continue to visit her, he would not impose upon her.

"Very well," replied she at last. "But I give no promises at present."

"I am not asking for a promise. We shall take it slowly, and whatever comes of it, so be it."

The lady nodded and then turned away. Fitzwilliam was feeling oddly relieved. Though he was still unable to determine his own wishes, it seemed he was not indifferent to her. It would be an interesting time, he was certain.

CHAPTER XXXI

$\mathcal{E}$ lizabeth's second assembly in Derbyshire was different from her first. Being a known and accepted member of society was one difference, the result of which was her increased confidence upon entering the room and being a more frequently sought after dance partner. The other difference was, of course, her engagement to William with whom she was to partner for the first dance. She had not known what a rare occurrence this was until Colonel Fitzwilliam informed her.

"I have a burning desire to see the tumult your dance with Darcy will bring," said the colonel as they were standing to the side of the dance floor soon after their arrival. William had been detained by some acquaintance, and thus she was nominally alone with Colonel Fitzwilliam, the other members of hers and the Pemberley parties standing not far distant.

"Why should it be of any great interest?" asked Elizabeth. No one knew of their engagement, so she was not certain how William's dancing with her—which he had done at the first assembly—should interest the gossips of the neighborhood.

"Because Darcy never dances the first."

Elizabeth turned to Colonel Fitzwilliam, noting his eyes twinkling with amusement. "Never?"

"I believe you have heard of how Darcy has been hounded by unmarried ladies and their mothers since receiving his inheritance?" When Elizabeth indicated she had, Colonel Fitzwilliam continued: "Because of this, he has made it a practice to never dance the first with anyone to avoid giving *any* young lady any indication of preference. He also never dances twice with the same lady."

"Both of which he will do tonight," said Elizabeth, a hint of trepidation building in her stomach.

"Exactly." Colonel Fitzwilliam's eyes darted to where Miss Bingley stood near her brother and Jane. "It will also be intriguing to see Miss Bingley's reaction to your first dance, not to mention the second. Every time he attends a function with her, she becomes less subtle in her attempts to induce him to stand up with her for the sets which you possess. I would not be surprised to see fireworks from the woman."

Miss Bingley was, Elizabeth noted with absent-minded interest, not behaving as she had during the functions in Hertfordshire. During those, her barely concealed contempt and overt arrogance had not made her many friends. Here, however, where there were attendees of a higher station, she was acting as if she belonged in such company, her bearing suggesting confidence, yet restraint. But the way her eyes often darted to where William still stood, the hungry look in her eyes, like a wolf, starving on a diet of field mice, spoke to her continuing ambitions.

"Poor Miss Bingley," said Elizabeth, not feeling sorry for the woman in the slightest.

"Poor Miss Bingley, indeed," said Colonel Fitzwilliam, laughing under his breath. "You must concede she is a most deserving recipient of the set-down she is likely to receive should she rise above herself tonight."

"Rise above herself?" asked Elizabeth. "By my account, she has *already* climbed the heights of conceit."

Colonel Fitzwilliam laughed. "I believe you are correct, Miss Bennet."

At that moment, a Mr. Smallwood, one of the gentlemen of the neighborhood with whom Elizabeth shared an acquaintance, approached and asked her for the first dance.

"I am sorry, sir, but my first dance is already taken, as are the next four."

"I see," said Mr. Smallwood, with an expressive glance at Colonel Fitzwilliam, which was returned by means of a grin. Elizabeth did not quite understand why were amused. "You are a popular partner, it seems. In that case, if I might, I should like to secure your first available dance."

"You may, sir. I would be happy to dance with you."

Mr. Smallwood thanked her and after bowing, he departed. Elizabeth turned back to Colonel Fitzwilliam and fixed him with a stern glare.

"I should like to know the reason for the byplay between you and Mr. Smallwood, sir."

"It is quite simple, Miss Bennet," replied the colonel, his readiness to respond proof he was enjoying himself. "Smallwood understands Darcy has been calling on you, and the purpose of his request was to see if you were *engaged* for the first dance. I believe he has his answer."

"But I might be dancing the first with my father!" exclaimed Elizabeth. "I *will* dance the second with him."

"Ah, but even if you danced the second with Darcy, it would be tantamount to dancing the first, given your father is in attendance. Your dances with me, Bingley, and Edward do not signify nearly so much, given Darcy's known attentions. I doubt there will be anyone in attendance who is not aware of your engagement by the end of the evening, even if you have not announced it by then."

Then with a smirk and a bow, Colonel Fitzwilliam turned and departed. Elizabeth watched him go, wondering at his temerity, until the sound of a most welcome voice interrupted her thoughts.

"Is Fitzwilliam being his usual insolent self?"

Elizabeth turned back to her fiancé and favored him with a smile. "Nothing more than usual. In fact, I find his observations to be amusing, and often quite correct."

"He does have his uses," said William.

With a laugh, Elizabeth touched William's arm and said in a fond tone: "I suppose he does."

Before they could exchange any further words, the screech of a high-pitched voice interrupted them, and a flurry of pastel green skirts forced their way in between Elizabeth and William.

"Oh, Mr. Darcy, what a wonderful locale this is! I dare say I have not seen anything to compare with Lambton for its quaintness and all of Derbyshire for beauty." Miss Bingley directed a scathing glance at Elizabeth. "It is certainly more beautiful than many other places I have recently seen, and the people here are more cultured, better bred, and quite obliging."

"I am happy you approve of our little corner of the kingdom, Miss

Bingley," replied William with that exaggerated patience Elizabeth had noted in his tone every time he was forced to speak with her.

"Who could not approve? I doubt there is anywhere which could hope to compare with it. I believe Derbyshire to be the best of all counties, and one where, if one is privileged to live, one would scarcely wish to leave it again."

"I believe you have stated my opinion quite succinctly, Miss Bingley."

Miss Bingley beamed at Mr. Darcy, as if he had just told her she was the most beautiful woman he had ever seen. "I believe the evening is about to start, sir. I so love to dance, and I am anticipating partnering with the best society has to offer."

Forced to stifle a laugh, Elizabeth put her hand before her face, wondering at the woman's utter lack of tact and delicacy. She clutched William's arm in a grip which might have been made of steel, and the impression she gave was of a sprig of mistletoe, hung from the ceiling at Christmastide. Should he raise his arm above his head, Elizabeth was certain she would hang off it, much like the aforementioned parasite.

"Then I wish you well in it," replied William. He gently disengaged Miss Bingley's claws from his arm—or as gently as one could, considering her tight grip—and approached Elizabeth. "Miss Bennet, the music for the first set has begun. I believe this is my dance."

"Of course, Mr. Darcy," said Elizabeth, laying her hand in his.

As he was leading her to the dance floor, past Miss Bingley, Elizabeth could see the utter shock on her countenance. But before she was out of sight, Miss Bingley's expression descended to utter rage like the sun falling past the horizon. She had always been at odds with Miss Bingley, ever since their first meeting. But the look on the lady's face suggested that whatever enmity they had possessed had now blossomed into full hatred. "That was smoothly done, Mr. Darcy," said Elizabeth, as they began the steps of the dance.

"Less smoothly than it could have been." William grimaced and shot a glance at the fuming woman. "In the past, I would dance with her, if only to do my duty to my good friend's sister. But I think tonight I will not even do that much. I have done everything short of telling her to her face that I am not interested in her, but still she persists."

"While I pity the woman, I do not blame you, sir." Elizabeth laughed. "I also do not blame her for fixing her sights on you, though her actions are irksome. You *are* quite the catch, if I do say so myself."

"If her motives were as pure as yours, I would agree. But she has nothing more than wealth, status, and a life of ease in mind."

"Then I would add the crime of not knowing you to the list of her offenses. I have seen you work very hard, indeed, when necessary."

"But she only sees parties, balls, being looked on with envy — the trappings of wealth. I am only the means to an end."

"Poor, William," replied Elizabeth, fixing him with a saucy smile. "To be chased after for such things must be a blow to your manly pride."

William grinned back. "I am counting on you, my dear, to put an end to such things. I cannot imagine a better woman to forever remove me from consideration from all fortune hunters."

"I will do my best."

Their immediate playful banter having run its course, Elizabeth turned her attention to those about her. There were many in attendance, and most of her friends were to be found on the dance floor dancing with those of the neighborhood. Jane was engaged with her husband, not far away, and Olivia danced with Edward, which brought a smile to Elizabeth's lips. The siblings had grown closer since she had arrived.

Of note, however, and to Elizabeth's surprise, she noticed Colonel Fitzwilliam dancing with Lady Emily, and wondered at it. She turned back to Darcy, noting his knowing look.

"I see you have seen my cousin and Lady Emily."

"I did, indeed, Mr. Darcy. Have there been any developments of which I am not aware?"

"There is nothing official, but Fitzwilliam has been calling on Lady Emily, with her father's approval, I might add. I do not know if Fitzwilliam's intentions have grown over time, but they do seem to be rather comfortable in each other's company."

Surprised, Elizabeth turned her attention on the couple, and she could immediately see what William had suggested. Colonel Fitzwilliam spoke with his usual animation, and though Lady Emily responded with much more reserve, as was her custom, she did not seem unhappy with his company. Elizabeth was unsure what to think. The residue of anger over Lady Emily's callous actions had been washed away, replaced by a sort of indifference to the woman. She was not certain a friendship could ever be re-established.

"Then I wish him the best," said Elizabeth. "It seems to me there may be some benefit to such an arrangement — on both sides, actually."

"I agree," replied William. "But I do not think he will propose unless he is assured of affection between them."

Elizabeth nodded. "Either way, I hope he finds what he is searching for. He is a good man, and I think highly of him."

"As do I," replied William. The subject was then dropped, and they spent the rest of the dance, alternating between comfortable silence, in which their eyes rarely left the other's, and playful banter.

Caroline Bingley was displeased. In fact, she was more than displeased. She was furious with that . . . that . . . chit!

This stay at Pemberley was to be Caroline's crowning glory and achievement, and she had waited more than long enough for it. Mr. Darcy was reticent. He was careful and patient. He was sober and serious. She understood all these things about him, but enough was enough. He was also wealthy. He was of the first circles. He possessed connections to the peerage. In short, he was everything Caroline had ever desired in a husband, and she had no intention of losing him to some upstart country miss with more impertinence than sophistication!

Miss Elizabeth Bennet. Oh, how Caroline hated that name! She had loathed the woman from the first time she had met her, and the intervening months had only increased her disdain. Jane was, because of her pliant nature, somewhat tolerable, though Caroline still railed against her brother's infatuation which had led him to attach himself to a most unsuitable woman. But Eliza was too much to be borne.

Worse, it seemed the chit had somehow managed to fool Mr. Darcy into thinking that she was a respectable woman, one who was worthy of receiving the attentions of a man who was as wealthy and high in society as Mr. Darcy. Caroline could not account for such blindness, but there it was. She had not wanted to believe it, but the talk at the assembly was rife with the attentions he had paid to her the last weeks. In particular, one conversation had caught Caroline's attention.

"I see Mr. Darcy continues his attentions to Elizabeth."

Fuming as she was over Mr. Darcy's snub and how he had subsequently escorted Eliza to the dance floor, Caroline almost missed the comment. Careful to keep her composure, she turned slightly to where two young women were standing nearby, watching the dancers. They were both dressed well, though not overly lavishly, and while both might be deemed pretty, Caroline did not think either was anything special—certainly nothing to herself on that evening.

"As he has every time we have seen them together. I am happy for her—she is a good friend and will make him a good wife."

"I think you may be putting the cart before the horse, Clara.

Nothing has been announced yet."

"Oh, pish tosh. I would be very surprised to learn they are not already engaged."

"Perhaps, but she would not wish it to be spread about until it is official."

The other first young lady — Clara — laughed. "She is a rare breed. If *I* were the recipient of Mr. Darcy's attentions, I would be spreading it far and wide as soon as may be!"

"Which is likely why it is she who is the happy recipient, rather than you. Mr. Darcy knows she will do nothing of the sort."

"I think you may be right, Deborah. But I am happy for her nonetheless."

While Caroline did not put much stock in this talk of engagements, it was still worrying nonetheless. Caroline had supreme confidence in her own abilities, and she knew that Eliza Bennet, though she might fancy herself clever, would never be a match for Caroline Bingley. It was clear Mr. Darcy needed a reminder of who was the superior woman by society's standards. And Caroline meant to remind him of it.

If it had not been so very pathetic, it might almost have been amusing. As Elizabeth moved through her succession of dances with her various partners, she watched Miss Bingley and her attempts to induce William to dance with her. Unfortunately for her, William remained impervious to whatever dubious charms she possessed, though that did not seem to cause her the slightest pause.

"Oh, Mr. Darcy," exclaimed she after a particularly lively dance, "how well you dance. It seems to me you are dancing far more often than usual."

"I am much more comfortable in Derbyshire society than I am in London, Miss Bingley," replied William.

From what Elizabeth remembered of her first assembly here, it was nothing less than the truth — Mr. Darcy *was* dancing with greater frequency. But where Miss Bingley could only see the number of times he stood up, Elizabeth noted that he danced with Olivia and Jane, and then had begun to ask some of Elizabeth's friends in the area for dances, knowing they were already aware of his attentions to Elizabeth, and that they would not expect anything more from him.

"These are your particular friends, so it is not surprising. I dare say you have known most of these ladies for some years."

"Many of them I have."

"Then I believe I have found the secret to your preferences, sir. There must be many with whom you have long been acquainted. I am certain they wait breathlessly for your attentions."

It was a lull in the dancing, the musicians having departed for a well-earned break, and Clara, who had been standing not far away, with Fiona, Deborah, and Erica in attendance, turned to Elizabeth. "That woman is your sister's new sister?"

"Caroline Bingley," said Elizabeth. "Mr. Bingley is Jane's husband of about six months."

"Your sister is everything that is proper and delightful," said Clara, glancing at where Jane stood with her husband. Elizabeth could only agree, though Jane's indifference persisted. "But Miss Bingley . . ."

Clara's eyes swung back to Miss Bingley, and a hardness appeared in them, much as it often did when she was confronted by Miss Russell and Miss Campbell. "She appears to be cut from a different cloth."

"Clara is only angry because Miss Bingley all but ignored her when they were introduced," said Fiona.

"She was not much better to you," rejoined Clara.

"No, but I was more willing to laugh at her rudeness. You took offense."

"Laughing at Miss Bingley is the only way to endure her," said Elizabeth. "If you think her behavior is wanting now, you should have observed her in Hertfordshire."

"What is her background?" asked Deborah.

"She is the daughter of a tradesman," said Elizabeth. "Her brother, Mr. Bingley, is leasing an estate near my father's. I believe he means to purchase soon."

"And her dowry?" asked Fiona.

"I have heard it said that she has twenty thousand pounds, and I dare say she can sniff the amount of dowry a lady possesses from one hundred paces."

The ladies laughed, but Clara still seemed offended.

"Then what right does she have to be above her company? Look at the woman! She is practically draped over Mr. Darcy. Has she no shame?"

"All the right of having attended a fancy seminary," said Elizabeth. "She seems to think that elevates her to the first circles. According to Mr. Darcy it has been ever thus. He has never given her a hint of encouragement, but she is determined."

Erica, who had not yet spoken, said: "She was quite . . . insistent upon claiming my friendship."

"That is because your dowry is more substantial than hers," said Clara, throwing Erica an exasperated look. "For those of us with equal or less, she quite considers herself above us."

At that moment, having disengaged himself from Miss Bingley, William approached the group of ladies and bowed to them. Elizabeth did not miss the slightly harried look around his eyes.

"Ladies, how do you do this evening?"

"Very well, Mr. Darcy," said Deborah. "But you need not feign interest in *us*. We all know you have no eyes for anyone but our Lizzy."

A burning started in Elizabeth's cheeks, and she glared at Deborah, who only returned her displeasure with a cheeky grin. The other three ladies raised their hands to their mouths to stifle their laughter. For his part, William seemed startled, but then he grinned.

"Miss Bennet is quite charming, and I am happy she has been added to our society. But I moved this way to seek dance partners for the upcoming sets. Would you, Miss Grant, be willing to stand up with me for the next?"

"Of course, Mr. Darcy," said Deborah, curtseying and throwing a look at Elizabeth.

"Excellent," said William. Then he turned to Clara. "I believe I not danced with you either, Miss Burbage. Might I claim the set after?"

"I would be delighted, Mr. Darcy. I will accept your gesture as the compliment to Lizzy I know it to be."

The girls all giggled again, and Elizabeth wondered if one could possibly die from mortification. Mr. Darcy only shook his head, amusement sparkling in his eyes, and he turned back to Elizabeth.

"Indeed, I would like to thank you, Miss Bennet, for providing me with these charming dance partners. I have already danced with Miss Allen and Miss MacDonald, and I am certain my future dances will be equally interesting."

"I hardly think *I* am the reason they are so charming, Mr. Darcy," replied Elizabeth, wondering what the man could possibly be about.

"No, that is all their own doing. But your presence has shown me what charming ladies they are, and furthermore, they are all willing to simply enjoy a dance between friends. I have you to thank for that."

Bowing, Mr. Darcy grasped her hand and bestowed a lingering kiss on its back before he turned and walked away, Elizabeth watching him as he went. The back of her hand burned where his lips had seared into it. It could not be proper in a public forum such as this, but Elizabeth found herself wishing he had kissed her on the lips as he had done occasionally.

"Elizabeth," said Clara, drawing her attention back to her friends.

With great difficulty, Elizabeth left of her contemplation off her fiancé and turned back to Clara, noting that her friend was sporting a wide grin. The other three ladies were no less amused.

"I believe it is time you told us the truth," said Clara. She grasped Elizabeth's arm and drew her to the side where there was a little open space and they were less likely to be overheard. "Mr. Darcy all but declared himself to you back there. You cannot simply treat it as if it was nothing."

"Has Mr. Darcy proposed to you?" asked Deborah. By her side, Erica and Fiona stood, watching with interest.

If she could not trust her closest friends, Elizabeth decided she could not trust anyone. She nodded, saying: "He has. We—"

With a surprised grunt Elizabeth was cut off as Clara flew into her arms, embracing her tightly, with tears appearing in her eyes. The other ladies all crowded around them, voicing their congratulations, though with quiet comments, which were not less heart felt due to their reserve.

"Congratulations," said Clara, fixing Elizabeth with a watery smile. "We have long suspected he would, but to hear it confirmed is wonderful."

"You will be a very happy woman, Elizabeth," added Erica. The others all chimed in with their own congratulations.

"But why has it not been announced?" asked Fiona.

"We decided to keep it a secret until my father's blessing could be obtained," said Elizabeth.

"But Mr. Bennet is here now," said Deborah.

"Yes, but there are other factors of which I cannot speak at present. It will be announced before long, but for the present I ask you to keep this confidence."

"Of course," declared Clara. "We are only happy you have chosen to share it with us. You shall remain in the neighborhood! I am so pleased we shall remain friends!"

"This is such a touching scene," a voice interrupted their excitement, and as one, the ladies looked to see Miss Bingley watching them, her usual sneer displayed for all to see. "I see you have managed to pass yourself off with some degree of credit in this society, Eliza."

"I have merely been myself, Caroline," said Elizabeth.

"And a better friend and confidant one could not find," said Erica, her look challenging Miss Bingley. It warmed Elizabeth's heart to hear such a vigorous defense from a young lady who was usually quite

356 ᯂ *Jann Rowland*

reticent. "We have all grown to love Elizabeth in the time she has been here."

"We would be distressed if she was to leave the neighborhood," added Clara. "She has become an integral part of our society, and I know I speak for us all when I say that we are happy to have her with us."

"Not all." Two more ladies approached, and Elizabeth glanced at them, revealing them to be Miss Russell and Miss Campbell. "Some of us have more discerning tastes than to accept the likes of Miss Bennet into our society."

"Oh, no one cares what *you* think, Hillary," said Deborah, contempt winding its way through her voice.

"You are only unhappy because Mr. Darcy chose to focus on Elizabeth," added Fiona. "You are still smarting due to the knowledge of your own insignificance."

Miss Russell's countenance purpled in her anger, but Miss Bingley chose that moment to inject her own venom. "Then I fear you have all been grievously misled. *She* is no lady. She is nothing more than a hoyden with nothing more to recommend her than being an excellent walker. Why, I remember not long after we moved to my brother's estate. Her sister had been dining with us, and our Eliza walked three miles in dirt and mud to attend to a sister who did not need her assistance. She was wild when she walked in, her petticoats six inches deep in mud!"

"To me it shows an admirable care for her sister," replied Clara. "Any of us would give much for a sister for whom we possessed such love and devotion."

"There was nothing wrong with my sister's appearance that day."

Jane stepped into their group and eyed Miss Bingley, and the creases in her forehead showed more displeasure for Miss Bingley than Elizabeth had ever seen her sister before display. "I was grateful to have her attendance, I assure you."

"So would anyone be," added Deborah. "And any of us would do likewise for a beloved sister."

Miss Bingley shot a dark look at Jane, but Jane for once did not seem to be affected by her displeasure. Her countenance smoothed, and she did not say anything further, but she also seemed to be feeling a hint of annoyance at her new sister.

But Miss Bingley was angry, and angry people will often say things they know they ought not. Such was the woman's pique that evening.

"I think perhaps you should all look to a woman's background when making a judgment upon her. I have personal knowledge of Eliza's ways, and these are exacerbated by a lack of education, an almost total disregard for propriety, and a want of common delicacy as to render her entirely unsuitable for polite company."

Though Elizabeth was angry enough to flay this unpleasant woman with the edge of her tongue, she was interrupted by the sight of another joining them. The newcomer was none other than Lady Emily, and as she stepped up, she fixed them all with a disapproving glance.

"You are all making a scene," said she, her voice faintly censorious.

Elizabeth looked up and caught sight of William, who stood some distance away, and she noted that many in the vicinity seemed to be watching with interest. She shook her head slightly at him, and rolled her eyes at Miss Bingley. He seemed to catch her meaning as he shook his head, but his vigilance never wavered.

"Miss Bennet," continued Lady Emily, "perhaps you would do me the honor of introducing me to your friend?"

Though Elizabeth wanted to take the word "friend" and trample it underfoot, she readily agreed, though she wondered what mischief Lady Emily intended. The lady had no reason to be friendly to her, after all.

"Of course, Lady Emily. This is Miss Caroline Bingley, my sister's new sister by marriage. And if I may, I would also like to present Mrs. Jane Bingley, my eldest sister who has lately married Miss Bingley's brother. Caroline, Jane, this is Lady Emily Teasdale, daughter to the earl of Chesterfield and Mr. Darcy's eastern neighbor."

The ladies curtseyed to each other, but their responses could not be any more different. Lady Emily was her usual enigmatic self, and even Elizabeth, who had now known her for some months, did not know if she supported Miss Bingley or disdained her. Jane was calm and controlled, as was *her* wont, but her countenance did show a little wonder at being introduced to the daughter of an earl. For her part, Miss Bingley was looking like that cat who had got into the cream, as she clearly expected to be the closest of friends with the earl's daughter. Her next words confirmed that supposition.

"It is, indeed, a pleasure to meet you, Lady Emily. I am certain we shall have much to speak of in the coming days, more so than *other* persons who are present."

Though Miss Bingley obviously expected some sort of agreement from the lady, she was destined to be disappointed. Lady Emily only regarded her through lidded eyes, seemingly contemplating her. When she finally spoke, it was not to Miss Bingley.

"Miss Russell, Miss Campbell." The ladies themselves replied with tolerable greetings, but having been acquainted with Lady Emily a little longer, they appeared to be more than a little apprehensive. "Jealousy is not an admirable attribute. You would do well to remember it, for those much higher in society than you might suffer from actions taken in anger."

No one understood the second part of Lady Emily's statement—other than Elizabeth, who knew Lady Emily spoke of herself—but the first part was clear to all. Miss Russell's color rose and her mouth thinned in mutinous anger, but Lady Emily only looked back at her, the challenge evident in her gaze. Miss Campbell nudged Miss Russell and the woman's defiance bled from her, though she still appeared cross.

Lady Emily's eyes then returned to Miss Bingley, and the woman returned her gaze, less certain of herself than she had been a moment earlier. That nervousness seemed to increase the longer Lady Emily remained silent.

"I overheard what you said to Miss Bennet," said Lady Emily at length. "Perhaps you would be wise to confine yourself to banal conversation while in an assembly room, for my words concerning jealousy apply to you as well. Miss Bennet has been in this neighborhood for some months now, and she is *almost* universally respected and liked. You have been here for a matter of days, and your performance tonight is not leaving a good impression.

"Furthermore," continued Lady Emily, and this time the ice in her voice and disdain in her glare was unmistakable, "you would do well to remember that an education does not make one a sterling example of a well-bred woman. It takes much more, not the least of which includes kindness, thoughtfulness, charity, and many other exemplary virtues. I have seen none of these qualities in you."

Then Lady Emily turned away from Miss Bingley as if she was of no consequence and smiled at Elizabeth. "I am happy to see you, Miss Bennet, and I would love to become better acquainted with your sister. Perhaps we might meet for tea sometime soon."

"I would be happy to," said Elizabeth, giving the woman a warm smile. It seemed she wished to make amends and put their past difficulties behind them, and Elizabeth was willing to do so, given her behavior at present.

"Excellent. I will send an invitation around."

With one final glare at Miss Bingley, Lady Emily departed, leaving a quieter and much subdued group of ladies. Miss Russell and Miss

Campbell soon left, though their injured glances at Elizabeth did not suggest they had learned anything, and Miss Bingley soon stalked off, her posture screaming her offense. With an unreadable look, Jane also walked away to join her husband, and could be seen in earnest conversation with him thereafter.

The other ladies stayed by Elizabeth's side.

"Was that Lady Emily?" asked Fiona. "I have rarely heard her speak so much at once."

"She can be quite pleasant," replied Erica.

"But she is more often reserved," said Clara. "It seems, Elizabeth, that you have won her approbation."

"There is nothing the matter with her behavior," replied Elizabeth. "I have counted her among my friends for some time now."

And it was true, Elizabeth decided. Before Lady Emily had begun showing her jealousy, Elizabeth *had* considered her a friend. She was happy she would in the future as well, for she thought that the lady truly was estimable.

CHAPTER XXXII

*F*eeling better than she had in some time, Elizabeth, in Olivia's company, went to Pemberley, eager to see her fiancé again and bask in the light of his presence. Of her sister, Elizabeth was feeling encouraged. Jane was at least showing emotion of late, especially the previous evening when she had engaged in a serious discussion with her husband after the confrontation with Miss Bingley. Of what that conversation consisted, she could not be certain, but the frequent glances Jane directed toward both Elizabeth and Miss Bingley — who had stood to the side, offense written upon her brow — spoke volumes. Anything was better than Jane's silence and indifference.

On their arrival, Elizabeth was informed of William's absence due to some matter of the estate, and she resigned herself to Miss Bingley's company. When she entered the room where the ladies sat, Elizabeth could feel the hostility in the air, and Miss Bingley's gimlet eyes, staring at her, disdain flowing off her like a waterfall, told Elizabeth that they would not be long in each other's company before sparks flew. Not far from Miss Bingley sat Georgiana and Jane, and though they were speaking quietly together, it was with a sense of hesitation. They too felt the tension in the room.

As soon as they arrived, Georgiana, clearly relieved to see them, claimed Olivia's company for herself and led her away to the music room so they could practice together. The looks she cast behind her as they left, however, spoke to the depth of her betrayal, for she was clearly not sorry at all to be leaving the sisters with the unpleasant woman. Elizabeth could not blame her. Jane, who played only little, wished them well and then returned to her recent behavior, closed countenance and reserved demeanor, even with Elizabeth, with whom she had always been open. She was, however, watchful and attentive, which Elizabeth had not recently witnessed in her sister's behavior.

Regardless, this time Elizabeth was not about to stand for it. She was determined to breach this wall of Jane's and discover what had happened to her elder sister.

"Jane, Miss Bingley," said she as she sat down with the two women. "How lovely it is to see you today."

Miss Bingley did not even condescend to make a response. Jane, however, allowed a slight smile to reach her lips. Elizabeth attempted to ignore this incivility and proceeded to speak with her sister, not allowing silence to fall between them again. She spoke of nothing of consequence—the weather, the pleasure she had received from knowing her cousins better, some anecdote Charlotte had written of the neighborhood of Meryton, among other subjects. But though Jane did not say much in response, Elizabeth was determined and kept speaking with her sister. All the while, Miss Bingley sat to the side watching Elizabeth chatter.

It was not a surprise when Miss Bingley's thinly held veneer of civility cracked and the true woman shone forth. In fact, Elizabeth had been waiting for the woman's vitriol to flow, and was prepared.

"Miss Eliza Bennet," said she, interrupting Elizabeth's words, "I do not know why you have suddenly become loquacious like your younger sisters, but I believe when one visits Pemberley, one must inject a little gravity into her manners and not carry on like a child. Perhaps you should return to your uncle's house." Miss Bingley sneered. "It is much more appropriate to your position in life."

Elizabeth did not miss the sudden darkness in Jane's countenance, but she turned her attention to Miss Bingley, knowing that if she was ever to bridge the distance with her sister, being rid of Miss Bingley was a necessity.

"It is interesting to hear you speak so, Miss Bingley. I must assume you have not been at Pemberley much. It is a home—a large and imposing one—but still a home. I have shared laughter here with Mr.

Darcy and his family, and in no way did any of us behave as if Pemberley was a mausoleum."

Affront blazed in Miss Bingley's eyes. "I have noticed that those who consider themselves witty often use humor to attempt to make themselves feel important."

"And I have noticed that those who consider themselves to be better than others will attempt to ridicule and belittle to make themselves feel as if they deserve the sphere to which they aspire."

"You are naught but a hoyden running barefoot through the fields. You attempt to draw Mr. Darcy's eyes, but I am certain that before long he will view you with nothing but disgust."

"And you are nothing but a pretender, grasping at the rungs of a ladder, not caring whom you trod upon in your attempt to reach the top." Elizabeth smiled thinly at the woman. "Unfortunately for you and your airs, I am already aware of how you are viewed by others, and it is not what you imagine.

The way Miss Bingley shot to her feet, Elizabeth knew she was more offended than she had ever been before. "I will see you thrown from Pemberley in disgrace!" hissed she. "And I will ensure you are never welcomed here again!"

And with those final words, Miss Bingley turned on her heel and marched from the room. It was apparent to Elizabeth that the woman had forgotten how one must behave with gravity and restraint while at Pemberley, for the door slamming behind her echoed throughout the room.

"Lizzy that was unkind."

Aghast, Elizabeth, turned back to her sister. "What unkindness do you call it?" demanded she.

Jane's eyes widened at Elizabeth's obvious fury, and she struggled to respond. Elizabeth, by this time, was beyond caring what her sister, or anyone else, thought.

"Perhaps you have missed your new sister's behavior, Jane, but Miss Bingley is barely tolerable when she is in the same room as I. Have you misunderstood her spiteful attacks at *me*? I might add, they are entirely unprovoked. Or is this the way those of high society behave? If so, I have no wish to be part of it."

It was obvious that Jane was taken aback by Elizabeth's vehemence, and well she should be. Elizabeth had rarely raised her voice to her sister. She had always considered Jane's propensity to look on others and ascribe the best possible motives to them to be a quaint and pretty innocence on Jane's part. Now she could not be certain.

"What has happened to you, Jane?" demanded Elizabeth when her sister did not respond. "What has happened to my closest sister, my confidant? Has your marriage turned you into this aloof creature? Or are you attempting to emulate your new sister and thus, have no time for the family in which you were reared?"

Anger flared in Jane's eyes. "You do not know what it is like, Lizzy! You cannot understand."

"I might surprise you."

Jane only shook her head. "It is useless. You have no part in the world I have joined. You cannot understand."

"Then my sister is lost to me." Elizabeth stood, looking down at Jane, now certain that her father's suppositions about Jane's behavior were true, feeling all the desolation of the loss of a wonderful friend and confidant. "I wish you all the happiness with your shrewish sister in your cold and unfeeling world, Jane. Remember this: you say I have no part in your world, and you may be right. But *you* will also have no part in *mine!*"

With those final words, words which seemed to pierce Jane to her core, Elizabeth spun on her heel to retreat from the room. She had no desire to see her sister again, and little wish to see Georgiana and Olivia either. Better to return to Kingsdown where she could attend to her grief in private, to mourn the loss of a sister she loved more than life itself.

As she reached the door, Elizabeth heard a choked sob behind her. She reached for the handle, determined that she was done with her sister, when something, she knew not what, stayed her hand. Perhaps it was an echo of what they had shared, or a hint of her compassion coming to the fore, but she never could leave Jane when she was distressed.

Jane's eyes were full and tears rolled down her cheeks unheeded, leaving wet, salty trails and dampening the front of her dress. The gaze with which she regarded Elizabeth was stricken, a thousand pains all gathered in one breast, crushing her with their dead weight, making her seem smaller than the elder sister Elizabeth had always known.

"I cannot do this any longer."

It was nothing more than a whisper, so quiet that Elizabeth had to strain to hear her sister. But Elizabeth was not willing to simply allow Jane to buy her way back into her affections with tears. "Do what?"

Jane started, as if she had forgotten Elizabeth was even in the room. She peered up at her, confusion warring with fear. Her mouth worked for several moments, but nothing issued forth. Then she released a keening wail and rose from the sofa, rushing past Elizabeth and out into the hall, leaving Elizabeth listening to the sound of her sobs as they faded in the distance.

There was now no question of leaving. Elizabeth turned and followed her sister, out through the doors and into the gardens of Pemberley.

It was a rare occurrence that Darcy resented his estate and the work which went into its management, but that morning, he found himself in that unfamiliar state. Elizabeth was coming to visit, he knew, and he had wished to be there to greet her. But he had received a message from one of his tenants, requesting his presence concerning a matter of importance, and Darcy knew he could not simply ignore it. So, he had dutifully saddled his horse and ridden out, accompanied by Fitzwilliam and Bingley.

He should not be worried, he knew. Though part of the reason he had wished to be at the house that morning was due to his desire to be in Elizabeth's presence, it was also because he knew that Miss Bingley had been in high dudgeon since the assembly the previous night, and he expected sparks to fly between them. Elizabeth was well able to fend for herself, especially against someone with such an overinflated opinion of herself as Miss Bingley. But that did not relieve the desire to be a protector for his beloved.

Now that the matter had been dealt with, he was free to return to the house and to Elizabeth, and he set a quick pace back, with his companions following behind.

"It seems to me that you are rather eager to return to Pemberley," said Fitzwilliam.

Darcy shot him a grin. "I will own to finding much more agreeable company there. Here I have naught but the glib tongue of an old soldier and a married man who is as eager to return to his wife as I am to return to my betrothed."

"Ah, so it is the lovely Miss Bennet which draws you home with such haste."

"Did you expect anything else?"

"Perhaps the desire to interfere with the unpleasantness which is likely occurring at this very minute?" asked Bingley in a tone of vinegar and lemon. "*My* sister is present at Pemberley, do not forget, and she and Elizabeth have never gotten on well."

Darcy eyed his friend, wondering what he should say in response to Bingley's — correct — statement.

"Oh, do not look at me that way, Darcy," replied his friend. "You need not say it, for I am perfectly aware of Caroline's behavior."

"Then what do you intend to do about it?" asked Darcy. He did not wish to accuse his friend or make him uncomfortable, but Miss Bingley was disrupting the peace in his home. It was a matter Darcy could not tolerate, especially since the woman's vitriol was aimed at that which was most precious in Darcy's life.

Bingley sighed. "I previously said, I have thought of sending her to my aunt in Scarborough. Caroline hates being there and decries it as the worst punishment, but since she cannot go to the Hursts and she is quickly making herself unwelcome here, there is nowhere else for her to go unless I set up her own establishment."

"Would it help if *I* spoke with her?"

"I doubt it," replied Bingley with a grimace. "It would likely only make her more difficult to bear."

Darcy shook his head. "I will leave her in your hands. But when you speak to her, make certain she understands that I will not tolerate her continued belittling of Elizabeth."

With a clipped nod, Bingley said: "I will."

They rode on in silence for some time, Bingley deep in thought, no doubt his sister being the center of his considerations. Darcy's deliberations, though, turned in a different direction, though he was loath to speak of it. Again, concern for Elizabeth led him to voice his thoughts.

"What of Mrs. Bingley?" asked he, pulling Bingley's unwilling gaze. "Though she does not disparage Elizabeth or act in a manner objectionable, I know her behavior gives Elizabeth much pain."

"On that front, I believe there may be some reason for optimism." Bingley paused and his brow furrowed. His horse whickered as it trotted along, and Bingley reached a hand down to pat its flank. Fitzwilliam, for his part, had drawn behind, seemingly understanding they needed to speak between them.

"Jane was asking me some odd questions last evening at the assembly."

"Questions?" asked Darcy. "Of what?"

"Of you, actually," replied Bingley. "She seems to have found your behavior . . . confusing."

Darcy frowned, wondering if his friend's wife was casting aspersions on his character. "I am sorry, Bingley, but I do not understand."

"Nor do I," admitted his friend. "But she seems to be confused about your good relations with the Drummonds, how readily you have accepted Elizabeth into your home, how you accepted my father-in-law, and how you have allowed your sister to befriend Olivia."

Uncertain what he was hearing, Darcy could only say: "She expected us to be proud and unapproachable?"

"I am uncertain exactly *what* she expected, but that is not an unreasonable assumption."

"Do you know the reason why she would expect us to behave in such a way?"

"I do not," replied Bingley. "Perhaps it is simply what she expects of someone of your level of society. It is not uncommon for those of your circles to be insufferable, you must acknowledge."

"I confess it freely," replied Darcy. "But I would hope she would wait to meet us before pronouncing judgment."

"My Jane is not judgmental!" exclaimed Bingley. "Far from it, in fact. She has always been so sweet and gentle, and she is almost naïve in how she looks for the best in others. I cannot explain it."

Suddenly an awful premonition fixed itself in Darcy's breast. The two were connected—Mrs. Bingley and Miss Bingley. How could he possibly have missed it?

The house was looming before them and Darcy, though he was not certain what he would say to his friend, happened to notice a figure hurrying out a side door toward the gardens. Then another exited the house chasing after the first figure. It was Mrs. Bingley—who seemed to be in some distress, though it was difficult to tell because of the distance—followed by Elizabeth.

"Jane?" said Bingley, starting as he looked toward the retreating sisters.

He shook the reins, but Darcy guided his horse toward his friend's, and restrained him. "I know you wish to comfort your wife, Bingley, but look: Elizabeth is following her. Perhaps they are on the verge of mending their differences."

"If you ask me," inserted Fitzwilliam, "it is long overdue."

Bingley was uncertain, but he still appeared as if he wished to chase them. Darcy, though, was certain that this was precisely what the sisters needed, and he grasped Bingley's reins himself, steering the man toward the stables.

"Come, Bingley, it will be for the best. Let us go to my study and have a drink. Once they return to the house, you may speak with your wife."

With the combined efforts of Darcy and Fitzwilliam, they guided

Bingley away from where the sisters had disappeared into the garden. Now that he was free to think about the matter a little more, Darcy wondered if Elizabeth had already made the same connection he had, or if she was about to learn of it. Miss Bingley's motives for poisoning Mrs. Bingley against Elizabeth were easily seen, but Darcy was not certain why she would have done the same against Darcy himself. Either way, if his suspicions were borne out, the woman would not be welcome at Pemberley any longer. Good riddance. He could barely tolerate her anyway.

When Elizabeth finally caught her sister, she found Jane on a bench in a secluded nook, hidden from the house. As she had when she had fled the sitting-room, Jane was sobbing as if her heart might break, her face hidden in her hands. It broke Elizabeth's heart to see her sister in such straits, so unlike Jane's usually optimistic outlook. But then again, nothing of Jane's recent actions could be construed as normal, so she was not certain what to think.

Carefully, not wishing to startle her sister or drive her away, Elizabeth settled on the bench next to her and put her arm around Jane's shoulder. It only made matters worse as Jane turned to Elizabeth and wailed: "Oh, Lizzy!" and flung her arms around Elizabeth, clinging to her as if afraid to let go. There was nothing to be done at present. Jane was almost hysterical in her distress, and there was no understanding what she was saying, so Elizabeth only embraced her sister and rubbed her back, trying to impart what comfort she could.

Elizabeth did not know how long they sat in that attitude, but at length Jane's storm of tears slowed and then stopped, leaving her sniffling and hiccupping in Elizabeth's arms. Elizabeth continued to hold her as if she were a young child, knowing that her sister needed comfort rather than explanations at present.

"I think I have been a fool, Lizzy."

Jane's words were so soft that Elizabeth almost missed them. "How were you foolish, Jane?"

Her sister let out a deep sigh, but she did not remove herself from her comfortable position in Elizabeth's arms. "I listened to someone to whom I should not have listened. In doing so I have allowed that which is most precious to slip away. How you must hate me now!"

"Indeed, I do not!" said Elizabeth. She pushed Jane away from her, forcing her sister to look her in the eyes, which was difficult as Jane's gaze immediately dropped to the ground beneath their feet. "I believe it is time you told me what has been happening, Jane. Why have you pushed us all away?"

"Because I thought it was expected of me."

Elizabeth stared at Jane, not certain she had heard her correctly. "You thought it was expected of you? I do not understand. Surely Mr. Bingley could not have made such a claim."

Jane shook her head. "Not Charles. I was deliriously happy, Elizabeth. But I am also aware of what Charles gave up in attaching himself to me. I wished to ensure he never regretted marrying me."

"That is admirable, and a sentiment I completely understand, dearest," replied Elizabeth.

With a dejected heave of her shoulders, Jane resumed her place in Elizabeth's arms. "Not long before the wedding, I was visiting Caroline and I confided my concerns to her. She was very solicitous and understanding. She claimed that those I met could not fail to see my worth."

"I believe I gave you the same advice, if you recall," replied Elizabeth.

"I do. But that is not all she said. She fell silent for a moment, frowning at nothing I could see, and when I asked her what was the matter, she confessed to worry for her brother's reputation. Though no one could fail to find *me* acceptable, my family was a different matter."

Elizabeth gasped. "She said that to you?"

"She did. You know that we have both despaired for Mama's behavior, not to mention that of Kitty and Lydia. She claimed that five minutes of their presence in London society would see the Bingleys shunned."

"What else did she say, Jane?" asked Elizabeth, certain her sister was holding something back.

"She said . . ." Jane paused and swallowed hard. "I could not disagree with her, but I noted that my family was not likely to be in London often. Then she mentioned how I had spoken of inviting you to live with us, and she was very direct in pointing out how *your* manners were also not fashionable."

"And you believed her?" asked Elizabeth incredulously.

"I did not wish to. I put the matter from my mind, and we went on our wedding trip, but when we returned, we spent a month in London. During that time, we attended a few events of the season, and while we were there, the subject was raised once again."

"From Miss Bingley?" asked Elizabeth.

"Actually, it was another lady of society. We had gone on some calls to one of Caroline's friends, and there were some other ladies there.

While Caroline was engaged speaking with some others, one of the ladies asked me about my family, and in the discussion, when I had told her about our background, she warned me to leave them in Hertfordshire, for they would not be accepted in London.

"I was shocked! I could not have imagined giving up my family. I was inclined to ignore her advice, but I watched those of society, noting how they behaved and how they interacted with each other. Then Caroline and I talked again, and she was most emphatic about what I must do. To preserve my husband's reputation, I had no other choice but to distance myself from you all. She claimed it would be easier if I made a clean break. That way I would not be inundated with requests from Kitty and Lydia to invite them to London. I would not have the pain of seeing *you* often and knowing you could never be part of my life."

Elizabeth was angry. She could not imagine how her sister could have been taken in by such lies. But though she wished for an outlet for that anger, she knew it would do no good to punish Jane, and their new rapport was something she did not wish to risk. Besides, Elizabeth knew *exactly* who should receive the brunt of her fury.

"Oh, Jane!" said Elizabeth. Once again she pushed her sister away and made her face her. "How could you have believed such lies?"

"I was afraid, Lizzy," replied Jane. "I did not wish to be the means of my husband losing his place in society. And you must confess that Kitty, Lydia, and Mama are not paragons of proper behavior."

"No, I do not dispute it at all. But Jane—to hear such things about our family and do nothing to defend us! Miss Bingley herself is not of the first circles. How could she possibly know what is acceptable and what is not? *We* are her superior in the eyes of society, no matter what earthly wealth she possesses. The Bingleys' status in society is dependent on Mr. Darcy's friendship. Charles is an estimable man, but he *is* the son of a tradesman. Nothing but time will change how society views him—time, good behavior, and continued connections to those such as Mr. Darcy. And it will only change for your descendants—at present, he is considered too close to trade."

"I know, Elizabeth. But . . ." Jane swallowed thickly. "Fear is a powerful motivator. I have . . . I have attempted to stay away from you all. I tried to be indifferent. But it was all so very hard. Then I came to Pemberley, and nothing was as I expected. Caroline assured me that you would not be welcome at Pemberley and that our uncle would only be tolerated because of his proximity to Mr. Darcy's estate. I was confused, and being close to you again was painful."

370 *🍃 Jann Rowland*

Elizabeth sighed. "I will not say you were not foolish, Jane, because it is clear you were. But it is clear to me that Miss Bingley preyed on your insecurities. I know you sometimes think I am too cynical and unforgiving, but I have always known that Miss Bingley is a grasping, artful, shrew, who was no friend of her brother's marriage to you. She is a detestable woman, and you allowed her to turn you against your family."

"I know," said Jane simply, rather than trying to deny Elizabeth's words. "I hope you can forgive me."

"Forgive you?" demanded Elizabeth with a laugh. "You must be jesting! When have I ever been required to forgive my perfect elder sister of anything?"

Jane smiled, though it was made wan by what appeared to be a bone weariness. "I am not perfect, Lizzy."

"As this episode shows," replied Elizabeth. "But neither am I. Of course, I forgive you, Jane. You are my beloved elder sister. We forgive those we love. I am only happy to have my sister back."

The sisters sat in the garden for some time, basking in their newly rediscovered closeness. The hurt was not gone—it would take some time for Elizabeth to push it to the past where it belonged, for Jane *had* hurt her terribly. But there was promise—the promise of renewed relationships, of future felicity, of a return to their former closeness. At the present, it was enough to look to the future with hope.

CHAPTER XXXIII

After some time, Elizabeth observed that her sister was on the verge of collapse from weariness. Coaxing Jane to her bedchamber was not difficult, for her sister went along without question like a small child trusting in its mother. They made their way slowly back down the garden paths and into the house, and when they reached Jane's rooms, Elizabeth ensured she was resting on the counterpane, insisting that she sleep for a time.

"You intend to confront Caroline," said Jane before Elizabeth could depart. Jane's tone was that of a simple statement, and not an accusation.

"I do," replied Elizabeth, realizing there was no reason to obfuscate. "Jane, the woman was hateful, not only to you, but to our entire family. Our suitability or lack thereof is not for her to judge. I have never met such a contemptible woman in all my life. This cannot go unanswered."

A sigh escaped Jane's lips, and she turned on her side. "No, I suppose it cannot. But I cannot dissociate my own culpability in this matter. The blame does not rest solely on Caroline's shoulders."

"No, but the clear majority of it *does*. Jane, she *used* you. She preyed upon your fears and inexperience and led you to believe you needed to throw your family off. I will not allow her to act in such a manner without consequences."

"I am certain Charles will handle it."

Privately, Elizabeth thought Mr. Bingley was of such an agreeable disposition that it was uncertain he would stand up to his sister. But Elizabeth could not say such a thing to Jane.

"No doubt he will, dearest." Elizabeth leaned over and embraced her sister. "Regardless, the response needs to come from a *Bennet*, and I reserve the right to make the response myself. I promise I will not behave as she. But she *will* know my displeasure."

"My fierce, indomitable sister," said Jane with a wan smile. "I know you will behave in an exceptional manner, as you always do. Please just leave part of Mr. Darcy's house standing, if you will."

"I cannot promise it will be *completely* intact," replied Elizabeth with a grin. "But I shall do my best."

Elizabeth fussed for a few more moments, seeing Jane settled, before she let herself out of the room. She quickly located Mrs. Reynolds and inquired of Miss Bingley's whereabouts, and though the woman, as a good servant, did not react, Elizabeth was certain the mere mention of Miss Bingley was distasteful to her. She was in good company.

"I understand she was seen returning to her suite."

"Thank you, Mrs. Reynolds."

It was a short walk to the woman's rooms, and though she would have preferred to walk in unannounced, Elizabeth's ingrained sense of polite behavior dictated that she knock first. It was a few moments later when Miss Bingley's maid answered the door.

"Is your mistress in her rooms?" asked Elizabeth.

"She is, ma'am."

"Thank you," said Elizabeth. Without any further ado, she reached forward and gently, but firmly, pushed the door opened, causing the startled maid to step back. There, pacing in front of the fireplace, was Miss Bingley, looking every bit as affronted as she had when she had left the sitting-room earlier.

"You may go now," said Elizabeth to the maid. "Your mistress will not require your services for a time."

The maid glanced at Miss Bingley, uncertain at being dismissed by someone else. Miss Bingley shot her a curt nod, and she curtseyed and hurried out, likely sensing the hostility which was already thick in the room.

Once the maid had left, Elizabeth wasted no time in making her displeasure known. "Miss Bingley," said she, "you are without a doubt the most contemptible, wretched, disgusting, unfeeling woman I have ever had the displeasure to meet."

While Elizabeth would have expected the woman to erupt in fury at being referred to in such terms, Miss Bingley only laughed. There was no true mirth in it, however — instead it was a cold, cruel sort of response.

"I am certain it must appear so to you, little Miss Eliza, but I care not. A simpleton such as you can have no understanding of the passions which motivate me." She turned around, facing away from Elizabeth. "Go back to Hertfordshire and live in the pitiful squalor of your father's house. If you are very lucky, you may even find a tenant who is willing to take you on."

Elizabeth's own laughter matched Miss Bingley's for harshness. "I am certain you believe that, Miss Bingley. I have no doubt it will bring you comfort, though little else will. I cannot tell you how much you disgust me. You have attempted to take a most precious sister from me, and you have done it with malice aforethought. I can never forgive you for this treachery."

"Treachery?" screeched the woman. She whirled on her heel, her glare a blast of frigid winter air. "I shall tell you what exactly treachery is. It is seeking to entrap *my brother* for your insipid sister. It is my brother betraying me, pulling our family name down into the filth and dirt of your situation. Do not insult me when your family is fit for nothing more than to be housed with the pigs!"

"Your overinflated opinion of yourself has always given me much mirth," said Elizabeth. "But regardless of what you think of me, I shall always have my dignity and my integrity. Unfortunately, honor is something of which you know nothing. You are too far immersed in your own selfish concerns to care for something so meaningless."

"How dare you!" said Miss Bingley. She stalked toward Elizabeth, her fists clenching and unclenching as she walked.

Elizabeth only laughed at her. "You have failed, Miss Bingley. I have my sister back, and she will never again pay any heed to your sibilant whisperings."

"Good riddance!" sneered the woman. "I have no need of your insipid sister. I will be happy to be rid of her and you when I take my place in society where I belong."

"Another of your failures," replied Elizabeth. Miss Bingley had driven all pity from Elizabeth's breast, not that she deserved it. "Not only is my relationship with my dearest sister restored, but you shall never have Mr. Darcy. Poor, deluded Miss Bingley. You never had a chance with him. He detests you *almost* as much as I do."

That brought Miss Bingley up short. She stared at Elizabeth for several moments, her eyes widened in terror. Then, as a dog shakes the water from its coat, Miss Bingley shook off Elizabeth's words, her fury coming over her again.

"Mr. Darcy would not attach himself to a simpleton with no dowry or connections."

"Nor would he attach himself to an arrogant termagant who is nothing more than the daughter of a tradesman giving herself airs.

"Regardless, you have missed your mark, Miss Bingley. I am, in fact, engaged to Mr. Darcy."

"Impossible!"

Elizabeth did not miss the note of desperation in the woman's voice. "It is not impossible. It is fact. He proposed to me not a week before you came. But even if he had not proposed to me, he would *never* have paid that compliment to *you*. You are everything he despises about society. You never stood a chance with him."

"Be silent!" shrieked Miss Bingley. "I will not listen to such lies!"

"You may call them lies if you wish," said Elizabeth. She purposely kept her tone offhand and deliberately turned her back on Miss Bingley, much as the woman had done to her not long ago. "But remember this, Miss Bingley: I will marry Mr. Darcy, and I have no doubt I will be very happy. My relationship with my sister has also been restored. What will you have?"

Elizabeth turned and regarded the woman, noting the anguish on her face. She knew she should be ashamed for the pitiless way in which she was destroying Miss Bingley's pretensions, but she was beyond caring.

"You will have nothing," said Elizabeth, answering her own question. "And after your reprehensible behavior, I cannot but believe that you *deserve* nothing."

With those final words, Elizabeth walked from the room. She quickly made her way down to the music room, where Olivia and Georgiana were still in each other's company. She quickly communicated to Olivia that she was welcome to stay, but Elizabeth was required to return to Kingsdown. Georgiana protested, but Elizabeth was firm, and within minutes she was in the carriage and on her way, having left a message with Georgiana for William. Though Elizabeth did not wish to leave her family and fiancé thus, her father needed to learn of what she had discovered.

*   *   *

Though Darcy had kept his friend with him in the study as long as he was able, at length Bingley left to attempt to find his wife. Darcy could not blame the man—seeing Elizabeth chasing after a fleeing Mrs. Bingley, who had obviously been crying, was more than a little disconcerting, and as his wife's behavior had been odd for some months, it was not in question Bingley would try to discover what had happened.

In the same vein, Darcy had thought to attempt to find Elizabeth himself, but his departure from his study, only moments after Bingley left, was forestalled by an enraged Miss Bingley. Not disposed to tolerating the woman at the best of times, her demands on that occasion rendered Darcy ready to eject Miss Bingley from his house forthwith.

"Mr. Darcy!" exclaimed she as she rushed through the door, almost colliding with Darcy, who had the presence of mind to jump out of her way. "I must insist you throw Miss Eliza Bennet from the house at once!"

Yet another attack against Darcy's beloved sent a scowl to his face, and the sound of the door impacting the frame, setting it to a loud rattling, did nothing to cool his temper. Eager to avoid being found in a room alone with the woman, Darcy avoided Miss Bingley's flailing arms and pulled the door open, leaving the interior fully exposed to anyone walking by. He then turned to Miss Bingley, noting her sour glance at the door and her accusatory glare, and he wondered if she had meant to attempt, in a final desperate ploy, to compromise him.

"I am sorry, Miss Bingley, but I fail to understand you. Not only do I doubt Miss Bennet could ever have done something which would warrant such a response, but *you* have no power to demand *anything* when you are in my home."

Miss Bingley swallowed the bile in her throat with some difficulty and attempted to cover her reprehensible demand through excessive anger. "You have my apologies, sir. If my errand were any less serious and the tidings I bring any less dire, I would never have spoken so. But when you hear what I must say, I am certain you will agree that all pretenses toward acquaintance with the Bennets must be disavowed without delay."

"Very well, Miss Bingley, you have my attention," replied Darcy, hoping to induce her to leave as soon as may be. "What is it that has offended you so?"

"Why, it is Miss Eliza trying to force your hand by speaking of an engagement with you!" cried Miss Bingley. She threw her hands into the air and began to stalk the room, the sounds of her slippered feet striking the tiles beneath her feet, reverberating in Darcy's ears much louder than should have been the case.

"I know it must be a falsehood, for you could never offer for one so unsuitable as she. She must think to claim a betrothal to engage your honor. You must disavow her and her entire family as soon as may be!"

"I am afraid you have wasted your time then, Miss Bingley," replied Darcy. The woman stopped her pacing in mid-step, and whirled to face him, incredulous at his words. Then her gaze turned hard. "Miss Bennet and I are, indeed, engaged, and she has said nothing which is not the truth.

"In fact," continued Darcy, his conversational tone seeming to infuriate her further, "I am pleased to hear that she is speaking of it openly. We already have her father's blessing, you see, and I was only waiting for Elizabeth's permission to make it known to all of society. Since she has spoken of it to *you*, she must be ready to have it published to all."

"Impossible!" breathed Miss Bingley. "You cannot have taken leave of your senses to be offering for such an unsuitable woman! I know you, Mr. Darcy—you are intelligent, sober, rational, and so very proper. The very notion is inconceivable."

"And yet it is true. Would you have me contradict my own inclinations, my own actions?"

"Yes! I would have you do it in an instant. I have waited for you to propose to *me* all this time since we were first introduced. I possess a handsome dowry, I have been trained to be the wife of a great man, and I have all the usual accomplishments necessary to make me a credit to your name.

"What does she have?" An ugly sneer came over the woman's countenance. "She has nothing—nothing other than relations to make a man blush, a paltry dowry, connections to trade and a country parson, and an impertinence which would make you the laughingstock of society. You cannot seriously be considering an alliance with her!"

"Miss Bingley!" said Darcy, his voice no less harsh for not having raised it. "I will thank you not to speak so of my *betrothed*. She is everything I have ever wanted in a wife, and the fact that *you* devalue her qualities does not affect *me* in the slightest."

"Qualities!" scoffed Miss Bingley. "Yes, she possesses qualities *any* man would wish to stamp out in the worst hoyden."

"Since you continue to demean them," said Darcy, this time his voice rising, "I will not speak of what I find irresistible about her. Suffice it to say that I am happy with what I will gain by having her as a wife. If you do not agree, it is nothing to *me*."

"Furthermore," continued Darcy, when she seemed poised to speak again, "I apologize if you have waited for a proposal from me, but I will inform you that I never considered you as a potential bride. I have no interest in marrying you, so your ambitions never had any chance of being fulfilled. And I would ask that you not attempt to demean my future wife in her future home. I will not tolerate it."

Miss Bingley let out a barking laugh, which held a hint of hysteria through its hardness. "She does not require *me* to demean her. She is fully capable of managing *that* herself!"

"Then you will no doubt be content to leave us to our fate." Darcy stepped closer to Miss Bingley, looking down at her, his stern glare daring her to protest. "I will inform you now, Miss Bingley, that I do not appreciate the behavior you have displayed since you have come to my house. I cannot and will not tolerate your continued attempts to belittle my betrothed. Regardless of what *you* believe, she is the most estimable woman I have ever met, and I *will* make her my wife. You may accept this with whatever grace you possess, or you will leave my home."

Any rational man might have expected several possible responses to such a set-down. Miss Bingley might have responded with rage, continuing to rail against his choice and words, overcome by the emotions of the moment. She might have swallowed her bile and dropped all her objections, maintaining her connection to the family by keeping her thoughts on his choice to herself. She might even have been expected to swing wildly about, looking to ingratiate herself with Elizabeth as an intimate though Darcy did not think her pride could be so readily dispelled. He supposed any one of those three possibilities — or another he had not considered — still might happen.

In the moment, however, Miss Bingley watched him, her eyes wide and her mouth slightly parted in shock. And then, apparently coming to the correct conclusion, she spun on her heel and marched from the room, leaving Darcy staring at her in bemusement. Perhaps she would conclude that her only hope lay in attempting to compromise him — she might think it would work, though Darcy knew it would not. Either way, he would need to take care.

With Miss Bingley mercifully returned to her room, Darcy left his study on his earlier, thwarted purpose, only to be disappointed again.

"Miss Bennet ordered her carriage and returned to her uncle's estate, sir," said Mrs. Reynolds when he inquired.

"When was this?"

"Oh, about fifteen minutes ago." Mrs. Reynolds paused, and then coming to a decision she continued: "The young miss asked after Miss Bingley and went to her room. Miss Bingley's maid came scurrying out soon after, and one of the upstairs maids heard raised voices in Miss Bingley's room.

Darcy thanked Mrs. Reynolds and returned to his study. It was clear to Darcy that Elizabeth had discovered something and confronted Miss Bingley about it, which led him to believe his own suppositions had some basis in fact. Why she had decided to return to Kingsdown in such an expeditious manner Darcy was not certain, but he thought it unlikely she would return that day.

Perhaps Bingley would confirm his suppositions, he mused as he looked out the windows onto the grounds. He wasn't certain there was any other way he would learn what happened that day.

Jane Bingley felt like a fool. She had always thought her patience and her ability to see the best in others to be a virtue, but it was obviously not nearly so desirable a trait as she had thought. It felt more naïve, sillier than it ever had before. She felt stupid and used, and the fact that Miss Bingley would not feel any remorse for what she had done made Jane feel even worse.

But even as she lay on her bed, sleep far away, even though she felt as weary as she ever had, Jane knew that she could not change her basic character. She would always tend to look for the good in others, and she did not think it was a contemptible trait. Unfortunately, it was one which could be used by another, more unscrupulous person, for their own purposes, as Jane had discovered. It was a mistake that Jane did not ever intend to make again.

In the end, then, though she could never be thankful to Miss Bingley for her actions, she decided that she had learned a valuable lesson. Never again would anyone prey on Jane Bingley for their own purposes. Starting with her beloved Charles and her wonderful sister Lizzy, no one would ever come between Jane and her family again. This she vowed.

Jane was not sure how long she lay in her bed thinking of the past months, but soon the door to the bedchamber opened and Charles stepped in. The dear man seemed to know that something had happened, for when he looked at her, she noted his hesitance. Feeling as if she had not seen him in weeks, Jane opened her arms to him, and he readily came and enfolded her in his embrace.

"Something happened between you and Lizzy," said he, wasting no time. "Can I assume it is good?"

"I don't know that anything good is to be had from this situation," said Jane. "I have been stupid and foolish, and I am fortunate to have a sister such as Lizzy, who is eager to forgive."

Charles drew away, and he looked in her eyes, a slight furrow in his brow. "Can you tell me what has happened?"

Jane burrowed into his chest yet again. "I am afraid of provoking your disappointment in me."

"Never!" exclaimed her wonderful husband. "If you have been foolish, I can only imagine there was some circumstance which clouded your judgment. Please tell me."

And so, Jane did. Her story of what had happened all those months ago, and what she had divulged to Elizabeth was told in stops and starts, embarrassed as Jane was about how she had been duped – and by his own sister! But all the while Charles listened with patience, though his countenance suggested a growing anger the longer she spoke. When she finally came to the end of her recitation, she fell silent, knowing his outburst of fury was to be expected. He did not disappoint.

"I can hardly fathom it!" said he. Jane could feel the shaking of his head, though she could not see, as she was still cocooned in the warmth of his arms. "How dare she suggest such things about my new family! Your mother and sisters are not the best behaved at times – it is true – but I value them because they are genuine. There is no malice or improper conceit among them, which is more than I can say for Caroline."

Then a thought occurred to him, and he looked down at Jane, demanding she return his gaze. "This lady with whom you spoke in London. Might I ask who it was?"

"I believe her name was Miss Carrington," replied Jane, wondering how it could signify.

Charles shook his head, dismay written in every movement. "Oh, Jane, I wish you had come to me about this. Not only would I *never* suggest that you cut your family from your life, but Frances Carrington is one of Caroline's oldest friends. They are thick as thieves and support each other in everything. I have no doubt they planned this in advance."

Shocked, Jane could only look at Charles. Then the anger descended, an anger such as Jane had never felt. "Then the betrayal has been far worse than I had ever imagined."

"It has." With a suddenness of motion, Charles disengaged from Jane and stood. "This cannot go unanswered, Jane. Caroline's behavior has become untenable. Darcy will be incensed by her attacks against Elizabeth, and I do not blame him."

"If you do not mind, I will stay here and rest," replied Jane. "I am exhausted from what has happened, and I would like to think of my own response to Caroline's perfidy."

"Of course, dearest." Charles leaned down and kissed her. "I will see to Caroline. She cannot stay, so I will send her to my aunt in Scarborough. What happens to her after that is entirely up to her."

After Charles left, Jane allowed herself to think a little more on the matter. Though they, neither of them, were as tenacious or direct as Elizabeth, this situation called for boldness. Though Jane knew her sister by marriage would never respect her, would never accept her, Jane would know how to act.

In time, the events of the day caught up to Jane, and she slept. But she did so knowing that her family was restored to her.

While the drama was happening at Pemberley, Colonel Fitzwilliam decided it was an excellent time to leave the estate and visit the woman he was courting. Darcy and Bingley did not require his presence, and though in other circumstances, Fitzwilliam would gleefully have watched events unfold, on this occasion he felt no need to do so.

Within a short period of time, he found himself walking with Lady Emily on the grounds of Teasdale Manor, and if he noted the earl watching them through one of the windows of his study, he could not blame the man. Fitzwilliam knew her father valued her more than all his worldly possessions.

"You seem to be overcome with other thoughts today, Colonel Fitzwilliam," said the lady at length, when conversation between them had ground to a halt. "Should I be concerned for your inattention?"

Fitzwilliam turned to regard her, noting her playful expression. Underneath it, however, he thought he detected a hint of concern. It heartened him—he had not seen much in her manners to suggest that she was at all warm to his attentions.

"Would you be concerned if I was inattentive?"

"A woman likes to know she is the center of the man's world, sir," replied she, her glibness revealing even more of herself to him. "We do not like to suppose there is anything more important."

"Then you need have no fear. I was merely thinking of some events at Pemberley this morning."

A frown was her response. "Is there something of which I should be concerned?"

"No, I am certain Darcy and his friend have things well in hand." When she turned a perplexed look on him, Fitzwilliam shook his head. "You must understand that I have no direct knowledge—only suspicions—and I am uncertain how much I should share with you. Suffice it to say that it seems Miss Bingley has managed to insult not only Bingley's wife, but also Elizabeth."

Lady Emily's distaste was clearly displayed. "The woman has no shame. Imagine her—the daughter of a tradesman, no less—thinking herself superior to gentleman's daughters! I cannot even begin to account for such effrontery!"

Amusement flowed through Fitzwilliam, though he stifled its release. Though she was not, in essentials, a proud or haughty woman, she was still every inch of an earl's daughter. This instance he agreed with her, though that may be as much due to Miss Bingley's disgusting character as anything else.

"Surely Mr. Darcy will not sit still for such behavior."

"No, I very much suspect that Miss Bingley will be leaving Pemberley at first light. I also think that Bingley will wash his hands of her."

"Good riddance!"

Fitzwilliam laughed, but he turned their discussion to other matters. "Were you truly worried about my distraction?" asked he, showing her a grin.

True to what he knew of her character, she only returned his playful comment with haughtiness. "I believe you overestimate your charm, sir."

"Of course, I do not," replied Fitzwilliam. "Be that as it may, let me inform you that I am every bit as engaged in our courtship as I ever was. I believe I am coming to esteem you, and though I do not think I love you now, I know it is possible—probable even. There, will that do to prop up your pride?"

The woman turned and directed a level look at him, but she did not immediately speak. She regarded him for several moments, seeming to consider her response, and when she did finally open her mouth, her words were not at all expected.

"I believe I am happy for Mr. Darcy and Miss Bennet. I have made overtures to Miss Bennet to restore our relationship, and I believe she was receptive. I have learned a valuable lesson, sir."

"Does that mean you do not wish for me to continue my attentions?" Fitzwilliam looked into her eyes, trying to divine her intentions. Her appearance seemed to soften a little, easing his own sudden consternation.

"No, it does not. It means that I have accepted that Miss Bennet and Mr. Darcy are to make a match, and that my pretensions were nothing more than that. It means that I can let go of the past and attempt to restore my good name in their eyes. It means I am ready to look toward the future and anticipate what may be."

"That, my dear Lady Emily, is all a *man* would ever wish to hear."

Fitzwilliam offered her his arm, which she readily took, and they continued to walk. Never had he felt such hope. When all was said and done, he knew all would be well.

CHAPTER XXXIV

Caroline Bingley left Pemberley the following day, and her going was not mourned by anyone. She left in disgrace, yet holding her head high, as if *she* was the one who was betrayed, rather than the reverse.

As expected, Mr. Bennet had been infuriated by the story Elizabeth had related to him on her return from Pemberley, and nothing would suffice but for him to go to Pemberley immediately to voice his own displeasure concerning her behavior. After Mr. Bingley's dressing down of his sister, William's few choice words, and Mr. Bennet's own displeasure, one might reasonably expect to see a chastened young woman who had learned her lesson. Instead, they were treated to the sight of Miss Bingley watching them all with cold disdain.

"Will you allow this man to speak to me in such a way?" asked Miss Bingley of her brother after Mr. Bennet had told her exactly what he thought of her.

"It is nothing less than you deserve," replied Mr. Bingley. "If you did not deserve it, you would not have been subjected to it."

Miss Bingley's sneer was not unexpected. "How typical of you, Charles. Not only do you choose an unsuitable woman for your wife, but you lack the ability to protect your own sister from unjustified attacks."

"Unjustified!" cried Mr. Bennet. "I have always known that your sister was an unpleasant sort of woman, sir, but I never imagined her to be delusional too."

Miss Bingley's lips tightened at his words, but Mr. Bingley only shook his head. "I never knew of it myself, though I am ashamed to own it. But you will no longer be required to endure her presence. She is for Scarborough tomorrow morning."

"Good," replied Mr. Bennet. "Please be aware that she will not be welcome in my house again."

"Nor mine," said William.

"She will also not be welcome in *mine*."

As one, the company turned to see Jane standing in the doorway. Elizabeth had never seen her sister looking on someone with such utter disdain as she did now. She could not help but be heartened by the sight, for she knew that Jane would never again be used in such a way by such a reprehensible person.

"Caroline, I find your actions disgusting, and your behavior appalling. I am ashamed of you."

Miss Bingley scoffed at her. "And you were eager and willing to fall in with whatever I said. Do not presume to blame me for your actions."

"I am aware of my own culpability," replied Jane, an implacability in her manner which was a revelation. "But I also know that if you had not betrayed me, I would never have behaved in such a manner. My guilt is great, but yours is greater.

"I will not ever have you in my house again. If Charles chooses, he may keep up his connection to you, but I will not have you distressing me, my family, or poisoning my children with your forked tongue."

"And I support my wife in this," was Mr. Bingley's short reply. "Caroline, you have gone beyond all decency in what you have done. You may live in Scarborough. If you prefer, I will release your dowry to your control and assist you in creating your own establishment in London. But I will not inflict you on my relations again."

"So, it seems you have simply passed your leading strings to another," mocked Miss Bingley. "For years, it was *my* apron to which you were tied. Now your little country wife holds the reins. How utterly predictable."

"Enough!" said Mr. Bingley. "I will tolerate no more of your vitriol. You may return to your room and direct your maid to begin packing. Do not bother to come down for dinner, as I shall ask Mrs. Reynolds to bring you a tray. If you are not prepared to depart in the morning, I will carry you to the coach myself."

Hatred simmered in Miss Bingley's eyes, but without another word she stood and left the room. It was the last time Elizabeth was ever in company with the woman, and she would see her only infrequently, and completely by coincidence, over the coming years.

After Miss Bingley's departure the next morning, those from Kingsdown joined the Pemberley party at William's estate, free from the specter of Miss Bingley. Though much still needed to be done to mend that which stood between them, Elizabeth thought they were well on their way to making a start. What she had not expected was for her sister to cling to her as if she thought Elizabeth would disappear in a puff of smoke without any provocation.

"I always knew the eldest Bennet sisters were close," remarked Mr. Bingley after they had been together for some time, "but I do declare it would be impossible to insert a sheet of paper between them at present."

"You have the pleasure of your wife's presence for the whole of your life, Mr. Bingley," said Elizabeth, shooting him an amused glance. "For now, I believe Jane and I require the reassurance of each other's affections."

"Well, then," said Mr. Bingley, reclining back in his chair and looking on them with fondness, "if such close sisters are not to be parted, I believe I will need to move forward with my purchase of an estate in this neighborhood."

Elizabeth gaped at him, but Jane was even more surprised. "Move to the neighborhood?" asked she.

"Yes, my dear," said Mr. Bingley. "As you are aware, I had originally leased Netherfield with the option to purchase. Recent events what they are, I had thought a change in scenery might be beneficial for your happiness, and I spoke with Darcy about the prospect of properties coming available in the north. There are a few possibilities, including a pair within thirty miles of Pemberley which might suit our needs. I thought we might look at them while we are here."

"Oh, Charles!" exclaimed Jane, and she abandoned her place by Elizabeth's side and threw herself into her laughing husband's arms.

"I will assume that the presence of my wife near Netherfield has not played a role in your decision," said Mr. Bennet. No one who heard him speak could have missed the sardonic note in his voice. "I will attempt not to take offense. But with you, and now Darcy here, taking away my most sensible daughters, I will have no one with whom to hold an intelligent conversation."

They all laughed at that, though Elizabeth noted that Mrs. Drummond only frowned at her brother.

"Surely you do not begrudge us this, Papa."

"Of course, I do not. But that does not mean I will not miss you."

"I feel the same way."

"I am not surprised. But you shall have ample sources of consolation in your new situation and will have, I am sure, no cause to repine."

"With the possible exception of being forced to endure my dour cousin," interjected Colonel Fitzwilliam.

"Oh, I think Darcy is not nearly so stern as you make him out to be, Colonel. I believe I shall like my third son-in-law, nearly as much as my second, though my first shall always hold a special place in my heart."

Colonel Fitzwilliam almost choked on his tea as he laughed. "I have been led to understand that your first son-in-law is my Aunt Catherine's parson, and given what I know of her preferences, I cannot imagine *his* society would be agreeable."

"And in that you would be correct, Colonel," replied Mr. Bennet. "But though he is all you say, he is also entertaining. I would not give up his acquaintance for anything."

"Oh, Papa!" said Elizabeth and Jane in tandem, while Colonel Fitzwilliam only grinned and raised his teacup in a toast to the absent Mr. Collins.

"It is clear you have much experience admonishing your father, girls," said Mr. Drummond, watching all with amusement.

"That is because he provides us so much opportunity," said Elizabeth with a wink.

The banter continued for some time, and Elizabeth participated in it as much as was her custom, finding joy in these relationships with beloved companions. Much had happened since she had come to Derbyshire, and she could not be happier. It was strange how such things worked out, but sometimes a ray of sunshine is found in the most unlikely of circumstances.

Later, Mr. Darcy crossed the room and took a seat by her side, and Elizabeth smiled at him, happy to be the recipient of his attentions and love.

"I do not believe I have told you, Elizabeth," said he, "but I am grateful you came to Derbyshire."

"No more grateful than I," replied Elizabeth. "And there is no need to despair—we would have met in time, even if I had not come. I am absolutely certain of it."

"Perhaps we would have. But this brings us to our happy resolution much more quickly, and I find I am impatient."

"As am I," replied Elizabeth, touching a hand to his face. "We shall be happy, Mr. Darcy. I have no doubt."

"And I have no doubt you would never allow unhappiness to reign," replied he. "It would not dare even try."

Elizabeth laughed. "Then it shall not have a chance, for we shall be united against it."

The newly acknowledged lovers spent many moments in the company of each other, and at times, the rest of those in the room faded away, leaving them feeling like they were the only ones present. And contented and happy they would be. His reserve and shyness would be overcome by the lady's happy disposition, and her previous depression had been overcome by means of his love, her sister's restoration, and the newness of her circumstances. Indeed, there could be no happier couple in existence.

Bennet watched his second daughter and her lover, and he felt a wistful sort of joy well up within him. It was hard, he decided, losing such a beloved part of his life to another, but he consoled himself in the knowledge that she had found exactly what she deserved. Darcy would care for her and make her happy, and that was enough for Bennet.

Of course, there were certain additional benefits to gaining such a son-in-law, not the least of which was the wonderful library the man possessed, not to mention his future expansion plans. Bennet's breath was almost literally taken away by the plans he had been shown, and he was certain that the future library of Pemberley, with its two levels of treasures available for his enjoyment, would be a thing of wonder to behold.

Everything had turned out well, from Jane's restoration to Elizabeth's engagement, and he supposed Mary was fortunate too in that she had been able to gain the attention of a respectable—albeit foolish—man. On the whole, his family had gained much, and he did not doubt that even Lydia and Kitty would benefit from their sisters' marriages.

There was one present, however, who seemed like she had not changed, and though Bennet knew it was likely a lost cause, he decided one more word into the woman's ears would not go amiss.

"I would like to thank you, Claire," said he as he sat down next to her.

She looked at him, as if wary he intended to be severe upon her. "For what?" was her blunt query.

"For accepting Elizabeth into your home and giving her this opportunity." Bennet waved her off when she opened her mouth to speak. "I am aware it was not your choice to do so. But even so, she has stayed under your roof and has blossomed into the future wife of a wealthy man, and for that I am grateful. I believe she deserves it."

Claire only grunted and turned away, her eyes fixed on the couple who were seated not far away, oblivious to the presence of anyone else. Bennet watched her, and he thought he noticed something different in her manner. He was not certain, but he hoped that she was reconsidering her actions, remembering the happy times rather than the objectionable ones. Bennet had never been certain if Claire had felt anything for the man who had declined to pursue her. She had never allowed herself to feel anything for her husband, though he was a good man. Perhaps she was feeling a hint of regret for her choices.

"I would like to give you a word of advice, if you will." Claire's eyes swung back to Bennet, and he chuckled at the warning therein. "Nothing so objectionable, I assure you. I merely wished to advise you to let go of the past, Sister. Allow yourself to be as happy as you can. Perhaps this life you have chosen for yourself has not been so bad after all."

Then nodding to her, Bennet rose and went to speak with the happy couple, and a moment later he was out the door of the sitting-room. The library was beckoning, after all, and he had no doubt there were many delights to be savored.

In the years to come, Elizabeth and Darcy would often speak of the events which had led to Elizabeth's coming to Derbyshire, and neither could view them with anything other than gratitude. For if Elizabeth's estrangement with Jane was a circumstance which had caused her great pain for a time, still it had, albeit indirectly, led to her decision to stay with her uncle, and through those means they had been able to find each other. Their affections and love strengthened daily, which helped them overcome the rough patches. Elizabeth would give Darcy four healthy children, all of whom were blessed with loving parents, and all of whom found their own paths in life. In the end, they were contented, and that is what Elizabeth thought was most important.

Of course, the Darcys were not allowed to arrive at the altar without exciting some drama, in the person of Darcy's aunt, Lady Catherine de Bourgh. The lady descended on Longbourn soon after Elizabeth's return to her father's house, full of demands and claims of a preexisting arrangement. Unfortunately for the lady, Darcy anticipated her offense and managed to ensure his presence at Longbourn when she arrived, and she was forced to resign the battlefield without carrying her point. They saw Lady Catherine but infrequently over the years, and she never did warm to Elizabeth. Miss de Bourgh, however, seemed to accept the situation with philosophy, and if Elizabeth did not find the woman to be exactly friendly, at least they shared a cordial relationship.

Regardless of Lady Catherine's displeasure, Elizabeth was glad that the Collinses chose to remain neutral in the affair. Though she was never certain—she did not ask, and Mary did not offer to elucidate—she suspected that Mary had convinced her cousin that he need not care for Lady Catherine's displeasure. After all, he was the heir to an estate and would be master himself someday. Given what Elizabeth knew of the man and had witnessed the year before her marriage, she thought it was remarkable, if, indeed, it was the truth. Of the Collinses, the Darcys saw little, which suited Elizabeth quite well. When they were in company with them, Mr. Collins had little to say, perhaps remembering the words they had exchanged at his wedding breakfast. This also suited Elizabeth quite well, indeed.

For Jane and Elizabeth, their reunion at Pemberley marked the resumption of a friendship which began at their earliest days and lasted for the rest of their lives. Jane made good on her promise never to allow another to come between her and her family, and in this she was supported by her husband. The Bingleys purchased an estate near Pemberley as Bingley had designed, and if Mrs. Bennet decried their going, they were happy living in the same neighborhood as their brother and sister. The Bingleys were also blessed with four children, who, in mingling with their Darcy cousins, forged lifelong friendships, though none of the cousins ever married each other.

Kitty and Lydia were also able to secure themselves good marriages. But while Kitty married the parson at Kympton, and soon removed to that town close by her second eldest sister, Lydia proved ungovernable, regardless of the measures Mr. Bennet had instituted to ensure her education. When she came of age, she left Longbourn and eloped with an army colonel, setting out on a fine adventure when he was transferred to a regiment in India. Word from the youngest Bennet sister was sparse thereafter, though she did occasionally send her sisters letters designed to make them all wild with envy. Whether this desire was realized shall be left to the reader's imagination to determine.

As for the elder Bennets, the realization of her daughters' advantageous marriages in no way changed Mrs. Bennet's character, and ever after she remained silly, prone to gossip, and nervous. One thing which did improve was her relationship with her second eldest, for the two women were able to use their conversation before Elizabeth's departure as a stepping stone to better understanding. Sadly, Mrs. Bennet predeceased her husband some fifteen years after Elizabeth's marriage, leaving Mr. Bennet a widower.

Though he surprised himself by missing the wife for whom he had possessed little affection, Mr. Bennet was quick in deciding his future. He called the Collinses home to Longbourn, turned the management of the estate over to his son-in-law, and left for Derbyshire as expeditiously as possible. His new home was made chiefly at Pemberley, though he was at times induced to stay with the Bingleys, and his daughter's prediction for his affinity for Pemberley's library — newly renovated with the second-floor balcony installed, per Darcy's plans — were proven correct in every particular. Mr. Bennet lived for an additional ten years after his wife's passing, and was able to enjoy the years of his retirement with his eldest daughter and numerous grandchildren.

And what of Colonel Fitzwilliam? The good colonel courted his lady for six months before they decided they had found the one person with whom they wished to spend the rest of their lives. Their wedding was a grand event, the wedding breakfast held at Pemberley, and the two earls who were fathers to the bride and groom were well pleased. The colonel was happy with his new wife and his children, and doubly so that he was able to begin a new dynasty of Earls of Chesterfield. Then when his eldest son was old enough to receive his inheritance, he was happy to retreat to Thorndell with his wife and live in peace and happiness. They always remained friends with the Darcys, and Lady Emily and Elizabeth came to their meeting of minds, each pleased with how their lives had turned out and able to forgive the past.

Miss Bingley, unfortunately for her, was never fully welcomed back into her brother's circle of friends. She stayed only six months in Scarborough, for the sedate pace of life did not suit her needs, nor did her poor temper suit her aunt, who had generously offered her a home. Miss Bingley returned to London, her sister allowing her to stay with her during the season, but Mrs. Hurst's conditions included a cessation of all harangues against Elizabeth Darcy, and a promise that Miss Bingley would attempt to find a husband. It was, perhaps, surprising to them all that she did so readily, and though the match was not the equal of the one to which she had previously aspired, the gentleman she married possessed an income of about five thousand pounds, so it was not inconsequential either.

Finally, the Darcys continued to have good relations with their Drummond family, particularly Mr. Drummond, Edward, Olivia, and Leah. Sensible of the fact that Mr. Drummond had been the means of putting them in a situation where they might grow to love each other, Elizabeth and Darcy both esteemed Mr. Drummond. Olivia and Leah, when she became old enough, both benefited from the Darcys' patronage, both making respectable marriages to gentlemen of the area. Mrs. Drummond ever after remained aloof, but her manners softened a little, and she was, eventually, able to maintain a cordial relationship with Elizabeth.

As she grew and had children, aged, and became a leading member of local society, Elizabeth found Derbyshire to be everything she had ever wanted in a home. The friends she had made also found their own husbands, and most of them stayed in the area. She received joy in these friendships for the rest of her life.

The End

Please enjoy the following excerpt from the upcoming novel On Tides of Fate, book three of the Earth and Sky trilogy.

Wisteria was much as Terrace remembered. She was heavyset, though not quite overweight, with the brown hair and eyes of her people, and though her younger sister was delicate and slender, Wisteria was rather like a battering ram in comparison. She was not unattractive, but Terrace knew many men would be put off by her plainer features and the contemptuous curl of her lips. If, indeed, they had not already been put off by her domineering manner and poisonous tongue. With some interest, Terrace noted a few pockmarked scars on Wisteria's face, including one—quite deep—just under her left eye. Terrace wondered whether she had been in a battle of some kind.

There were a number of noble men and women standing by in the room, gazing on Terrace, as though wondering what she would do. Wisteria held her hand out to a nearby servant, who placed a goblet in her hand, backing away deferentially, almost genuflecting before the woman.

Terrace watched this scene with shock. Groundbreathers had never required such strong obeisance from their subjects. Most of those who lived in the castle were Groundbreathers themselves, descended from the same people who had originally been blessed by Terrain. Tillman's requirements for respect had been almost perfunctory in nature, though Sequoia had always been more stringent. But even *that* imperious woman, who Terrace knew to be a good person at heart, had not acted the way her oldest daughter did. The girl almost seemed to think that she was Terrain himself.

"Welcome, Aunt," Wisteria said, her contemptuous amusement not hidden when she paused to drink deeply from the goblet that had been provided to her. "To what do I owe the honor of this unannounced visit?"

"I am sure you understand exactly why I am here, Wisteria. I wish to know what happened to my brother, and I want to know what you have done with River."

Wisteria cocked her head to the side. "You were informed, were you not?"

"I was. But I would hear it from you nonetheless."

Wisteria shrugged. "It is as you were told. There was an attempt to take over the castle, and my father was an unfortunate casualty."

"You speak of him as if he was nothing more than a Groundwalker," Terrace spat. "He was *king* of our people!"

"You had best moderate your tone," the chamberlain said. "Your niece is to be addressed with the respect she deserves and referred to as 'Your Majesty.'"

"I changed her soiled linens when she was a child and swatted her bottom when she misbehaved," Terrace snapped. "You had best mind your manners, or my niece will need a new toady to do her bidding."

The man stiffened at the insult, but Terrace's glare must have been fierce enough that he knew better than to speak any further. The sullen glare he directed at her, however, informed Terrace that she had made an enemy. But she did not fear what a man who kissed her niece's feet could do, and she turned her stony gaze back on Wisteria.

"Well, Wisteria?" Terrace prompted. "I am waiting for your answer."

"I do not make light of my father's death," Wisteria responded. "I mourn his passing as much as anyone, but as *I* am the eldest and the leadership of our people must be maintained, I have put my personal feelings aside for the good of the people and so that I might act in obedience to Terrain."

Terrace glared at her niece. Wisteria had rarely been obedient to anyone, and Terrace had always thought her devotion to the earth god to be little more than superficial.

"Where is River?" Terrace asked, deciding a different tack was required. "Where are Sequoia and Tierra?"

Watching for Wisteria's reaction as she was, Terrace was not surprised when an expression of almost insane revulsion crossed the young woman's face. Wisteria had always hated Tierra with an antipathy so deep that Terrace suspected Wisteria would not shed a tear if Tierra fell over dead.

"My mother disappeared in the chaos," Wisteria replied, though her short tone indicated her patience was being exhausted. "As for River and *Tierra*, they are safe at present. That is all you need to know."

"River is my daughter, and I demand —"

"You are in a position to demand nothing!"

Aunt and niece glared at each other, neither giving an inch. Wisteria stared with cold eyes, her gaze almost seeming to bore through Terrace as though she were not even there. Belatedly, Terrace realized that this woman now held absolute power over the castle and its surrounding environs. These strange Iron Swords guaranteed that.

Wisteria would not be loved by her people. She did not have the ability to inspire such loyalty. Rather, she would rule by fear and her implacable will. Judging by the atmosphere in the throne room, she had already made a start down that path.

It was time to take greater care. Terrace could not do anything from the inside of a cell, and Wisteria would have no compunction about incarcerating her own aunt if her displeasure grew too great.

"I am merely concerned over my daughter," Terrace said. Her attempt at a conciliatory tone was likely an abject failure, but Terrace thought Wisteria would care more about outward respect than inner feelings.

"I know you are concerned," Wisteria replied, her grating attempt at a soothing tone nearly causing Terrace to grimace, "but at present, you must trust me. River will be returned to you, and I promise you she has not been harmed."

Terrace did not miss how Wisteria did not even attempt to mollify her concerning the fate of Tierra. "And when will that be?"

Again, Wisteria's composure cracked, though she controlled her tone. "That is yet to be determined. I will keep you informed of her status. At present, I believe it would be best to return to your home."

Though it galled Terrace to be forced to retreat in such a manner, there was nothing more to be done. "Very well. But I must insist you inform me the moment there is any news."

Terrace inclined her head in farewell and turned to leave, but she was arrested by the sound of Wisteria's voice.

"Aunt, I am afraid I must ask you to remember that my father is dead . . . and *I* am now the queen. My father's reign was marred by laxness, not only in the manner in which his subjects were allowed to behave, but also in . . . other matters that he championed before his death. I have restored the order of our kingdom now. I require all my subjects to behave properly, as our god would require it. I will not hesitate to enforce my dictates. Am I understood?"

Once again, Wisteria and Terrace stared at each other, Terrace searching for any hint of weakness. If there was any, it was well-hidden, for Wisteria's expression was unreadable. It appeared Tillman was correct after all. He had often mentioned his concerns over the fitness of his daughter to rule when he passed away, and Terrace could see nothing before her but the realization of those fears. Wisteria was not to be trifled with, and if she were not stopped, then she had the potential to become the worst despot in the history of their people.

"Perfectly," Terrace replied.

"Excellent! Then we shall see each other anon. Changes are coming,

Aunt, and we must do our part to bring about our god's designs."

Terrace nodded and turned to leave the room, her retinue trailing behind her. She did not understand what Wisteria meant concerning Terrain, but she feared it nonetheless. It was at times like this that she wished Heath was still with her. He had always known what to do, and he had possessed an instinctual ability to read others and determine their motivations with a single glance. Terrace missed him; she had loved and cherished him, and theirs had been a marriage of the hearts.

But there was no point in dwelling on her loss. Terrace had to take action. First, Terrace needed to try to find Sequoia. She was the key. If Terrace could find Sequoia, then Tierra and River could be located afterward.

But first, Terrace needed to involve Basil. As it was his fiancée who was missing, Basil had a direct interest in the matter, and Terrace would not leave him out of it.

And so Terrace departed the castle. But it would not be for the last time. She was now convinced that Wisteria had played a part in Tillman's demise. Terrace meant to find out what had happened to her brother. Wisteria would be held responsible, even if she had only failed to act to save him.

FROM ONE GOOD SONNET PUBLISHING

http://onegoodsonnet.com/

FOR READERS WHO LIKED
IN THE WILDS OF DERBYSHIRE

Chaos Comes to Kent
Mr. Collins invites his cousin to stay at his parsonage and the Bennets go to Kent and are introduced to an amiable Lady Catherine de Bourgh. When Mr. Darcy and his cousin, Colonel Fitzwilliam, visit Lady Catherine at the same time, they each begin to focus on a Bennet sister, prodded by well-meaning relations, but spurred on by their own feelings.

Coincidence
Fitzwilliam Darcy finds Miss Elizabeth Bennet visiting her friend, Mrs. Collins, in Kent, only to realize that she detests him. It is not long before he is bewitched by her all over again, and he resolves to change her opinion of him and win her at all costs. Though she only wishes to visit her friend, Elizabeth Bennet is soon made uncomfortable by the presence of Mr. Darcy, who always seems to be near. As their acquaintance deepens, them much learn ore about each other in order to find their happiness.

My Brother's Keeper
When Fitzwilliam Darcy accompanies Charles Bingley to Netherfield, he is accompanied by George Wickham, a friend of many years. At first, Darcy does not see Elizabeth Bennet for the jewel she is, but his eyes are soon opened to her true worth. As Darcy and Elizabeth grow closer and love begins to blossom between them, the actions of a scoundrel threaten their happiness. All is in the balance when one who they call friend is forced to make a decision which will affect their felicity.

The Angel of Longbourn
When Elizabeth Bennet finds Fitzwilliam Darcy unconscious and suffering from a serious illness, the Bennets quickly return him to their house, where they care for him like he is one of their own. Mr. Darcy soon forms an attachment with the young woman he comes to view as his personal angel. But the course of true love cannot proceed smoothly, for others have an interest in Darcy for their own selfish reasons…

The Mistress of Longbourn
When the Netherfield party arrives in Hertfordshire, the family they find at Longbourn is small, composed only of Elizabeth and her younger sister. A change in the circumstances of the entail has left Elizabeth Bennet as the mistress of Longbourn, beholden to no one. But the challenge before Elizabeth is to recognize a deep and abiding love when it finds her.

For more details, visit

http://www.onegoodsonnet.com/genres/pride-and-prejudice-variations

ALSO BY ONE GOOD SONNET PUBLISHING

THE SMOTHERED ROSE TRILOGY

BOOK 1: THORNY

In this retelling of "Beauty and the Beast," a spoiled boy who is forced to watch over a flock of sheep finds himself more interested in catching the eye of a girl with lovely ground-trailing tresses than he is in protecting his charges. But when he cries "wolf" twice, a determined fairy decides to teach him a lesson once and for all.

BOOK 2: UNSOILED

When Elle finds herself practically enslaved by her stepmother, she scarcely has time to even clean the soot off her hands before she collapses in exhaustion. So when Thorny tries to convince her to go on a quest and leave her identity as Cinderbella behind her, she consents. Little does she know that she will face challenges such as a determined huntsman, hungry dwarves, and powerful curses . . . .

BOOK 3: ROSEBLOOD

Both Elle and Thorny are unhappy with the way their lives are going, and the revelations they have had about each other have only served to drive them apart. What is a mother to do? Reunite them, of course. Unfortunately, things are not quite so simple when a magical lettuce called "rapunzel" is involved.

If you're a fan of thieves with a heart of gold, then you don't want to Miss . . .

THE PRINCES AND THE PEAS
A TALE OF ROBIN HOOD

A NOVEL OF THIEVES, ROYALTY, AND
IRREPRESSIBLE LEGUMES

BY LELIA EYE

An infamous thief faces his greatest challenge yet when he is pitted against forty-nine princes and the queen of a kingdom with an unnatural obsession with legumes. Sleeping on top of a pea hidden beneath a pile of mattresses? Easy. Faking a singing contest? He could do that in his sleep. But stealing something precious out from under "Old Maid" Marian's nose . . . now that is a challenge that even the great Robin Hood might not be able to surmount.

When Robin Hood comes up with a scheme that involves disguising himself as a prince and participating in a series of contests for a queen's hand, his Merry Men provide him their support. Unfortunately, however, Prince John attends the contests with the Sheriff of Nottingham in tow, and as all of the Merry Men know, Robin Hood's pride will never let him remain inconspicuous. From sneaking peas onto his neighbors' plates to tweaking the noses of prideful men like the queen's chamberlain, Robin Hood is certain to make an impression on everyone attending the contests. But whether he can escape from the kingdom of Clorinda with his prize in hand before his true identity comes to light is another matter entirely.

About the Author

Jann Rowland

Jann Rowland is a Canadian who enjoys reading and sports, and dabbles a little in music, taking pleasure in singing and playing the piano.

Though Jann did not start writing until his mid-twenties, writing has grown from a hobby to an all-consuming passion. His interest in Jane Austen stems from his university days when he took a class in which *Pride and Prejudice* was required reading. However, his first love is fantasy fiction, which he hopes to pursue writing in the future.

He now lives in Alberta with his wife of more than twenty years and his three children.

For more information on Jann Rowland, please visit:
http://onegoodsonnet.com.

Made in the USA
San Bernardino, CA
11 June 2018